THE
GOOD
NEIGHBOR

Also by William Kowalski

THE
GOOD
NEIGHBOR

A NOVEL

WILLIAM KOWALSKI

HarperCollins*Publishers*

HarperCollins books may be purchased for educational, business, or sales pro-
motional use. For information, please write: Special Markets Department,
HarperCollins Publishers Inc., 10 East 53rd Street, New York, NY 10022.

FIRST EDITION

Designed by Joy O'Meara

Printed on acid-free paper

Library of Congress Cataloging-in-Publication Data
Kowalski, William.
    The good neighbor: a novel / William Kowalski—1st ed.
        p. cm.
    ISBN 0-06-621137-9 (acid-free paper)
    1. Pennsylvania—Fiction. I. Title.
PS3561.O866G66 2004
813'.54—dc22
                        200402896

04 05 06 07 08 ❖/RRD 10 9 8 7 6 5 4 3 2

For Kasia, my little girl,

and also
young Ethan Lars

AUTHOR'S NOTE

I would like to express my appreciation to my wife, Alexandra, my agent, Anne Hawkins, and my editor, Marjorie Braman, for their continued support during the writing of this book. Nathan Sidoli and Michael Wolfe were also helpful, and Paul Romaine gave generously of his time and energy in helping me see the world through the eyes of a professional stock trader. Larry Finlay, my editor in the U.K., has been a constant source of optimism and encouragement. Without these people and others, this novel would not have come to be, and they have my full and unending gratitude.

The town of Plainsburg, Pennsylvania, is fictitious, and should not be confused with any actual place.

William Kowalski

CONTENTS

PART THREE

PART FOUR

PART ONE

1

GOING HOME

In the morning, the river seemed flat and still. At this early hour, there was no depth to it; it was as if one could bend down and pinch the water between thumb and forefinger and just peel it away, like a bandage, and underneath, the earth would be dry. There would be bones down there, and other secrets, too, whispering of the things that had already happened in that place, as well as things that were to come—but they wouldn't have known any of this, not yet.

They came around that last bend in the road, where the bluff ends and the river plain begins, and the valley opened up before them like a drawing from a long-forgotten children's book. There was the house on one side of the road, and the thin, silent river on the other. Growing along the river were trees in profusion— Francie saw wise sycamores, tentative birches, and weeping willows, as well as several sprightly young oaks and one stately old one. In their brilliant headdresses, they seemed to her like torches that had been stuck in the earth and left there to glower against the ragged gray belly of the sky. It was fall, the best time of the year in that part of the world.

Later, like jealous explorers, they would argue about who had seen the house first, Francine or Coltrane. It was difficult to determine, because the house wasn't the only thing to come to the eye once one had swung around the bend. There was too much else to look at. There were the rumpled mountains in the distance, for example, unstriking in either height or appearance, but lending a softening distraction to the scene, as if they were not real but a background image done in paint or chalk. They looked like something you could jump into, Francie thought, like the park scene in *Mary Poppins*. Also, there was the river, and all around them, the broad, fecund fields, whose varying greenness was still defiant and bright, so early was it still in this new season of dying. There was the road, which unspooled over the hilltop in the foreground like a runaway ribbon. But, really, it was the trees that got you first, with their colors of priestly saffron and Martian red.

Francie would later tell Colt that he could not possibly have seen the house first, because he was driving, and it was tucked away on her side of the car. She let him have credit for discovering the river, because she didn't care about the river. She only cared about the house, and from the moment she saw it—it really *was* she who saw it first, though they both exclaimed about it at the same time—it was as if she'd never cared about any other place in her life until now.

"Pull over!" said Francie, although Colt was already doing it.

They parked at the side of the road, not daring the driveway, just looking up at the house. Then, after they'd sat in silence for several moments, she said to her husband, "I'd love to live here someday."

She expected him to make fun of her for this, but instead, to her astonishment, he said:

"Yeah, so would I."

■ ■ ■

One could see that this house was old, cut patiently by hand from living hardwood and frozen stone. There was a wraparound porch, ornamented with Victorian-style gingerbread cutouts and a swing on a chain, but the gingerbread was new and pretentious, clearly out of place. Whoever had put it there was trying too hard, Francie thought. If it was up to her, she'd take it down. There were *three* stories, plus what looked to be an attic, or a half-story of some sort. A small round window hinted that it might be interesting up there.

"That's where they kept the demonic stepchild," said Colt. "Until it killed all of them in their sleep."

"Shut up," said Francie. "Don't ruin it." *Like you ruin everything else*, she thought.

"Can a place like this actually be *empty*?" Colt wondered.

Timidly, they got out of the car and headed across the vast front lawn. Nobody came out to see what they wanted. No dogs barked. They went up the steps, Francie first, fearless now, and she pounded on the door. Without waiting for an answer, she went to one of the windows and put her face up to it, shading her eyes from the glare on the wrinkled old glass. She already knew that everyone was gone.

"Don't be so nosy," said Colt. "Maw and Paw will come after us with a shotgun."

"It's vacant," said Francie. "Nobody lives here."

She showed Colt the sitting room. Clean outlines on the walls and floor proved that it had been occupied in exactly the same way for a long time, and then had suddenly been emptied all at once, like a sink whose plug had been pulled.

"They were all murdered," Colt said darkly. "I can tell."

"They were *not*," said Francie. Normally it worked when Colt was trying to scare her, but this time she knew he was lying. "It's got a . . . a feel to it. Alive. They liked it here."

"They? They who?"

"Everyone. Right down to the cats," she said. "Even the mice were happy."

"I wonder if it has termites," said Colt. "Probably does."

Without bothering to stop and ask each other what they were doing, they wandered around to the back.

■ ■ ■

Colt and Francie hadn't been in the market for a house. They lived in the city and had no intention of leaving it, in any permanent sense; they had only been out for a drive, which was Francie's whimsical idea, because she was sick of breathing truck exhaust and wanted to go for a walk somewhere quiet. Again, to her surprise, Colt had agreed. Usually, he didn't want to be bothered with leaving the city. It seemed to take all morning just to get ready, and then they had to go a mile to the garage where he kept his beloved car, and then drive in weekend traffic through the Holland Tunnel, across New Jersey, through the Delaware Water Gap and into Pennsylvania, which was where they both knew they would end up that day, though they hadn't discussed it. Pennsylvania held a kind of magic for Francie, because it was woodsy and quiet, or so she thought of it, and also because it reminded her of a childhood that hadn't quite happened but easily could have. She even liked the way the word sounded, rolling out of her mouth like a cheekful of liquid silver: *Pennsylvania.*

Colt never thought about Pennsylvania in poetic terms. He simply hadn't driven his car, a rebuilt 1970 Camaro with a two-hundred horsepower V-8, in a whole month, and he was aching to feel it open up on the road underneath him. The engine and body of the car had a way of vibrating together at a certain speed—miniscule waves of motion shuddering throughout the whole machine, intersecting with each other perfectly and canceling each other out—so that it felt, for brief moments, like the car wasn't even moving at all, when in reality it was roaring along like a bat out of hell. It was like hitting the sweet spot on a baseball bat or a golf club. Depending on the temperature, it happened at around seventy-seven miles per hour, and Colt loved this feeling so much that sometimes he fell asleep thinking about it.

■ ■ ■

When they went around to the back of the house and saw what was there, they gasped. Francie reached for Colt's hand. Their eyes, so accustomed to the unnatural foreshortening of the urban horizon, felt at first as though they were being stretched, cartoon-like, out of their heads. It didn't seem possible that all this space could go with one house. The yard simply went on and on until it disappeared, the end of it hidden by a thick blur of trees that, for all they knew, might even be part of the property. Think of it! they said to each other. Owning trees! It was too good to be true.

About a hundred yards from the house, and hidden behind it, there was a barn, velvet with age—a rough and unsteady creation of the last century that would certainly not make it through the next. It was already halfway through the process of collapsing, and seemed to have halted now merely out of surprise, or embarrassment. There was also a small and weathered fruit orchard consisting of perhaps two dozen trees, organized not in neat rows but all in a huddle, like old men having a fire drill. Near them was a little pond, overgrown with algae and reeds. As they approached, they heard the sound of dozens of tiny divers taking refuge in the murky water.

"What's that noise?" said Colt. "Fish?"

"It's not a noise, it's a sound. And it's not fish, it's frogs," said Francie, who knew about such things. Sweet memories of her childhood again came back to her, whether real or not, she couldn't say, and she wiped her eyes. Colt had grown up in the city, and when, at that moment, Francie realized he'd spent his entire life without ever once hearing the sounds of frog-song on a midsummer night, she felt something not unlike pity, but with a sharper edge, whereas once upon a time she might have found it amusing that he didn't know frogs from fish.

"They're scared of us," she explained.

"I wonder how many acres this is," said Colt. He spun around slowly, scanning the horizon. "There are," he announced, "no neighbors, except that one house on that hill. Which you can barely see. It's quiet." He said "quiet" with trepidation, like one beginning a bold experiment. The house he pointed to was indeed scarcely visible, though Francie knew that, in country terms, the owners had probably considered themselves to be practically rubbing elbows. They would have known each other's every intimate detail, every irregular thought. They would have been neighbors all their lives. They might even have been related.

"It's perfect," she said. "Isn't it?"

Colt shrugged. "There's enough room back here for a whole golf course, practically."

"No! An English country garden."

"I could at least put in a putting green."

"Cross-country skiing in winter."

"Jesus," said Colt, "we could build a whole *resort* back here."

"Let's not," said Francie.

"Are we moving?" asked Colt. "Somehow, when I got up this morning . . ."

"Can we at least talk about it?" Francie asked in return, knowing that he had already convinced himself, and that therefore the hardest part of it was already done.

■ ■ ■

Leaving the driveway in the Camaro, pausing to let pass a pickup truck that was weighed down with various items of junk, they noticed what they hadn't earlier: a battered, rusty mailbox, leaning like a drunk away from the road.

"Hold on," said Francie. She got out and went to look at the name as the driver of the pickup truck slowed curiously, peered at them from under a baseball hat, and sped up again. On the door of the truck were written the words FLEBBERMAN TOWING. Colt could tell what he was thinking: *Strangers.* He felt unnerved. In the city, people were not supposed to notice each other that obviously.

"It says 'Musgrove,'" Francie called, kneeling next to the rust-red, loaf-shaped mailbox. She hadn't noticed the pickup truck. "Or at least it used to say that." She got back in the car. "You can still see the paint. Barely. It was the Musgrove house," she said.

"Yeah, I heard you," Colt said.

His tone was sarcastic and impatient. Francie wondered, hurt, what had happened in the preceding three seconds to make him suddenly testy. They'd gotten through the whole morning without a fight. For a Saturday, the only full day of the week they spent together, that was pretty good. She couldn't have understood that it was the driver of the pickup truck, staring at Colt in what he had already come to think of as his own driveway. He'd wanted to challenge the man, but he was gone too soon, and now he had adrenaline in his system, which made him touchy. To punish him, she kept her daydreams to herself for the next fifteen minutes. But they were both too excited to stay quiet for long, and soon they were chattering like schoolchildren on holiday as they wended their way back toward the city. She even got Colt to apologize, though he didn't understand what for.

2

■

THE END OF THE GOLDEN AGE

The next Monday was September 25, 2000, a date that would later bear particular significance in Francie's and Colt's minds as a kind of freeze-frame snapshot of the planetary alignments that had determined the course of their future; it was a picture of late youth to regard in their geriatric years, when they would look back on themselves as they once were, and wonder what strange forces had caused everything to change. After all, no one is more attuned to the vagaries of the universe than poets, of whom Francie generously considered herself one—despite the fact that she had written perhaps ten poems in nine years, all of them failures of inspiration and style. And for Colt's part, there is no self-respecting financial trader who doesn't hold at least a little stock in the mysterious powers of the cosmos; they all understand that no part of the universe is unconnected to any other part, that when you pull one string down another goes up, that all things under the sun, eventually, are reflected in the market, and that the market, in fact, is really only a reflection of everything, a model of the universe in miniature. Hence the good-luck charm he wore discreetly around his neck, tucked into his shirt—a simple gold ring on a chain, to remind him that all was one, and that success was only a fingernail's breadth away.

This was Coltrane and Francie, in a nutshell, on the day they waited in the driveway of the house for the real estate agent, who was late; and their entire futures hung balanced, like a triangle standing on its apex, ready to topple one way or the other.

███

Francie and Colt had met almost ten years earlier, during Francie's big post-graduate fling in New York. That trip was only supposed to last most of the summer, nine sultry weeks of big-city independence before heading back home to earn a master's degree in English literature or poetry, or maybe even a doctorate; but somehow it had turned into almost a decade of being someone's wife, in a city that still felt strange. She still wasn't sure how it had happened, either. That is, she knew the facts of it, but not the meaning behind it—if there was any meaning to be found.

The facts were that through the influence of one of her professors, she had been "awarded" an unpaid internship at the Metropolitan Museum of Art, which meant that she'd been granted the privilege of standing stock still every day amid the glassy-eyed fowl and plump nudes of the Renaissance painting exhibit, her feet screaming, her spirit slipping further each day into darkness and despair. And then Colt had come and rescued her. She'd noticed him because he was tall, and she'd fallen in love with him because he knew how to take charge. What did she know? In many of the novels she'd read, people got married for far less than that. Yet she had not seen herself as an urban housewife, which was what she had become, and it was at moments like this, when the triangle was about to topple, that she looked back at the preceding years and shook her head.

Francie had graduated from the University of Indianapolis in

June of 1991, putting an end to four years of blissful extended infancy, a period she thought of now as her Golden Age. She had
never left home before. Even while at school, she continued to live
with her family, ostensibly because it was cheaper but really because she was afraid to leave. And also, there was Michael, her
baby brother—not really a baby, but five years her junior, whom
all the kids picked on and who needed her protection and comfort.
When he was ten, Michael had developed a penchant for getting
beaten up. He seemed to attract bullies like a light attracts moths,
and Francie was the only one he could complain to; their father
would just whap him on the back of the head and tell him to be a
man, their mother would only worry ineffectually, the teachers
didn't care. What would Mikey do if he couldn't crawl into
Francie's bed every night after the lights were out, whimpering
the litany of wrongs committed against him that day?

"When are you going to come to school and beat them all up for
me?" Michael would ask, his wet face buried in her hair. "Why
don't you help me?"

But the very idea of her beating anyone up was ridiculous. Poets
did not behave in such a fashion. All she could do was comfort
him with dreams.

"When we grow up, we'll live in a house together," she
promised him. "Just you and me. And no one will be allowed in,
and we'll never have to leave it."

"Can we have armed guards? And dogs?"

"Yes."

"Where will it be?"

"In the country somewhere," Francie would say. "Somewhere
no one can find us."

"That sounds really good," said the young Michael, and then he
was able to fall asleep, snoring, choking occasionally on his sister's
hair.

This conversation had been repeated a hundred times, maybe a
thousand. But Michael's need of her notwithstanding, Francie had

often lingered on campus in the evenings, in rapt adoration at the proverbial knee of some brilliant professor or enlightened graduate student, or in the dim watering holes that other literary hopefuls frequented, watching them imbibe to excess. She herself did not drink. Or—especially in her last two years—she spent her time in the library, where she scribbled in one of the dozens of spiral-bound notebooks she filled with musings, verses, and occasional paragraphs of unwieldy prose.

But fiction in general she found too strenuous and unlovely. If poetry was like sculpting small statues in clay, then fiction was pouring cement. She would leave such heavy work to coarser types. Besides, all the budding novelists she had met in school were wild, drunken narcissists who either tried (and failed) to lay her, or looked down their noses at her because she could take up to a week to write four whole lines, while they churned out pages in a single day.

It was really the common, free-form stanza that enthralled Francie most. She was reminded of butterflies; she saw herself in a garden, surrounded by fluttering, diaphanous phrases that had emerged from her ears and mouth. These were her ideas, and they were perfect. The greatest triumph of her life came in her senior year, just before her twenty-first birthday, when a small press in Chicago agreed to publish a collection of her poems in the form of a chapbook—not quite a hardcover, but not really a paperback, either. It was more like construction paper, actually, but at least it had her picture on the back. "Achingly beautiful," the press's publisher had called her work; and also "filled with the sweetness of surrender." The chapbook was entitled *Poems from My Sinister Hand*, which was not a confession of secret crimes but merely a clever Latin reference to the fact that Francie was left-handed.

This was the sort of thing that young poets dreamed of, and old ones too, and Francie suddenly had the feeling that her life was moving along according to some sort of plan that was better than anything she could have come up with herself. She became famous, within the tiny, rarefied sphere that was her world. Freshmen sat at her knee in the same dim watering holes, hoping for some pearl of wisdom to fall from her lips. The drunken novelists renewed their maddened efforts to lay her, and failed again. One of her professors did succeed in seducing her, however, and thus her surrender was made even more sweet: one Tuesday evening in spring, Francie McDermott lost her virginity to a balding, forty-five-year-old classics professor who smelled of wool and pipe tobacco, and who called her "my dear" as though it was the most passionate phrase he could think of. The pretext of their tryst was a romantic dinner at his place, but she was home in time to watch Leno with her father that night. It was all rather quick, really, maybe a little too quick, but then again, life had been moving faster of late. The Chicago press printed five hundred copies of her chapbook, giving her twenty-five in payment. And, to make the surrendering even sweeter, the school literary magazine published six poems from her book and offered her a small cash award—which she astonished everyone by declining. Publication she could accept, but it was better, she believed, to go unpaid, for fame and money were the two great enemies of the creative mind.

Of course, Francie made this gesture with the expectation that she was actually about to embark on the greatest literary career of the twentieth century. As the divinely ordained love-child of Dickinson, Plath, and Leonard Cohen, it had simply never occurred to her that she might never again be published anywhere, by anybody. She'd forgotten that the world was not a university campus, and had little use for types like her. The real world had Jerry Springer and drive-in wedding chapels and crack cocaine in it, and no one knew—or cared—that you were Francine McDermott, poetess, and that the ichor of two American genius-women and a brilliant Canadian Jew filled the hollows of your bones. You were only a customer, and that was America. No one anywhere in the entire damned country was reading poetry, it seemed, except in university classrooms. To her knowledge, not one copy of *Poems from My Sinister Hand* had ever been sold.

A copy of it still sat in a bookstore in Manhattan, run by her friend Walter, who had graciously given her five inches of counter space and promised that he would never move it. Walter believed in poetry the way other people believed in religion. If ever she saw it was gone, he told her, she would know that it had been sold.

But it had been a long time since she'd been able to bring herself to go to Walter's bookstore and see if, in fact, *Poems from My Sinister Hand* was still there.

■ ■ ■

After graduation, Francie decided to have a carefully planned yet wild adventure in New York City, birthplace of a hundred famous poets and a million unknown ones. Her parents approved—relieved, perhaps, that she was finally showing some inclination to leave home. The classics professor who stole her maidenhead wrote a letter to a friend at the Met, asking if he could make room for her somewhere. The friend wrote back and said that he could. Her friends in the literature and art departments back home all drooled with jealousy. They were sure she was going to get discovered and become famous. How this was to happen, nobody knew; poets were not normally "discovered," like Lana Turner sitting at the soda fountain. But sometimes these things happened anyway. And everyone was sure it was going to happen to Francie, simply because she was leaving Indianapolis and going to New York. At the very least, they all believed, she could now be assured of dying in glorious obscurity. That in itself was more than any of them could hope for. It was beautiful to be obscure in New York, but to be obscure in Indianapolis was the normal state of affairs.

Instead of getting discovered, she cried herself to sleep every night in the furnished apartment her father had sublet for her in Midtown. By the time she did manage to drift off, around four A.M., she'd usually cried so hard and for so long that she was dehydrated, and her ribs were sore from sobbing. She hadn't the faintest idea what she was upset about. She thought it was probably homesickness, but her mother, Penelope, told her over the phone that people didn't get *that* homesick. She probably had something else wrong with her, Penelope said. Possibly something serious.

Francie agreed. She'd begun work at the museum on a Monday, and by that Friday she'd already lost the urge to go on. She just lay in bed all day in a strange person's apartment, lacking even the will to shower. She'd been in New York less than one hundred fifty hours, and already all she wanted was to die.

Her parents flew in from Indianapolis and tried to figure her out. Her father was stymied, but Penelope thought she had a pretty good idea what was going on. It was a hereditary illness, one that had mercifully skipped over Penelope herself. Her own mother, Francie's grandmother Minnie, had acted like this sometimes. They called it the Galloping Sobs, because it seemed to come up on you out of nowhere and run you into the ground. When a fit of the Sobs came over Minnie, everyone knew to be extra quiet and extra nice for as long as it took it to go away. Sometimes it took days. Later, it got to be weeks. When this kind of thing happened over and over, though, everyone stopped caring; Penelope remembered this cruel fact all too well. You went back to acting like yourself, being a normal kid and doing normal kid things, and that was when Minnie *really* broke down. The slightest noise was enough to make her crazy. When Minnie had the Sobs, even her own children were her mortal enemies.

But that, Penelope knew, was before the great pharmaceutical corporations of America had begun to turn their attention toward what had been referred to in a general way as "hysteria," that peculiarly feminine disease that once seemed to doctors to originate in the womb and spread, like a virus, into the brain. Penelope did not suffer from the Sobs herself, thank God. But she knew the signs, and she would do anything in her power to spare her only daughter the hell that had been her mother's life. She would get her some pills. Pills could fix just about anything these days, the Sobs included.

"I just want to go home," Francie had said.

"You're not going home," said Penelope. "You're going to lick this thing."

"I don't *want* to lick it," said Francie. She thought of how odd that phrase was, "to lick it." She imagined herself holding It up to her mouth, whatever It was, and running her tongue over It. It would be a slimy black thing, like a leech. The image made her gag. At this point she hadn't showered in a week. Her face shone and her hair was limp with grease. She lay on her side and let one arm trail over the edge of the bed.

Her father, who up till now had been pacing ineffectually between the front door and back wall of this tiny apartment, which was smaller than his own dining room, said, "You'd goddam well better lick it. I didn't spend three thousand of my hard-earned dollars on this shoebox just so you could lay around in bed all day. Who cares if you're depressed? Get up and get to work. There's time enough to get emotional later. You can't just give up on life every time you realize things in the world aren't perfect."

"Stewart," said Penelope, "for goodness' sake, shut up."

"No, I won't. I'll have my say," said Stewart. "This is the same kind of act your mother used to pull, Penny. Remember?"

"Remember? How could I forget?" said Penelope.

"It's not an *act*!" Francie wailed. "I want to *die!*"

"All right," said Penelope. "If you want to die, there's nothing anyone else can do about it. You're the only one who can make that decision. But as long as I'm alive, I'm not going to sit idly by while you let yourself waste away into nothing. I've made an appointment this afternoon with a very good doctor, and you're going to go see him. After that, if you still want to die, go right ahead. Just let me do this one last thing for you, so I can ease my conscience after you're buried."

"What kind of doctor?" Stewart asked.

"A psychiatrist," said Penelope.

Stewart muttered darkly to himself, but said nothing. He was a successful real estate broker who felt out of place in New York. The sheer size of the buildings here had put him in a bad mood the minute he stepped off the plane, because they reminded him that there were so many men in the world whose success dwarfed his. Right now, he was absorbed by the notion that all the money he'd amassed over his lifetime would disappear in less than five years if, for some bizarre and unpredictable reason, he should be forced to move to this city and live on his savings. Stewart enjoyed torturing himself sometimes with thoughts of this nature. Five years, and then he'd be on the street. The thought was so horrifying that he felt he might be getting depressed himself. Think of it! All those years of work down the drain. His money was already being squandered in a shameless fashion by this daughter of his, who, all right, let's admit it, really did have something wrong with her upstairs, had *always* been too sensitive, cried at everything, never showed much in the way of gumption or ambition, but then you couldn't blame her for that—she was a female. Girls were impossible. Lord above, you could go crazy trying to understand them.

■ ■ ■

The long and short of it was that Francie agreed to go to the psychiatrist, whose diagnosis was prompt: she was manic-depressive, with bipolar aspects. The psychiatrist was a slight man, and in spite of her natural fear of doctors, Francie liked him. He was wise, kind and small, somewhat like Yoda, though instead of green he was a soft, pale pink. The doctor postulated gently that the mania part of her illness would normally take over during times of great excitement, such as the weeks leading up to the move to New York. Did this sound familiar to her? Indeed, Francie remembered that period as the best part of her Golden Age, when everything had seemed rosy and nothing could possibly go wrong. Then came the depression, after all the excitement had died down, after the move was over, and she was on her own in a huge city where she knew absolutely no one, and where she sensed, with the instinct common to all mammals, that she was in great danger. She knew that if she were to slip and fall into the cogs of the great machine that was New York, she would be chewed up and spit out in an instant. She had become obsessed with the fear of tripping. If she tripped just once, say on the stairs as she was coming out of the subway, the hordes marching along behind would flatten her under their heels with no more mercy than Hitler's brownshirts. She didn't think she was crazy for feeling this way. She thought it more likely that she was the only one who understood how bad things really were.

That was when she first heard the magic word that was going to change her life: Benedor. Other magic words in the history of the world had never had any effect on her: "open sesame," "abracadabra," "abraxas," "please," "I love you." But times had changed. The old alchemical incantations had been replaced by the modern buzzwords of mental chemistry. And weren't the pills a nice color? her mother asked. Francie agreed, because it was true. After only a few days on Benedor, *everything* was a nice color. The sky was a little bluer, the buildings not quite so stark and gray. Within a month, the kind, wise, small doctor told her her system would be thoroughly permeated by the drug, and everything would be just fine. Until then, she should be prepared for a few rocky moments; nothing was immediate. And she should keep coming to see him as long as she was in the city, so he could check up on her.

"But it's up to you," the doctor told her, "whether you live or die. No one can tell you what to do. You have to tell yourself."

This was just what her mother had said, of course, and so Francie knew it was true; one or the other of them might be lying to her, but not both. She told herself once more to go to work, and this time it worked. Her mother went with her and had a private chat with the head of her department, behind closed doors, while

Francie waited in the hallway. Since Francie was working for free, the museum couldn't exactly fire her, but there was a certain amount of smoothing-over to do. She was reinstated to her former position, which had consisted of standing in one of the Renaissance rooms and making sure no one touched anything. She wore a badge and a ridiculous maroon blazer that didn't go with anything she owned, and she carried a heavy walkie-talkie in her pocket that pulled her spine out of alignment, giving her a neckache. That was all right. She didn't care. She took her Benedor in the morning and again in the evening, and she protected the integrity of the Renaissance, and she waited patiently to be discovered.

Her parents went back home to Indiana, confident that they had helped their little girl out of the last serious scrape of her childhood, and that she was now equipped with all the tools she needed to deal with the world. Now all they had to do was get Michael whipped into shape, and they could retire in peace.

In fifty-three days, Francie was to go home again. Then she would have to go back to school, and that was a whole other thing to be dealt with. She'd already enrolled in a master's program she had no interest in, for no other reason than that she needed something to do. Maybe she would drop out of that. Perhaps she could get a job instead, and write poems on the side. For now, though, she was content to stand and stare at the paintings, and hope that no one would try to touch anything so that she wouldn't have to speak to them about it.

And then Colt walked in, leading a group of wide-eyed Japanese investors. He sized her up from across the room; she could feel his eyes burning her skin. Francie didn't know it, but she was pretty, in a wide-eyed, corn-fed kind of way, and she had an innocence about her that stood out in a place like New York. Her reddish brown hair caught the light and held it long after it had passed over the rest of her; her nose was small and upturned; her ears delicate, stomach and hips trim, breasts high and firm. Colt himself was tall and broad-shouldered, with flecks of gray along his temples, and an intensity to his eyes that she mistook at first for kindness. It was the first time in her life that she had ever wanted to be approached by a total stranger. God, I hope that man comes over here and talks to me, she thought, and the very next thing you know, he did, and suddenly everything seemed all right again, more all right than it ever had before, because even though she didn't know his name she could tell he was not afraid of anything, and what was more, he liked her. He really liked her. She didn't know how he possibly could—Francie did not believe herself lovable, or even attractive—but he did.

Several of the Japanese investors took pictures of Francie and Colt speaking to each other, believing that she was some sort of important artistic authority. During that conversation, Francie smiled for the first time in two weeks. A few hours later, she was telling Colt over dinner that she'd been led to believe by the small, wise doctor that she could—in theory, at least—learn to take care of herself, but now that she had met Colt, she knew the truth: *he* was the only one who could take care of her, really and truly. She held nothing back from him. She told him everything right away, and she was glad she did. She saw the fire this statement put in his eyes, the protective swell of his chest, the way he took her arm as he walked her back to her sublet. He fell in love with her because he needed to be needed, and she needed him; he hadn't read as many novels as she, but this made perfect sense to him, too.

"That beautiful face of yours is going to be in photo albums all over Japan," he told her. "What do you think of that?"

"I think it's neato," said Francie, because it was all part of the magic.

He invited himself in, as she had known he would, and he availed himself of her, kindly, behaving as if he held the title to her body. That was all right with her, too. She didn't have to worry about it anymore. It was his body now. In the morning, when she woke up, he was still there, and then she knew that things really were going to be all right, because he hadn't left her in the middle of the night. She made him breakfast the next morning, and he woke to the smell of coffee.

So this was the big thing that happened to her when she went to New York, not getting published, but getting attached; and within a few weeks, she knew that she was never going home again, because Colt had said out loud that he loved her, and she had said it back. She was going to stay in the city instead, and things were going to be just fine, and her future was going to be perfect.

Back in Indianapolis, her parents rejoiced that their strange and wayward daughter had finally found a man to take care of her. Michael moped and wept, to no avail; his sister had found another man, and there was to be no house in the country after all. Francie's poems stopped altogether, of course, killed off by the pills as if they were vermin. No more chapbooks. No more adoring publishers. And so every age must end.

3

■

THE BRASS RING

Colt stood in the front yard of the house that he already knew he was going to buy, up to his ankles in leaves, craning his neck to see the peeling white paint on the widow's walk. A light breeze toyed with his carefully barbered hair, still mostly its original chestnut, and dimpled his white Brooks Brothers shirt around his gym-sculpted chest; his sleeves were painstakingly rolled to just below the elbow, in order to convey a sense of relaxation. He was thinking that this house was a far cry from the apartment building on Avenue A where he'd been born thirty-nine years earlier, and where he'd grown up. He rarely thought of that place these days. He didn't know what made him think of it now, unless it was the wondrous sense of full-circularity, the feeling that he'd finally arrived. Of course, having already arrived years ago, it was really only a new way of feeling it—the feeling being so exceedingly pleasant that he sought constantly to re-create it every day, in ways small and large, right down to the manner in which he flung his change at convenience store clerks. If only his parents could have seen this place. They would have been astounded at

his success. Nothing like this had been envisioned for their only
son. Nothing had been envisioned for him at all, in fact; but it had
already been many years since he'd forced himself to forget about
that.

This huge old house, now, Colt mused, was just the thing he
needed to get away to once in a while, and to show off a little. It
might even help him make partner—you had to show the higher-
ups that you knew yourself what you were worth before you
could hope for them to acknowledge it. In his early days, when
he'd just been starting out as a stockbroker, Colt had noticed that
all the men he respected most owned a country place. It was the
ultimate brass ring, even better than a fancy car, or a big apartment, or a beautiful wife. All those things were good to have, but
a country place was proof that one had transcended the carnage of
life in the city, and could lift out of earthly orbit at will, to fly off
to a calmer, cooler, cleaner place. His first boss, at the brokerage
firm he'd worked in after he'd finished school, had owned a
monthlong timeshare in a tiny cottage on Long Island, just east of
the Hamptons. He could walk out of his front door, turn right, go
five hundred paces, and walk smack into the ocean. At the time,
that had seemed to Colt like the highest state of luxury. The ocean
was a place one went when times were good, and there was
plenty of money. Colt himself had not seen the ocean with his
own eyes until he was twenty-two years old.

His boss now, Forszak, co-owner and senior partner of Anchor
Capital Investments, had a palatial mansion in the Adirondacks
that had once been featured on the television program *America's
Castles*. That was impressive, but Forszak also owned an apartment in Hong Kong, which he used perhaps once a year. This was
in addition to his penthouse overlooking Central Park, of course, a
twenty-room apartment with a hot tub on the deck and a dining
table that sat twenty-two. Forszak was wealthy beyond all
earthly proportion; his holdings actually verged on the interplane-
tary. This was no mere exaggeration, for his name was on a list of

people waiting to fly to the moon, in a Russian spaceship that had yet to be built, at a cost of roughly $50 million per passenger. It was his serious ambition to be the first Hungarian Gypsy on the moon, and at age sixty-something, the oldest person to boot. Once his feet were firmly planted on the loose, gray dust of the lunar surface, he intended to say his Roma prayers for all those who had been murdered by the Nazis, and to look down with a sense of supreme satisfaction on the planet whence his people had sprung, and where they had nearly expired, and revel in the fact that they, in the form of Forszak himself, had made it through, after all—barely. As the Nazis exterminated the Gypsies along with the Jews, twenty-seven Forszaks had gone into Dachau and Auschwitz. Only one had come out, but that one had achieved such success as was almost never heard of, and had arisen to the most exclusive of country places. It could be said of Forszak that his latest "country place" was to be so exclusive and remote that it didn't even have any oxygen.

Already, the newspapers had made much of his ambition. But Forszak's real concern was not his reputation; it was to say his prayers for the dead while gazing upon the planet that had been the scene of the crime, hoping perhaps that their scope would be greater from that perspective, and that they would get that much more quickly to God's ear, not having the interference of the atmosphere to contend with.

Colt and Francie had been to Forszak's Central Park place once and his Adirondack place twice, with a standing invite to come again any time they wanted. The Adirondack place was like a mansion, Colt had marveled afterward, but one made entirely of massive logs. *Endangered* logs, Forszak told him slyly, though he was probably joking. That was what you got when you were routinely one of the top five performers in a capital investment firm of over two hundred people. Even your boss tried to impress you a little.

Of course, it wasn't the kind of invitation you took advantage

of. One didn't want to wear out one's welcome with Forszak. It
was enough just to have been invited to the Log Palace once. It
was like a badge one could wear around the office. *Out at Forszak's
last weekend. Great time. Great fishing. Great guy.* These words,
dropped casually into water-cooler conversation, had the effect of
putting on stilts; Colt was suddenly elevated ten feet above everyone else, breathing the same heady ether that inflated the lungs of
all the great men of finance. The rank stench of the Cuban cigars
that Forszak loved and handed out freely to his darlings was also
the taste of wealth, all the more titillating because they were just
the teensiest bit illegal. *Don't think of it as helping Castro's economy*,
Forszak told him. *Think of it as burning his fields.* Colt laughed duly
and lit up; the smoke deadened his tongue and lingered in his
mouth, and he thought of it as a harsh but necessary poison that
killed off any cells of mediocrity that might still be polluting his
genetic structure.

■ ■ ■

Kicking through a pile of leaves now, Colt stumbled over a metal
FOR SALE sign. He pulled it up disdainfully, soiling his hands on the
moist organic detritus underneath. A small community of potato
bugs and centipedes briefly considered their options, then panicked and fled from the gilded sunlight. Like some kind of medieval disease, a pox of rust had spread across the face of the sign,
rendering it O ALE.

"Would you look at this?" Colt remarked to Francie, who was
sitting half in and half out of the car, trying without much luck to
raise various preset stations on the radio. One slender leg extended
from the car, the other resting inside. Her reddish blond hair was
pulled into a ponytail, revealing the freckles that were scattered
like snow across her usually concealed forehead, and the back of
her neck. She noted with delight that they were out of the city's
broadcasting range.

"Someone didn't want to sell this place," Colt said.

"What makes you say that?" Francie asked, without much interest. She usually only half heard things Colt said until he had repeated them two or three times; it was a reflex she'd developed some years ago, after noticing that he rarely remembered what she said to him, or, for that matter, what he himself said to anyone.

Colt cocked a hip impatiently. "Well, look," he said. "They hid this sign under the leaves."

Francie looked, paying attention now. "If someone really wanted to hide it they would have thrown it away," she said. "Probably it just fell over and got covered up."

This being the likeliest scenario, Colt decided she was wrong; he decided furthermore that it was evidence of some kind of plot. He would investigate later. For now, he considered wandering behind the house to explore the backyard again, but he didn't want to miss the agent when she finally pulled up, because he wanted to give her a good dose of the Eye of Doom, which was one of his most effective business techniques. It was the look he used when he had fixed on making a deal, no matter what the body count. The agent's name was Marge Westerbrook, and after their initial chat on the phone, Colt thought he had her number pretty well: divorced, raising one child on her own, lonely. One of those women who pretended real estate was an actual career. It wasn't that he was psychic. It was that Marge Westerbrook felt obliged to tell everyone her personal details over the phone, before she'd even met them. This was a habit Colt despised—people talking too much about themselves.

"She's fucking late," he snarled for the third time.

Francie sighed. It had been her hope that exposure to the country air would teach Coltrane how not to be in a hurry all the time. She could see now that this would take longer than a few minutes.

"Do you still like it here?" she asked him, hoping to distract him from his own impatience. "The house, I mean?"

He paused, lifting his head, smelling the air like an animal. "Sure," he said. "Kind of place I always wanted."

"Really?"

"Uh-huh." Colt got back in the driver's seat, sniffed again, and let loose with a sneeze that rocked the car.

"Jesus," he gasped. "I wonder if I'm allergic to something."

"I didn't know that about you," she said.

"I've never been around these many damn plants before," he said, looking in the glove compartment for a tissue. "Plants everywhere you look. It's like they're invading or something."

"No, I mean about the house. I didn't know you *always* wanted a place like this."

"Oh, that." He found one and blew his nose. "Yeah. Always thought, you know, when I was a kid, I'd have a country place someday. Everyone who's anyone has one. Forszak has one, remember? Good idea. Somewhere to get away to."

She wanted to ask him, *But do you love it? Or do you just want it because of Forszak?* But questions along these lines irritated him because they were analytical, and she had no right to be analyzing anybody. Instead, she got out of the car and leaned on the roof, looking across the road where the river lay hidden from view below the embankment. Instantly she felt better about everything, even the dwindling number of things in her life that had nothing wrong with them. You could be invisible over there, she thought. You could be down there soaking your feet in the water and no one would be able to see you. Not a soul.

"Here she comes," said Francie.

She had spied a yellow Volkswagen, one of the new models, raising dust as it came around the bluff. Colt got out of the car and slammed the door.

"Half an hour she made us sit here," he said. "Could of called. She has my cell number."

"Colt, please," said Francie. "Be kind."

"Good Lord, she drives a bug," said Colt.

The Volkswagen scrabbled to a halt in the gravel driveway. A large, florid woman got out, already trilling at them before she closed her door. She had red hair, wore a flowery-yellow printed top with black slacks, and in the crook of one arm she cradled a clipboard to her oversized bosom as though it was a nursing child. "Helloo!" she called. "I'm so sorry, my son wouldn't change his shirt, I just . . .oh, teenagers. Hello there, sir, are you Mr. Hart?"

"Hello," Colt said, shaking her hand. The Eye of Doom, he felt, had gone unnoticed, but he had only loaded one shot; he didn't really feel like causing trouble today. He would save that for negotiating. Marge Westerbrook shook Francie's hand by the fingertips and called her Fanny.

"Pleased to meet you," said Francie. "We're so glad you could come out."

"Oh, my goodness," gasped Marge Westerbrook, "this is my *pleasure*, this is my *job*, and all the way from New York you are, too. Oh, my. I am late, aren't I?"

"Yes," said Colt.

"It's really okay," said Francie quickly. "We've got the day off. Colt does, I mean."

"Oh, how nice!" said Marge. "And what do you do, Mr. Hart?"

"Finance."

"Oh, my, New York City *and* finance! How interesting. Listen, let's go in, shall we?" She lowered her voice and leaned in toward Francie. "And we'll just leave him out here, until he changes his attitude," she said.

For one uplifting moment, Francie thought she meant Colt, until she looked in the Volkswagen and realized there was a giant, sullen teenager lurking there, so hunched over that despite his size he was practically hidden by the dashboard. The teenager perked his head up, sensing he was being discussed, and then ducked again when the stares of two strangers confirmed it. Francie caught a luridly red flash of acne splashed across his cheeks like buckshot. Instantly she felt sorry for him; her cheeks had looked like that once, when she was young, and she remembered all too well how much easier it was to stay hidden.

"Oh, he doesn't have to," she said. "He can come in, too, I mean. Don't keep him out here on our account."

"I wouldn't think of it," said Marge, her voice suddenly tight as a jib. Whatever the teenager had done, he'd sinned mightily, that much was clear. "I've got the keys right here. Mr. Hart, would you do the honors, please?" She handed him a key. "The door sticks," she explained. "You'll probably have to put your shoulder into it."

Colt mounted the steps, inserted the key, "put his shoulder into it" three or four times, and the ancient, heavy door swung open.

"Needs to be planed," he muttered.

He became aware that the house was breathing on him open-mouthed, exhaling the taste of unknown years of emptiness. It was a bitter fragrance, not unpleasant, and it reminded him of something too deep to retrieve at the moment. He stepped down the house's throat, a long foyer that led into a central room. The two women came along behind him as he paused for a moment, uncertain, and then strode forward, a willing Jonah now. He was already trying to imagine himself living here.

"The For Sale sign was hidden under some leaves," he told Marge Westerbrook over his shoulder.

"Kids," said Marge, though she didn't say which kids; possibly she meant her own, thought Francie.

Marge crossed the room to a massive fieldstone fireplace and lay one plump hand on the mantel, which was a single slab of rock nearly six feet in length and about four inches thick. The fireplace opened on the back to an opposite room; apparently it was meant to provide heat to both areas. Its grate was clean, Francie noticed. No one had had fires here for a long time.

"Now, this is the living room, or one of them, I should say. You can see the other through there, plus there's an upstairs parlor. This house has nearly ten thousand square feet in all." Marge paused and bowed her head, as if such a place deserved her reverence. "Four bathrooms, six bedrooms, a study *and* a den, a beautiful dining room, pantry, servant's quarters on every floor, a games room, an unfinished basement, an unfinished attic, a kitchen you'll have to *see to believe*. And the property itself is almost fifty acres."

Francie gasped. "Fifty acres! Colt, did you hear that?"

Colt had only half heard. He was scanning the beams in the ceiling and corners of the living room as he listened. For an old house, the room was high. He was exactly six feet tall, and yet if he reached upward he could barely brush the ceiling with his fingers. He ran his hands over a corner beam and felt the long scallops in the wood that told him it had been shaped by hand. Colt had once had a client who was a collector of wooden antiques, and she'd taught him, or tried to teach him, some of the basic distinctions to be made when dealing with objects of wood; he was astonished to discover, ten years later, that he'd learned something.

"This is real," he said, more to himself than the other two.

"All original beamwork," said Marge Westerbrook proudly, as if she was responsible for it. "Well preserved, no dry rot, no termites. The place has really been looked after nicely. It's a *real find*. You people have excellent taste!" She led them into the kitchen, their feet echoing on the floorboards until they came across slate tiles the color of angry November. Francie cooed; Colt stomped experimentally, to see if anything came loose; Marge elaborated on the need for plumbing repairs, no sense in being deceitful, she didn't believe in doing business that way—the place would need *work*. The last improvements were completed (here she consulted her clipboard) in the mid-1970s. She turned on the tap over the sink, and all three attended to a rush of air, like the hiss of radio signals from a distant star. After a moment it was replaced by a low, gurgling note, the pitch changing as the source of it approached at rapid speed from somewhere below their feet. They were rewarded with a gout of brown water that smelled briefly of pond. Then, as if by magic, it ran clear.

"You have well water!" cried Marge Westerbrook, making Francie jump. They each held their hand under the stream for a moment, allowing it to impart its subterranean chill to their finger bones. Colt tasted it, cautious. It was sweet and clean, slightly chalky. There was none of the metallic, chemical flavor of city water, no chlorine, no fluoride. No one had touched this water before him, no government official had approved it as fit for his consumption. There had never been a liquid like this in his life before. He swirled it over his tongue like a vintage wine, closed his eyes, and thought of cave fish, stalactites, stalagmites. They had well water.

Marge led them triumphantly through the rest of the house: the master bedroom, spacious and bright; the guest bedrooms, small, numerous, and dim; the parlor, impossibly oak-paneled, as was the den; the bathrooms, which were merely bathrooms. They even went to the attic, a warm, rustic space, floored with unplaned boards. Light flooded through the bull's-eye windows at either end in surprising quantity. In one corner, a plastic tarp had been draped over a pile of something. Pulling this back, Francie found a stack of cardboard boxes. Opening one, she found comic books, mostly of the sci-fi variety from the 1950s and '60s. Francie gave a coo of delight; she wouldn't be surprised if some of them turned out to be collector's items, provided they hadn't mildewed. There was also an aged steamer trunk, the kind she had seen on *Antiques Roadshow* many a time. She pulled up the fragile domed lid and saw that it was empty. She tried, with her poet's mind, to imagine what kind of person had owned this trunk, and from where they had come with it, and why. Or perhaps it had been purchased for a journey that was never taken, and that was why it was still here, empty. You looked at a trunk and you thought these things, because a trunk meant traveling and dreaming, she thought. It smelled of cedar, as every good trunk should, and was lined in peeling paper, printed in a pattern not unlike Marge Westerbrook's blouse.

Francie looked quickly at Colt and Marge, who were at the

other end of the long attic, talking about something. Unobserved, she grabbed a random comic book and stuck it in the waistband of her jeans, under her shirt. Then she closed the lid of the trunk and replaced the tarp. If they bought the house, the trunk and books would be theirs, and it wouldn't be stealing. She didn't intend to keep it, anyway—she was just going to take it to her friend Walter, who owned a used-book store in the city, and was an expert on everything that was printed, from Superman to Shakespeare. He would know what, if anything, they were worth. She pulled her shirt out of her jeans to hide it, and then it was time to go downstairs again.

They had already decided, back in the city, that if they liked the place they would put in an offer right away. They had never discussed *why* they wanted it; they just did, and in the elation of finally agreeing on something, they did not examine the matter any further. Also, Colt believed they would get a deal, which in his mind was reason enough to buy it. Who knew how long the place had been empty? Years. Whoever owned it would probably be desperate to sell. It was off the beaten path, far from conveniences, the perfect country retreat. Few, if any, interested buyers would have simply happened by, as they had.

Francie would leave that part of it to him; he was the master deal-maker, the negotiator, the man who could cause publicly held companies to flourish or wither on the vine with a single phone call. Colt arched his eyebrows at her inquiringly, and she nodded back decisively, trying not to giggle at her own seriousness. Marge Westerbrook, expert at detecting these types of exchanges, pretended to study the floor.

"Let's talk turkey," Colt said to Marge.

"I'll wait outside," said Francie, and she left with her purloined comic.

4

■

THE BLOOD OF ANGELS

Afterward, they stopped for lunch in Plainsburg, which, like every other middle-sized town in Pennsylvania—or in America, for that matter—had two parts to it. The first was old, dating back in this case to the late nineteenth century, all false wooden storefronts and one or two old stone warehouses-turned-retail-spaces, and a charming, broad brick sidewalk running down both sides of Main Street, itself lined with imitation gas lamps. The second was new, with a four-lane highway on the outskirts of town that boasted a frizzled, litter-strewn grass median, strip malls on either side stretching into the distance as far as the eye could see, and four lanes of traffic moving along in a snarl.

They chose the old part to have lunch in, but not without arguing about it, and so, sick of each other, they talked little as they ate, not even about the house. Colt was unusually dreamy—unusually for him, anyway—and a poem had drifted into the room and found Francie. They always came to her this way, accosting her like beggar children, arms outstretched. She spent the meal picking absentmindedly at her french fries, trying to capture this one on a napkin before it left again. Something about veins running through wood. Wood that was like flesh. As usual, it had seemed brilliant at first, but now that she had the shape of it she could see that once again she had failed. It was another abortion. *Argh. Feh.* She cast a sidelong glance at her husband, who was gobbling his cheeseburger as though there was no such thing as poetry. Or manners. Colt never asked how her poems turned out, she thought resentfully; he didn't care that for years now they'd been a series of mutants, a lineage of misbegotten circus freaks. Of course, someone like him could not be expected to understand. To him they were just words.

■ ■ ■

"What did you talk about?" she asked him as they sped east, homeward.

Colt turned to look at her and smiled lasciviously. He reached for her thigh and gave it a suggestive squeeze. Francie was surprised at this; he rarely touched her with any kind of spontaneity anymore. If he brushed against her in the apartment, he was more likely to mutter "Excuse me" than to reach out and caress her. What on earth was going on with him?

"You and Marge," she prompted him. "What did you say to her?"

"I made an offer," he said. "She's going to take it back to the owners."

His hand was still there on her thigh, squeezing, rubbing, suggesting. They hadn't had sex in a month, probably. Maybe six weeks. And now he wanted to mess around in the car, like teenagers? Not likely. Yet despite her indignation, Francie felt herself growing warm. It was the house that was really doing it to him, she told herself. Or the deal. Spending money always made him horny.

"Just like that?" she said. "It's done?"

"No, it's not done," he said. "All I did was make an offer. That's only the first step."

"Who owns it, anyway?"

"A bank. A bank I own stock in, as a matter of fact." He slid his hand farther up her leg and began to massage her inner thigh. Through her jeans, she could feel the friction on that never-sunned part of her body, as pearlish and tender as the inside of an oyster shell. She clamped her legs shut like a flytrap and pulled the hair on his wrist. "A bank? Do you think they even know what it looks like?" she asked.

"I'm sure," said Colt, shaking free of her, "that they have a very clear financial picture of the place."

"But what it *looks* like, I said. Not how much it's worth."

"They're not stupid people. That's why I own their stock."

"How much did you offer?"

"Don't worry about it," he said. "If you knew it would keep you up tonight."

"Oh, Coltrane!"

"I said don't worry. We can afford it. We can afford ten houses like this. About time we started spending some money, don't you think?"

"I guess so," said Francie, surprised. It seemed to her that something in Colt had changed recently without her noticing, until now. First he had agreed to drive her out to the country, and then he had noticed the house at the same time she did, and now this. She wondered what had brought it about. It was one of the greater ironies of Colt's character that he took no pleasure in spending money, only in earning it. For him to really get turned on, he had to make a killing at work. He already had piles of money, scads of it, oodles. He had literally more money than he knew what to do with. It was sitting in all kinds of different accounts, earning yet more money in interest and dividends, and making the two of them rather disgustingly rich, to be honest. But Colt had never before wanted to buy anything big; and Francie had never been the furs-and-jewelry type. They didn't even own the apartment they lived in, though they could have easily enough. It occurred to her now that perhaps Colt was entering some sort of Golden Age of his own. If so, she wanted a glimpse of it—just to see. She knew she would never be a part of it, even if he bought them both everything they'd ever wanted. It would always be *his* money, and the things they bought with it would always be *his* things.

Except the house in Pennsylvania. That was already hers. She'd felt it from the moment she set foot on the porch. It was like coming home.

■ ■ ■

They rounded the Delaware Water Gap again, the water choppy and cold-looking in the slanting sunlight that lay over it as thin as gold foil. A couple of optimistic powerboaters were out, determined to make the most of the waning season.

"That looks like fun," Francie said.

"I never saw the point to having a boat," said Colt. He reached over to stroke the side of her breast with the backs of his fingers. She took his thumb in her mouth and bit it, gently but seriously, and he pulled away again. "Look at those guys. They drive all the way down here from God knows where with a boat on a trailer, just so they can put it in the water and race up and down. It seems dumb."

"Why are you coming on to me here, like this?"

"What do you mean, why? You're my wife, aren't you?"

"Yeah, but."

"But what?"

"Maybe they like it," Francie said, looking out at the boats.

"Well, they're idiots."

"Don't you ever want to get a boat?"

Frustrated, Colt put his hand back on the wheel. "If I was

gonna have a boat, I'd want it to be down in the Keys. Somewhere warm. And I'd want a real fishing boat, not one of these dinky little tubs. A charter-type thing, with two decks and a wheelhouse and . . . all the other stuff you can get."

"You can get to the ocean through the Water Gap," she said. "It's a long ways, but you can do it."

"You can? How?"

"Down the river," said Francie. "The Delaware River."

"Why can't I touch you?"

"You have to earn it."

Colt smirked. "How do I do that?"

Francie giggled at his impatience. "Through acts of grace," she said. "Are we going to buy this house?"

"I don't know yet."

"Then you don't get to have sex with me," Francie said, returning her gaze to the highway.

They had just entered New Jersey. Colt veered swiftly off the road, making her gasp, and they pulled into the parking lot of the first motel that appeared on the roadside. He turned and leered at her like a high-schooler.

"Coltrane! What am I, a cheap date?"

"I was not aware that we were dating."

She stayed where she was. Colt got out and opened her door. The manager of the motel came to the office door and stared at them—a short, squat man in a T-shirt and long shorts, with kneecaps like softballs. Colt crossed the parking lot on winged feet and handed him a couple of twenties. The man reached inside the office for a key and handed it over.

They went down a cracked concrete sidewalk with weeds growing up through it to a room that smelled of stale cigarettes and chilled air. Colt slammed the door shut and tossed her onto the bed, shedding his clothes, then slowly divesting her of her own. When he discovered the comic book in her shorts, he said, "What the hell's this?"

"Oh, that. I forgot. I stole it."

"Bad girl. You need a spanking."

"Don't hurt me," she said, closing her eyes.

■ ■ ■

They were in there for half an hour. When Coltrane finally collapsed on the mattress, spent, Francie opened her eyes again and stared thoughtfully up at the ceiling. She was preoccupied by the notion that Colt hadn't used a condom. That was rather odd, actually, she thought. Colt always used condoms, because she was afraid of the Pill (not another pill, she told him), and the other implements of birth control, jellies and sponges and diaphragms, were all too cold and squishy and intimidating. Had something else changed too, then? Now that they might own this house, were they finally to talk about having a baby? It wouldn't do to ask him directly; when you wanted something from Colt and thought he might say no, the last thing you did was ask him directly. Maybe he had just forgotten. He wasn't in the habit of carrying condoms around with him, after all.

At least, she hoped he wasn't.

She felt between her legs and touched the wetness that had dripped onto her thighs, rubbing it between her fingers. His semen. She hadn't felt it in some time. When she was younger, she'd imagined that the marrow in her bones would look just like this, not red like blood but white and shimmery, iridescent.

Oh, shut up, she told herself. You think too much. And don't ask him about it, or he'll get mad, and the day will be ruined.

"How come we only ever do it after you spend a lot of money?" she asked instead, running her finger through the swirls of hair on his back. Last time, it had been the purchase of his very expensive cell phone that sparked things. The time before that . . . she didn't remember.

"Mmf," he said.

"Coltrane."

"Hm."

"Do I still excite you? On a day-to-day basis?"

"Hum," he said. "I'm sleepy."

"But do I?"

"Of course you do," he said. "Why do you always feel the need to quiz me on our relationship after we have sex?"

"I do not."

"Always."

"I'm sorry," she said, looking up at the ceiling again. "Are we going to stay here for a while?"

"I wanna take a nap."

He lay with his back to her. Francie grabbed the remote and flicked on the TV. A man and a woman lay in bed and nuzzled each other. The woman was wearing a silk nightgown and the man was wearing silk boxer shorts. The sheets of their bed were silky-looking, too. They lived in a silk world. Francie muted the television and watched with envy as these people talked gently to each other, imagining what they were saying, trying to read their lips, trying to figure out how it was really done.

5

A HISTORICAL DIGRESSION

Adencourt was built, in its slapdash fashion, on the orders (and with the considerable family fortune, got by the slave trade) of Captain Victor T. Musgrove, gentleman-hero of the Mexican-American War of 1848, and of several unnamed Indian campaigns before then. Captain Musgrove knew a fair bit about one or two things, including Indian warfare and a couple of native languages, but was completely ignorant of everything else, including the principles of architecture. This didn't matter in the slightest, as far as building the house was concerned; for the Captain considered himself to be a man of impeccable taste, and no one was rich enough to contradict him.

Adencourt was one of those spectacularly solid and impenetrable homes of which it was said, even one hundred fifty years ago, that it would last at least one hundred fifty years. One could tell this just by looking at it. It was a breathing, alert thing, looking something like a submarine monster: the vast, oaken panel of the front door like a mouth agape; the windows, its many blank eyes; the roof, by turns gabled, peaked, flattened, and widow's-walked, a ridiculous hairline; and the two large wings, northern and southern, a pair of clawless appendages. Its skeleton of hand-smoothed beams was connected by a kind of joint known as mortis-and-tenon, carved with mallet and chisel by carpenters skilled in arts hardly anyone remembers today, except Luddites and Amishmen. The carapace was motley clapboard of a half-dozen tones, all variations on the theme of dirty white. Were you to go over the whole thing with a metal detector, you'd find scarcely a nail in it. It was put together with hand-whittled pegs, like some sort of giant Chinese puzzle. The frame, that is. The drywall had to be hung with nails; there just wasn't any other way. But that, of course, was a recent addition.

The house's bones were cherry, ash, and oak, grown from the very earth on which it stood now. Some of its beams, the ones you rarely saw unless you descended deep into its bowels, were thicker than a man—these were the spine and ribs of the house. It was a strong house, a house built like a ship, or even better than a ship; it was a house that would float if set on the sea, a house that could never be broken. It was, in fact, a fortress. In certain rooms, the walls were still the original mixture of horsehair and plaster of paris, so springy that if you tried to drive a nail in, it came flying right back out at you, like a bullet.

Until 1945, an old-fashioned carriage house with a turnabout had stood next to the barn. The carriage house had been knocked down with the intention of replacing it with a modern garage, but at the dawn of the twenty-first century, this improvement had yet to be accomplished. The barn was still there, however. It was older than the house by three years, and would likely continue to exist a while longer in its present form as a pile of ancient lumber, unless someone took a match to it—or it was hit by merciful lightning.

Captain Victor T. Musgrove was commonly referred to by his neighbors as a "hero," but his last war was one that, strictly speaking, had not offered the standard opportunities for heroism that a good war ought: namely, an honorable reason for fighting. The war against Mexico had really only been a thinly disguised land grab, an embarrassing mark on the report card of a country already founded on land grabs—a nation whose entire philosophy of growth, in fact, was based in thievery and genocide, just like all nations. Captain Musgrove knew this, and so did everyone else in the United States of America, though it can be said, with almost complete certainty, that none of them *knew* that they knew it.

It had, of course, been Captain Musgrove's opinion that America had an excellent reason to fight the Mexicans, who in his eyes were not even a true race, but only the bastard descendants of the Spanish conquistadores and the native women they had raped centuries earlier. It was because they had plenty of land, and America wanted some of it. Nothing could be simpler. Captain Musgrove was a professional Indian-killer—a title that once carried great distinction—and he had firm ideas about the destiny of white men in North America. There was clear evidence that the continent belonged to them, the primary pillar of which was that they were there. *Do not try to argue with Captain Musgrove about Manifest Destiny*, people used to say of him, four and five generations ago. *First he'll argue you to death, and then he'll shoot you, and then he'll scalp you*—a trick he had learned from the very same Indians he once used to hunt, as though they were rabbits. *And then he'll argue with you some more.*

Not that anyone was interested in arguing with the Captain. The doctrine of Manifest Destiny was *so* manifest it didn't even need to be discussed. It was a self-evident truth, as dear to the heart of the Great White Father in Washington as the one that stated all beings were created equal, as long as those beings were white property-owning males. Every white American man believed, back then, that the whole world belonged to him, or at least as much of it as he could farm and hunt. It must be remembered that most of these Americans were really only transplanted Europeans or their immediate descendants, and that they'd been tricked into this belief by the stupendous size and wealth of the continent of which they found themselves the de facto heirs. To stare over the oceanic vastness of the Great Plains—with the wind roaring in the long grass like surf, and the humped spines of buffalo just visible over the tips of the wild sedge and amaranth grasses, like sleeping whales—was a vision miraculous enough to convince the most timid serf or humble peasant that he'd become wealthy almost by accident, particularly because no one had farmed here yet. In Europe, there was no such thing as unfarmed land. That continent had been overpopulated and overcultivated since the Middle Ages. America was too good to be true, a broad-hipped, buxom temptress wearing absolutely nothing, who did not even try to hide her fruits but urged men on to blind abandon in the plundering of her. It was enough to make even the most virtuous of men greedy; those who were already weak in character didn't stand a chance.

Captain Musgrove, who certainly saw himself as among the most virtuous of men, retired from the U.S. Cavalry in 1851 at the age of forty-three, already moving and thinking like an old man, thrice gravely wounded, twice healed. The name "Adencourt" had been circulating in his mind for some years now, though he didn't yet know what it meant. It came to him from time to time, usually when he was a-horse, like a one-word lyric poem that fit the beat of thudding hooves. It pleased him to form it with his tongue, as though he were going to say it, but he never did, not out loud.

The Captain's left arm, chest, and both legs were scarred and weakened by arrow, musket ball, and sabre. His last wound, the one from which he'd never fully recuperated, had been received in hand-to-hand combat with a Mexican officer. They'd come at each other on foot, screaming like charging bulls. He'd shot at the Mexican and missed. He threw his empty pistol at his head, and missed again. Then, like an amateur, he fumbled with his sword. The Mexican had taken this opportunity to stick his own blade between the Captain's ribs. The Captain promptly passed out—

not from pain, which was something he had never acknowledged, but from the certainty that he was finally, blissfully dead.

The Captain did not believe in heaven, since he had never received any reliable reports of its existence. He expected, when he awoke, to find that he was in hell, but he was not. He was in Texas. The Mexican officer was nowhere to be seen. The field, in fact, was mostly empty. The Captain was never able to offer himself a reasonable explanation of that day. In fact, he was to puzzle over it for the rest of his life. What had happened to his enemy? Had someone else killed him? Had he himself been left for dead? Had Jesus come while he was unconscious and taken away all the righteous, leaving only the damned?

It was one of those incidents that might have caused ordinary men to take stock of themselves and perhaps mend their ways, out of sheer gratitude. Not so the Captain. He'd been trying to kill himself ever since puberty, when he'd first taken up soldiering. In truth, he wasn't much given to introspection. He was aware now only of a dim but familiar disappointment at finding himself still breathing. He'd come close to death so many times that he felt he could salute it by its first name, that he could recognize it from a distance at which, to most men, it would only resemble a faint disturbance in the atmosphere. Like a desired whore, like America itself, death was, to the Captain, almost an unattainable ideal, something he could strive for all his life and never achieve. The irony of that was not lost on him, philosophical ineptitude notwithstanding. He wasn't a stupid man. It was that he believed the only life that had been well lived was one that ended bloodily, in the service of something greater than oneself.

Now retired, having reached his mid-forties, it was hard for the Captain to breathe. A military sawbones told him his left lung was partly ruined. Someday it would kill him. He couldn't raise his left arm above his head. It took him half an hour to get dressed in the mornings. He didn't care. It was only a body. The rest of him learned to compensate.

■ ■ ■

The Captain was born in easternmost Pennsylvania, and he'd always intended to return home, buy some land, and grow some sort of crop on it when he became too old to fight, if that was to be his miserable fate. (Suicide was out of the question, unless he'd been defeated in battle.) He was, he often thanked God, of purely English extraction. In those days, the ethnic makeup of that part of the country was different. All the Indians from around there were already dead, of course, or nearly all. And you didn't have so many of your Eastern Europeans then, not yet—the Poles and the Bohemians and the other miscegenated rabble that would soon invade the East came over to work the coal mines only later, when the invention of steamships made the trip affordable for anyone who could scrape together a few dollars. In that part of Pennsylvania you mostly just had your Germans, your Scots, your shanty Irish (as if there were any other kind of Irish, the Captain frequently opined), and many English. There were a few lingering French, left over from the days when those people had ruled the fur-trapping trade. Some of the Scottish families had already been in the New World long enough to have migrated all over again, from the Ozarks in the South to the Catskills and the Adirondacks and the Poconos in New York and Pennsylvania. These people had mountains in their blood, and they still sang the Gaelic songs of the Highland clans from the days of Bonnie Prince Charlie, as well as the songs of their cousins from the northern Irish counties. They sang them at their whiskey-soaked gatherings year after year, generation after generation, until gradually the sound of their voices and the rhythm of their tunes evolved into a different kind of music altogether, one that would have been only slightly recognizable to their ancestors, yet would have set their feet to tapping all the same.

And then there were the families descended from the oppressors of these people, which was the kind of people the Musgroves were: English lairds, nobles who'd been granted land in Scotland and Ireland that they would never even see. Early Musgroves had assisted in the systematic eradication of every trace of indigenous culture from the Scottish Highlands with sword and English Bible as their weapons, just as they would cleanse the North American continent of red-skinned heathens centuries later. The Captain knew his family history intimately, and was proud of every bit of it. His was a family of winners. They would never sink. Some of what they'd done wasn't pretty, he knew, but this was the price of progress, and it was better to be on top than on the bottom. That was a motto he repeated to himself every night, in the only Latin he knew, to pacify the pangs of conscience that were plucked in his head like a harp. *Melior in summo quam in fundo*: Better to be on top than on the bottom.

■ ■ ■

Musgrove would name the house Adencourt because it sounded like something he'd heard about that had happened once in France. *He* had not been to France—but *it* had happened there, a battle or something, he wasn't sure what. He just liked the name. It had resounded in his skull now for years, ricocheting like a musket ball in a bell, ringing with all the force of destiny.

The word he sought was "Agincourt," of course, which was the name of a battle between France and England in 1415; it had been a complete rout for the French, who were demoralized and embarrassed by not having made good on their threat to cut off the middle and index fingers of every English longbowman on the field, so that they would never pluck anything again, be it bow-, harp, or heartstring. It was a shame the Captain wasn't familiar with this story, because he would have enjoyed it thoroughly, especially the part about the French losing.

But he also would have liked the idea of cutting off fingers. In his youth, like many others, the Captain was a practitioner of battlefield mutilation. For many years, from the rafters of the long porch of his new house near Plainsburg, there hung oddlooking things, something like horsetails with a bit of horse still attached. These were human scalps. The Captain had taken them himself, from three warriors of some Apache tribe, at the battle of San Fernando. In those early days of America, to hang body parts of your enemies in public places was, though perhaps excessive, still socially acceptable. Visiting ladies politely averted their eyes from the grisly trophies, and the more squeamish business gentlemen up for a few days from Philadelphia or New York (who often stopped in to meet the old war hero on their way to points west) would take a great deal of time working up the courage to ask what, exactly, it felt like to rip off a man's scalp. The Captain was only too proud to describe it, in his diffident, frontier manner:

"Feels just like skinnin' a possum. Makes the same kind of noise, too. Yeh make a gash with your hatchet at the front of the head, not too hard, for yeh don't want to dash his brains out. Yeh want him to feel it, yeh see. Then yeh get your knife blade under there, just 'twixt the skin and the skull bone. Yeh run it up under and around, holdin' onto the feller's hair all the while. Like as not he's kickin' and screamin' about it, so, why, yeh just got to kneel on his chest and hold 'im down. Then, yeh just give a mighty tug, and off she comes, hair and all, and if you done it right, it's just as neat as can be. They usually fall pretty quiet about then, and you just run your blade acrost his throat, and that's the end of 'im, an' a fittin' end it is, too, the filthy bastards."

Said one truly horrified gentleman, a dandy lawyer from New York City:

"Why, then, sir, do you not simply remove the entire head, and carry that around with you?"

The Captain was as unfamiliar with the principles of sarcasm as he was with architecture. He explained:

"Yeh cain't put a human head in a saddlebag, nor tie it to a saddle horn. It spooks the horse."

∎ ∎ ∎

Upon his retirement, Captain Musgrove decided to move back East and marry. With all the deliberation and forethought that men now give to purchasing automobiles, he chose a wife from a family whose background was as similar to his as possible. This meant that he married his first cousin, because who else but other Musgroves could possibly be suitable for a Musgrove? Most everyone else in the world suffered from weak blood and water-on-the-brain, anyway. That was not for the Captain; he wanted strong children. Musgroves wanted their line to prosper. It was the only right way.

Her name was Marly. She was sixteen to his forty-three, which was considered by everyone, including Marly, to be a perfect match. Marly was short and thick-waisted, with a wide, sturdy pelvis and strong forearms; her features were a little too heavy to be considered attractive, but to the Captain, who had spent most of his life in the company of men, she was the epitome of womanhood, and he gladly took possession of her from her father. This girl would eventually bear the Captain ten children—including two sets of twins—and would assist in running the farm, as well as overseeing the few hired hands. Marly succeeded admirably in all these tasks, until she died under the hooves of a runaway horse when she was fifty-three, carrying an infant grandchild in her arms. That grandchild, Lincoln Flavia-Hermann, survived the accident without a scratch, and lived long enough to see the assassination of President John F. Kennedy replayed on television some eighty years later. Lincoln would watch it on his little black-and-white set in his nursing home, and he would remember the story of the tragedy that had attended his infancy, marveling at how easily death came to some, while others, such as himself, had to pray for it.

Of Marly's ten children, two died at birth, one died before she had learned to walk, one died of tuberculosis, and one drowned in the nearby river, which was deeper and faster then than it is now. This was not to mention the two who died in the flower of adulthood, during the outbreak of the Spanish Flu of 1918, which killed more people in the United States than all twentieth-century wars combined, yet which is almost never spoken of, or indeed remembered, by anyone now alive. Of ten Musgrove children, in fact, only three lived long enough to die of old age: Hamish and Ellen, who were fraternal twins, and their younger sister, Lucia.

The Captain and his wife buried their young children, one by one, in a little cemetery on the far end of the property, which in later years would become hidden by creeping wisteria and lilac, as well as the second growth of the trees that had been cut down to build the house. The five Musgroves who survived early childhood—Hamish, Ellen, Lucia, Olivia, and Margaret—were accustomed to visiting the cemetery often in their youth. They played their loud and carefree games six feet above the decomposing bodies of their siblings, imagining, with a sense of duty, that they were keeping them company, that they were all having fun together.

■ ■ ■

One day in 1859, a traveling salesman stopped into Adencourt for a glass of water. The Captain, rocking on the porch, saw him walking up the road; he hailed the yellow-haired man with a roar and the casual two-fingered salute that he'd adapted from his Army days, which had become his trademark. As it turned out, the man had seen some of the same western country the Captain had; they fell to talking about the vastness of the world, and lying frankly to each other about how well they were acquainted with it. The Captain appreciated a good liar, as long as he was honest about it; so the salesman, whose name was McNally, was invited to spend the night.

Noting the Captain's physical discomfort at dinner, McNally

alluded to the fact that he had a smattering of medical knowledge. The Captain allowed as how he wasn't one to complain, but seeing that the gentleman was in the medical way, he might as well tell him about his various aches and pains, to see what might be done about them—he hadn't had any luck with regular doctors. When the towheaded salesman left the next morning, it was with a full belly and a brand-new pair of shoes. In exchange, he'd left behind six bottles of McNally's Special Oriental Health Tonic, which was approximately 80 percent alcohol, 19 percent water, and 1 percent opium.

The stuff was the answer to the Captain's prayers. It eased his labored breathing and it allowed him to sleep the whole night through for the first time in years. He was not a drinking man, but since he didn't know what was in McNally's Tonic, that didn't matter. The salesman had assured him that it was a secret mixture of herbs known only to a few Eastern wise men, with whom he, McNally, had entered into an exclusive agreement during his world travels. He would be passing by this way again in several weeks; he would be happy to stop in on the Captain and replenish his supply of the tonic, though next time, being a man of business, he would have to charge him full price. Surely the Captain would understand.

A few weeks passed. After noticing that the tonic had become less effective, the Captain began to up his dosage. He went from one tablespoon in the evenings to two, and added one in the afternoons. Soon he stopped using the spoon and started using a glass. By the time he'd emptied three bottles, he was back to being an insomniac, only this time he suffered from cold sweats, paranoia, and headaches that threatened to rip him down the middle. He sometimes fancied that all the men he'd ever killed were standing in a circle around his house, waiting—Indian and Mexican side by side, united in their wish to gather him unto their cold and ragged bosoms. His old pain was gone, but it had been replaced by a creeping sense of doom, plus a horrible, empty feeling that the Captain had no name for, but one that consumed him all the same: addiction. He didn't want to drink any more of McNally's tonic, but he was afraid to stop. He forced himself to drink it even when he didn't feel like it, in order to stave off the inevitable shakes and bouts of anxiety that came every few hours. By the time he had upended the last of the six bottles, the Captain had begun both to fear and pray for the reappearance of the salesman.

Marly, now twenty-six years old, hardly knew what to think. She hadn't been to school beyond the age of twelve, and she knew nothing about the mysterious world of medicine. All she knew was that in a short time, her husband had become incapacitated, and the running of the farm was left to her. It was too much to handle. She took to keeping a loaded shotgun by the door, and a sharp eye out.

McNally showed up exactly when he said he would, no doubt already calculating the profits he would make from this easy sale. He was greeted at the door, where he stood with his hat in his hands, by the business end of the shotgun, which he found aimed at his mouth. At the other end of it was Marly Musgrove, pregnant then for the eighth and final time.

"Turn about, McNally," she said. "March."

McNally smirked. The sun glinted off his hair as though it was spun gold. "What are yeh goin' to do, missy?" he asked, raising his hands slowly. "Does yer mister know yer playin' with his scatter-gun?"

"The Captain doesn't know his own name, hardly," said Marly. "Now get moving."

She marched the salesman across the road to the river and down behind the trees, where no one would see or hear them. She made him take off his clothes and throw them in the water, along with his traveling suitcase. By this time, McNally's smirk had disappeared, and he had developed a bad feeling about his future, for it appeared the woman was serious. Though naked, he kept his hat on out of modesty. His quivering hands were raised high above his head.

"Look here at me," said Marly.

McNally did so. When he saw the expression on Marly's face, he began to cry, because he knew she was going to kill him.

"What's the cure?" she asked him.

"There ain't no cure, lady," said McNally, trying unsuccessfully to stifle his sobs. "You got to lock him in a room till he gets over it. There ain't no other way."

"Will he die of it?" Marly asked.

"I don't know," sobbed McNally. "Maybe."

That was all Marly needed to hear. She pulled both triggers simultaneously, knocking herself onto her back. When she managed to sit up again, the salesman had already floated a hundred feet down the river, amid a great red, blue, and green slick of blood and entrails.

Marly got to her feet and went back into the house, gun still smoking, shoulder aching. She could not bring herself to look at him. Her children would have heard the blast; she would tell them she'd shot at a fox. The Captain would be upstairs in bed, three days into his enforced drying-out period. She wouldn't tell him anything, because he would think he'd dreamed the noise. She would have to hope that the body would never be found, though there was a good chance that it would be. If so, she knew, she herself would be among the least likely suspects. She was the Captain's wife, after all. And without clothes, the man might be anybody: a gambler, a convict, a bank robber, a gypsy. He would be buried in a paupers' cemetery, and she was hopeful it would be assumed that someone had merely given him his just desserts.

Which, of course, someone had.

A couple of weeks later, when the Captain was finally starting to feel like himself again, he said: "If that damned salesman ever dares to show his face around here again, I'll blast him with the shotgun."

"I guess he won't," said Marly quietly. "Likely someone else'll get him first."

"What was his name again?" asked the Captain. "I forget."
But Marly wouldn't say it.

■ ■ ■

Two years later, the Civil War erupted, and the Captain decided he
was going to war for the third time in his life. To tell the truth, he'd
been praying for something like this. He could barely contain his excitement. His body may have been largely useless by then, his
breath nothing more than a feeble butterfly-wing breeze, but he
could, by God, still command. The battlefield was where he was
most at home, anyway. Domestic life drove him crazy, mostly because he had to deal with so many women—he understood women
far less than men or horses, and he didn't particularly like horses.

Before marrying his cousin, the Captain had never experienced
the peace and quiet of a farm. Not as a grown man, that is. He'd
entered the Army at fourteen, and had hoped, even at that tender
age, to die in its service. While the virtues of home life had been
extolled by the older soldiers in the form of songs and stories
around the campfire, he realized now that it was only the contrast
to violence and uncertainty that made it seem so pleasant. In
truth, he was dying of boredom, and with scarcely a word to anyone, he put on his old uniform and went to Philadelphia, never to
be seen again.

In time, his family was to learn—without much emotion—
that he'd been killed in Gettysburg, a no-account Pennsylvania
county to the south and middle of the state. When Hamish Musgrove, then ten years old, heard the news about his father, he
went onto the porch and lay underneath the withered Indian
scalps, looking up at them as they wandered gently in the breeze.
These belong to dead people, he thought, *and now my father is dead*.
For several minutes he lay there, trying to make a connection.
When none was forthcoming, he gave up. He hadn't cared for his
father very much, anyway. No one had.

This left Hamish, Ellen, and Lucia; the twins, Olivia and Margaret, who would later die of influenza; and Marly. Marly cut down the Indian scalps from the rafters and tossed them onto a refuse fire, where they gave off an unexpectedly sweet, purifying smell, like burning sage. The house settled comfortably around them like a blanket. It had an air of childhood about it, a feeling of renaissance. Things had gotten lighter. Life, now that the Captain was gone, was quiet and good.

These were the first people to live in the house, and so they are important. A house becomes like those who build it, true, but also like those who inhabit it. To take the elements of the earth and reshape them into something as magnificent and comfortable as a house is a feat of wonder. Yet creating something, or watching it be created, is not the same as owning it. It's the spirit that comes into a house after it's born that determines what kind of house it will be, what kind of life it will have. It's the people who move through it day after day, like a stream of blood through a many-chambered heart, that make it have a feel and a smell and a way. Eventually, the Captain wore off, and though no story about the house would be complete without him at the beginning of it, he plays no part in the end.

■ ■ ■

When they were just eighteen years old, Hamish and Ellen moved first to Harrisburg and then to Pittsburgh, where they shared an apartment and did not object when people mistook them for husband and wife. This was in 1870. After a time, they stopped coming home for holidays, and even their own family gradually forgot about them. Lucia, their sister, later married an immigrant farmer and settled in the house, which by now had lost all traces of the Captain—a lucky thing, since he would have been mortified at her choice of husband, who had not a drop of English blood in his body, only Bavarian. Lucia had three children. Of those, her eldest son, Lincoln—survivor of the runaway-horse incident—inherited the farm and house.

When Lincoln was put into the nursing home where he would witness the last significant event of his lifetime, he passed the house on to Helen, his oldest daughter, a beautiful woman with a taste for cruel men. Helen attempted to sell the old place several times, but she found, to her consternation, that she couldn't. There was no explanation for it; her hand simply refused to sign the papers, time and again, until realtors and bankers began to regard her as eccentric and manipulative. She couldn't have known it was the pull of the old children's cemetery, now forgotten and hidden by undergrowth, that prevented her. It still exerted its influence on all who shared Musgrove blood, like a small moon over a private sea. It would not be abandoned.

Instead, Helen had Adencourt remodeled. The house had never been glorious or beautiful; it had merely been new, once. She tried to recapture that state as much as she could, replacing rotted wood and shoring up the first floor from the basement, fumigating for termites, repainting, reroofing, adding drywall in some rooms, and modernizing the plumbing and electrical works that had been added around the turn of the century.

This, as it turned out, was the major task of Helen's life. She would never accomplish anything more useful than this. She was not the marrying sort, though it took her several tries to find that out. She wasn't the mothering sort, either. It's pleasant to think that an angel came to Helen one night and whispered warnings in her ear, that if she procreated, her children would be violent and hungry, that they would be a plague on the world, and that as a result, she denied her urge to reproduce; but there are no indications that the world works this way. Everything seems to be a strange blend of free will and chance, and it was this heady mixture that led Helen to make one last bad decision about a man who beat her to death in a SoHo hotel room one night. She was in her fifties then, near the same age her great-grandmother Marly had been when she was trampled. *She should have been home baking a pie and knitting, not lying in a pool of her own blood with a stomach full of Scotch.* This is what was said by one of the cops who helped lift her body, who noted in her a resemblance to his own mother, and was disturbed by it.

The year was 1975. For the first time in nearly a century and a quarter, the Musgrove house stood empty. It was not a showpiece house, but it was big. It was haunted by kind, anonymous spirits, the sort who merely watch, curious and lonely, never making a sound or disturbing anything. For a handful of years, the ghosts had the run of the place, until, like the old Captain, they began to grow bored, and slowly dissipated. The energy of the house and grounds experienced a brief surge whenever someone stopped to look, as though it were desperate to be lived in again. This was, in fact, the case. A house is like a person in this respect. It must be useful, or it dies. But finally Adencourt began to dim, like a candle drowning in its own wax, until the day the Harts showed up and peered in the windows. Francie thought she could almost certainly see things getting brighter inside before her very eyes, though she attributed that to the sun coming out from behind the clouds. Coltrane was already too busy calculating mortgage rates in his head to notice anything of the sort.

PART TWO

6

THE PRESCRIPTION

Coltrane and Francie did not prepare to leave New York until more than two months later. By then it was late November, and the weather had turned cold, threatening dire punishment on faithful and faithless alike. The bank had accepted Colt's first offer for the Pennsylvania house, with no attempt at negotiation—even though he'd deliberately underbid. Colt was surprised by this, and even a little suspicious, but not so Francie.

"It's proof the universe wants us to own it," she said, delighted. "I knew it was going to work out like this! I just knew it."

"It's proof there must be something wrong with it," Colt said. "Think for a minute. It's been sitting empty for twenty-five years. Why wouldn't someone else have bought it by now?"

"Because it was waiting for us," Francie said. "Why do you always have to look for a reason for everything?"

"Because there *is* a reason for everything. Things don't just happen by themselves, Francie. They happen because something made them happen."

"I don't care, I don't care," she sang. "It's ours, and I love it."

She looked around at the apartment that they had shared for the past nine years. It had grown so cluttered with things that it was nearly impossible for a person to move: a dining room table that was far too big for their dining room; a credenza; a highboy; an overstuffed leather couch and chair; endless shelves of knick-knacks and boxes of books that were all Francie's, that had nowhere to live because the bookcases were already crammed full. When Colt had lived here alone, she remembered, he'd owned a couch, a bed, a television, and a refrigerator—nothing more. Man furniture. The place had looked like a gangster's hideout.

These were all things that Francie had bought whimsically, but she could see now that they were destined not for the apartment but for some unknown dream home that she must have sensed in her future. At least, it seemed that way to her now. Finally, she thought, we will have *room*. To celebrate, she'd put on an old party hat and draped herself in a string of Christmas lights from the coat closet. She stood now, treelike, festooned in blinking red and green.

"I should have looked it over more carefully," Colt grumbled, ignoring her antics—although he had, in fact, hired a building inspector to go over the house with a finetooth comb. The inspector had found nothing wrong, at least nothing that wouldn't be expected in a house as old as that. The wiring and plumbing were all up to code; the structural supports were sound. The basement didn't leak and there were no termites. It was going to need a lot of cosmetic work, but there was no reason they couldn't go live in it tomorrow, if they wanted to. In fact, said the inspector, he'd never seen a house of similar age in better condition, and he'd seen plenty much worse. All of this had only deepened Francie's conviction that the place had been waiting for them all along; but Colt, his instincts honed on stone and whetted with blood, was waiting for the other shoe to drop.

"Come on," she said, holding out another string of lights. "Put these on. Let's have a party."

"You look ridiculous."

"*You* look ridiculous. Sitting there as though something was wrong, when there clearly isn't. A person would think you're upset, after getting such good news."

"I can be upset if I want to."

"But what are you upset *about*?"

"Nothing. I just don't want to put on any damn Christmas lights."

"Fine," said Francie, unplugging herself from the wall. "Be a party pooper. Be a big old bucket of poo. All I care about is we got it, Coltrane. We got it!"

"Yes," said Colt. "We got it, all right. The question is, what did we get?"

■ ■ ■

Next day, Francie went furniture shopping for their new place, armed with a handful of sketches of what she wanted. This was something she was good at, picking out furniture. She had the ability to look at an empty room and envision it as it should be, sketching blank walls and filling them with interesting shapes, and then filling the shapes with furniture. It was almost as satisfying as writing a good poem, as long as she tried not to think about what a pathetic substitute it actually was. She went to a department store and purchased couches, coffee tables, chairs, a credenza, knickknacks, and a glass-fronted case to hold them. She bought an oversized wingback reading chair and a duvet cover. After much wrangling, she succeeded in hiring—"bribing" was more accurate—the store's deliverymen to bring everything all the way out to Pennsylvania, since there was certainly no room for any of it in New York. She was told it would arrive "soon." In the lingua franca of furniture deliverymen, this meant sometime before all parties concerned were dead of old age, though there were not even any guarantees of that. Yet Francie knew it was best not to press for details, lest the deliverymen grow spiteful.

Colt was in favor of waiting for everything to arrive at the new house before they went back to it, since otherwise, as he pointed out, there wouldn't even be anything to sit on. But Francie complained that the walls of the city were beginning to close in on her. Besides, she was too excited. She didn't think she could wait any longer, she said; they should take the extra furniture from the apartment out there now and get set up.

"Yeah, but to tell the truth I sort of saw this as a summer place," Colt said. "To hang out in during nice weather. I mean . . . well, it's gotten cold out."

"Oh, I don't see it as a summer place at *all*," Francie said.

She was going through the receipts of her purchases, but she paused now, horrified at the thought that she might have to wait until spring to go back. Already she'd had dreams of herself out there in the wilds; she'd filled a notebook with drawings of the living rooms, the parlors, and the den, all furnished in ten different styles apiece, from Louis Quinze to modern Scandinavian.

"Colt, are you serious? I thought . . . I mean, I *know* I could finally do some really good writing there. It's such a . . . I don't know, a *rich* place. Just thinking about it makes me feel productive!" she said.

"Do you have any idea how much it's going to cost to heat it? Houses like that are totally inefficient. Old windows. Bad insulation," Colt said.

"But . . . Colt!"

"Well, I'm just saying, is all. What are you so worked up about? That house has been sitting there for a hundred and fifty years, Francie. It's not going anywhere before spring."

How was she to explain it to him? In the short time the house had been theirs, ideas had started to come to her again. The well was beginning to fill once more. She could sense it, and for the first time in years she was beginning to get that old feeling again, the one she hadn't had since her Golden Age. It was, quite simply, the feeling of being inspired, and that was not the kind of thing you put on hold until it was warm outside.

"I sort of want to live there," she said. "All the time, I mean."

Colt looked at her as if she was mad.

"You never said that," he said.

"Didn't I?" She was surprised at herself; it must have seemed so obvious that it hadn't needed mentioning. "Colt, we . . . we *bought a house*. What did you think we were buying it for, if not to live in? At least part of the time?"

"A *vacation* place, Francie, for God's sake," he said. "For summer weekends and stuff. And to have people out there for parties."

By "people," Francie knew Colt meant "work people": the tall, brittle men of finance and their brassy-voiced wives. She had a vision of the graceful driveway filling with expensive city cars, and of herself standing on the porch steps, a mink stole around her shoulders, a glass of bubbly in her hand, welcoming all with air kisses. Weekends of lawn bowling and adultery and feuding among the servants, ending with a good murder or two. No. More likely it would be loud alcoholic dinners and houseguests who didn't rise before noon, with Colt bragging all the while about this and that to anyone who would listen and Francie hiding in her room with a book until everyone went home again. God, what a fate, she thought. With her unerring sense for compromise, she came up with a rapid plan on the spot.

"Let's just go out there and get settled," she said. "Clean the place up and organize everything. Spend a few days. Celebrate. Then we can come back to the city. This is a big deal, Colt. You're due some vacation, aren't you?"

"Yeah, but . . ." Colt let his voice trail off. The fact was, he hated vacations, which Francie knew very well. He preferred work to anything else, and when he did take time off, he always wanted to go to some tacky resort in the Caribbean, with beaches crammed to the treeline with the sunburned bodies of other rich Americans. It was occurring to Francie for the first time that they had wanted this house for very different reasons. Oh dear, she thought. It would appear I have miscalculated. This place is just another trophy for him, isn't it? Just another thing to hang on the proverbial wall and admire. Like the Camaro. Or me.

"Come on," she said. "Please? For me? It would make me so happy, Colt."

The promise of domestic bliss was a trump card she rarely played. Never, in fact. So, after examining their schedules—Francie's empty, while Colt grumbled about shoving around his various meetings and planning sessions, et cetera, talking as if anyone actually *cared*, she thought—they planned to depart on the following Wednesday, the last one in a month that had already turned the earth as hard as iron, but had yet to produce any snow.

■ ■ ■

That Tuesday evening, just as they were sitting down to dinner, there came an unexpected buzzing on the intercom.

Who the hell is that?" Colt asked, irritated.

"My psychic powers are failing me just now," Francie said, getting up.

"No, don't answer it. Whoever it is, it's not someone we're expecting."

Francie stopped and glared at him.

"That's what makes life interesting," she said. She pressed the intercom on the wall. "Hello?"

"It's me," said a voice in a burst of static.

"Me who?"

"Me! Michael!"

"Mikey!" Francie screamed into the box. "Is that really you?"

"Let me in, Sissie," came Michael's wan voice. "It's freezing out here!"

Francie buzzed him in and began a frenetic happy-dance around the apartment. Now it was Colt's turn to glare at her.

"It's Mikey!" she told Colt. "He's visiting us!"

"Joy," he said, without feeling any.

"Mikey" was Francie's brother Michael. Once again, the wide-eyed wanderer had appeared out of nowhere, with no warning. These surprise visits were part of Michael's self-described style; he knew how to make no other kind of visit, in fact, since he seemed largely incapable of following most social conventions. It was the fifth or sixth time since their marriage that he had simply shown up.

"Again he does this?" Colt said, resting his forehead in his hand. "It's too much trouble for him to call?"

"That's my brother for you," said Francie, out of breath, exhilarated. "He's a free spirit."

"You say that like it's a good thing. What if we weren't in the mood for visitors?"

"He's *family*," Francie told her husband. "That's not the same as visitors."

"No. It's worse."

"If you had a brother, you'd be glad to see him, wouldn't you?"

"Yeah, but I don't."

The buzzer sounded and Francie yanked open the door, screeching with delight, for there stood her baby-faced, slope-shouldered little brother, soft and pudgy in the stomach, ambitiously whiskery, his thin lips plastered tight against his teeth in a stoned approximation of a smile. Colt noted that Michael was still sporting the same long, greasy hair, and the same old knit poncho—swept dramatically over one shoulder, as if it were a cape, and he minor nobility. Colt wouldn't have been surprised to learn that Michael hadn't showered much since the last time they'd seen him; hygiene, or rather the lack of it, was as much a part of his style as itinerancy. This never seemed to bother Francie, who attacked him now with kisses, practically bending him over backward in the hallway, Gable-like, before he even had a chance to enter the apartment.

"Mikey!" she screamed. "How are you? Where have you been?"

"Whoa," said Michael, pleased at her assault but fending her off. "Hi, Sissie. Hey, Colt."

"Hi," said Colt.

"Come in!" said Francie. "Are you hungry? Are you tired? Do you want a drink?"

"Shit, yeah," said Michael. "D, all of the above. I started out in Ohio this morning, and my bus is on its last legs. Kind of a tense trip. Wassup, Colt?"

"Nothing, as you so quaintly inquire, is 'up,'" said Colt. "You still driving that same old hunk of crap?"

"Yup," Michael said. "Almost two hundred fifty thousand miles on her now. Big hole in the floor, too. Rusted right out. You can practically drop things through it, if you want."

"Sit down, Mikey," said Francie, closing the door and pushing him into a chair.

"Right on," said Michael. "Sit down I will. Colt, my man. Nice to see you."

"Right on," said Colt. "You're on vacation from work, I take it? Got a couple of weeks off from the old grind?"

"No, dude," said Michael. He gave a phlegmy smoker's laugh, like a motorcycle chugging underwater. "I'm not working at the moment."

Colt put his hands to his face in a gesture of mock surprise. "What!" he said. "Mikey McDermott, without a job? Shocked, I am!"

"At the *moment*, I said," said Michael. "I'm on tour, dude. Making a cultural survey, you might say. Exploring this great land of ours. You know."

"No, I don't. I've never had the luxury," said Colt.

"Finding out what makes America America, man," said Michael. "I've seen the most amazing shit. You wouldn't believe it."

"I can't wait to hear all about it," said Francie.

"Something tells me we won't have to," said Colt.

■ ■ ■

They resumed their interrupted dinner, with Francie floating now between table and counter, helping Michael to more meat loaf, more juice, more salad; she even opened a bottle of champagne, one of the expensive ones Colt had been saving for a special occasion. From the look on Colt's face as the cork popped, it was clear that this visit didn't fall into that category, but Francie either failed to notice or didn't care; if it was up to Colt to decide when and how they would celebrate the small blessings in life, she knew, every day would be like a funeral. Michael talked and ate; Francie cooed; Colt listened, trying and failing to hide the sneer of contempt that kept sliding across his face like an eclipse.

"Meat loaf and champagne," he said. "I wonder if that's on the menu at Le Cirque."

"Tell us everything," said Francie, ignoring her husband. "I haven't talked to you in ages. The last time I spoke to Mom she said you were out West."

"I was in Denver," Michael said.

"Ooh, Denver! I've never been there. What's it like?"

"Mountainy. And cold."

"'Mountainy'?" Colt echoed.

"Yeah. With snowcaps. And mountain goats. Totally wild."

"How did you end up there?" Francie asked.

"I was hanging out in Phoenix, and I heard Phish was playing a concert up there, so I just went. And I met this girl out in the parking lot. Yolanda, her name was. She was cool, so I decided to stick around for a while."

"Wow, a parking-lot romance," said Colt. "Did she have hairy armpits?"

"I hope you were *careful*," said Francie.

"Aw, c'mon," said Michael, blushing. "They have parties in the parking lot," he explained to Colt. "It's not like she was just sitting there on the curb or something. There's dancing. And food. Sometimes there's even other bands."

"Oh, well, in that case," said Colt.

"So what happened?" Francie asked. "You didn't want to bring her along home with you?"

Michael shrugged and forked another slice of meat loaf onto his plate. "Y'know," he said. "It ran its course, I guess. We hung out for a few weeks, and then it was time to move on."

"Aw," said Francie. "Did she hurt you, sweetie?"

Colt snorted with laughter.

"No, it's cool," said Michael, shooting him an icy glare. "No attachments, no regrets. Y'know. Things happen the way they're supposed to happen. I wasn't upset about it."

"Good," Francie said. Colt picked up a butter knife and made sawing motions on his wrist. Francie continued to ignore him. "Go on," she said. "What else did you do?"

"Lessee. I went to this sweat ceremony with these Indians, where you're like crammed into this tiny little underground room with about thirty other people, and there's no air? We were in there for like six hours. And you have to like confront your own death and everything? And I fainted!"

"Oh, my God!" said Francie. "Were you all right?"

"He's here, isn't he?" Colt said.

"Sure, I was okay. I got in touch with my totem animal. It was a snake."

"This is spellbinding," said Colt, toying with his mashed potatoes.

"Seriously, man. All kinds of crazy shit happened to me out West."

"Was it 'heavy-duty,' man?" asked Colt. "Was it 'far out'?"

"Is he making fun of me?" Michael asked Francie. "Sometimes I can't even tell."

"Just ignore him," said Francie. "That's what I do."

"Yeah, that's the Coltster for you. I ended up catching two concerts, too. And I hooked up with these really cool people who let me stay with them for a while. Yolanda's friends. They had this great house. Really old."

"I bet it's beautiful out there," said Francie dreamily. "I've never been out West."

"It's awesome, Sissie. Everywhere you go looks like a movie set."

"Except, of course, it's real," said Colt. "Right?"

"Yeah, man, that's what I mean. Just that it *looks* fake, 'cause it's so beautiful."

"Yes, I got that. I just think it's kind of pathetic that your only frame of reference for describing natural beauty is the work of a bunch of Hollywood set designers," Colt said.

"Jeez, get a load of the Coltster," said Michael. "What's up your ass?"

"Nothing at all, as far as I know," Colt said mildly. "Last time I checked, anyway."

"Coltrane, shut up if you can't be nice," said Francie. "Mikey, *we* bought a house. A great big old house, out in the country. In Pennsylvania."

"No shit?" said Michael. "When did this happen?"

"In the last couple of months. We just saw it and fell in love with it. And we're moving some of our stuff out there. The antiques, and the extra furniture."

"Tomorrow, as a matter of fact," said Colt.

"No fucking way!" said Michael. "That is so cool! Hey, what about this apartment? Are you gonna keep it?"

"Of course. But we'll be going out to the country for a few days, to get things set up."

"Hey, no shit," said Michael. "In that case, can I crash here for a while? Just until I figure out where I'm going next?"

"Of course you—"

"No," said Colt, interrupting his wife. "Absolutely not."

"Coltrane!" said Francie. "Why not?"

"No, listen, really," said Colt. "I've got to put my foot down. If you're going to show up unannounced and uninvited, the least you can do is make yourself useful. We've got a shitload of stuff to

move tomorrow morning. All the crap your sister has bought over
the last ten years that we didn't have room for. And I'm not running a hotel here." He gave Francie the Eye of Doom, but she de-
flected it with practiced ease, resting her chin on her hand and
staring blankly at him as if waiting for him to get to the true
point. "And most of *my* stuff is staying here, including my very expensive stereo system," he added, "and I don't want you messing
around with it. Plus, I seem to recall a couple of CDs that you
'borrowed' the last time you were here. You didn't happen to
bring them with you this time, did you? My Steely Dan greatest
hits, for example?"

"Oops," said Michael. "Okay, man, chill. Of course I'll help you
move."

"That would be most appreciated," said Colt.

"The harshness in here is a little what you might call stifling,"
said Michael to his sister, taking yet another slice of meat loaf.
"Kind of like having a whole other dad, isn't it?"

"He really does go away if you ignore him," Francie said.

Michael snorted with laughter. "Good one, Sissie," he said. "I'll
have to remember that."

■ ■ ■

"He's got a learning disability," Francie reminded Colt later, as
they were lying in bed. "He's dyslexic, *and* he's got ADD. It's really not his fault he's so erratic. And I don't appreciate you being
so tough on him."

"They've got a name for everything now, don't they?" Colt
said. "Nobody has to be responsible for anything anymore. Listen,
the only real problem that kid has is that your father is still
shelling out an allowance every month. He doesn't even have to
work. It's pathetic. He doesn't contribute anything to the world.
He just . . . *coasts*."

"He *will* contribute something someday," said Francie. "He just needs encouragement."

"You know what would encourage him? Starvation."

"Colt! That's terrible!"

"All I mean is, he needs a job."

"Well, if you have any bright ideas, maybe you should share them with him. He needs some pointers, Colt. He needs guidance. It doesn't help that you make fun of him all the time. You might not know this, but he actually looks up to you. You'd get a lot further with him if you weren't so hostile."

"He does *not* look up to me," said Colt. "He talks to me like I'm eighty years old. He *patronizes* me."

Francie sighed. "You could show a little patience. Help him figure out what to do."

"It doesn't *matter* what he does," Colt said in exasperation. "That's the thing he doesn't seem to understand! He acts like he's waiting for his dream job to be handed to him on a silver platter. All that really matters is that he earn his keep, at least for starters. *Anything* would be better than doing nothing. He could pump gas, or work at a fast-food place. Once he got a taste of that, he'd be motivated pretty quick to find something better. Eventually he'd find something he liked." He paused. "Or not. It's not like it matters whether he even likes what he does. Life isn't a fucking cocktail party, after all. We're not here to have fun all the time. It's . . . it's just not like that."

"That's your point of view, Coltrane, not his. Not everyone sees the world like it's a punishment to be here. Some people actually enjoy their lives." She sighed. "Besides, he doesn't even know where to start, Colt. He says every time he thinks about it his brain freezes up."

"Well, did he actually major in something during his . . . how many years of college? Six, was it?"

"World Cultures."

"World Cultures is a *major*?!"

"Shh, Colt. He'll hear you. These walls are thin."

"This is my home, for God's sake. I can talk as loud as I want. What exactly does majoring in World Cultures qualify you for, if it's not too insensitive of me to ask?"

"It gives you an appreciation of the world we live in," Francie said, "which is something you could use a little more of yourself."

Colt fell silent, clenching the sheet in his fists as he stared up at the darkened ceiling. An appreciation for the world we live in? he thought incredulously. This was one of the many problems with America today, he thought: colleges and universities were too strapped for cash to turn anyone away. They even had to invent bullshit subjects like World Cultures so they could keep the money coming in. People like Michael didn't belong in school, he thought. They belonged in factories, or the army. Places where they would at least be useful.

"For God's sake," he managed finally. "How are you supposed to make money appreciating the world we live in?"

"There are other things in this world that are more important than making money, Coltrane."

This was unbearably familiar terrain, and rather than traverse it again Colt opted for a good night's sleep, in preparation for what was sure to be a strenuous day of heavy lifting and further arguments. He rolled over and put a pillow over his head, muttering a good night.

"Promise me you'll try to be nice to him," said Francie.

"What?" Colt pulled the pillow off his head. "What did you say?"

"I said I want you to be nice to him. It'll make things a lot easier on me. I can't take any tension right now, Colt. This is such a happy time. I don't want anything to ruin it."

"Oh, God," said Colt, "all right, I promise."

■ ■ ■

In the deepest part of the night, Francie had a dream that jolted her awake; but by the time she lifted her head off the pillow, she'd forgotten what it was. She lay back and twirled her hair in her fingers, staring up into the blackness. Colt was snoring heavily at her side. Irritated, she reached for her foam earplugs. Just before she stuck them in, she heard Michael through the wall, muttering something in his sleep. She had tucked him into the guest bed, marveling at how he'd gone unconscious almost immediately. He'd always been that way, ever since he was a baby; she remembered the day of his first homecoming perfectly, even though she'd only been five—his puckered red face, his thin, reedy cry, like someone blowing on a blade of grass between their thumbs. Even then, she'd felt that it was up to her to take care of him. She would sneak him out of his crib at night and take him into her own bed, and their parents would find them like that, morning after morning—she curled around him, despite all their warnings and threats about suffocation and accidental squashings. *She thinks she's his mother,* her father used to say. *Lord knows how she got that idea.*

Lord knows indeed. She pressed the foam in until she felt pressure on her eardrums. We're moving tomorrow, she thought. Of course *Colt's* not happy about it. He treats it like everything else: like it's a nuisance. He was happy about it for about five minutes. Why is it he sees the world as though we were all laboring together on some kind of assembly line? He never used to be that way. Or if he was, I didn't notice. That hardly seems possible. But it's been almost ten years. People can change a great deal in that time, or, what's more likely, they *stop* changing; they drop the mask they used to lure you in with, and you see their true, terrible face.

Now what kind of talk is that? she thought, astonished at herself. Shut up and go to sleep, would you?

Aided now by artificial silence, she did.

■ ■ ■

The movers showed up the next morning only an hour late, a minor miracle and a good omen—two brown-skinned Indian men in
a truck that bore the logo TWO SMALL BROTHERS WITH STRONG
BACKS MOVING CO. and a caricature of themselves, big-headed and
tiny-bodied, laboring mightily under a massive grand piano. It
was an ad that inspired confidence in those who favored under-
dogs. The men finished loading the extra furniture and the guest
bed into the truck around noon, and then left. Francie cruised
once more through the apartment, which now seemed unfamil-
iarly bare. She found, to her mild surprise, that she could now
move through the place without banging her shins on anything.
They left the city soon after in a convoy made up of themselves,
the Camaro, and Michael's ancient Volkswagen bus.

Somewhere in New Jersey, Coltrane asked, "So, did he say how
long he's going to be visiting us?"

"Michael? A few days," she said, pawing through the contents
of her purse. "You know, he seems kind of upset about something.
Like something bad happened, but he doesn't want to talk about
it. Did you notice?"

"My heart overflows with concern," said Colt. "He seemsd like
his normal worthless self to me."

"Well, a sister can tell these things."

"I'll take your word for it."

"Honey? I don't mean to alarm you, but I forgot to get my prescription refilled before we left."

"They have pharmacies in Pennsylvania, too," said Colt. "How
long is 'a few days,' anyway?"

"A week, maybe," said Francie. "I just . . . I just hope I have my
actual prescription slip somewhere. Come to think of it, I haven't
seen it in a while."

"Well in that case, *he* can sleep in the basement," said Colt. "Or
no, let's put him in the barn. Your prescription is probably in one
of your ten zillion boxes. How many pills do you have left?"

"One," she said. She put her purse down and leaned back, running her hands distractedly through her hair. "And I have to take it tonight. So I have none for tomorrow."

"Don't worry about it," Colt said. "I'll get you some more this weekend when I come back into the city. Plenty of time."

"I'm not supposed to miss a day. It throws me off."

"Francie?"

"Yeah?"

"You were the one who said you didn't want anything to ruin your good mood. So don't worry about it. Really. Missing a few days won't hurt you. You've been on that stuff so long your body won't even notice."

It's not my body, it's my brain, Francie thought; but she only smiled weakly.

The bare trees of New Jersey stood like sentinels along the road, bare arms flexed as if they were supporting the weight of the sky. They sped around the Delaware Water Gap once more, its surface chilled thick and oily, abandoned now by all but the hardiest birds. Anyone could see that winter would be coming early this year, that it was nearly time to hunker down and burrow in.

"Would you tell me something?" she asked Colt quietly.

"Tell you what?"

"You know what."

He knew what she wanted to hear; once upon a time he had been able to read her mind, nearly always, and he would guess what she was thinking. Feeling a sudden rush of—what? warmth? pity?—Colt reached over and took her hand in his, squeezing it.

"Yes, I love you," he said.

Francie smiled.

7

■

THINGS AS THEY OUGHT TO BE

It seemed as if the Pennsylvania heavens had been burned black by the time they pulled into the driveway of the house in Pennsylvania, early that afternoon. A mighty storm was creeping out of the northeast, turning the sky to the dull sheen of charcoal. Francie got out of the car and stood in the driveway, looking up, entranced, as a raft of marbled clouds sailed westward, so low she could nearly touch them. It had been sunny in New York, though cold; but they'd entered the season of rogue weather, when no one could tell what was going to happen.

She breathed deeply, and at that moment she smelled something for the first time in years: the coming of snow. It was a fragile scent, easily destroyed by smog, but here there was none. Nor were there those endless city buildings bristling like forests of needles, threatening to rend the tender belly of the sky. And the sky itself was bigger, too. The horizon simply went on until it disappeared, like it was meant to, and the clouds flowed over the distant curve of the earth like water pouring downhill. She half heard the slamming of doors as Colt and the Indians disembarked and opened the sliding door at the back of the truck. In the distance she could hear the clicking metallic whine of Michael's bus as he struggled up the road; he'd managed to keep pace, despite Colt's subtle efforts to lose him on the highway.

This was her first time seeing the house as someone who lived in it, rather than a visitor, and she paused long enough to let that sink in, too. She already knew that she was never going back to the city. She would welsh on her deal with Colt; that was no problem. She had no intention of staying in the country only "a few days." When they'd emerged from under the river and she'd turned to see the city behind her—finally—she'd breathed freely for the first time in years. She'd never succeeded in becoming a New Yorker, she realized, as the skyline receded. Other people could move to the city and fit in within a week, so that it was already in their blood. But for her, it was always like a party she was looking in on from the outside, half afraid she would never be invited and half afraid she would. Now this place, with its squared edges and rounded windows, its three and a half stories, its incongruous widow's walk that was at least three hours from the ocean: this place was in her blood the moment she saw it, and they were going to have to drag her out of here in a straitjacket, or carry her out feet first, before she would go back to that apartment.

When she opened the front door, she found that it swung easily this time, without effort. Francie stepped into the foyer and down its length, then into the outer living room, listening to the sound of her own footsteps reverberating through distant, empty spaces. It was up to her now to fill this house with furniture, and art, and things; it might very well take years. Excitement roiled in her at the thought of it. *This is it*, she told herself. *This is the place where things will finally be as they ought to be.*

Hand in her coat pocket, Francie fingered the plastic cylinder that had once held fifty pills, and now held one; she could feel the lone survivor rattling around against her palm, a single, tiny pink pebble.

And suddenly, she was reminded of something.

When she was a little girl, she'd been in the habit of saving her lost milk teeth, carrying them around in a baby-food jar as if she couldn't bear to part with them. It was an old and familiar gesture, this veneration of artifacts of the self. She went through compulsive phases sometimes, saving hair, fingernail clippings, sometimes used tissues by the dozens; but only now did she remember how that had started. The problem was that in those days, she couldn't believe that the Tooth Fairy would really come to her, not when one considered how very many children there were in the world whose teeth had also fallen out. And if she did come, Francie couldn't bear the thought of a part of herself being taken away by a total stranger—even a part she didn't need anymore.

Her father had finally taken her teeth himself. He said it wasn't normal—she'd been bringing them to school, to church, even taking them to bed, and the other children teased her about it. Francie didn't disagree with him. Even then, she was waiting for someone to tell her it was all right to let things go, that it wasn't necessary to hang onto *everything*. When he finally took them, it was a relief, but it was not the last time she would have to be told how to feel.

Which was why, in a manner of speaking, she was on the pills now: she didn't feel anything. They made it so that she didn't have to wonder how she had to be. She could just *be*.

But they were treacherous, duplicitous little tablets. Everything was actually their fault, she thought. Her life as it was now was all because of them. *They* were why she hadn't written any good poems, for one thing. Also, they were what allowed her to agree with Colt on so very many issues. Like having babies, for one. *He* didn't want any children, not ever; he was always saying he didn't have the energy for both career and family. True, he worked so much that if they *were* to have kids, he would never see them. Twelve-hour days were normal; fourteen, or even sixteen, not unusual. But what about me? she thought. *I* don't work sixteen hours a day. *I* don't do *anything*! I could have a baby, and take care of it myself. Couldn't I? Why shouldn't I be allowed to try, at least? Don't I get to have a say in that, too? Why should he be the one who gets to decide everything, just because he's the one who makes all the money?

It must have been a sign, her losing the prescription. Just like getting the house. It must mean that she wasn't supposed to take them anymore. What if she were to go off the pills? She was a different person now than she was at twenty-one, anyway. She was no longer a helpless girl. She was a woman now. She could stop taking them for a while and see what happened. If it didn't work out—if things started getting bad again—she could simply go back on them. It would be good to take a break. It would be symbolic, even—like she was making a whole new start in life, along with moving into the new house.

Secretly, before the men came in, Francie stole into the bathroom near the kitchen. She took the plastic cylinder out of her pocket and opened the childproof cap. Then, carefully, she tipped the last pill into the toilet and flushed it away.

What a bad girl am I, she thought, delighted with herself.

"What're you doing, Sissie?" Michael asked.

Francie whirled around, startled to see her brother standing behind her. Quickly she put the plastic container back in her pocket.

"Nothing, Mikey," she said. "You shouldn't sneak up on me like that!"

"Sorry. I thought you heard me," said Michael. "What was that you just flushed away? 'Ludes?" He giggled.

"Cold medicine," said Francie. "I had a cold. It's gone now."

"Oh. And you're planning on never having another cold again?"

"It . . . had side effects," said Francie.

"Oh. Listen, man, this is a hell of a house. Really something."

"Don't you just love it?"

"Yeah. Looks like we finally got that country place, huh?"

Michael grinned at her, delighted. Francie smiled uneasily.

"It's big. And cold. Who lived here before?" he went on.

"We don't know," said Francie. "I mean, we sort of know. It was a family called the Musgroves. But they haven't lived here in a long time."

"Place is clean," said Michael. "Doesn't look like it's been empty."

"The bank said there was a caretaker. Someone's been keeping it up for them, in case they ever sold it."

"It suits you. Couldn't see why you ever moved to New York in the first place."

"It was a whim," said Francie. "It was good for a while. But I'm done with it now. I think I can be happy here. I can really . . . open up."

"And you're happy with Colt?"

Francie was startled. "Of course I am, honey," she said. She reached out and tucked a wayward strand of hair behind her brother's ear. "Why on earth would you think I wasn't?"

"I just wondered, that's all," said Michael. "He's so . . . edgy, I guess. Really businessy. He never really has anything nice to say about anything, didja ever notice? A real negative type. Tell the truth, I didn't see you ending up with a guy like him, either." He lowered his voice on this last thought, looking over his shoulder to make sure they were alone. They were—sounds of shuffling feet and grunting came from the front of the house, where Colt and the movers were struggling with a sofa. "You're really sensitive and artistic, and he's . . ."

"I know," said Francie. "Businessy. But we complement each other, honey. You don't want to marry someone who's just like you. You want them to fill in your missing pieces. Kind of like a jigsaw puzzle."

"I guess so," said Michael.

"Don't worry about me," said Francie. "Your big sister can take care of herself. I was wondering about you, though. Is there something on your mind? Something bugging you?"

"Little help!" called Colt from the living room. "Hello! Francie! Mike!"

Michael shuddered. "I hate it when he calls me 'Mike,'" he said. "Makes me feel like one of his poker buddies."

"Mikey? Was there something?"

Michael looked at the floor, then around at the walls. Francie knew this expression all too well; whatever it was, he was afraid to tell her. She waited.

"Not now," he muttered. "Later."

"We'll talk," said Francie. "Gimme a kiss." She pulled her brother's ear to bend him down to her, and they bussed lightly. Then they went back out to the front of the house.

In the living room, they came upon Colt, who was crawling on his hands and knees, his nose six inches from the floor.

"Lose something?" Francie asked.

"My charm," said Colt. "It just fell off. The chain broke."

Michael guffawed. "I don't believe it," he said. "You carry a good-luck charm?"

Colt glared at him. "Yes," he said, daring him to make something of it.

"They all carry them at his office," Francie told her brother. "They believe in them."

"Of course we believe in them," said Colt. "That's because they work."

"Are you sure you lost it in here, honey?"

"Francie, if I was sure where I lost it, then it wouldn't be lost anymore, now would it?" Colt said exasperatedly.

"There's no reason to get snappy," Francie told him. "I was just asking."

They looked high and low, but found nothing. Colt's charm was gone.

8

SURVIVAL OF THE FITTEST

The movers, not wishing to be stranded in Pennsylvania, worked fast under the threat of the looming storm, finishing just as flurries began to thicken the air—not the storm itself, but only the advance guard. The two men accepted a wad of cash from Colt and pulled out of the driveway in a hurry. Though it was not yet twilight, it had already gone dim inside. Shadows crept out from the walls and gently spread themselves across the floor. Already he could hear the creaks of the old wood as the house adjusted to the dropping temperature. How many snowstorms had this house survived? he wondered. A hundred? A thousand? Was there a limit to how many a house could endure?

"Power on?" he called, as he came back inside, slapping snow off his shoulders.

"I don't know," Francie answered him, from somewhere.

"Of course you don't," he muttered. "You'd just sit in the dark until someone came along and turned the lights on for you."

"What?"

"Nothing!"

Colt felt along the wall until he came to a switch, and was gratified to be hit with a splash of light from a bare bulb that hung by wires from the ceiling. "Yes, it's on," he called back. Other switches were flicked in other rooms, and the three of them came together in the kitchen, lost in its massiveness, shivering, grateful at least for the brightness.

"What kinda heat you got in this place?" Michael asked.

"Electric baseboard," said Colt. "Plus fireplaces. A lot of fireplaces."

"Oh, let's make a fire!" said Francie. "Please? There's firewood in the basement. I saw a stack of it when we came through with the real estate agent."

"That's not a bad idea. Okay, you," said Colt, pointing to Michael, "go downstairs and get some wood. Bring it up to the living room."

"By myself?" Michael said. He turned and looked at the basement door. Opening it, he peered down the rickety wooden stairs into the blackness. "Oh, Jesus," he said, dubious.

"Don't worry, there's nothing down there," Colt said. "Ha ha."

"Colt, you help him," said Francie.

"Why? It's a one-man job. It's easy."

"He's scared."

"I'm not scared, Sissie," said Michael. "Relax." He flicked the switch on the wall and tromped down the stairway, which was made of nothing more than two-by-sixes; they could hear it quake under his weight like a leaf in a thunderstorm. Colt smirked at Francie.

"If this was a movie, this is where he would get eaten by the monster," he said.

"Shut up," said Francie. "You really are being an asshole."

"I am not," Colt protested. "Or if I am, it's working. He helped us unload, didn't he? First honest work he's done in years. Maybe I'm rubbing off on him."

"Rubbing him the wrong way is more like it."

"Fine. Whatever it takes."

Francie moved around the kitchen, running her hands over the curved lines of the ancient refrigerator. It was silent. She bent down, reached behind it, and plugged it in. It rattled and whirred into life. Opening it, she frowned at its emptiness. "What are we going to do about dinner?" she asked. "We forgot to bring food."

"Order in," Colt said automatically.

"From where, dear husband? We're in the country, you know."

"I dunno. There must be some Chinese around here or something."

"I don't think so, Colt. There might be a place in town, but that's miles away."

"Yeah, but . . . well, you can get delivery anywhere, can't you?"

Francie was dismayed to note that there was a hint of panic in his voice. Was it only occurring to him now that there were places in the world that didn't fall into someone's delivery radius? she wondered.

"Look in the phone book," she said.

"We don't have a phone book. We don't have a phone, for that matter." Colt felt in his pocket and came up with his cell phone. Flicking it on, he held it to his ear and cursed. "Out of range. I thought I had roaming on this thing."

"That's an extra feature. You have to sign up for it."

"Well, thanks for telling me now, Ma Bell."

"There's a supermarket in town," said Francie, sighing with exaggerated patience.

"All right, I'll go," said Colt glumly. "Got any cash? I gave all mine to the movers."

"No, I'll go."

Colt was startled. "What? That's crazy. It's snowing out."

"Colt, we need food. And I'm better at driving in snow than you are."

"That's not true."

"Yes, it is," Francie said patiently, knowing she could win this one. "I grew up driving. You grew up riding the subway. We've had this argument before. Remember?"

"Oh, all right," said Colt. "If you're so determined."

"I just want to do something, that's all. I want to explore a little."

"At night? With a blizzard coming? Fine. Be my guest."

"Boy, it's creepy down there," said Michael, coming back up the stairs with an armload of logs. "And this wood is pretty ancient. It's like rotten or something."

"I'm leaving," said Francie. "See you guys in a bit."

"Where you going, Sissie?" Michael asked, a note of alarm in his voice.

"Sissie going to da soopeymarket," Colt said. "To buy Mikey some foodies."

"Colt!" Francie said.

"Just messing around," he said, hearing the broken glass in her voice. "Trying to inject a little levity into the situation. Jeez."

"You want me to come, too?" asked Michael.

"No, sweetie, you stay here. I'll be fine. You can help Colt."

"Help Colt with *what*?"

"We make fire," said Colt. "Eat buffalo. Do war dance."

"You're acting like an idiot," said Francie.

"He's not acting," said Michael.

"Good-bye, boys," Francie said, pulling the keys from Colt's jacket. "Try not to kill each other while I'm gone."

■ ■ ■

Michael watched with a sense of grim foreboding as Francie pulled out of the driveway in the Camaro, disappearing into the snowflakes that swirled along the road as though stirred up by the skirts of invisible dancers. Then he turned to watch the spectacle of Colt trying to light a fire. It was abundantly clear to him that this was a man who bought his fire prepackaged, just like everything else. In a half-assed approximation of every Hollywood cowboy movie he'd ever seen, Colt had built a kind of log pyramid on the grate, and he was now holding a lighter to it, waiting for it to catch. He burned his thumb and stuck it in his mouth. When he caught Michael trying not to grin, he threw the lighter at him.

"Here," he said around his thumb. "You think you're so smart, you try it."

"Kindling, dude," said Michael. "You need kindling."

"What's that?"

Michael snorted. "Tell me you're joking," he said. "You don't know what kindling is? Didn't you ever go camping when you were a kid?"

"I was too busy," said Colt. "I skipped childhood and went straight into my twenties."

"Sucks to be you."

"Sucks more to be you."

Michael shredded some bark off the logs and broke up a couple of the smaller pieces. Within moments he'd created a blaze that grew rapidly, filling the room with the sound of snapping fingers. Colt nursed his seared digit and stared at the flames in a state of sulky hypnosis.

"Boy Scouts," said Michael. "I can build a rabbit trap, too."

Colt didn't answer.

"Seriously, your dad didn't ever take you camping?" Michael asked.

"Nope," said Colt.

"Why not?"

"Because he's dead."

"Whoa. Bummer. I didn't know."

"You didn't notice he wasn't at our wedding? Or my mother, for that matter?"

"Your wedding was a long time ago, dude. I was what, sixteen? So you're like an orphan?"

"At my age you're not called an orphan. You just don't have parents anymore."

"Right. But did they die when you were young?"

"Yes," said Colt. "You could say that."

"That's too bad, man."

Colt didn't answer. They stood in awkward silence for a few moments. Michael sighed.

"Well, unless we're gonna sing 'Kumbaya,' I'm gonna get turned on," he said. From somewhere within the folds of his poncho, he produced a thick, bent joint. He wet one end and lit the other, inhaling deeply; then he offered it to Colt, who waved it away.

"How long you been smoking that stuff, anyway?" he asked.

"Thirteen years," Michael said, exhaling a cloud of smoke in the direction of the fire. "More or less. I think."

"That long? Jesus."

"It was the thing to do, back when I started."

"It was the thing to do when you were *twelve*?"

Michael shrugged and took another toke. "What can I say? I ran with an advanced crowd."

"Advanced, my ass. Your brains probably look like a marshmallow by now. You ever think about what that stuff does to you?"

"You mean to tell me you've never taken drugs? Not once?" Michael asked. "Not even coke? I thought all you financial types spent your lunch hour doing lines in the executive washroom. It's in all the movies."

Colt guffawed. "Sure," he said. "I've done coke. Kid stuff."

"Kid stuff?"

"It's what all the junior types do. To make themselves feel like big shots." He shook his head. "It was the eighties," he said. "What can I say? I only did it a few times."

"Well, then, you've got no room to lecture me. Besides, pot helps me think."

"How can smoking pot help you think?"

Michael shrugged. "It focuses me," he said.

Colt snorted. "Please," he said. "That stuff slows you down, if anything. You have to think in terms of survival. You think you could defend yourself if you were stoned?"

Michael looked around. "Defend myself against what?" he asked, laughing.

"Saber-toothed tigers. Woolly mammoths. Enemy attack. You wanna get ahead, you have to think like a caveman. Survival of the fittest."

"Man, you *are* a caveman. We're not under attack, dude. We're like right here in your living room."

"Yeah, but I'm talking about *survival of the fittest.*"

Colt began dancing around Michael, throwing punches at his face, pulling them at the last second.

"Cut it out," said Michael nervously.

"You think our species got ahead because everyone sat around getting messed up all the time? You have to be ready. You never know when someone's gonna try and steal your woman. Oh, wait, I forgot. You don't have a woman. There was just . . . Yolanda. Yolanda with the hairy armpits."

"Quit it, man," said Michael, stepping back from him. "She did not have hairy armpits! And you're harshing my buzz!"

"Come on. Seriously. You ever box?"

"No, and I'm not starting tonight!"

"I boxed a little in college. I could show you a few things. Throw some with me. Come on, tough guy. Let me have one. Move around like this."

Colt shuffled his feet rapidly and hit Michael lightly in the stomach a couple of times. They were only butterfly blows, but Michael wasn't ready for them, and he was startled. "Jesus," he said, a note of anger sounding in his voice. "Knock that shit off, will you?"

"That's it. Get mad. Get pissed off." Colt kept moving around him, landing a couple more light blows. But Michael refused to engage him. He stared steadfastly ahead at some invisible point on the wall, gritting his teeth with each punch. "You gotta get mad if you wanna be a killer. You gotta get mad if you wanna be a killer. You gotta get mad if you wanna be a killer."

"*I don't wanna be a killer!*" Michael shouted.

"Hit me!" said Colt.

Michael, breathing hard, swung suddenly and wildly at Colt, a haymaker punch that he ducked easily, almost without trying.

"You're telegraphing," said Colt. "I saw that punch coming before you even threw it. You gotta be sneaky, like this."

He came up from underneath and stuck his fist somewhere in Michael's poncho, a little harder this time. The air came out of his brother-in-law in a gentle *whuff*.

"You asshole," said Michael. "That hurt!"

"That's it! Get mad!"

"I don't wanna get mad!" Michael said, his voice high with panic now. "I wanna mellow out!"

"Here," said Colt, "I'll give you an easy one. Now get out of the way."

He sent a slow punch at Michael's face, but even at half-speed it was too fast for the pudgy younger man, and it caught him squarely on the nose. Blood spurted out from under Colt's knuckles as Michael dropped to his knees, as if answering a call to prayer.

"Oh, fuck!" he said into his hands. "My nose!"

Oops, thought Colt.

In his head, he heard his father's voice: *Way to go, Coltie boy. Way to show him who's boss.*

■ ■ ■

It took Colt several minutes to locate a roll of paper towels amid the chaos of the move. He brought them back into the living room, eyeing his brother-in-law with a mixture of disdain and regret. Michael was lying in front of the fire now, hands over his face.

"Here," said Colt, handing him the paper towels. "Take these. We don't have any ice yet. Fridge hasn't been on long enough."

Michael grudgingly took the towels and held them to his nose.

"Tilt your head back and breathe through your mouth."

"I know how to get rid of a bloody nose," said Michael. "I've had plenty of practice, thanks to pricks like you. Jesus Christ, man, what's the matter with you?"

"C'mon, we were just messing around, right?" said Colt. "You know I wasn't really trying to hurt you. Right?"

"Coulda fooled me," Michael snuffled. He sat up and spit bloody mucus into the fire. Then he lay down again, closing his eyes.

"Appreciate it if you wouldn't say anything to Francie about it. I really am sorry."

Michael sighed.

"Is it broken?" Colt asked.

"I don't think so."

"I didn't hit you that hard."

"Why did you have to hit me at *all*?"

"I didn't mean to," said Colt. "Look, if it makes you feel better, you can have a free shot at me. Go ahead. I won't duck. Take a poke."

"Fuck you," said Michael.

Colt ran his hands through his hair in frustration. "It was just a game," he said.

"Some game."

Yeah, some game, came the voice again. *Is that how I raised you? To hurt people for fun? Oh, yeah, you're a big man, all right.*

Oh, shut up, Colt thought. *Where do you get off? You didn't raise me at all.*

■ ■ ■

He left Michael lying on the floor and went back into the kitchen, where he paced back and forth between the counter and the opposite wall. It had been months since his father's voice had troubled him last, and he had dared to hope he was rid of it once and for all; but sheer willpower had never been enough to banish it completely.

You didn't have to hit him. You just wanted to, to show him how big and strong you are. Look at you, almost forty years old and still acting like a teenager! You might as well still be in high school!

"Shut up!" Colt said, hands to his head. "He had it coming. He needed a little shake-up. I didn't really hurt him."

No, you didn't really hurt him. That's why there's blood all over your hands.

Colt looked down, and saw that there was indeed a large, amorphous smear of Michael's blood on the back of his right hand, from where he had punched him. He went to the sink and scrubbed it off under a stream of freezing water. He felt his temples; blood had caked there, too, where his hair was going gray. He must have been running his hands through his hair, something he did when he was worried. He wet his fingers and rubbed it away. Then he went to the mirror in the bathroom, checking to make sure it was all gone.

"There," he said to his reflection. "You happy? Now shut the fuck up. I don't need any input from you."

The voice fell silent.

Colt went back into the kitchen and leaned on the sink, rocking back and forth on the balls of his toes. He watched the snow swirl downward, the flakes as round and thick as quarters. He could see himself faintly in the glass, and he bared his teeth at himself in a mirthless grin.

"It was a dark and stormy night," he said.

9

THE CHICKEN OF DESPAIR

Parking between two antiquated pickup trucks in the supermarket parking lot, Francie dashed through the automatic doors just ahead of a blast of cold air that made her long skirt swirl around her legs dramatically, something that always gave her the delicious sensation of being a suicidal poet on the brink of despair. It was the whole reason she wore long skirts in the first place—most poets wore them, she imagined. Also, there was just something immensely perfect about the way a long skirt felt. You were exposed and protected at the same time.

The temperature had dropped at least fifteen degrees since they'd left the city that morning. Snowflakes had begun to fall in earnest, batting against cars and buildings and falling fractured to the earth. She imagined she could hear them colliding, like moths. A mousy-haired girl at the cash register looked up in alarm from her cuticles as Francie made her Gothic entrance, as if anyone who would brave weather like this was someone to fear.

"We gotta close in five minutes," said the girl. "We're all gettin' sent home early 'cause of the storm."

"I'll be quick, then," said Francie. She smiled, to show that she didn't take the store's closing personally. The girl stared at her. Still smiling, Francie disentangled the last in a long line of carts and began whipping up and down the aisles, composing a dinner in her head as she went. She grabbed some red peppers, a giant pack of drumsticks, a bag of salad mix, carrots. Something about the weather had trickled deep into her, and she felt dark and delightful. Big action on the horizon. In the car, on the way here, the eastern sky was so heavy and murderous that it seemed to absorb light from the rest of the world, sucking brightness into itself like a ravenous black hole. It was beautiful. Francie knew it would be months before she adjusted to the lack of buildings, to the immediacy of the sky. She looked forward to this opening of herself. She was a winter blossom. She felt as though she'd been uncaged. Her heart fluttered free above the rice-and-foreign-food aisle like the dove released from the Ark, looking for that first hint of land. She was Francie Hart, and she lived in the country now. She could really say that.

At the end of the aisle, she came up against a pharmacy counter. Next to the oversized bargain tubs of vitamin C and the herbal medications, a rack of condoms greeted her with polite audacity, a phalanx of furled penises awaiting the call to action. A kind-looking older man, with a fringe of white hair that ran in a perfect circle from the top of his head to his chin, was doing what looked like closing-up things behind the counter. A pharmacist. He looked Amish, though Francie knew that was impossible. Amish people couldn't work in pharmacies. Their religion forbade it. Mennonites could, though, the less strict ones anyway. Maybe that was what he was. A Mennonite pharmacist. Good heavens. What more surprises did this new country life hold?

Francie stopped. Had she found her prescription, she could have had it filled right now. But she still didn't know where it was. She was going to have to go back into the city and see her doctor again.

Wait. She wasn't going to take them anymore, remember?

Oh, right.

That.

No, actually the more she thought about that idea, the more insane it seemed. Remember how bad things were before? she asked herself. *Before* you went on them? Is that how you want them to be again?

This line of thought quelled her mood, and suddenly she was keenly aware that it was cold in the supermarket. Over the piped-in music that sounded as though it was filtered through aluminum foil, she could hear the wind tearing at the roof in fits and starts.

"Excuse me," Francie said timidly. "I wonder if you could help me?"

"We're closing," said the Mennonite-looking man, but he didn't ignore her. He simply stood there, smiling, and Francie felt encouraged to go on.

"I really just had a question," she said. "I . . . well, do you have any sort of a computer database thingie where you could type in my name and maybe get a copy of my prescription? I used to go to a place in New York, but I lost the actual paper and I don't know where it is. I was sure I'd put it in my purse, but when I looked later it wasn't there, and it wasn't in the boxes with all my important papers either, and I . . . " She trailed off, aware that she was babbling.

"What was the name of your other pharmacy?" asked the man.

She could see it in her mind, a small corner store on Seventh Avenue, made of red brick. The owner's name was Bernie. He had a brother who'd retired to Orlando. The pharmacy was about a thousand years old, and it smelled horribly of some kind of ointment. Did it even have a name? If it did, she'd never known it.

"I can't remember," said Francie. "I'm having a block." She tried to laugh. "Don't you just hate it when that happens? I've been there a million times and I never even thought to find out what it was called."

The man smiled understandingly and moved to his computer. "If you could just spell your last name for me," he said, "I'll see if you're in our system."

"H-A-R-T. Hart," said Francie. "First name, Francine."

She watched the pharmacist's plump fingers as they dashed over the keyboard, and she wondered idly, as she was prone to do during in-between moments, what this man must think of his life. He probably got lots of people with things wrong with them coming to see him every day, she thought. Everything you could think of, from hemorrhoids to cancer. And there were probably plenty of people like her, too, the kind with problems you couldn't see. Those would be the hardest to deal with, she decided. You could never tell with people like her when they were going to lose it. People who were crazy.

"I'm sorry," said the pharmacist. "You're not in our database."

"I see," said Francie. She felt pain in her fingers. She looked down to see that her knuckles were white around the handle of the shopping cart. "I see," she said again, forcing herself to let go, gently. Her hands fell from the handle and hung at her sides, while a feeling she had not felt in many years, one she'd hoped never to feel again, began to peck at the underside of her lungs. It was like having a chicken trapped in her abdominal cavity, she thought. That was precisely how it felt when she became anxious. The pink pills were what fed the chicken. When it was sated, everything was fine, and the chicken stayed quiet. But she had never failed to feed it before, not once in nine years, and she noted with alarm that the chicken was suddenly hungry. It hadn't been fed in ages, and now it was thinking about making a break for it.

She said quickly, "Well, is there any way you can . . . look, I'm out, and . . . I haven't ever run out of . . . I've been taking these for a long time, you know? I thought I might try going off them, but I can see now that was a mistake. So it's like, something bad might happen if I stop taking them. I don't even *know* what would happen." She laughed here, trying to make it sound like a joke.

The pharmacist smiled again, but not as broadly as before. He looked quickly at the telephone. Francie noticed this, and suddenly the chicken grew larger and more violent. She could actually feel its claws digging into her duodenum.

"I'm sorry, dear," said the man.

Did men like him look at her and have grandfather fantasies? she wondered. Did they daydream about taking her shopping for granddaughter things and sending her checks at Christmas? Then she realized that that was an insane thought. Only a crazy person would think something like that. Grandfather fantasies, indeed.

"I'm sure you know I can't do anything without a prescription. What exactly is the name of the drug?" the man said.

"Benedor," said Francie, wild hope surging in her. Maybe he had some he could slip her! In a paper bag, through the back door!

"Oh, no, definitely not with Benedor," said the man. "That's a psychoactive."

Her heart fell. "I know," said Francie. "It's just that . . . we just moved here from the city. Today, in fact. And I forgot to get my prescription filled before we left. I've run out. And I lost it, anyway. I have no idea where it is." Her voice had begun to tremble, she realized. She was repeating herself. She was going to cry. Oh, shit.

"I'm really very sorry," said the man. "I wish I could help. Can't you just go see your doctor? Tomorrow, maybe?"

"Oh, my God," said Francie. "Oh, my God!"

She said this because the chicken had just burst out of her, through her abdominal wall and out into the clean, white air of the supermarket. She was amazed the pharmacist couldn't see it, or, if he could, why he didn't say anything. It was covered in her blood and visceral matter, this chicken, and it strutted oddly along the tiles of the floor, its claws clacking wetly, tentative in the brave new world of reality. Francie put one hand on where she imagined the hole in herself to be and sank slowly to the floor. A poetess on the edge of the cliff. An actress, dying her best onstage death. But this was real, or seemed to be, and it was no fun at all.

"Ma'am¿" said the pharmacist, leaning over the counter to look at her. "Are you all right¿"

Francie sat down, her legs spread out in front of her like a child. She watched dully as the chicken turned left and wandered out of sight down the detergents-and-soaps aisle. She began to cry.

"Ma'am¿" The pharmacist had somehow appeared on the other side of the counter. Had he actually leapt over it¿ How heroic. A heroic Mennonite pharmacist. Francie felt his hands on her shoulders, trying to comfort her. He was asking her grandfatherly questions. Are you sick¿ Do you need water¿ Do you need to lie down¿ She ignored him. The pain where the chicken had exploded out of her was unbearable. She couldn't breathe.

"What's your phone number¿" the pharmacist was asking her. He was holding her hand. She saw him looking at her wedding ring. "I'll call your husband."

Francie sobbed. "I don't know!" she said. "We don't even have a phone!" She was going to have to live at the supermarket! She would never have the courage to leave it, not now. Not after the world had seen her weakness.

"Come in the back and lie down," said the pharmacist. "We'll get you taken care of, my dear. Don't you worry about a thing. Nothing at all is wrong."

"Yes, something is," Francie said. She allowed herself to be helped to her feet and led by the hand, like a child, through the waist-high swinging doors of the pharmacy counter, into the employee break room. The pharmacist put her on the couch and took her shoes off. He brought her a glass of water.

"Here you go," he said.

"Something is terribly wrong," Francie told him, taking the glass. "Something has *always* been wrong. I've just never been able to figure out what it is." She sipped carefully at the water, hoping it wouldn't leak out of the hole in her middle. It would surely cause a mess if it did. "That's been the problem with me all along," she told the pharmacist. "Only no one knows how to fix it."

"Just relax," said the pharmacist.

Francie let her head loll back slowly against the wall.

You stupid, stupid man, she thought. You don't know what you're messing with.

10

DRINK THIS TO MAKE IT BETTER

Michael had retreated to a corner of the inner living room, separated by a wall from his marauding brother-in-law; and there he sat in semidarkness, sulking, waiting for his sister to come home. Colt sponged up some drops of blood from the floor that he'd discovered only after walking through them, assuaging his mild revulsion with the hope that this act of penance would partly absolve him of his violent sin. Darkness had fallen, and Francie wasn't home yet. Now Colt paced before the fire, worrying that something might have happened to her, worrying about what would happen to *him* when she returned. She was, he knew, going to be angry. When the headlights of the Camaro finally illuminated the driveway, it was with mixed emotions of relief and apprehension that he came to the door. He watched her get out of the car and mount the porch steps, bearing bags of groceries. At least two inches of snow had accumulated in the driveway. More was falling, whipped into miniature tornadoes by the ever-increasing wind.

"Jesus Christ," Colt said, as she came into the foyer, "where have you been? I thought you were lost!"

Francie didn't answer. She pushed past him silently, heading straight for the kitchen.

"What's the matter? Is the car all right?" Colt asked, following her. "You didn't have an accident, did you?"

"Go check it yourself, if you're so concerned," said Francie. She put the groceries on the counter. Colt tailed her closely, suspicious.

"What happened?" he demanded.

"Nothing happened."

"No. Something happened. I can tell. You seem . . . funny."

Francie was holding her coat tightly around her middle, as if to prevent her insides from leaking out. She was of two minds concerning the hole through which the chicken had emerged: her rational mind knew that it was a delusion, but her poet mind believed it was real, and at the moment the poet mind was winning the argument hands down.

"Funny how?" she asked. "Milton Berle funny or Hannibal Lecter funny?"

"I mean . . . weird."

"I'm fine, Coltrane." She waited for him to go away, but he stayed, hovering in her face like an insistent prosecutor.

"What do you have in your coat?"

"Nothing."

"Open it. Let me see."

Abruptly she surrendered, as she always did, simply because it was the easiest way to be with him. Pushing her arms aside, he pulled her coat open and looked. She closed her eyes and waited.

Colt frowned. "Is something bothering you? Inside?"

"No. I just . . ." So he didn't see it. So it wasn't real.

"What?"

"I had a moment. That's all."

Colt frowned, let go of her coat. He went to the counter and began to unpack the groceries. Francie sagged against the counter, depleted.

"A moment? What kind of moment?"

"It's nothing, Coltrane."

"Oh, I get it. Some kind of woman thing, is it?" he asked over his shoulder.

Francie rolled her eyes. "Yes, that's it," she said. "Some kind of woman thing. That's all. Nothing to be taken seriously."

"Well, in that case, why don't you have a glass of wine?" he said. "I can make dinner."

"A glass of wine," she said. "What will that do?"

"What do you mean, what'll it do? It'll relax you. You could use it."

"I see," said Francie. "Is that your assessment of what I need?"

Colt gave her an odd look.

"You really are in a weird mood," he said.

"How very perceptive of you, Coltrane," Francie said. "That's the most sensitive thing you've said all day."

"Touchy, too. You know, in the old days, they used to make menstruating women leave the village and go into a hut. So they could leave everyone else in peace and quiet." He grinned. "Maybe I oughta build you a hut of your own," he said. "In the backyard. Now that we have a backyard."

Francie bit her tongue then, because otherwise she was going to scream.

◼ ◼ ◼

A few moments later she carried two glasses of wine into the living room, looking for Michael among the shadows. She squinted; he had melted away, he was nowhere to be found.

"Mikey? Where are you?"

"In here," came the muffled reply, through the fireplace. Francie went around the wall, where she found her brother staring into the flames, hugging his knees.

"Mikey? You want a drink?"

Michael looked up at her, pathetic. She recognized this expression. It was the same one he used to have after the neighborhood boys had been at him, painting him with mud, poking him with sticks.

"What's the matter?"

"Nothing's the matter," he said. "Everything's fine."

She sat down next to him, leaned over and kissed him on the cheek. Dried blood lingered on the wispy hairs of his mustache. Francie touched his face.

"What on earth happened to you?" she asked with concern.

"I . . . I bumped my nose."

"Aw, honey. I *thought* you must have done something to yourself. Does it hurt?"

"Yes, it hurts."

Francie touched it, lightly. "Is it broken?"

Michael winced and pulled away. "I don't know. I don't think so. Maybe."

"Poor little honey. Here, drink this to make it better."

How many times had she said that very phrase to him? A hundred, perhaps a thousand. As a girl, she was always making infusions over an imaginary fire, brewing up innumerable potions in a cast-off aluminum pot to heal his plentiful ills. Grass and dandelions for hurt feelings, bark and roots for boredom, mud and rocks for anger and bad grades. They never worked, but she was still trying. She handed him the wine now, cool in the glass. Michael drained half of it in one gulp as Francie sipped hers daintily. The pain in her middle had begun to fade. To her surprise, she found, suddenly, that she felt fine. It was as if she had expressed something poisonous, and now that it was out of her, she was cleaner, more natural. Maybe that chicken coming out was a *good* thing, she thought. Although it certainly hadn't felt good at the time. Worst pain ever, in fact. Yet there was something purifying about it. She felt, quite literally, as if she'd been purged.

But there was no point in getting into any of this with Michael. It was not his job to listen to her. That was no one's job; it was a position that hadn't been filled yet.

"You were gone a long time," he said.

"I know."

"I was worried."

"Well, that makes one of you. *He* was more concerned about his car."

Michael snorted and drained the rest of his wine. "Now that I believe," he said.

"Listen. Before I forget—what were you going to tell me before, when we were talking in the bathroom?" she asked.

"What do you mean?"

"You seemed kind of upset. Like something had happened in Colorado. I had the impression you were about to tell me about it."

"Oh, that. Well . . . never mind. It's not worth getting into," said Michael.

"What does *that* mean?"

"It means it's something I have to deal with myself. You can't help me out of it."

"Mikey," said Francie.

She was about to say "I'm your big sister," another timeworn phrase, when the lights went out and a background hum that none of them had actually noticed, which was the furnace in the basement, fell silent.

"Shit!" Colt barked from the kitchen. "The power!"

Michael groaned. "Now what?" he said. "This is turning into a fucking nightmare!"

"It's okay, it'll come back on," Francie said. "Don't worry."

She put her wine down and felt her way to the stack of boxes in the hallway. She could hear Colt stumbling around in the kitchen, cursing, bumping into things. Francie opened box after box in the blackness and felt through the contents of each, until she came to the one she was looking for; she'd remembered that she had packed a bag of tea lights, and she found them finally and brought them to the living room. She and Michael lit them methodically until the walls glowed orange. Then she went with two of them, incandescent in her hand, down the hall and into the kitchen, where Colt still floundered helplessly, cursing.

"Jesus, you look like a ghost," he told her, out of the gloom. "I don't know what we're going to eat now. And I'm starving."

"I bought vegetables. And potato chips. We can eat those."

"You couldn't have thought to buy precooked chicken, of course."

"Well, Colt . . . I wasn't planning on the power going out."

"No. You wouldn't."

"What's *that* supposed to mean?"

"Nothing. Only you always seem to expect things are just . . . going to work out, somehow. You have to think ahead, damn it. Bad weather, wind, heavy snow. Of course the power's going to go out!"

"Are you seriously trying to blame me for that? It's snowing out, the lines go down. It happens all the time."

"I'm not talking about the *power*, I'm talking about *dinner*."

"Colt," said Francie, putting her hands to her forehead. "Please. Just shut up."

"Yeah," said Michael, appearing behind her in the doorway as another glowing form, underlit by a handful of candles. "Why don't you shut up? And quit being such a prick to us. Or I'll tell her what really happened to my nose."

"What really happened to your—"

"Oh, damn it," said Colt.

"Go on, tell her, big man!" said Michael.

"Colt?" Francie crossed her arms. "What did you do to my brother?"

"We were just messing around," said Colt lamely. "It was an accident."

"*He* was messing around," said Michael. "*I* was trying to mind my own business. But he just couldn't leave me alone. He always has to fuck with me somehow. Always has to be giving me shit. And he hit me!"

"I didn't *hit* you, I *tapped* you," said Colt. "And it was an accident. If I'd really hit you, you'd still be stretched out right now."

"See? There he goes again!" said Michael. "Always making threatening statements! Always trying to prove how tough he is!"

"You *hit* my *brother*?" Francie was aghast. "Coltrane Hart, what in the name of God is wrong with you? Why would you do such a thing?"

"We were boxing," Colt said lamely.

"*He* was boxing, Sissie," said Michael. "*I* had no interest in boxing, and I told him so about a hundred times, but he can't let anything alone. He always has to start shit. Always! He's like a ten-year-old!"

"Now, just hold on," said Colt.

"Colt, you asshole," said Francie calmly. "You complete and total dick."

Colt's eyes became slits, his eyebrows lowering like floodgates. "Francie, watch it. Just because—"

"Here," said Francie, "see how you like it." She reached out in the semidarkness and tried to slap him, but missed. Colt grabbed her hand to stop her and ended up pulling her off balance, so that she stumbled and nearly fell. She gasped in surprise and wrenched free of him.

"Hey!" shouted Michael. "What are you going to do, beat her up now too?"

"No!" said Colt. "I wasn't—"

"Take your hands off me," said Francie, though she was already loose. "I don't want to see you again tonight, Colt. I don't care where you go, to the basement or the attic or one of the bedrooms. But I don't want to see you. You really make me sick sometimes. Really sick. Now just beat it." She was fighting to keep the tears out of her voice, but they were tears of rage, not sadness—not that he would have known the difference.

"I'm not going anywhere. This is *my* house—"

"Your house!" Francie yelled. "*Your* house⸮"

"Yes! Jesus! Who do you think paid for it⸮ *You⸮* You haven't got a dime to your name, and you haven't worked in years! You're no better than him!" Colt pointed to Michael. "You're like a couple of children! You both think everyone owes you a living!"

"I do not think everyone owes me a living," Michael said.

"Yes, you do!"

"*Who's* a child⸮" Francie said. This comment had infuriated her to the point that her voice was shaking, the tears just behind. "Who are you calling a child⸮ You're the one who thinks the world revolves around him! You're the one who thinks he's the most important person in the universe!"

Colt stared at her in disbelief. "What's *that* supposed to mean⸮" he asked.

"Your needs," said Francie. "It's always about *your* needs!"

"No, it isn't always about my needs."

"Yes, it is!"

"All right. What are you talking about⸮"

Francie felt herself vibrating with emotion now, like a violin string tuned too tightly; she felt as if at any moment she might part in the middle, and fly off in different directions.

"You think you're the one who gets to decide our future! You're the one who makes all the decisions! What about *me*⸮ What about what *I* want⸮"

"Let me tell you something," Colt said. "If I didn't make the decisions, then no one would. If I left everything up to you, it'd be like . . . we were *hibernating*, or something. Nothing would ever get done!"

Francie burst out laughing; she wasn't going to give him the satisfaction of tears. "Hibernating⸮ What the hell are you talking about, hibernating⸮"

"I mean sitting around always waiting for something to happen. You have to be proactive in life, Francie. You have to take matters into your own hands sometimes. You have to get things done!"

"I know how to be 'proactive, damn it," said Francie. "I know how to get things done. It's just hard when I have to always fight you every step of the way! Because you think you're more important than me!"

Michael had fallen silent now, sensing that the argument had moved into the realm of the ultrapersonal. He retreated to the doorway, where he stood half in and half out of the kitchen, listening.

"I do not think I'm more important than you," Colt said. "You have no right to say that."

"Oh, is that right¿" Francie said. Here came the tears now; she couldn't hold them back any longer. "What about what I want for us¿ For myself¿ What about my dreams¿" She wiped her nose on the sleeve of her sweatshirt.

Colt rolled his eyes. "Not this again," he said. "Please, not now. In front of your brother you want to start this¿"

"Why not¿" Her voice became shrill. "He might as well know." She turned to Michael, whose eyes had grown wide, like a child witnessing a fight between two giants. "You know what, Mikey¿ Colt won't let me have any children. Because *he* doesn't want them. *He* would find it inconvenient. Because *his* work is the most important thing in his life."

Colt threw his hands up. "'I won't let you,'" he echoed. "You hear how you're talking¿ As if everything was really up to me. That's the real problem. You're angry at yourself, Francie. You're pissed off at yourself for being too passive. The reason you don't feel like you have an equal say in things is because you never open your mouth until it's too late! And then you take it out on me!"

"Well, I'm opening it now!" Francie said. "It's not fair, Coltrane! I am a woman! I want certain things! I *need* certain things!"

"And you're just going to sit around waiting until I give them to you," said Colt. He picked up a fork and ripped open the plastic wrap that covered the chicken. "Instead of going to get them for yourself. That's the problem. Passive instead of proactive. Always the victim, never the victor."

"How am I supposed to go and get a baby for myself?" Francie shrieked. "How? It takes two, Colt! It takes you and me!"

"Exactly. It takes two. And we both have to want it."

"And you don't! So where does that leave me?"

Colt shrugged. It was more than Francie could take, this seeming indifference. She swung at him again, connecting with his shoulder this time, spraining two of her knuckles on his scapula. More tears sprang to her eyes and she yelped in pain. Colt put the fork down and stood staring at the raw chicken, hands gripping the countertop, trying to control himself.

"I never hit you," he whispered. "In almost ten years, I have never once even thought about hitting you." He slammed his fist into the counter, so that the empty cupboards rattled.

"And you play games with my head sometimes!" Francie went on, as if she hadn't heard. "What about that time in the motel? After we found this house? Remember?"

"Remember *what*?" Colt hissed.

"You didn't use a condom!"

"Oh, man," said Michael. "Maybe I should—"

"No, Mikey, you stay," said Francie. "I want him to explain what he did." She turned to Colt again. "Remember, you bastard? You fucked me! Without a condom! Remember that? Why did you do that? Just so you could get my hopes up? Or did you forget, just that once? You *never* forget, Colt! It's like a religion with you! How was I supposed to interpret that? What was I supposed to think?"

"Jesus, Francie," said Coltrane, despairing now. "I can't believe you're doing this."

"I want to know why! I want to know right now why you did that!"

"All right," said Colt. "You want to know why? Because it doesn't matter anymore whether I use a condom or not, that's why."

"And why not? *Why* doesn't it matter?"

"Because," Colt said, "I had a vasectomy."

There was a long silence, during which Michael silently melted away into the darkness of the hallway. Francie stared at Colt. She couldn't believe her ears. The pain in her middle swelled again like an ocean wave. She grabbed at her gut, suddenly nauseous.

"You had a what?" she said finally. "When?"

Colt sighed, sagging against the counter. "When I went to San Francisco, last summer."

"I thought . . . I thought that was a business trip."

"Yeah, it was, partly. And partly for the other reason."

"So you, what, you just . . . decided on the spur of the moment? On a whim?"

"No. I planned it."

"You planned it. Without consulting me. Without telling me."

Colt braced himself, as if against a strong wind. "I didn't see why I should have to. It was my decision. It's my body. You women are always going on about how your bodies belong to you, how no one else has the right to decide what happens to you. Abortions and birth control and all that shit. Well, why should it be any different for us men? It's our bodies, too. We can decide what happens to us. I don't have to ask your permission. Besides, I knew what you would say. I knew what it would lead to. This."

"Colt," said Francie. "How could you do this to me?"

Colt looked at her now. "Because," he said firmly. "I don't want children. Ever. And I wanted to be sure there would be no mistakes. I wanted to make sure I wasn't going to get . . ."

His words trailed off. Francie waited.

"Get what?" she prodded him. "You wanted to make sure you wouldn't get what?"

Colt cleared his throat.

"Trapped," he said.

Francie felt now as if she, too, were melting away, as if there were nothing left. She leaned against the counter for support.

"Trapped," she repeated.

"That's right," Colt said. "Yes."

"Having children with me would be a trap."

"For me, at this time in my life, yes."

"And you knew what this would lead to if you told me," Francie said. "And so you wanted to put it off."

He didn't answer.

"You knew that I would leave you," Francie said. "That's why you didn't tell me."

Colt still didn't answer. He looked down at the floor.

"Well," said Francie, "who's the passive one now, then?"

11

■

THE VISITOR

The long pause that followed this question was interrupted by a sudden banging from the front of the house. Neither of them moved. They could hear Michael's breath, drawn sharply in surprise.

"You guys?" he said querulously, from where he had been listening around the corner. He sounded as if he'd been crying, like a child caught in a parental crossfire. "I think someone's at the door!"

The banging came again, more insistent now. Colt picked up a candle and brushed past his wife, heading for the foyer. Through the glass he could see someone standing on the porch, holding a flashlight.

"Hello?" he called.

The response was too muffled to make out. Colt, city-cautious, opened the door a crack.

"What did you say?" he asked. "Can I help you?"

"I—I just come by ta check up on the place," said the person. It was a small man, wearing a thick snowsuit of the sort that utility maintenance workers wore. He was shining his flashlight at his feet, and his face was lost in shadow. "Live just up the road there. Flebberman. I seen you movin' in earlier. You, ah . . . you the new folks?"

"Yeah, that's us," said Colt. "The new folks."

"Oh. Right. Well. Hi, there."

"Hello," Colt said.

The man was clearly uncomfortable, as if he were performing an unpleasant but necessary task. He cast several glances backward over his shoulder, plotting a quick getaway.

"Well, ah . . . the juice ran dry, so I thought I might as well come down and check up on ya. See how yer makin' out." He cleared his throat nervously and stomped his feet on the porch, which sounded as hollow as a drum.

"Oh," said Colt. "You're the neighbor."

He opened the door wide, remembering the name he'd seen on the truck that had passed them when they were first looking at the house—FLEBBERMAN TOWING. There'd been a man who'd stared at them, not exactly hostile but not exactly welcoming, either. So this was Flebberman. Colt had thought, without knowing why, that he would be bigger.

"Come on in," he said.

Flebberman stepped in shyly and followed Colt through the foyer into the living room, where his features were illuminated by the gentle glow of the fire. He looked about fortyish; his spade-shaped face was covered with three or four days' worth of beard, and his shoulders and head were covered in snow, which he made no move to brush off. Francie and Michael came in together and stood at the entrance of the kitchen hallway. She'd dried her eyes in record time, Colt thought.

"Hello," Francie said calmly, in a tone that chilled Colt's bones. "Mister—"

"Randy."

"Mr. Randy."

"No, I mean Randy Flebberman," said Flebberman. "Nobody calls me mister. Just . . . Randy."

"I'm Francie. This is my brother Michael, and . . . Coltrane Hart." She spat his name out like a poison seed.

"Hi," said Michael.

"Din't mean ta startle ya," Flebberman said. "Saw yer movin' truck earlier, an' I thought, uh-oh, this ain't no time to be movin'. With the storm comin' an' all. An' then the power goes out. Ah, well." He shrugged philosophically. "Waddaya gonna do?"

"We were just making dinner," Francie said. "Would you like to stay?"

Colt shot her a look that went unnoticed, but it was not necessary.

"Naw, thanks," said Flebberman. "Wife has dinner ready. I just come down real quick ta see how things was goin'."

"We *were* making dinner," Colt said. "But then the power went out."

"You got a gas stove," said Flebberman. "You can still cook. Don't need power for a gas stove. Jus' gotta light it yerself, 'cause the pilot'll be out."

"Oh," said Colt, sheepishly. "Right."

"How'd *you* know we have a gas stove?" asked Francie.

"Bank hired me ta take care a the place," said Flebberman. "I been lookin' after it since I dunno when. Long time."

"Right," said Francie. "That's why there was so little dust. You've been keeping it clean?"

Flebberman looked at the floor, scuffing his foot. "Yuh," he said. They waited, but he offered no further explanation.

"Any idea when the power'll come back on?" Colt asked.

Flebberman shrugged again, and laughed wryly. "Could be fi' minutes, could be tomorra," he said. "Y'never really know. Power never does go out on a nice summer day, after all. Always at night, in weather like this. Haw haw. Crew's gotta come out from all over creation. Takes 'em at least an hour just ta get mobilized. I oughta know. I useta work for the county."

He was running on nervously, it seemed to Colt. He attempted to interject, but Flebberman went on.

"Worked plowin' the roads for 'em, sorta freelance, y'know, 'cause they were always short-staffed on purpose to save the budget, but then a course when it actually snowed they'd be screwed. They might even call me out for this one. Who knows؟ Gov-'mint's run by a buncha goddamn morons. Pardon my French."

"Would you like a glass of wine, Randy؟" Francie asked.

Flebberman seemed taken aback. "Wine؟" he said, almost laughing. "Naw. Everything else's awright؟ Water on؟"

"Yes," said Colt. "The water's on."

"Well," said Flebberman. "I grew up in this house, y'know."

This admission startled them all, since it seemed to come out of nowhere. Francie smiled at the little man.

"Really," she said. "How interesting. I didn't know that."

"Well, I din't really *live* here. But I spent a lotta time here when I was a kid. My old Aunt Helen was the last one to own the place. Great-aunt, actually. My mother useta leave me with her sometimes, when she was workin'. Nice old place. Lotta history to it. Woulda bought it m'self, if I coulda 'forded it." Flebberman shuffled his booted feet again, pondering his own poverty; then, abruptly, he appeared to become embarrassed. "Nice car you got out there," he said, almost wistfully.

"Thanks," said Michael.

"He was talking about *my* car, you dumbass," Colt said.

"The Camaro؟" Flebberman said. "Nineteen-seventy؟ 'Bout two hundred horses؟"

"The man knows his cars," said Colt.

Flebberman flushed and scuffed his foot again; then, realizing he was leaving marks on the floor, he abruptly stopped and put his foot over the streak he'd left.

"You folks got any plans for redoin' the place?" he inquired tentatively. "Any renovations er whatnot?"

"Not really," said Colt. "Not yet, anyway. Hadn't had the time to think about it, actually. Why do you ask?"

"Just curious, is all."

"It's in pretty good shape, for such an old place," Francie volunteered.

Flebberman appeared gratified. "Oh, yuh," he said. "I been keepin' it up, like I said. Takes a lotta work ta keep an old house like this in any kinda condition."

"You did a wonderful job," said Francie. "It's almost like it was waiting for us. We appreciate it. Really."

This compliment seemed to embarrass Flebberman almost beyond speech. He ducked his head and nodded. "Well," he said, clearing his throat, "I'm startin' ta melt all over yer floor here. I'll be gettin' back home. We're just up the road there, you know, at the top of the hill. Give us a holler if you need anything."

"We will," said Francie.

"Yeah," said Colt. "Sure will."

Flebberman gave them all a curious sort of two-fingered salute as he clomped back down the hall and down the stairs, back into the teeth of the blizzard. The three of them watched through the window as he got into his tow truck and headed up the road. They were left alone again.

"I don't know if we just met Barney Fife or Gomer Pyle," Colt said.

"Fuck you," said Francie, leaving the room.

12

WHITE MEN FROM THE FUTURE

With the cold fingers of betrayal firmly wrapped around her heart, Francie headed upstairs to the attic. All she wanted was to be alone, like a dying dog—for that was how she felt. Like her guts really had been ripped out her middle. Small flames guttered in the saucer that she held, waiter-style, on her fingertips, and her rippling shadow followed her at a discreet distance, keeping to the wall. So he didn't want children with her, ever? All right, then. If he felt that strongly about it, why didn't he just say so? What kind of a man would willingly have his scrotum sliced open rather than risk having to share his life with other people?

And, as long as that was the case, why were they still married?

Let's not go there just yet, Francie told herself. One thing at a time. You've only just had a mental breakdown, and now there's this. Should we file divorce papers tonight, too? I think not.

That could wait until the morning, at least.

■ ■ ■

It wasn't that she'd wanted children *all* that badly. Sometimes she did, of course; that was only natural. It would hit her, at random moments, that she was missing something indefinable, that she was not just bored but unfulfilled, that she had more to offer to the world than just sitting around in the apartment in a state of creative constipation. But there were other times when she was glad she didn't have them, usually when she was tired and frustrated and frazzled by the ten thousand and one complicated things that were involved in living in a modern city. For example: when she was trying to get her Metro card out of her purse to run it through the subway turnstile, avoiding being jostled from behind by impatient commuters, avoiding the homeless man up ahead who always seemed to single her out of the crowd no matter how hard she tried not to catch his eye; after which she would have to push her way onto the car, always ending up between some ancient woman who was only five foot four on one side and a sweaty construction worker covered in a natural hair suit on the other, so that she was forced to stand curled sideways, like a question mark, and she would think out of nowhere, *Imagine lugging around a baby on top of all this*, and she would wonder how it was ever done at all.

Yet, from time to time, she treasured the possibilities contained within her womb. It was really just the idea of babies—for she did like to think about them sometimes, and he had held out hope to her, time and time again, when he had known that there really was none. And that was a lie.

He'd lied to her. He might as well have cheated on her.

Francie probed her abdomen as she ascended the stairs. The chicken hole, briefly healed, seemed to have been reopened by the argument. She fancied that she ran her fingers lightly over the bottoms of her lungs, feeling the ragged area where the chicken's beak had pecked away at them. She caressed her liver, thumbed her pancreas, became intimate with the half-hidden nubs of her kidneys. And here was her uterus, tiny and triangular, dangling like an empty purse.

It was all madness, of course. She knew full well that only crazy people felt this way. But she couldn't escape the impression that this wasn't a delusion; or, if it *was* a delusion, it was a very good one. The most convincing she'd ever had, in fact.

"I'm crazy crazy crazy," she whispered.

The attic was where she was headed, and she knew it would be freezing up there, so she stopped in the master bedroom on the third floor, where she put on a sweater, jogging pants, a pair of wool socks. She put her bathrobe back on over all of this, added a knit hat, and continued upward, watching her breath spout out before her in a plume of white, as if she were a walking teakettle. Climbing the final set of stairs, she set the dish of tea lights on the attic floor and opened one of the boxes she'd noticed when they'd first come through with Marge Westerbrook. Anything that would distract her now was welcome. Too much thinking at a time like this could drive her back over the edge over which she had only just clawed herself.

Reaching in blindly, she came up with a double handful of comic books. With a connoisseur's nose, she sniffed their bouquet of decaying newsprint and antiquated ink. Someone had wanted to preserve these old things; someone had thought they were worth saving.

Francie had been a great fan of science fiction in her early teens. It was just another thing about her that had concerned her parents, and had made other girls hesitate in inviting her to parties. Girls were not supposed to like science fiction, which was precisely why she did; or half the reason, anyway. She'd never understood why boys were so fascinated with Mars and ray guns and rocket ships and alien beings, while girls ignored such things. The only possible answer was that boys were keeping it all for themselves, because they didn't want to share. Typical. Boys were dolts—it was their fault the world was not a nice place.

In rebellion against this fact and others, Francie had read everything she could get her hands on, from the classic works of H. G.

Wells to the comic-book adventures of *Rom the Spaceknight*. She'd particularly liked Rom, who had been turned into a cyborg, the poor dear, and as if that wasn't misfortune enough, he also suffered the indignity of being practically anonymous in the world of comic book superheroes. No one else had ever heard of him; Rom never made it into the pantheon of critically accepted do-gooders. She'd found him one day in the comic book rack of an Indianapolis convenience store, hidden away behind *Sgt. Rock and Easy Company* and *The Unknown Soldier*. Here, Francie felt, was someone who deserved her sympathy, a neglected galactic savior she could nurture. She'd bought the first issue for fifty cents in 1978, so new it was still damp, and she hoped vaguely it would become a classic someday. As far as she knew, it was still somewhere in her childhood bedroom back in Indiana—the only first issue of anything she'd ever bought. When it had sat in obscurity long enough, perhaps it would become a classic. This was the same curious dichotomy to which Francie found herself subjected. The world would not be ready for her poetry until she had suffered in silence throughout her life, and then died, alone.

And childless, apparently.

But she had decided to put that out of her mind.

Many of these books featured astronauts on the covers. Despite herself, she had to giggle at these clean-cut white men from the future, with their military-style brush cuts, their perfect, twenty-fifth-century teeth, their form-fitting suits that somehow protected them against the depressurization of outer space while sacrificing nothing of comfort or athleticism. Francie flipped through idly, discarding them when the action failed to grab her. Going deeper into the box, she found even older books, boys' adventure stories in hardcover: *The Iron Boys in the Steel Mills. The Dreadnought Boys. The Boy Allies*. The original *Hardy Boys* series. *Tom Swift and His Amazing Flying Machine*. These books contained no illustrations, save for an engraved frontispiece; they were from the era before comic books. Checking the publication dates, Francie saw that some of them were over eighty years old. Automatically she checked the flyleaves, a habit she'd picked up over a lifetime of browsing books to see if any former owners had left their mark. The name RANDALL FLEBBERMAN had been inscribed into each one, in careful, uneven block letters.

■ ■ ■

She'd not been up there more than five minutes when she heard footsteps on the stairs. Turning, she saw Michael, bearing more candles, light puddled under his chin and illuminating the searching tendrils of his scraggly beard. Francie drew her robe more tightly about her.

"Hi, Sissie," said Michael. "Came up to see if you're okay."

"I was reading," she said. Michael sat next to her. "How's your nose?"

"It's fine. Way to lay into him. You showed him a thing or two, I guess. You, uh . . . you really okay?"

She nodded, pressing her lips together.

"I just wanted to tell you . . . I don't know. Sorry, I guess. I never knew you wanted a baby that bad. But I guess it makes sense. I mean, you'd be a great mom and everything." He cleared his throat. "Uh . . . you do know that vasectomies can be undone, right? Like, they're not permanent? I think I saw that on the Discovery channel."

"No," said Francie. "It's better this way."

"What d'you mean?"

She shook her head. "Nothing. It just wasn't meant to be, that's all. Not with him."

Michael nodded. "He wouldn't be much of a dad."

"And I wouldn't be much of a mother," she said. "Not in the condition I've been in."

Michael's brow furrowed. "Why not?"

Francie sighed. "Never mind. I don't want to talk about it."

"All right. Holy crap, look at these old books!" Michael said, switching gears without a pause. Francie had always envied his ability to drop things once they became boring, without a moment's guilt or hesitation. "They gotta be worth a million bucks by now!"

"I doubt it," she said. "I hardly recognize any of them. It's only the famous ones that are worth anything. This Tom Swift, maybe." She passed her fingers over the cool cloth-covered cardboard. It was in decent condition. Walter would know something about it, surely.

"What are you gonna do with them?"

"They're not mine."

"Yes, they are. It's your house, isn't it?"

"Randy Flebberman's name is in them. They must have been his when he was a kid. I guess they got left behind here."

"So?"

"So, they're still his," said Francie. "If he wants them."

Michael opened a comic book and held it close to his candle. He scanned the dot-matrix images, pulling yet another joint from behind his ear like a magician, wetting one end of it on his tongue. He interrupted his reading to hold the joint to a candle and take a deep drag, the dried flowers inside popping and crackling. He offered it to Francie, who surprised him—and herself—by taking it. Normally she steered clear of the stuff. But what did she have to lose now? she thought. Nothing. She could be dying, after all. No one could survive what she'd gone through tonight. The harsh smoke spilled into her lungs and began almost immediately to leak out their perforated bottoms. She pulled her robe even tighter and handed the joint back to Michael.

"You really should stop smoking this stuff," she said. "You're gonna get into trouble."

"With who?" he snorted. "Mommy and Daddy?"

"It's your health I'm really worried about. Once in a while is okay, but you do it too much."

"It's part of my personality," said Michael, unperturbed, not looking up from his comic book. "It's who I am. I do what I do, and you do what you do, and nobody should be judging anybody."

"It's just not good for you, that's all," she said. "I don't like to see you hurting yourself."

"Remember when we used to sit up and read under your covers with the flashlight?" Michael asked.

"You didn't read. You made me read to you."

"That's because I *couldn't* read. The letters were all backwards."

"I know. Poor kid."

"Don't poor kid me."

"I can't help it," said Francie. "You're so cute."

"Shut up." He lay on his back and tried to read that way, then abruptly sat up again and threw the comic book to the side. "It's still really hard," he complained. "Mom and Dad always thought I was faking it. They thought I was lazy."

"They know better now," she said. "That you had a disease. It wasn't just in your head."

"Whatever," he said. "They're not exactly role models themselves."

"What do you mean?"

"I mean, of how to live a perfect life. Dad's a racist prejudiced bigoted asshole. If he met some of my friends he'd have a heart attack."

So would I, probably, Francie thought, though she knew Michael was right about their father.

"And Mom—she's just a country club gal. Christ. Take them out of Indianapolis and they're like fish out of water. All they do is find fault with everything. Complain. Did I ever tell you about the time they came to visit me at school, what a nightmare that was? Dad couldn't believe I had a black roommate. Like, he thought I was playing a joke on him. He thought Al *worked* there. I wanted to kill him."

"I know. I heard all about it from Mom. They do the best they can, is all. They're middle-aged Midwesterners, Michael. They were raised a certain way, to believe certain things. You really can't change people, much as you might want to."

"Unfortunately."

"Now listen," she said. "What were you telling me about before, when the power went out?"

"What?"

"Before. You sounded like there was something wrong. Like you were about to tell me there's something going on. This is the third time I've asked you now. So, out with it."

"Oh, yeah." Michael sighed heavily. "Well, I, uh . . . I got into a little mess in Denver."

"What kind of mess?"

"Well, after I hooked up with Yolanda, she took me over to these guys' house where she lived sometimes, right? And so I ended up staying for a few weeks. They were really cool to me. I ran a few errands for them, you know. Helped out a little. But, ah . . . well, there was this raid, right? The whole street was all blocked off with cop cars and shit. I missed it just by a second. I was just coming back from a . . . an *errand*, and I saw all the sirens in the street, so I just kept on going. Lucky is not the word, really. I was like, holy shit! You never fucking know, man. I came *this close* to getting popped."

"And you were selling drugs for them," Francie said.

Michael stared at her, as if amazed by her mental powers. "No, not really, Sissie, I was just—"

"'Running errands,'" she finished. "Right?"

"Well, I never actually *saw* what I was delivering," said Michael, "so it's not my fault, right? They can't prove anything."

"Michael, this is serious! *Really* serious! Do the police know who you are?"

"Well, here's the messed-up thing about that. The day before the raid, this meter reader came to the house, right? And he asked me if I lived there, and I said yeah, sort of, and he asked if I could give him my name just so he could put it down as the person he talked to, and I said sure, and like an idiot I let him see my driver's license. And then he read the meter and went away." Michael paused, thinking. "He was a nice guy, actually."

"But he wasn't a meter reader."

"I don't think so. I think he was a cop. In disguise, like."

"Yeah, well, Michael? For future reference, meter readers don't ask to see ID."

"I know that *now*, Sissie."

"So, they know who you are. They have your address."

"My old school address. That's what's on my license."

"Still. They have your name. They can track you."

"I know," Michael said. "That's why I came out East again. I sorta need to lay low for a while. Don't tell Colt, okay? He'll kill me."

"Believe me, I won't say a word. But Michael . . ."

"Yeah?"

"If the cops show up here . . ."

"I know. I don't even wanna think about it. I doubt they will, but still, you never know. I was gonna ask if . . . I mean, I figured I'm better off with you guys for a while, even with the caveman downstairs. Do you think I could crash with you? I mean like, longer than a few days? Like . . . indefinitely?" He reached out and took one of Francie's hands in his, interlacing their fingers. "I'm really fucked here, Sissie. I don't know what to do."

"Colt won't like it," said Francie.

"I know, but . . ."

"But who cares," said Francie. "You're my brother. It's my house, too, no matter what he says. He's going back to the city on Monday, anyway. And he'll be gone until Thursday."

"Right," Michael said, sighing with relief. "I forgot that."

"So if we can make it through the rest of this week and the weekend, it can be just the two of us. For a few days, at least."

"How romantic," said Michael. "Just like the old days. Listen, there's something else, too."

Francie rubbed her face tiredly. "Something else? How can there be more?"

"You know how I was saying I had to just keep on going instead of stopping, when I saw the cops on their street? The day of the bust?"

"Yeah?"

"Well," said Michael, "that was because I just happened to have ten kilos of dope in the car at the time, and I didn't know what else to do with it. So . . . I kind of brought it all with me. It's in my bus now." He looked at her with a self-satisfied expression. "There," he said. "*Now* I've come clean."

"Oh, my God, Mikey," said Francie, turning pale. "Tell me you're joking."

"No," said Michael. "I wish I was."

"What on earth are you—"

"I'm gonna give it back," he said.

"And how are you going to do *that*?"

"Well," Michael said, "I figure they're going to look me up sooner or later, just like you said. Not the cops. I mean, the guys who own it. It's worth a lot of cabbage to them. And when they find me, it's all going to be there. Every bit. I'm not going to touch any of it. And I can just sort of hand it over and explain the whole thing, and hopefully they'll understand. I mean, these aren't like cold-blooded killers or anything. They're nice guys. I *know* these guys."

"You knew them for . . . how long? A few weeks?"

"Yeah. Something like that."

"And on that basis you would trust them with your life."

"Sissie, come on. This isn't Scarface we're talking here. It's not Al Capone. It's just . . . *guys*."

"Guys who deal very large amounts of drugs."

"Well, yeah."

Francie put her head in her hands.

"Michael," she said, "you're never going to learn."

"I know," Michael said—sheepish, grinning, mischievous. "But I'm still really cute, right? Aren't I? And aren't you proud of me for coming clean?"

"You have to get rid of it," Francie told him. "I don't care how, but you have to. Jesus, Michael, you can't have that much dope sitting around on our property! What the hell were you thinking? Do you know we could lose our house if the police found it here?"

"Sissie, I told you, I was *running*—"

"You're always running," said Francie. "You never stop and think. What if what you're running into is worse than what you're running from? And what about how this could affect other people's lives? You have to start thinking about that, too. Or eventually you're going to have no one left to help you."

Michael was silent. He stared at the floor, sulking.

"Get rid of it," said Francie. "Promise me."

"But what am I supposed to do with it?"

"I don't care. Dump it out at sea. Bury it. Just don't try and sell it, whatever you do. You'll get caught, and that will be the end of you. You'll go to jail for a long time, and no one will be able to get you out. Promise me."

"All right," said Michael. "I promise."

"And if you said you're not going to touch any of it, then what are you smoking right now?"

"Well, they won't mind me helping myself to a *little*," said Michael. "I mean, after all, I did save it from the cops. And 'Thou shalt not muzzleth the ox that treadeth the corn.' Remember that one from the Bible? Ha ha! And you thought I didn't know anything!"

Francie covered her face in her hands. Then she grabbed the joint out of Michael's fingers and stubbed it out on her tea saucer.

"Stop," she said. "Just stop."

"Are you mad?"

"Yes. I'm mad."

"How mad?"

"Really mad."

"I'm sorry."

"Oh, well," Francie said, "in that case, I guess everything's all right." She sighed. "Let's go to sleep. I'm exhausted."

▌ ▌ ▌

When they went downstairs, Colt had disappeared. Michael dragged his air mattress in from the bus, trudging through snow that had now piled up in drifts over a foot high. He set it in front of the fire, and he and Francie snuggled in on top of it together, a couple of blankets thrown over them, using their arms for pillows.

Francie, chilled, was still wearing her sweatshirt. She rolled over now and put one arm over her brother, who already slept the deep sleep of the drugged. She almost managed to drift off, despite the noise made by Colt, who was apparently stomping from room to room on the third floor, shoving around the few articles of furniture they'd brought with them.

What the hell does *he* have to be mad about? she thought. He's not the one who's just had his heart ripped out of his chest. He's not the one who's been gutted.

And yet it soothed her, in an odd way, to know that he was feeling something. At least he wasn't sitting there ignoring her and the world around him, watching television, which was what he always did after an argument.

The last thing of which she was aware was that the power came back on. Light flooded the room, and beneath her, Francie could hear the faint hum of the polybrachial furnace as it sprang into life once more. She got up quickly, shivering, and turned the overhead light off, then dove back onto the mattress. The furniture noises upstairs stopped abruptly and were replaced by the ticking of the vents as the house began to warm again. Comforted by this, and by her brother pressed against her, she slept.

13

———————■———————

THE DIARY OF MARLY MUSGROVE

As is common with secret doors, Francie found hers by accident.

The day had begun with her waking sometime before sunrise. Michael was snuffing and puffing gently beside her, his arm flung over his face as if still trying to protect his battered nose. She slid off the air mattress carefully, so she wouldn't wake him, and waited for a moment on her hands and knees to see if he would stir. The house was dark and cold—even though the furnace was struggling gamely—but it was far from silent. Mysterious creaks and groans came from every beam, and the floor crackled under her feet as she went to her pants and felt in her pocket. Already the hair was rising on the back of her neck, the same way it did when she was watching a scary movie, or when she imagined that she was being watched by spirits. And yet she was not afraid.

On her key chain was a tiny flashlight, the kind you squeezed in the middle. Francie took it out of her jeans pocket now and shone it around the living room, slicing through the blackness as if it were jungle undergrowth. She was an explorer; she would do some exploring. She padded slowly through the other living room and into the den. She had no idea what time it was, but the sky was still black. She marveled once again at the deep, dark sheen of the den's oak paneling, ran her fingers over its smooth richness. Then she went into the kitchen, shivering as her feet came into contact with the frigid slate, simply looking around at how different everything seemed under the feeble beam of the flashlight.

The uncharted second floor beckoned her next, with its long hallway of closed doors. Here were the bedrooms, which must once have been full of children but now were empty of everything, even beds. The rooms were narrow and tight, each with a single window at the end. There were six of them. She stuck her head into each, like a prison warden. Through a window at the end of the hall she caught a glimpse of a single high-flying cloud, no bigger than a man's fist, reflecting the first pinks of the rising sun as it spilled over the eastern edge of the world. At the same time she became aware of a raucous and stentorian snoring from upstairs. The hair on her neck rose again. Colt. Oh yes. She'd almost forgotten about him.

Francie tiptoed upstairs to the third floor and looked tentatively into the master bedroom. There he was, sprawled diagonally, bachelor-wise, on the mattress that they'd brought from the guest bedroom, just his nose visible as it emerged from under the edge of the duvet. Look at him, sleeping away as if he hadn't a care in the world, she thought. How dare he be so relaxed? She would just have to fix that.

She picked up the empty suitcase that sat on the floor and thunked it down again, but he didn't move. Vindictiveness for yesterday's crimes surged in her suddenly, and she felt a strong urge to throw something. She picked up the suitcase again and flung it with all her might into the open closet, where it smacked heavily against the wall. Still, he didn't move. Intending now to drop it on his head, or something like that, she went into the closet to retrieve the suitcase and, turning on the light, saw where it had struck the wall. It had left a mark, and when she touched it to see if it was permanent, she felt the wall itself give slightly. Oh, dear, she thought, all anger fled now, I've broken something. And, pressing experimentally upon the spot, a door about three feet tall swung inward.

Francie sank to the floor in astonishment. Childhood memories, again possibly hers, probably not, flooded her mind: a wardrobe in England, with a Christly lion on the other side. Sweet nostalgia overcame her as she remembered: yes, there *was* a better place than this, and she could still find it, if only she looked hard enough.

And now, apparently, she had.

For some moments she was too surprised to do anything. Colt had finally begun to rustle in the bed. Francie hastily pulled the closet door shut behind her. Now she didn't want him awake, for he would ruin this, too. Crouching, she reached up and yanked the chain that turned off the closet light. Then, suddenly timid, she shone her flashlight into the little doorway that had just magically revealed itself.

"You have got to be kidding, house," she whispered. "No way. *No way.*"

But the house wasn't kidding. Her light revealed a cramped, narrow stairway, heading down. It was a tight fit, and ahead of her lay utter darkness, but without a second thought she ducked in.

The air in the stairway was close and musty, and, unbearably, it was full of cobwebs, which to her had always felt like skeins of human hair—*dead* human hair. She couldn't bear the way they clung to her. But for something as unexpectedly wonderful as a secret stairway, she could put up with it.

Down, down she went, shining the finger-thin beam ahead of her. She was aware that the stairway wound around once and then twice, by which time she was disoriented. Her breath came quickly as she wondered what she would find at the bottom of it.

Surely it would be marvelous; surely it would change her life, like an angel's wing brushing her forehead. There would be talking animals, and witches, both good and bad. Perhaps she would find a whole race of beings who'd been waiting patiently for centuries for her to come lead them to freedom. Her blood boiled with a fever she hadn't known since girlhood.

And then, quite suddenly, she found herself in a little room.

She thought that she must be back on the first floor by now, only it was a part of the first floor that none of them had ever seen. The room was no more than five feet tall at its highest end; at the other, it petered out into the point of a triangle. Judging by the ziggurat-shaped ceiling, she was underneath the main stairway. If she stretched her arms out to either side she could touch the walls simultaneously. So it was a crawl space, more or less—a hiding place. It could be nothing else. Obviously, no one was supposed to know it was there.

Yet *someone* had known, for they had been here, and left artifacts. In the glare of her little flashlight Francie saw an old greenglass bottle, lying on its side. Near it, propped against the wall as though taking a break, were three creepy little figures, which Francie recognized as old-fashioned rag dolls, their cloth faces blank as thumbnails. Someone had wrought these with great skill out of sewing scraps, for despite their facelessness they were easily recognizable as a man, woman, and child—a little rag family, each in their own suit of clothes. Picking up the child doll, Francie gasped as she stuck her finger on a wooden splinter in the floor. A globe of blood swelled like dew on her fingertip. She licked it off, the sour taste of copper mingling with a bit of grit. Grimacing, she hawked and spat. Her saliva pooled in the thick dust; here was one place where the tender ministrations of Flebberman had not reached. No one had ever cleaned in here.

Which meant it was *really* secret.

Francie tucked the child doll into the sleeve of her sweatshirt, deciding to leave the other two where they sat. She didn't want

Colt to know anything about this. He didn't deserve it. It was *her* world, she thought; he would only do something to ruin it. Then, casting her light around, she noticed the bottle again. Wiping its face clean, she read the yellowed label:

McNally's SPECIAL ORIENTAL TONIC
Cure-all for MIND, BODY and SOUL!
Guaranteed to Fix What Ails You!
Made From A SECRET Ressapie
OF ONE HUNDRED HERBS of the ORIENT!
THIS ELIKSIR OF HEALTH has been Used From Time
Out of Mind in the East by
Sages, Wise Men, Kings and Queens!
As Well As Princes and Conquering Heroes!
It Is Unknown in Europe!
ONLY IN AMERICA!
All Ailments Healed!
Youth Restored!
MANLY VIM AND VIGOR Will Return to You
Upon Taking Only
ONE draught of this
SPECIAL RARE Potion!
PRICE ONLY $1.00
Excellent Also for Sleepless Children, Toothache,
Fever, Stummickache and
The Pains of Childbearing Womon!

What kind of snake oil was this? Francie wondered. A dried cork still plugged the bottle's mouth, but crumbled to dust when she removed it. Inside she could make out the encrusted remnants of whatever dubious substance it had once held, long thickened into solid sludge. She sniffed it carefully, and some faint, medicinal odor drifted into her nostrils. She set the bottle down again and wiped a hand on her sweatshirt.

Conscious now that she had stumbled onto some kind of treasure trove, Francie felt a delighted tightening in her bowels. She was, she knew, in the very heart of the house. Some child had played in here once—probably a girl, judging from the dolls. This was confirmed when she next discovered a brooch, missing half its paste diamonds, and a hairpin with a butterfly on it. These were the kinds of things only a girl would appreciate. Picking up the latter, she realized that the butterfly was woven from human hair. Its wings were looped around and around, like tiny strands of rope, and they were twisted expertly together in the middle to form the delicate body. She overcame her momentary revulsion to wonder at the patience that had been required to make such a tiny thing. Whose hair was it? she wondered. Carefully she blew the dust from it, and saw that the hair was a beautiful gold—time had dimmed it only a little.

And then she saw the book.

She'd nearly missed it, for it was covered in such a thick layer of dust that it blended in perfectly with the floor. It was a big book, a thick book. Another thrill ran through her. Running her finger along its spine, she felt the dried leather of the binding, and a shiver ran like a current down her own spine. She lifted it, marveling at its weight. This was no cheap paperback. It was a real book, made the way books used to be. Judging by its heaviness, Francie knew that the pages were made of materials other than just paper; perhaps linen, too. She had learned something about bookmaking while she was in college—not much, but enough to realize that this was the kind of book they didn't make anymore.

Neither the spine nor the cover bore any sort of inscription. Opening it to the first page, she read:

Sunday May 1851
This week we have buried our firstborn son Charles William Musgrove, aged one month and two days. He rests now in our back plot at Adencourt. God speed his soul to heaven.

Francie froze, disbelieving. Could this book really be that old? Could it have been sitting down here this long? Obviously it was a diary; the Musgroves had lived here for even longer than she could have guessed, then. The handwriting was blocky and awkward, as if done by someone unaccustomed to holding a pen.

Francie paged through several more entries. All were short, no more than two or three lines, and all were made on Sundays. Whoever it was, it had been a woman; that was obvious. The entries had to do with nothing more earthshaking than the thousand mundane chores of running a household one hundred fifty years ago: sewing, baking, churning butter, washing, gardening, harvesting, ironing, et cetera. But they were fascinating; time had rendered their banality profound. Some entries contained notes on family members:

4th Sunday January 1853
A boy, Hamish, born to us this week. Lay abed, wrought lacework.

And then:

3rd Sunday December 1853
Hamish stood. Baked bread, made butter. Captain poorly in the chest. Am with child.

Am with child? Francie thought. Gave birth, made lace? Baked bread, made butter, am with child—less than a year after having a baby? Clearly, *this* woman's husband didn't have any issues with raising a family. Her pregnancies merited no more mention than her other chores. And who was this Captain, and why was his chest poorly?

"You have got to be kidding," Francie whispered again.

She closed the diary and hugged it, thinking. Something like this came along once in a lifetime, if ever. Perhaps it belonged in a museum—it was certainly old enough. The daily life of a woman who lived a century and a half ago. She'd never found anything as exciting as this before. She'd never found anything exciting before, period. Things like this did not happen to boring people like her.

She opened the diary again to the first page and reread the first entry. No statement of ownership, no "This Book Belongs To:" on the flyleaf, no acknowledgment whatsoever that this thing was in any way important. And yet, to the author, it must have been priceless. A book like this would have been expensive. It would have been jealously hidden away from the grubby hands of children—and the prying eyes of a husband, perhaps.

And how sad that it should begin with the death of a child. A tiny newborn infant, only a month old. Their first. Perhaps it was that event which motivated the writer to begin recording the rest of her days—the realization that everything is temporary, and likely to be forgotten if not carefully noted. Even something like the loss of a baby—would that fade with time, or would it remain fresh forever, a wound that refused to scab over?

The "back plot." Francie pondered that. In those times, she knew, it was not unusual for people to bury their dead on their own property. Was that what she was referring to? Was this lost infant still here, somewhere in the vast tract of the yard? And who else might be with him, one hundred fifty years later?

"Adencourt," she whispered. "This house is called Adencourt." The word escaped her lips and hovered in front of her, like a bee; and all around her she felt the walls swell outward and then relax, like dusty lungs drawing a breath.

"Yes," Francie said. "Wake up, house."

■ ■ ■

"Michael," Francie whispered into her brother's ear.

The diary was tucked inside her sweatshirt, cold against her abdomen. She had carried away the other treasures, too, the bottle and the rag doll and the hairpin, and stuck them in her suitcase. It was the one place she was sure Colt wouldn't look, since she knew he would never bother to help her unpack. "Mikey!"

Michael stirred, whimpering. Francie joggled his shoulder.

"Get up, sweetie," she said. "We've got some exploring to do."

Michael rolled over and pulled the sleeping bag over his face. Francie pulled it down again and blew in his ear. He jolted awake, alarmed. Then he sat up and looked around.

"I was dreaming," he said peevishly. "What'd you wake me up for?"

"There's something I want to find," Francie said. "Come on, get dressed."

"What time is it?"

"Who cares?" She yanked the sleeping bag off of him. Michael covered his crotch with his hands and rolled over again, pulling it back over him.

"Sissie, Jesus," he said, "I've still got my morning woody!"

"Well, get rid of it," Francie said, unperturbed. "There's no time for your little fantasies. I'll make some coffee."

Michael groaned.

"Yolanda," he muttered.

Rolling her eyes, Francie went into the kitchen and started a pot brewing. The sun was almost fully up now, revealing a world of white outside the kitchen window. Snow had fallen all night. She could see the apple orchard, or what remained of it—the dwarfed and shriveled trees clothed now in robes of purity, like newly ordained clergymen, and the little pond frozen over. Even the old barn had become dignified in death, the snow drawn over it like a sheet.

She poured steaming coffee into two mugs and brought one to Michael, urging him to drink. He burned his mouth, as she'd known he would; then she had to wait and listen as he described every single detail of his dreams, which had been utterly commonplace. Finally she bullied him into his clothes and got into hers, and they stepped out the back door and sank in snow nearly to their knees before their feet touched solid earth.

"Wow," said Michael. "This is crazy."

"It really snowed," said Francie.

She'd forgotten what snow could be like. Marveling at its depth, its texture, she forged a path beyond the barn and the orchard, out toward the far reaches of the property. Michael huffed along behind her, stepping in her footprints. All he had brought to wear were sneakers; he was not equipped to go hiking through the Arctic. The snow was getting in his socks, he complained. He was cold. He wanted to go in.

"This is not the Arctic. This is hardly anything," said Francie.

"Yeah? How would you know?"

"Because I've been to the Arctic."

"Yeah? Really?" She could hear the uncertainty in his voice. Her heart nearly broke at how easy it was to fool him.

"Yes," she said. "Colt and I went there on vacation last summer. To get away from the heat and the—"

Francie stopped suddenly, remembering, and stuck her hand in her jacket, under her sweatshirt. It was gone. Not the diary, which she still carried against her skin; the hole in her middle.

My God, she thought. Maybe I'm not crazy anymore. Maybe I never was to begin with! Maybe it was all in my head!

At that, she had to laugh. The craziness was in her head! That was a good one. Funny on several levels. Of course it was in her head. Where else could it be—in her liver?

"What is it?" Michael asked, stopping. "What's so funny?"

"Nothing," she said. "Never mind."

There was no point in explaining any of this to him. Michael needed to know that his Sissie was in one piece and able to take care of herself, and of him. The poor dear was feeling a little fragile just now, what with all the nasty drug dealers and sneaky Colorado policemen after him.

"I'm just trying to think," she said.

She turned to look back at the house, but there were no clues there, no signs, not that she had expected any. She turned and faced northward again, toward the tree line. Nothing broke the surface of the snow. To the west there was a low, creeping jungle of undergrowth, all of it dead brown in this season except for the evergreens, weighed down under inches of snowfall. Perhaps the cemetery had been there, and was overgrown. She forged ahead in a new direction now, angling toward this little wilderness.

"What are we looking for, anyway?" Michael gasped. "Bigfoot?"

"Tombstones," Francie said.

Her brother stopped short. "What?"

"There's a little cemetery back here somewhere. I'm sure of it. It can't be that hard to find."

"Jesus Christ," said Michael. "You mean there's actual dead bodies hiding back here? That's creepy."

"No, it isn't. It's beautiful. It's touching. And they're not hiding. They're just . . . lost."

"Who's buried in it?"

"A child," said Francie. "A little boy named Charles."

■ ■ ■

They found it ten minutes later. The same plant life that had hidden the cemetery from view in autumn had shielded the stones from the bulk of last night's storm; the effect now was that of being inside a small chapel, with walls of interwoven branches. A roof of snow filtered the light and gave it an aqua coloring, as though they were underwater. There was even a sort of natural doorway, through which one could walk nearly upright.

Francie entered first, and then Michael. It was, she thought, like being in a holy igloo. They waited without speaking, listening to the light wind scour the surface of the snow outside.

"Wow," Michael whispered.

At their feet, dusted lightly as though with sugar, were seven stone markers of varying sizes—two large, the rest smaller. Francie dropped to her knees and read the inscriptions. Most had suffered greatly from the weathering decades, their letters drying up and dropping off one by one, the survivors clinging like desiccated insect shells to the fragile stone. Francie read:

C T. VIC GROVE
18   –

And:

H   MUS
BR TH
18   –1

And:

L   M   GR
[Illegible]
18   –1925

There was one that was completely illegible, its face worn smooth as paper. And finally:

MARLY
BELOVED MOTHER
1835–1888

The letters of this last one had survived better than the others, for no more reason than that the stone had been partially sheltered by a fat old tree stump—which, in those days, would still have been a tree. If she were to count the rings on it, Francie knew, she would find more than a hundred, perhaps almost two. She sat on the stump, overcome.

"This is her," Francie said. "Marly's the one. It has to be."

"The one what?" said Michael. "Sissie, have you got some kind of *Shining* thing going on here? Because you're kinda creeping me out."

"The one who wrote the diary. Marly Musgrove. She wrote about the funeral of her child. Her first son." Francie turned and looked toward the house again. Here they were obscured from its numerous window-eyes, but back then, this cemetery would have been obvious, out in the open, looked after. It would have been trimmed and maintained. It would have had a little fence around it, maybe. They would have come a few times a year to put flowers on the graves. People kept their dead close in those days.

"What diary?" Michael asked, but she could tell he didn't really care, and so she didn't answer him.

Of the smaller stones, only three bore names, none of them legible. The other two each said BABY, but did not indicate a name or even a gender, and only one of them a year: 1855. Five children, thought Francie. Out of how many? Maybe twice that number. Maybe even more. Those were the days when women had children in the double digits. Yet five children seemed a horrible toll, even before medicines and vaccines. If every family had suffered such a loss, there would scarcely be any people left on the earth at all.

"Mikey," Francie said, "we've made an important discovery."

"Okay, that's great," said Michael. "Can we go back in now, please? I'm freezing my ass off."

"In a few minutes," said Francie. "I want to be here for a little while."

"You go right ahead. I'm going in. See ya."

"Michael?"

"Yeah."

"Maybe we shouldn't tell anyone about this."

"Sure, Sissie," said Michael. "Whatever you say."

"I'm serious. Especially Colt."

"Why especially Colt?"

"Because . . . he won't appreciate it." *He'll want to ruin it some-how*, she thought, *and it's perfect just the way it is.*

"Okay," said Michael. "Whatever. See ya."

He exited the little enclave, leaving Francie alone in the church-like silence. She knelt, took a mitten off, ran her fingers over the cold letters of Marly's flaking white stone. Then she leaned forward and touched her tongue to it, gently, just to feel. She was surprised at how alive the stone seemed, even though it was frozen, and she pulled back quickly, before she could stick to it—guilty and pleased at her own weirdness.

When she was little, she'd had a fort that was kind of like this place, in the hedges of her mother's garden. She could go back there for hours and no one would know where she was. When Michael was old enough, she'd allowed him in, too, though it was supposed to be for girls only. Michael was always in need of a place to hide out. Often it wasn't safe for him to venture into the company of other boys, who were more like wolves than people. But Francie didn't have any girlfriends to come in there with her, so she took to keeping a raggedy spare dress on hand for Michael's visits. When he wanted to come in, he had to put the dress on. That way he was in semicompliance with the rules, and Francie could feel like she was having a real live tea party, instead of one that had been polluted by the presence of a boy.

"You can be my people," she whispered to the stones. "I'll take care of you from now on."

And the stones, though of course she knew better, seemed to whisper back.

14

■

THE CEMETERY

Coltrane Hart could count on one hand the number of times he'd left New York City for pleasure. Over the course of his distinguished career, he'd taken many business trips to many cities: Paris, Hong Kong, London, Berlin, Amsterdam. But, since all he ever saw of these places were corporate boardrooms—all furnished in remarkably similar style, with long tables of veneered wood and plush leather chairs—it was his opinion that the world outside New York was, for the most part, a cheap imitation of the real thing. He had noted, to his dismay, that people in other places often didn't speak English at all, or if they did, it was with varying degrees of fluency, none particularly satisfying (especially the Londoners); and when you sent out for lunch, you were bound to be disappointed, since nowhere in these cities could you find a predictable hamburger—only the unmentionable things that the natives ate. Colt was always unpleasantly surprised to find himself out of New York; it was amazing to him that people could live anywhere else, and not mind it.

And now here he was in Pennsylvania—where he neither knew

nor cared what the natives ate—standing on a porch that he owned, wearing his terry cloth bathrobe, pondering the bleakness of his latest acquisition. The first shocker had come last night, when he'd realized that for the first time in his life he was not within delivery range of a restaurant. And now, there was all this weather. In New York, the elements were mostly ornamental, but here they could really change things, and that made him nervous. He'd lived all his life half believing that the weather had been conquered, like polio, or the Nazis. Yet there had never been this much snow in Colt's life before, or as much openness, or quiet, or sky. To be honest, it was already driving him crazy. And the lack of familiarity bothered him, too. Not only did he not recognize anything, there was nothing to recognize. Everything was missing. There was simply nothing here—no buildings, no streets, nothing. Was it possible that buying this place had been a mistake? Well, theoretically, you couldn't go wrong with real estate these days, as long as you weren't buying in a ghetto. As a living situation, it might be a different story. Still, he'd never said he was moving out here permanently, had he? It was only a vacation home—an experiment.

A trophy. Except now Francie had this stupid idea that she wanted to *live* here.

Looking out across the road, all Colt could see was nothing. The riverbed was sunken out of sight, below road level, and there were the pathetic trees. Beyond that were some fields, and far off in the distance the mountains. Other than that, there was not a goddam thing out here, and what little there was was all covered in white. Everything in the world looked like it was the same size and color. It was like being on the moon. Who in their right mind would want to live in a place like this? His wife, that's who—she who hadn't been in her right mind for some time, anyway.

Colt was standing in the freezing cold in his bathrobe, watching Randall Flebberman swoop up and down the driveway in his truck as he plowed away the remnants of last night's storm. There was someone in the cab with him, a hulking thick figure of a man, ex-cept it wasn't a man—it was a teenager. Maybe he was Flebber-man's assistant. Flebberman and Company. Jesus, what a way to make a living, Colt thought. Here was this Flebberman, whose greatest mark on the world to date was a clean driveway, probably, or something equal to it. In other words, nothing. A real loser. Yet on Flebberman's face, he saw nothing like despair—only a sense of presence, almost sublime in its totality, a look that said "I am plowing this driveway" and nothing more or less. Almost as if he had no idea he was supposed to be unhappy. Colt had slaved all his life to get somewhere, and by his own reckoning he still had some ways to go; yet to judge by the look on Flebberman's face, one would think he'd already arrived. It was positively maddening.

Colt shivered in his bathrobe, the chill wind whipping up under-neath to caress his unprotected genitals. This created in him a shriveling feeling, akin to fear, and so he poured the remains of his coffee into the snow and went inside. Yet he continued to watch Flebberman and the teenager through the picture window in the outer living room. *Jesus Christ*, he thought, *the son of a bitch actually looks like he's enjoying himself*. It was making him sick to his stom-ach.

He heard Francie's footsteps as she came in through the back door, through the kitchen, and down the long hallway to where he stood now, but he didn't turn around.

"Morning," he said quietly.

"Yes," said Francie. "It is, isn't it?"

Couldn't argue with that logic. After a moment Colt cleared his throat.

"I wonder how much this guy got paid by the bank to take care of this place. Might be worth it to keep him on. I certainly won't have time to do it myself."

"Colt, can we talk?"

"We are talking."

"I mean about last night."

"Oh, that," said Colt. "Actually, I don't have time."

"Why not?"

"I'm going back to the city."

"Already?"

"What do you mean, already?"

"I thought—Colt, can you look at me, please?"

Colt turned and looked at her. He could tell she wanted to get into it again: Why did you do it? What made you do it? Why can't we have a baby? But he'd said all he had to say.

"I . . . thought you were going to stick around a few days," she said. "Help me unpack, and get things in order."

"That's what your brother's here for," Colt said. "Might as well make himself useful. I want to get back to work. This place isn't going to pay for itself, you know."

"Oh," said Francie. "All right, then."

Colt was surprised. He'd been expecting another fight.

"Yes," he said, with a mixture of relief and disappointment. "All right."

"See you around," said Francie, heading back toward the kitchen.

▪ ▪ ▪

Colt went upstairs, into the large bathroom off the master bedroom. It also bore the marks of the haphazard renovations of the 1970s, though to what degree it had benefited was clearly a matter for debate. There was a large tub, and a flexible, European-style showerhead, but the walls were tiled in pink pastel, and the rug, truly an abomination, was some kind of greenish shag. Who the hell put rugs in bathrooms, anyway? Old ladies, that's who. That would be first on his list of things to have done around here—to redo this bathroom into something he could tolerate. Turning on the tap, he found he had to wait an unacceptably long time for hot water as he stood, naked and uncomfortable, with earth-chilled well water splashing around his feet. When hot water did come, it was gone within ten minutes. So the water heater would need replacing, too. That would be number two on the list. Colt groused as he put on the one suit he'd brought from the city. Money, money, money. This house was going to keep on costing him. Nothing, damn it, was ever finished being paid for.

When he came downstairs again, he saw through the window that Flebberman and the giant teenager were now talking to Michael and Francie. The teenager towered a full six inches over the older man, although he slumped against the hood of the truck as if in the middle of a heart attack. Colt stepped briskly outside, pulling out his wallet.

"Colt, this is Marge Westerbrook's son," said Francie. "Owen. You remember? We sort of met him the day we looked at the house. He helps Randy out sometimes when he's not in school."

"Oh, yeah."

"Hi," said the teenager, in a voice as deep and thick as molasses.

"Hi, kid. What do I owe you for the plowing?" Colt asked Flebberman.

Flebberman lifted a hand. "Nothin'," he said.

Colt paused, impatient. "Come on. Really."

"I been plowin' this driveway a long time," said Flebberman. "I just like to keep it clean. Kinda used to it by now. Makes the place look lived in."

"It *is* lived in," said Colt.

"Colt, what Mr. Flebberman means is, he did it as a favor. And when someone does something nice for you, the proper response is 'Thank You,'" said Francie.

Colt shot Francie a dirty look.

"'Snothin'," said Flebberman.

"I wanted to ask you if you'd be willing to keep on minding the property for me, on a permanent basis. I won't have much time for it myself. You know, plowing and yard work and . . . all that," Colt said.

"Oh, *I* can do some of it," said Francie quickly. "Some of the yard work, anyway. I was looking forward to doing it in the spring. Having a garden and all."

"Mr. Flebberman is a professional," Colt told his wife pointedly. "He knows what he's doing."

"So do I," said Francie.

"Aw," said Flebberman. "We'll see, I guess."

Colt frowned. "I'm offering you work here," he said. "What does 'We'll see' mean? Do you want the job or not?"

Flebberman looked down at his boots, shuffling them through the snow. He and Owen exchanged glances. Then he shot another look at Colt, his thin, almost invisible eyebrows lowered.

"Sure," he said, resentful. "If yer offerin'."

"How much was the bank paying you?"

Flebberman looked upward now, calculating. "Two hunnerd bucks a month," he said.

"I'll give you one seventy-five."

"Coltrane!" Francie said, shocked.

"What? I'm bargaining, here. Do you mind?"

"Not with our neighbor, you're not. It's rude."

Flebberman said nothing, his eyes going from Colt to Francie like they were engaged in a tennis match. He looked at Owen again, as if to say *I told you they'd be like this.*

"No, it isn't," said Francie. "It's a crime, is what it is. We'll pay you . . . we'll pay you two fifty a month, Mr. Flebberman. Would that be all right? If you kept the driveway clear in winter, and mowed the lawn, and helped me with trimming the brush and all that? Once spring comes, I mean?"

"Oh, for Christ's sake," said Colt. "I see my own wife is cutting my legs out from under me. All right, Mr. Flebberman, what do you say? Two hundred fifty a month, all in."

Flebberman still said nothing; he looked down at his boots again, then wistfully at his truck, which—though the engine had been idling all this time—was in such an excellent state of repair that one could hardly hear it running. Colt noticed that Owen Westerbrook was staring at Francie as though he had never seen a woman before, which out here in the boonies was a distinct possibility. Francie smiled at him; Owen turned a deep shade of red and looked away. Colt smirked.

"Awright," Flebberman said, his voice barely audible.

"Good," said Francie. "Thank you, Mr. Flebberman."

"Maybe he can clean up that old cemetery," Michael said. "Clear the branches out of it and all."

"Well, it's great to see you again, Mr. Flebberman," Francie said quickly. "And nice to meet you, Owen. We appreciate you coming by."

"What cemetery?" asked Colt. "Did you say 'cemetery'?"

Flebberman looked at Michael. "So you found it," he said in a low, almost resigned voice.

"Found what?" said Colt, as Francie's heart sank. She shot Michael a murderous look, but he missed it.

"There's a little cemetery way out back. We just found it this morning," Michael said excitedly. "A real old one. Sissie and I—" He stopped short, remembering, too late, that it was supposed to be kept secret. "Oh," he said. "Oops."

"You mean on this property?" Colt said, incredulous. "There's dead people *on this property?*"

"Yuh. That'd be my fambly," Flebberman said. "The Captain and his wife and kids. I ain't been back there for some time. Since when I was a little kid, and Aunt Helen was still alive." He turned to Owen, who had now draped his entire frame over the hood of the truck, like a dishrag. "You remember that old cemetery, Owen?"

"Yuh," Owen said. "I seen it once or twice."

"It's very charming," said Francie. "It's *peaceful,*" she added.

"It's gone," said Colt.

Francie, Flebberman, Owen, and Michael all looked at him at the same time, as if he had just shouted some horrible obscenity about their mothers.

"Uh, what's that now?" said Flebberman.

"I said, it's gone. Gonzo. Outa here," Colt said. "I don't want something like that on my property. Jesus, that's disgusting!"

"Colt, people used to have cemeteries all the time, in the old days," said Francie. "It's nothing to worry about."

"Francie, we have *well water*, for Chrissakes," said Colt.

"Oh, they ain't gettin' in your water," said Flebberman. "They're back far enough. They knew better than that."

"I don't care. I'm having it moved," said Colt. "It makes me sick just to think of it. Jesus! All those maggots and—ech!" He shivered, as if these maggots were now crawling along his neck. "No wonder the bank didn't want to haggle," he said to Francie. "Remember how I said something would come up? That it was too good to be true? This is it. This is exactly what I was talking about. God damn it, I am going to sue the pants off that bitch of an agent!"

"Hey," said Owen Westerbrook. "That's my mom yer talkin' about."

"*Coltrane!* I am so sorry. My husband is from the city," Francie said to them, as if that explained everything.

Flebberman's cheeks had colored. "Waddaya mean, yer havin' it moved?"

"I mean like, dug up and relocated," said Colt. "That's what I mean."

"Oh," said Flebberman. He balled his fists and his voice began to shake. "I sure wish you wouldn't do that."

"There's absolutely no reason to," said Francie desperately. "Colt, be reasonable. It's been there forever. They're all gone by now, anyway. Decomposed."

"No, they aren't," said Colt. "Bones can last for centuries, sometimes. And even if they are, it's like . . . *pollution*, or *contamination*!"

"Hey, now," said Flebberman. "They're not contaminatin' anything."

"Colt, those people are Mr. Flebberman's family," said Francie.

"Dang, dude, chill out," said Michael, greatly amused at this squeamish side of his brother-in-law. "They're not going to like grab you from under your bed or anything."

Colt shook his head and sighed. Then he headed for his car. "I'm going to make a few calls, think about it," he said over his shoulder. "Bottom line is, it's on my property. So it's my decision."

"Colt," said Francie.

"Uh," said Flebberman anxiously.

Colt opened the door of his Camaro and waited.

"Yes?" he said.

Flebberman's face hardened.

"Well, forget it. If that's the way it's gonna be," he said, "then I quit."

Colt snorted. "Quit what?"

"You just hired me. Now I quit. That's what."

"Oh, I see. Well, I guess I'll just have to hire some other guy with a snowplow on the front of his truck," said Colt. "That shouldn't be too much of a challenge. I saw about forty of them yesterday." He got in his car and slammed the door. Then he revved the engine and backed out onto the road, taking off without a backward glance.

15

∎

BREATHING

An awkward silence fell over the four of them in the driveway. Owen Westerbrook's eyes were wide. His mouth hung open in a perfect O, as if he'd just seen a traffic accident. Francie turned to Flebberman, who had gone pale with shock and rage.

"I am so sorry," she said to him. She looked at Michael, who cringed. "It was supposed to be a *secret*."

"Hunnerd fifty years they been buried there, some of 'em," said Flebberman. "Nobody ever bothered with 'em before. No need to. Now you folks just move in here and think you can do whatever you want¿ It's not right!"

"I'm on your side, Mr. Flebberman," said Francie soothingly. "Believe me. I'll work on him. I won't allow this to happen."

"They're my people," said Flebberman. "This was their place. They're restin', for Chrissakes! You can't just move 'em! Just 'cause he buys the place . . ."

"He called my mom a bitch, too," said Owen Westerbrook. "I don't 'preciate that."

"I'm sorry about that, Owen. I'll take care of this, don't you worry," said Francie. "I'll fix everything. I promise."

"How?" asked Flebberman. He looked sick to his stomach.

"I'm not sure," said Francie, biting her lip. "But—I'll think of something. I promise. I'm really sorry."

"Well, you—you oughta be," said Flebberman. "You damn well oughta be!"

He got into his truck. Owen got in the passenger side and slammed the door, his chin high with righteous indignation. Flebberman rolled down his window.

"You goddamn people move in here and right away you think you can do whatever the hell you want!" he shouted. "Who the hell you think you are, anyway? Whyncha go back where you came from!"

"Mis—Mister Flebberman!" said Francie. "Please, don't. He's not—he doesn't understand—"

Flebberman and Owen pulled out of the driveway before she could finish, the heavy wheels of the truck spinning in the packed snow, then grabbing and propelling them up the hill. The silence they left behind them was as loud as a waterfall. When they were gone, Francie turned to Michael, who was still smothered in shame, head hanging.

"I can't believe you," said Francie. "What's the matter with you? Didn't I ask you not to tell anybody?"

"I'm sorry, Sissie, I just . . . got carried away, I guess," said Michael. "I don't see what the big deal is, anyway. You think he wasn't going to find it, sooner or later? You think you can hide something like a cemetery? And besides, it's not my fault he freaked like that. Dude's crazy, or something. It's like he almost had an allergic reaction."

"But I told you not to tell him, dammit!"

"Jeez, Francie," Michael said. "You don't have to get all mad on me!"

"I'm sorry. It's just—he just doesn't *understand* this place," Francie said—not sure that she quite understood it herself. Perhaps it was that she felt connected already—to the diary, to the hidey-hole, to the cemetery and the people in it. And she knew that Colt would never feel that way. "He thinks this place is going to be like a . . . I don't know, a medal around his neck. He wants to bring his business buddies out here and show off. He wanted to put a golf course back there, for heaven's sake. Colt is not the kind of person who appreciates history."

"That Flebberman guy was pretty upset."

"He *should* be upset," Francie said. "Look at it from his point of view, Michael. And from mine, too. We show up here and in less than twenty-four hours we're already making enemies. This is not good. I didn't want to have these kinds of problems. I am not a confrontational person."

"Well, maybe he'll get over it," said Michael. He yawned and stretched his arms. "Anyway, listen, Sissie, I'm going back to sleep. You got me up way too early."

Francie laughed disbelievingly.

"What's the matter with you?" she said again. "Is that all you can think of? Sleep?"

"Well, jeez," he said, "Waddaya want me to do? You woke me up at like five A.M."

"I don't know!" she said. "But do something! Say something intelligent and perceptive! Something that lets me know you're in there somewhere!"

"Well, excuse me," Michael said, hurt. "Maybe you should go back to Indiana so you can hang out with all your smart college friends, then!"

"That's not what I mean!" Francie said. "I didn't . . . "

Michael stood, waiting for whatever she was going to say. But she saw that there was no point in saying it; he would just take it, and wait for her to stop being mad at him, and then things would go back to being the same as they always had. You never got anywhere yelling at Michael. It was better just to let him be himself, and not expect too much.

But suddenly Francie decided she had had enough of that. Why should she expect any less of him just because he was her little brother? Maybe it was going off the pills; maybe it was revenge for telling about the cemetery. She would never know what made her cross the driveway to his Volkswagen bus and wrench open the sliding door. But once she did, she passed the point of no return. Instantly she was overwhelmed by a pungent odor that made her wrinkle her nose. There, in a neat stack, she saw ten brick-shaped bundles, wrapped in plastic garbage bags and duct tape, each about a foot long and six or eight inches high.

Michael came up behind her. "What are you doing?" he asked.

"Looking. To see if you were serious."

"Well, I was," he said.

"You don't even try to hide it?"

"What's the point? If a cop pulled me over, he'd smell it before he even left his car. He wouldn't even need to call for the dogs."

Francie turned to face her brother.

"Michael," Francie said, "I want you to go and get rid of this stuff. Today. Right now."

Michael's eyes widened. "What?" he said, incredulous. "Right this minute? Are you kidding?"

Francie crossed her arms. "Do I look like I'm kidding?" she asked.

"Well, Sissie . . . what am I supposed to *do* with it?"

"You should just . . . turn it in. Just go to the cops and let them have it. Come clean with them. Tell them everything."

"Come clean with the *cops*? Are you nuts? You know what they'll do to me?"

"Whatever it is, it won't be as bad as you think. Come on, Michael, we have murderers and rapists walking the streets. They just check into jail and check out again. What do you think they're going to do, send you to the guillotine? You'll feel better if you get this resolved. Then you won't have it hanging over your head anymore."

Michael laughed, as if still hoping it was some kind of joke—but another look at Francie told him she was in no mood.

"Wait. You're serious," he said.

"Yeah, I'm serious," said Francie, "and another thing. You never should have brought it here to begin with. Think about how selfish that was, Michael. Really think about it, for once in your life. If you got caught here, we would all get in trouble. They'd think we were *all* dealers. They could confiscate the house and property, and we'd never get it back. Do you realize that?"

"Well—Sissie," Michael said, "I didn't have anywhere else to go. What was I supposed to do, take it to Mom and Dad's place?"

"Why should you have to take it anywhere? Why should this be anyone else's problem but your own?"

"Okay, well," he said. "Think about the guys who own it! Whatever they're gonna do to me is a lot worse than what the cops would do. I'm tellin' you, Francie. They have to get it back."

"I thought you said they were nice guys."

"Yeah, well, business is business."

"Well then, take it back to Denver," she said. "I mean it. Today, right now. Take it somewhere. Anywhere but here."

Michael looked at her woefully.

"Denver is like three days away," he said. "Francie, I'm broke. I'm flat busted. I don't get another check from Dad for a whole month."

"Don't," she said. "Don't even try it."

"Try *what*?" Michael shrieked. He threw his arms up in the air and began marching back and forth. "I'm not trying *anything*! Francie, come on! I need a break here!" He stopped suddenly and glared at her, suspicious. "You're mad I told him about the cemetery, aren't you? That's what this is really about."

"Of course it's not about the cemetery," she said, though in fact it was—at least a little bit.

"What, then?"

Francie sighed. "Michael, I'm going to tell you something, and I want you to listen. I mean, *really listen*. Okay?"

"Okay," Michael said. "I'm listening."

"Something happened to me yesterday, while I was in the supermarket. Something . . . huge. And things are different with me
now. Everything, as a matter of fact. You understand? My entire
life. Something shifted, somehow. I don't quite understand it, but
that doesn't matter. All you have to know is that things are not
going to be like they were before. Not anymore."

"That must have been some supermarket," Michael said.

"No, you *idiot*," Francie said, "the *supermarket* had nothing to do
with it. It's—well, I don't know what it was. I thought it was a
breakdown, but really it was a break*through*. And there are certain
things that just can't happen anymore. And you having a busload
of drugs on my property is one of them. I love this place, Michael.
I belong here. So I want you to do this, before you do anything
else. And I don't want you to come back until it's taken care of."

Michael sighed.

"Can I at least have some breakfast first?" he asked.

She crossed her arms again, not smiling back. "I'll loan you a
hundred dollars," she said. "That's it. Add it to the thousands I've
given you over the years. And I expect you to pay me back for all
of it. Eventually."

Michael threw his arms up in the air again.

"Oh, my God! Fucking shit!" he screamed at the sky. "What the
fuck is going on all of a sudden? It's like . . . a nightmare, or something!"

"Michael! You don't have to talk like that!"

"Tell me why, Francie. Why? Why does everything have to be
different all of a sudden, just like that? What did I do? Huh? Tell
me that! What did I do that was so wrong?"

"Everything has to change, eventually," she said. "You have to
take responsibility, Michael. This is your mess."

"IT'S SNOWY!" Michael yelled at her. "THERE'S A HOLE IN
MY FLOOR! I'LL DIE!"

"No, you won't," she said.

"I might!"

"Michael," Francie said, "it's time for you to grow up."

He stared at her, a small noise of disbelief escaping from the back of his throat.

"Fine," he said. "Be a fucking bitch about it, then."

"I'll pretend you didn't just say that," said Francie.

She went into the house and took five twenties from her purse. When she came out again, Michael was scraping ice off the side windows of his bus. Francie watched, saying nothing. When he was done, he pushed past her, went into the house, and came out again, dragging his air mattress after him. She held the money out and he grabbed it from her without a word as he went by, like a relay racer. He opened the sliding side door of the bus and threw the mattress in. Then he got in the driver's side and started up the engine. It took several moments for it to catch, and he held her gaze all that time, eyebrows lowered. Finally he unrolled his window.

"I'm leaving. Okay? You happy now?" he said.

"I'm a long way from happy," said Francie. "But I'm getting there."

"What the hell does that mean?"

"Michael," said Francie, "good-bye."

Michael's lower lip began to quiver.

"You remember when we were kids?" he said. "And you used to tell me that we would get a house in the country someday, where we could be alone and no one would bother us?"

"Michael—"

"First you leave me to fend for myself," he said, "and now you throw me out? This was supposed to be our place, and now you're sharing it with him? Great! Thanks a lot, Francie."

"Mikey, that was *years* ago," she said.

But, having planted his dagger, Michael was content to leave. He backed out of the driveway and onto the road, where he did a K-turn and began moving slowly along the river. She could see him looking back at her, waiting for some sign that she was just kidding, that she had taken pity on him again. But she gave no such sign, because she wasn't kidding. And soon he was out of sight.

And here I am, alone with my house, she thought.

Francie climbed the steps and closed the door after her. She stopped in the foyer and listened. There was nothing to hear, except her own breathing.

16

■

ZERO-G

Colt, driving along the New Jersey Turnpike, was hearing his father's voice again.

Whatsa matter¿ it said. Afraid of a few dead bodies¿ Afraid they're gonna come out and get you¿

"Don't you start," Colt said.

Why not¿ Too grown up to listen to your father¿

"You're not my father," said Colt. "You're a voice in my head. Which means . . . guess what¿ You're not real."

Yeah, but what is real¿ Isn't everything just a voice in our head, when you come right down to it¿ Isn't the whole world just an illusion we have to keep convincing ourselves of, over and over¿

"Now you're gonna start handing me that hippie bullshit¿ I don't think so."

Actually, it's not "hippie bullshit." It's Berkeley.

"Fuck you and your philosophers," Colt said. "Where were you when I had to deal with Mom's body, anyway¿ Huh¿ And where was your philosophy when you were supposed to be raising me¿"

He turned on the radio and stabbed at the buttons, trying to find a song with screeching guitars. This was the only thing that worked—turning the volume up to such a level that no one else could have tolerated it.

It was only when he was alone that he started hearing Nova Hart's voice. The bastard never bothered him when he was with other people. He was like the singing frog in the old cartoon, the one that sang "Hello, My Ragtime Gal" when there was no one around, but didn't make so much as a peep when you put him in front of an audience.

The dead are troublesome, Colt thought.

His father wasn't actually dead. He merely thought of him that way. It was Colt's fervent wish, for reasons he chose not to revisit, that he should never see his father again; "dead" was the most convenient way to think of him. In reality, Colt's father was living some hours upstate, if you could call his current arrangements "living."That was something not even Francie knew; she thought Nova was dead, too. And it was something that Colt never allowed himself to think about, which was why he turned the car stereo up as loud as he could bear it.

But a person didn't have to be dead to haunt you. That was a disconcerting fact Colt had discovered in recent years. This voice that took over his head sometimes—there was only one way to deal with that, and that was to make as much noise as possible until it went away. And New York was the one blessed place where you could count on never getting a single moment of peace and quiet.

Colt's heart sang with relief as he neared Manhattan, its jagged lines jutting upward like the petrified jaw of some extinct beast. He sped faster toward it, a parched man on his way to an oasis. Hurry, he thought. Hurry, before it starts again. Forget about Francie, forget about the house, forget about everything else. Just hurry up and get there.

Anchor Capital, the investment firm for which Colt worked, was located in one of the glass-and-steel monoliths that dominate Sixth Avenue, a suitably loud thoroughfare constantly bustling with people, cabs, sidewalk vendors, construction crews, and tourists; every so often the surface rumbled queasily as a subway tore through its bowels. Colt's boss, Forszak, who owned 51 percent of Anchor, rented a portion of the thirtieth floor of one of these magnificent structures, and it was here that his minions toiled endlessly in the Snake Pit, manipulating the fortunes of the world in their own subtle way, through their tentacles of fiber-optic cable. Forszak himself, the head of the financial octopus, occupied a hidden corner office, where, via electronic means, he watched and listened to everything that was said and done through everyone's computers and telephones, and cackled, and patted his belly—and occasionally ate homeless children for lunch, if rumors were to be believed. Mostly, though, he just counted his money. Colt knew—he had been in Forszak's office and seen the figures zooming across the screens. There had been digits followed by more glorious zeroes than he'd ever seen before, even in his dreams. It was enough to make him drool. Someday, he, too, would lead these figures in a merry dance, like the Pied Piper and his legion of rats; someday, Colt would be a Forszak.

He nodded to the receptionist, who greeted him with a respectful smile and buzzed him through the glass double doors. Colt went straight into the Snake Pit and hung up his coat. When Anchor Capital had moved here six years earlier, Forszak had ordered all partitions removed, all desks pushed together, four by four, creating a large, open space in which no one could hide from anyone and everything was known; all the traders were thrown in together, writhing around in a heaving, chaotic mess. There were no less than thirty-seven men, and two harried and driven women, all shouting and cursing in the peculiar language of finance. It was blissfully loud in the Snake Pit, a veritable Babel. It had the same effect on Colt that the sound of waves had on sea turtles.

He made his way to his desk, feeling the uproar smother him motheringly as it closed behind him. Nothing could bother him here, because there simply wasn't time to think about anything. On Colt's desk, just like on every other, were three computer monitors and a wireless keyboard. Behind him was a television, tuned at all times to MSNBC. On the wall in front of him was another television, this one tuned to CNN. Between these five electronic oracles, Colt and his comrades were able to keep a handle on everything of note that happened in the world, for there was no telling how anything—an earthquake in Argentina or a war in Africa or a bushfire in California—could affect the entire market. You had to be adept at interpreting how these events would ripple throughout the financial world, and hedge your bets accordingly, if at all possible. It usually *wasn't* possible, but that didn't keep the traders from trying. They were the diviners at the temple gates, reading the day's events in the spilled entrails of sacrificial animals. Nothing that happened was insignificant: a pencil dropped in Singapore, a woman forgetting to buy steamed rice in Delhi, a butterfly falling out of the sky over the Pacific Ocean—all these things were connected, and no matter how small they seemed, they all meant something. And eventually the effects of these things found their way into the stock market. Theoretically, the most adept trader in the world could lie on a hillside watching the clouds go by, and know every single thing that was happening everywhere, at any given moment. That person hadn't been born yet, of course, but he was out there somewhere, the Reader, the One—He Who Didn't Even Need to Set Foot in an Office to Make Fortunes with Every Breath He Drew. Or maybe it was a She. There was no way to know. All of the traders in Forszak's office dreamed of becoming this One, and all of them knew it would never happen to them.

But they kept on showing up for work anyway, just in case.

Colt sat down and nodded to Herbert on his right, the balding, pudgy Asian man whom everyone called "Buddha."

"Hiya, Coltie," Buddha said. "How's it hangin'?"

"Bood. What's news?"

Buddha shrugged. "Nothin'," he said. "I'm long and wrong on Cisco."

"Yeah?"

"Yeah."

"Well, let's see here."

Colt punched a random key and his screens flickered into wakefulness. One was connected to the Reuters line, another to various market indices, the third to his Web browser. He'd liquidated most of his holdings before they moved out to the new house; it wouldn't do to be hanging onto stocks if he wasn't there to control his position. They were in the moving business, after all, not the storage business. That was one of Forszak's favorite lines— *moving, not storage. We don't hang on to things here, we buy 'em and sell 'em.* Colt had kept a few penny stocks on the line like minnows, just to see what fortune they attracted, and he saw now with mild pleasure that one of them had advanced sufficiently for him to it sell off. He cast two hundred shares out into the electronic sea and watched as they were snapped up by some shark out of Philadelphia. Nice. He'd been at work for less than a minute and already he'd made a hundred dollars. That was how it went, day in, day out—sometimes the numbers were big and sometimes they were small, but all that really mattered was that they had a plus sign in front of them. He wrote "+ 100" on a piece of paper and leaned back, cracking his knuckles.

"I suck," he announced, for it was office superstition that the more one debased oneself, the more likely the market gods were to shower one with favor.

"Coltie," said Joe, the older man who sat across from him. "You move awright?"

"Yeah, we moved."

"How'd it go?"

"Fine, I guess. Pain in the ass. Brother-in-law shows up outa nowhere, wife throws a hissy last night. Things are crazy. I was gonna take a few days off, but I had to get outa there for a while."

Joe nodded. "Story of my life," he said. "You know things are rough when you'd rather be at work than at home." He reached out and touched the plastic head of the little dippy-bird that he kept on his desk; this was a kind of perpetual-motion toy in the shape of an ostrich and filled with red-colored water, which continually bobbed up and down. It drove the others crazy, but Joe claimed it was his good-luck charm, which removed it from the realm of criticism altogether. Everyone was allowed their charm.

"Joe moved once," said Buddha. "After his wife found his gay porn collection. Dincha, Joe?"

"Zing," said Colt.

"Don't let the Bood get away with that shit, Joe," said Raoul, on Colt's left.

Joe himself, frowning at his screens, seemed unperturbed by this assault on his character. He had started out as an order boy on the exchange floor decades ago, when positions were still being recorded in chalk on a big blackboard. Now over sixty, thrice divorced, Joe was a big earner, a *huge* earner; only Buddha was allowed to zing him, because Buddha was hilarious, when he wanted to be.

"Fuck you, you Chink," said Joe absently.

"Great comeback, Joe," said Colt. "Real good one there."

Buddha snorted. "He's a regular Don Rickles, is Joe," he said. "Mind as sharp as a noodle."

"Whoa," said Raoul. "Lookit Dell."

Colt peered at the Reuters line. The price of Dell shares had dropped five cents—somewhere in the universe something was happening, and this was the ripple of it, washing up on shore. Frantically he hopped on five hundred shares, and was rewarded a moment later by seeing it appear in his holdings column.

"Hot diggety," he said. "I got some."

"Me, too," said Raoul.

"Sell me yours," said Colt. "I like Dell. I'll give you two and half over your purchase."

"Done and done," said Raoul, striking a few keys. "Now good day, sir."

"Anybody know anything about the Bomber?" asked Buddha.

"What the fuck is the Bomber?" asked Joe.

"I heard some guys talkin' about it in the elevator. Bombardier. They make subway cars, or something. Canadian company."

Raoul and Joe guffawed. "Canadian!" they said, simultaneously.

"Whatsa matter, Buddha, those American stocks getting too much for you?" asked Colt. "Old red, white, and blue too expensive for your yellow blood?"

"The official animal of Canada is the beaver," said Joe.

"Well, there ya go," said Buddha. "My official animal is the trouser snake. It's a match made in heaven."

"Don't bet on fuckin' elevator gossip, Bood," said Raoul. "Next thing you know you'll be goin' to the cleaning ladies for tips."

"Naw, you go, Bood," said Colt. "And send us a postcard when you get there."

They fell silent, preoccupied by the action on their screens. Half an hour later, when the price of Dell had risen again, Colt dangled a few shares, but was disappointed to see that no one was interested. Traders all over the country were waiting to see what would happen next. He leaned back again and folded his arms, waiting for a strike.

"Buddha, you been playin' any cards this week?" he asked.

"Oh, Coltie, lemme tellya. I was in this all-nighter last weekend."

"Here we go," said Joe, rolling his eyes. "The cannelloni story again. I only heard this five times already."

"Shut up, Joe. Listen, Colt. I was playing cards out in Brooklyn, a regular game I hit sometimes. Good buncha guys, usually the same ones." Buddha was an excellent gambler; it was well known that he supplemented his already considerable income by playing poker, and if his own stories were to be believed, sometimes he made as much as ten thousand dollars on a good weekend. Buddha didn't discuss his bad weekends. "Lawyers and accountants and shit. A judge. Sometimes a congressman. Most of 'em I've known for years. Y'know?"

"Yeah," said Colt.

"Which congressman?" asked Raoul.

"I ain't sayin', numbnuts. The Brooklyn game, I'm talkin' about. So last time they've got this new guy, someone I never met before. Right away, I see I'm gonna have a problem with this guy. He's bluffin' all over the place and winning on dumb luck. Can't read him at all. And he never shuts up. I mean never. His mouth is running the whole time. You get his whole life story—how he went to Bermuda and banged a movie star, how he's got four Porsches, how his whole family is in prison."

"His whole family's in *prison*?"

"His last name is Buonarotti. He even showed me his driver's license."

"Fuck me," said Colt. "*Those* Buonarottis?"

"Yeah, *and*," said Joe. "Wait for it, Coltie."

"So then he starts goin' on and on about how his second great-uncle twice removed is the Mob boss and he's all mobbed up himself, and if he ever wanted anybody whacked, all he had to do was ask. See what I mean? A real sweetheart."

"Does this story never end?" asked Raoul.

"Fuck you, Raoul. So about two in the morning we order out for some food. An Italian place that delivers all night, if they know ya. The food comes, our little Mob buddy insists on paying himself, he's calling the delivery guy 'paisan' and all that shit, he even tips him a hundred bucks just to make himself look good. Really doing it up. And he opens up one of the containers and he looks inside, and he says, What the hell is this?"

"Tell 'im, Buddha," said Joe.

"What was it?" asked Colt.

"Cannelloni," said Buddha. "Fuckin' guy is supposed to be in the Mob and he doesn't even know what fuckin' cannelloni is? Yeah, right."

"I love this story," said Joe.

"Did *you* know what it was?" asked Colt.

"Yeah, I fuckin' knew what it was," said Buddha. "I've eaten so much Italian food in my life I got it comin' outa my ears. Don't let these slanty eyes fool ya. I'm practically half dago."

"It was *stuffed* cannelloni," said Raoul. "Tell the story right, Buddha."

"Excuse me. It was *stuffed* cannelloni. I left out that very significant piece of information. So I figure, this guy's gotta be full of shit. I mean, how can you be in the Mob and not know what cannelloni is? It don't figure."

"Beats me," said Colt.

"Anyway," said Buddha, "once I realized what a liar he was, I took him for five grand."

"Whoop! There it is!" said Raoul.

"I toleja, I love that story," said Joe. "Buddha figured out his tell. Dincha, Bood?"

"His tell was that he was breathin'," said Buddha. "His tell was that he was a fuckin' idiot. Every time he opened his mouth he was lyin'. *That* was his tell. He bluffed *every time*, Coltie. I was like a kid in a candy store."

"You gotta love fools with money," said Colt.

"I know," Buddha chuckled gleefully. "What with them bein' parted so soon, and all."

■ ■ ■

Later, after everyone else had gone home, Colt was still at his desk when Forszak came out of the gloom of his office.

"Good," Forszak said upon seeing him. "I said to myself, I said, 'Self, if Coltie is still out here when I'm done for the day, I'm gonna invite him for a drink.' And here you are."

"Here I am, sir," said Colt.

"So, let's go."

Colt sprang to his feet. He'd been watching the action on the screen in Hong Kong—part of his never-ending scheme of trying to figure out when would be a good time to jump into the whole mess in Japan—but you didn't turn down an offer from Forszak for anything, because you might not get another one.

They took the elevator to the prefabricated Irish pub in the lobby and sat on a vinyl banquette, Colt sipping a Guinness, Forszak a bitters-and-soda. To the unspoken relief of everyone in the office, Forszak had recently stopped wearing a toupee that hadn't entirely covered the expanse of mottled toad-skin on top of his head; no one had the guts to say anything about it, but no one could bring themselves to look him in the eye during the agonizing weeks he wore it, either. Forszak was the one man in the office whom no one teased, for obvious reasons. His dome gleamed dully now in the twilight of the bar as he stared ahead, thinking. Colt sipped his drink and waited, geishalike, for his master to speak first.

"Normally I like a little Scotch in my soda, but I'm in training," Forszak said after a while.

"Right. How's that going?"

Forszak smiled ruefully. "I run five miles a day, I'm on a diet, I'm in hell," he said. "I have to drop ten pounds before I can even fit into the suit. But the docs gave my heart the okay last week. I never smoked, see. And it's gonna be worth it. You know what I'm doing next Tuesday?"

"No, sir."

"Next Tuesday, I am going to take a flight in a zero-g simulator. You know what that is?"

"Nope."

"It's a plane," Forszak said. "It's a plane that flies straight up to the goddamn edge of the atmosphere, and then it goes straight down again, and you take off your seat belt and for about thirty seconds you're weightless. Because you're in free fall, see? You can float around and everything. Just like they do in outer space. It's practice for the real thing."

"Sounds fun," Colt said.

"Fun? More likely I'm gonna shit my pants. I tellya, Coltrane, I'm so excited I can hardly sleep at night. Me, going to the moon! They're almost done with building that ship, did I tell you?"

"No, sir, you didn't."

"It's called the *Komet*," Forszak said. "The irony of it all is just fuckin' killin' me. First I have to run from the Nazis, then from the Russians, and here I am going to the moon in a goddam commie spacecraft that was built with Nazi technology. Did you know that the Yoo Nited States practickly got its whole space program from captured Nazi scientists? From the V-two program, to be exact?"

"No, sir. I didn't know that."

"Well, that's irony for you. If it wasn't for Adolf Hitler, I wouldn't be goin' to the moon. Ha. That's true in more ways than one. Think about it."

Colt nodded. "Yeah," he said.

"Well, things are different now, anyway," said Forszak. "Russians aren't even commies anymore. I don't even know what the fuck they are. Ah, well. If my parents could only see me now. They'd never believe it."

"It is pretty amazing, when you think about it," said Colt. "You're going to be famous."

"Yeah. Or dead." Forszak shuddered and reached out for a piece of wood, but there was none to be found, only laminated plastic that had been painted an "authentic" smoky black-brown. "Oh, shit," he said, falling back against the banquette. "Remind me to touch a tree or something, next time I see one."

"Yes, sir."

"So. How's your new place?"

"It's great, thanks. Needs a little work."

Forszak grunted. "Don't they all. How old?"

"Hundred fifty years."

Forszak whistled softly. "That's almost as old as me. Still in good shape?"

"Seems like it."

"I thought you were gonna take some time off."

"I, uh . . . I don't know. I wasn't gonna come in today but . . . I changed my mind." He looked down at his drink. "I sit around too long, I start to go crazy."

"That's why I like you, Colt," said Forszak. "You love to work. You got a great work ethic."

"Thank you, sir," said Colt. He paused, choosing his words carefully. "Matter of fact, I was going to ask if you and Mrs. Forszak would like to come out for a weekend sometime, maybe when the weather gets warmer. I'm going to put in a putting green in the back. Tons of room out there. Peace and quiet. I think you'd like it."

"Well, why not?" said Forszak grandly. "When one of my top performers asks me out to his country place, who am I to say no?"

Gratified, Colt smiled. "There's lots to do in winter, too, of course," he said. "Cross-country skiing and stuff like that. I might get a snowmobile or two. "

"Sounds like a great place for kids," Forszak said absently. "Speaking of which, you and the missus have any plans along those lines?"

Colt blanched. *Yeah, Coltie,* said his father's voice. *What about those kids?*

"Ah," he said too loudly. "No. Not really. Not yet, I mean. How—how are *your* kids doing?"

Forszak sighed. "Wish I knew," he said. "I don't hear much from 'em. Son lives a mile away and I never see him. Too busy. My daughter's in San Francisco now, did I tell you?"

"No, sir."

"Yeah," said the older man. "Well, I didn't know myself until last month. Can you imagine that? A daughter moves across the country and she doesn't even tell her own father?" He brooded silently. "She and I don't talk much, obviously," he explained. "She's got some . . . resentments. What was her phrase? Oh, yeah. I was 'emotionally absent.' " He shook his head in mock wonder. "Some goddam pop psychology bullshit she picked up somewhere. Lemme tellya something. Those kids have no idea what I went through. No idea."

Colt remained silent. Sneaking a glance at his boss, he saw that his face had grown dark and empty. Hurriedly he looked away again. But out of the corner of his eye, he could see that Forszak was nodding to himself, as if in agreement with whatever he was hearing inside his own head. Maybe the whole world is hearing voices, Colt thought. Maybe the entire planet isn't actually run by people, but by the voices in their heads. Wouldn't that be a scream?

"I ever tell you I didn't even learn English until I was thirteen years old?" Forszak asked.

"No, sir," Colt said, though he had, several times—and though the guttural hints of some other tongue still lurked in the back of Forszak's throat, emerging only when he was excited.

"I came to this country with nothing. I lived in a fuckin' orphanage in France for two years. Not even in a building—in a tent. There was hundreds of us. All our parents gone. It was like being in a prison. It wasn't near as bad as the camps, but it wasn't good, either. Finally I just snuck out, and lied about my age to get a job. And then I lied again to get over here. Said I had family in New York. I didn't have no family. I didn't have no money, either, Coltie. Nothing. I wasn't even old enough to shave."

Colt tried to imagine the world that was being conjured up, and failed. He sipped his drink again.

"I lived on the street," Forszak said. "I spoke three languages, and none of them English." He managed a woeful smile. "All I knew was, 'Hey, Joe, got chocolate?' 'Hey, Joe, you buy cigarette?' That don't get you too far in this town, I can tell you."

"No, sir," said Colt.

"And now all she can say is 'emotionally absent.' As if I wasn't busy working my ass off so my kids wouldn't have to end up in a tent, too. So they could enjoy the best of things, instead of living covered in mud and shit every day of their lives, like I did." Forszak reached his right hand up under his left jacket sleeve, absently rubbing his forearm. In the gloom Colt could just make out a series of digits in blue ink, tattooed into his skin. Again he looked away, feeling as if he had just seen the man naked.

Forszak smacked the table with his open hand and straightened up. "Listen to me," he said. "I sound like an old man."

"No, sir, you don't," said Colt. "It's very inspiring to hear you talk, as a matter of fact. I always love to hear stories about people who made it with nothing."

"Yeah, right. You're sitting here wondering when the hell I'm gonna shut up so you can get on with your life."

"Not at all."

"Bullshit. Anyway. Let's get onto other things. Your country place."

"Anytime you wanna come out," said Colt. "Just let me know."

"Yeah. How about next weekend?"

Colt froze.

"Next weekend?" he croaked.

"Not this coming, but the next one. Okay? Thing is, I'm gonna be busy all through December, and I'm going to Russia in January," Forszak said. "For more training. And I do wanna come. I like old houses. Besides, I wanna see what old Coltie has done for himself. It's good for me to see my guys happy and successful. Makes me feel like it's all worth something. Know what I mean?"

"Sure."

"You guys are like my family," Forszak said. "My own family

won't even call me on my birthday. Waddaya think of that?" He patted Colt on the shoulder. "Seriously. You're like a son to me, Coltie. You and all the other younger guys that started out here. I love to see you succeed. It does my heart good. I hope your old man knows how lucky he is to have a son like you."

Embarrassed, Colt muttered something.

"Besides, it ain't healthy to stay cooped up in the office all the time. You've had time to get the place set up already?"

"Oh, yeah," said Colt quickly. "That's no problem. I mean . . . it'll still be a little rough. But you'll be quite comfortable."

"Good," said Forszak. "Next weekend it is, then." He drained the rest of his bitters and hopped off the banquette. "I gotta go," he said. "We're going to a play tonight, me and my wife. You be in tomorrow?"

"Yes, sir, I sure will."

"Awright. You email me the directions. Look forward to it." Colt felt another hearty slap on his shoulder, and then Forszak, concentration-camp survivor and future astronaut, was gone.

Colt rested his forehead on his hands. Furniture, he thought despairingly. Food. Rugs. Paint.

Then he sat up, alarmed, thinking:

Oh, yes, and there still happens to be a goddamn cemetery in my backyard.

17

■

A HISTORICAL DIGRESSION
(CONTINUED)

Ellen Musgrove, eldest daughter of Captain Victor T. Musgrove, was in her eighth year the first time McNally, the tonic salesman, came walking down the dusty road to Adencourt, toting his large suitcase. Just for variety, she'd been sitting on the porch roof, a place that was strictly off-limits; this, of course, was what gave it its attraction. Ellen had to be quiet, for her father, a stern old man with handlebar mustaches and iron eyes, had come out onto the porch and seated himself in his rocking chair. This meant she was trapped. If she moved, she would be caught, and she would get whipped for certain.

The Captain roused himself at the sound of approaching footsteps. Ellen flattened her body against the shingles as the stranger climbed the porch, and she listened with one ear pressed against the warm wood shakes. Their deep male voices echoed loudly, but they were muffled and she could understand little of what they said. When her father and the stranger went inside, Ellen crawled back in through the bedroom window and went downstairs, where she was introduced to the visitor. He was tall and sun-burned, with eyes set close together—a trait that signified un-trustworthiness. Ellen didn't like the way he looked at her, or at any of them, or the house. He had a way of running his eyes over things as though trying to figure out how much they were worth. She found him so frightening that she feigned a stomachache that evening just so she wouldn't have to sit at the dinner table. The obligatory dose of castor oil was a small price to pay for escaping the stranger's company. Instead of staying in bed, however, she crawled down into the wall, into the secret space that had been created when the house was built.

To get into the secret space, one had to go into the built-in clothes closet in the master bedroom and through a hidden door in the wall. A closet was an unusual and highly modern feature in those days. People generally had wardrobes instead, but the Cap-tain, in a rare stroke of foresight, had insisted that his wife have what amounted to a separate room just for her dresses. Marly, em-barrassed by this largesse on the part of a man who otherwise barely spoke to her, used it as a general storage space—among other things, she kept her dressmaker's dummy in there, which scared the children because it looked like a headless nude woman. She hardly owned enough dresses to justify a closet, anyway. Ellen had wondered if her father was planning on buying her more, just to fill it up. That would have been exciting. But no such wonders were forthcoming. Instead, the closet went mostly un-used, which suited the furtive child perfectly.

The secret space itself was not really a secret. The Captain, who was inclined to think of all places in terms of military de-fense, had included it in the plans of the house as a hiding place of last resort for women and children, in the event that his home should be attacked by the Indians, or the Mexicans, or the French. It mattered not a whit to him that no military threat had existed in eastern Pennsylvania since Revolutionary times. In the Cap-tain's view, one could never be too careful—he believed that it was not a matter of *if* war came to Adencourt, but *when*. Every so often, perhaps once a year, he conducted defense drills, during which he banged on an iron pot with a spoon and shouted orders as the other members of the family scrambled to their stations. Marly and the older children took up brooms, symbolizing rifles, and went to the third-floor windows, where they dutifully put the bristles to their shoulders and said "Bang! Bang!" The smaller children ran into the bedroom closet and scurried like mice into the crawl space, which was a narrow stairway that led back down through the walls of the second floor below, to a tiny room under the main stairs on the first floor.

Most Musgroves, big and small, found being in the secret passage a terrifying experience. The only light available was that which leaked through chinks in the wall, it being unsafe for candles, and there was scarcely enough room to turn around; you had to be truly tiny to avoid an attack of claustrophobia. But it was possible to hear things that were done and said in other rooms while remaining undetected, and if one wasn't bothered by cobwebs, dust, and dark, confined spaces, the crawl space was the perfect place to play.

Ellen sat in there the night McNally ate dinner with her parents, concealed like a mouse behind the wall, and she listened as her father recited the litany of things that were wrong with him: sore bones, aching joints, shortness of breath, headaches, dizziness, a broken arrowhead in his left thigh, shrapnel from burst musket balls sprinkled throughout his body like salt. She had to move quietly, because even though she was invisible she was not inaudible, and her mother had the ears of a bat. She heard the *glug-glug* of a bottle; this was McNally dosing the Captain for the first time with Oriental Tonic. Dinner finished, she scrambled back up to bed. The next day, she was relieved to learn that McNally was gone, and her stomachache miraculously disappeared.

In later weeks, when the Captain became strung out and disoriented, Ellen was prevented from entering the crawl space because the only way to reach it was through her parent's bedroom, and she couldn't go in there while her father was abed. This was a tragedy, for she'd cached her rag dolls there, as well as various trinkets pilfered from her mother's meager beauty chest: a broken comb, and a brooch missing half its paste diamonds. She was forced to fall back once more on her second-favorite place, the porch roof. It was more exposed, but on the other hand she could see for a long ways. That was how she came to be the first to be aware of McNally's return some weeks later, and how she also happened to see her mother frog-march him across the road and down to the river shortly after, a shotgun clamped firmly under her arm.

This was a strange new development, and the young girl could make no sense of it. Ellen watched as the blond-headed salesman took off his clothes and raised his arms. From where she sat, she had a clear view of McNally's penis. Ellen found this sight so revolting that she drew her breath in preparation for giving a loud scream. Only the fear of discovery, and punishment, prevented her. Growing up on a farm, Ellen had seen plenty of penises, all of them attached to animals; she knew that baby boys also had penises; but it was news to her that men had them, too. In fact, the adult male penis appeared to have nothing in common with the tiny little mushrooms her brothers possessed. It looked like a different organ altogether.

McNally happened to have an extremely long, thin penis that cascaded several inches from his groin. It seemed to belong more on a horse than a man. It was *so* long, in fact, that Ellen believed she was witnessing an "abomination of nature," a phrase she'd heard her father use often, but had never understood—until this moment. Here was a man who looked, quite literally, as if he were half-equine; he was proof that nature could, and sometimes did, go awry.

Then there was a puff of smoke, and half an instant later she heard the double blast of the shotgun. Horrified, Ellen saw what the now-horizontal Marly herself did not, which was the hail of shot busting through McNally's body as though he was no more durable than a watermelon. It knocked him backward and into the nameless river, which promptly swept him away.

Marly picked herself up and came quickly into the house. Ellen stayed flat on the porch roof until she was sure she could sneak back in without being discovered. Then she made a beeline for the closet, too scared to worry about her father, who didn't notice her, anyway; he tossed and moaned in his bed in the strange kind of half sleep that had overtaken him lately—nothing of which had been explained to the children, except that the Captain was "poorly." Losing no time, Ellen scrambled into the hidey-hole and down into the tiny secret room, where she caught her breath and tried to explain to herself what had just happened.

The reasons, once she had thought them out, made sense. Mother had killed McNally because of his penis. Ellen, being a farm girl, knew full well what penises were for: peeing into females, who then made babies. What she did not understand was just how pregnant her mother was, of course. Marly Musgrove was not in the habit of announcing her frequent conceptions to her children until she was well along, and she had the kind of figure that made it difficult to tell that she was with child. It seemed to Ellen that McNally must have peed into her mother weeks earlier, during his first visit, and this meant that Marly was going to have McNally's baby.

Clearly, this was not good news. For one thing, the baby would be an "abomination of nature," like its father. For another, Marly herself must not be happy about it, else she wouldn't have killed McNally. It went without saying that McNally had peed into Marly against her will—*all* intercourse appeared to the young Ellen as a kind of barnyard rape, a painful indignity that the female animals were forced to endure. No one could blame Marly for not wanting to put up with it. *She* was not a horse, after all. She was Mother, and her actions must be right.

What it all came down to, Ellen told herself, was that Marly had acted in self-defense—against McNally's penis. He must have wanted to pee into her again. That all men would have penises did not occur to her; she was to believe, for a good part of her life, that simple possession of a penis was an act of treachery, and that only bad men had them. The eight-year-old Ellen vowed to herself then and there, as she hid under the stairs, that if she ever saw a penis again, she would find the strength to defend herself against it, just as her mother had. Ellen didn't want to shoot anybody—but if she had to, she would.

It was hours before Ellen found the courage to come out of the secret space and into the light again. When she did, she found Marly sitting in a rocking chair, calm as a statue, with Lucia opposite her. The two of them were carding wool.

"Did you hear?" Lucia asked her sister. "Mother shot a fox."

Ellen looked at her mother carefully. Marly glanced at her daughter.

"Child, where have you been? You're all dirt and cobwebs," she said. "Draw some water and wash your face."

"Yes, Mother," said Ellen. So this was how she was to play it; very well. She, too, could act as if nothing had happened. "Was it a big fox?" she asked.

"Big enough," said Marly, studiously avoiding her daughter's eyes now. "Go do as you're told."

"Mind Mother, Ellen," said Lucia, who though just a year younger was a terrible boss.

Ellen went to the pump in the yard and drew a bucket of water. She rubbed her hands together in the cold, clear water and vigorously scrubbed her face with her palms. Waiting for the ripples in the bucket to subside, she looked down at her reflection, holding her breath. The transparent version of herself looked back up at her from the silvery surface. Ellen stared into her own shocked eyes for a long minute, knowing that she had seen something she was not meant to see, and that she was therefore changed. She was checking to see if she looked any different. If there were some way to freeze everything right there, she thought, she would do it; she prayed desperately that she would never grow one second older, not if womanhood was the eventual result. She tried all the tricks she knew of to stop time, including holding her breath. But nothing worked.

No one knew what Ellen had seen, because Ellen never told; and no one knew what Marly did, either—except Ellen, who had succeeded better than she knew at stopping time. For the rest of her life, even as her body aged, in her mind she would always remain that eight-year-old girl looking into the bucket, holding her breath and wishing that things would go back to the way they were, before McNally came to Adencourt.

■ ■ ■

Ellen and Hamish, her twin brother, left Adencourt together, following Hamish's graduation from high school with a certificate in bookkeeping. Hamish intended to find himself a job, hopefully in a bank, and Ellen—who had not gone to school beyond the age of fourteen—was to keep house for him until she found herself a husband. They were glad enough to have each other, for they had no idea what city living held in store, and they were both excited and scared. All they knew for sure about their futures was that they had no desire to remain at home—though, at the time, only Ellen understood why.

In 1870, when they were eighteen years old, the twins bid farewell to their family and moved westward, first to Harrisburg, where steady work was not forthcoming, and then to Pittsburgh, where Hamish finally found a job keeping books for a small factory—really a large smithing shop. Without actually consulting her on the matter, Hamish made the assumption that his sister was interested in meeting eligible young men, and as her brother and male guardian it was his obligation to get her married. In fact,

he had promised their mother he would. He made efforts to introduce her to the more well-heeled members of their social class—
not quite nobility, of course, but definitely above the common cut,
since they were the children of a war hero, after all. In the first
few years, he made the casual acquaintance of several young men
through work; occasionally, he brought one home to sample her
cooking. Ellen, who had no intention of marrying anyone, retali-
ated against this show of proprietorship with subterfuge. She
sprinkled the dinners of their guests with alum on the sly, knowing that a bad cook would never win a mate.

She was right. The bitter powder, harmless but with a poisonous taste, did its work. No young man ever came for dinner
twice. After several valiant efforts, Hamish gave up, not without
some relief. He hadn't particularly wanted to get rid of his sister,
with whom he shared the unspoken bonds of twinship; he'd
merely acted out of a sense of duty. Once it became clear that no
one was ever going to marry her, he felt free to regard her as his
own helpmate—as he already had for some time.

And Ellen, meanwhile, rested secure in the knowledge that she
would never be forced to defend herself against the world of men
in the same way that her mother had, with violence and blood.

■ ■ ■

At first, Ellen and Hamish took the train back to Plainsburg from
Pittsburgh just once a year, at Christmas. They kept this tradition
up with a grim sense of duty, each of them hating it for their own
reasons, anxiously awaiting the moment when they could return
to the city they now thought of as home.

Of the five Musgrove children left—Hamish and Ellen, Lucia,
and Olivia and Margaret, who were also fraternal twins—only
Lucia had stayed behind to live with their mother. Olivia and
Margaret had married Philadelphia businessmen and become well-
to-do society matrons. They wore fancy dresses and hats, and

sprinkled their speech with French phrases that sounded mighty grand, though no one could understand them. Olivia and Margaret had little to say to their siblings, in French or otherwise; it was obvious that they couldn't wait to get back to the city. Their discomfort was increased by the fact that Lucia had married a new neighbor, a rather uncouth Bavarian named Kloot Flavia-Hermann, who specialized in pigs. In a reversal of the usual order of things, Flavia-Hermann had moved into his mother-in-law's house, and so for a time the grounds of Adencourt were home to a smallish herd of swine. This was really more than the Philadelphia sisters could be expected to take, and shortly after this unfortunate union they began to make excuses for why they could no longer make the journey home.

Before they began to drift apart, however, it was an inviolable part of the Christmas tradition for the Musgrove children to visit the cemetery where their five siblings lay. All of them hated doing it, but none wanted to be the first to say so. Hamish often had the uncomfortable feeling, when they were all together again—five above, five below—that the dead ones formed their mirror image. In his more poetic moments, he wondered if perhaps *they,* the dead, were looking up at *them,* the living, with the same sort of pitying expression on their pale faces; for there was no proof, he reflected glumly, that the world he lived in was the better one.

There were actually six stones in the cemetery now. A new one had been added to commemorate the loss of the Captain, whose body had been buried where it fell, at Gettysburg. The Captain had been an atheist, and while he was alive no preacher was ever permitted to speak over the graves. But upon his passing, it came out that Marly had been a believer all along, and had kept her faith a secret, lest—like some kind of early Christian—she be persecuted by her Roman emperor of a husband. This faith grew stronger in her as she aged. The notion that her littlest ones had been buried without consecration ate away at her, until finally she couldn't take it anymore. In 1887, she called her surviving children together for what she referred to as the "Blessing of the Stones," which was meant to be sort of a group memorial service.

A Methodist minister from Plainsburg was invited out to Adencourt. The children, now in their twenties and thirties, grudgingly heeded their mother's summons. Olivia and Margaret, who were to die of influenza in the great epidemic of 1917–18, brought their wealthy husbands along. Hamish and Ellen came, too; Lucia, of course, was already there, pregnant with her first child—she and Flavia-Hermann had been trying gamely for years to conceive, and had only recently succeeded.

The Philadelphia husbands wandered the property, commenting to each other on the profitability of it, or the lack thereof. It was clear that the dark foreigner who had married their sister-in-law was wasting a great deal of potential. He ought to have been selling off the trees for lumber, and drilling for oil, and mining for gold or coal, and raising cattle instead of pigs, but he had done none of these things. Instead, he'd accumulated a massive collection of ruined farming equipment, which he kept in the barn—mowers and plows and harrows, and the like. Apparently he intended to fix these items up and resell them, but there was no telling when he meant to put this plan into action. That was the way with foreigners, the Philadelphia husbands declared. They simply weren't in possession of enough good, old-fashioned American get-up-and-go.

The ceremony itself was a disaster. Marly dressed all in black for the occasion, something she had not done even at the death of the Captain. This struck her children as particularly morbid. The rest of them had brought clothes that were suited to a serious, important occasion—but not to another funeral. It was clear now that their mother had changed in recent years. And none of the children knew the Methodist minister, who nevertheless insisted on embracing each of them for a long and uncomfortable moment. Olivia would later swear that there was something positively indecent about the way the man pressed himself into her bosom. And Ellen—Ellen, who of all of them had been a model of stoicism—collapsed in tears and screams when the minister intoned the names of the dead children. She remained on the ground, inconsolable, pressing her face into the earth as if she was *kissing* it—"carrying on like a Catholic," Margaret would later say to her mortified Philadelphia husband. Hamish finally had to half carry and half drag her into the house, no small feat for a man who spent ten hours a day moving nothing heavier than a pen. Even after he managed to put her in bed, Ellen continued to sob and moan. No one else thought to follow them into the house. Ellen had long been Hamish's problem.

"Ellie, Ellie, dear," he said, standing over her, wringing his hands. "Whatever is the matter? What can I do?"

"That—poor—little—fellow," Ellen hiccupped.

"Which little fellow?"

"The—one—who—drowned!"

"Do you mean Henry? Why, Ellie, that was years ago! Why on earth should that make you so sad now?"

"Oh, Hamish," said Ellen. "Never mind it—but we must leave! I want to go home! It's too terrible here! I can't stand it another day!"

"All right, then, all right, my dear," Hamish said. He had little experience in consoling Ellen. He'd certainly never seen her behave like this before. Hamish had no idea what to do except to obey her. He pushed his spectacles more firmly onto his nose. "We'll leave tomorrow," he said. "I'm sure Mother will understand."

"Do you promise?"

"I do. I'll take it upon myself to explain to her."

Ellen sighed with relief then, and became more composed. But Hamish sat next to her for several hours, holding her hand and soothing her at each sign of returning grief. In the meantime, he tried to figure out why his sister should only now be struck so hard at the loss of the little brother who had wandered away from the house nearly thirty years earlier, and who had been found later in the river, in the eddy of a large, rounded boulder. It was the same eddy, in fact, where another body had been found a few years before, that of a strange, yellow-haired man with a ghastly wound in his chest, whom no one was able to identify. That was odd, but there was nothing odd about this coincidence. All manner of things collected in that eddy, being brought there by the direction of the current.

But the drowning itself, he remembered, had fallen hard on the family. Everyone had taken a share of the guilt upon themselves, because although none of them had been specifically charged with watching the boy, who was just over a year old, all of them knew that the accident wouldn't have happened had they kept a sharper eye out. Things had been different after that, Hamish remembered. Other children had died before Henry, but he was the first who was lost to simple carelessness, and afterward everything was different. None of them played in the river anymore, for one thing, nor would they eat any fish out of it. And security had grown tighter—all of them had fallen into the habit of doing head counts at least once a day, to make sure no one else had been "taken."

That was how it felt to be a Musgrove, Hamish thought, as he slowly nodded off in his bedside chair. You never knew when you were going to be taken, or by what means. It was as if there were something about their line that had offended the very order of things, and nature was setting itself to rights—restoring the balance, as it were. Sitting there in the tiny second-floor bedroom that had once belonged to Lucia, Hamish felt oppressed by his very name. He wished that he had been born into any other clan but this.

Hamish and Ellen went home the next day, back to the apartment they shared, back to the gloom that had gradually descended over them, back to their loveless and spiritless existences. For the next many years, their lives varied little in routine; Hamish went to work, Ellen kept house for him, and neither dared to venture far from the safe but tiny world they had created for themselves, for they grew so accustomed to their sadness that its absence would have felt strange. Until 1917, that is, when Hamish was sixty-five years old. This was when he accidentally discovered Sigmund Freud in a Pittsburgh bookstore, and his life was changed forever.

It happened when he was walking home from work one day, just weeks before his retirement. His route took him past a certain bookstore that he was in the habit of stopping into, at least once a week. There, without looking carefully, he purchased a small, thin book called *Dora: An Analysis of a Case of Hysteria*, believing it to be some sort of newfangled romance novel. Romance novels were Hamish's secret vice. He devoured them by the dozen, an embarrassing habit. Each month, the bookstore owner slipped him a new shipment in plain brown paper, as discreet as a druggist. The books were filled with passionate phrases and heaving bosoms, and occasionally, holy of holies, a long, deep kiss. Hamish was ashamed of himself for reading such womanish tripe, but he couldn't stop.

The problem was that like his sister, Hamish had never married, but unlike her he would have liked nothing better. Yet he had been sadly unsuccessful in his early attempts with the women of Pittsburgh, who were a little more brash and far more sophisticated than the girls he had known back at home. Having been rebuffed on a few occasions—no more so than any other man, but more often than he was equipped to deal with—he had retreated, clamlike, into the world of his imagination. The only women he'd had were between the covers of his books. It may have been less satisfying than the real thing, but there, at least, he could shine.

Yet *Dora* was not a romance, as it turned out. It was actually the case history of a young Viennese woman who'd come to the famous Dr. Freud for psychiatric treatment. There was little romance, but plenty of darker stuff: namely, incest and lesbianism— or *gynaecophilia*, as Freud referred to it. By the time Hamish discovered his error, he'd already been swept up in the voyeuristic thrill of learning all the sordid details of a total stranger's life, and a crazy stranger at that. Before he'd even finished the little book, he considered himself to have become a devout disciple of the new science of "psychoanalysis."

This science, which Hamish defined simply as "the art of figuring out what's wrong with you," was something he'd never heard of before. Indeed, hardly anyone had heard of psychoanalysis in those days—especially in Pittsburgh, where life revolved mostly around steel. To Hamish it was like a revelation from the heavens. Finally, he'd come across something that might explain why he hadn't yet found love, and why he was so unhappy. He felt unspeakably relieved, even at this late point in his adulthood—just six weeks away from retirement—to be one step closer to unlocking the riddle of his own life. There was nothing in particular about Dora's case that applied to Hamish, but that was not the point. It was that somewhere out there was a man who understood that people could be *fixed*, and perhaps this man could fix *him*.

Years earlier, when Hamish was just a boy, he'd begun to suspect that there was something wrong with Musgroves in general. Lately, he had become sure of it. He would always remember the day on which he'd learned of his father's death, how he'd lain on the boards of the porch and looked up at the dried, withered scalps of the aborigines the Captain had murdered in some far-off place, waving back and forth in the breeze like an unholy wind chime. It was a moment that came back to him frequently throughout his life. He often thought of it in the middle of doing something else, though he didn't know why, and he had to force himself to put the image out of his mind. But it wasn't until late in life that he finally made the connection he'd sought between worlds on that long-ago day, one so obvious he couldn't believe he hadn't spotted it sooner: the Musgroves were doomed because they were killers.

Yet Hamish didn't even know how right he was. He thought his father was the only one who had ever murdered anyone, a fact that he sought to verify with his sister after he finished Freud's book.

"Did Father ever tell you stories about the old days?" he asked Ellen, who, though she was his fraternal twin, had never looked anything like him: she was short and round like their mother, while Hamish was lanky and lean, with a hawkish nose. The only physical characteristic they shared, in fact, was that they were both left-handed—a trait her teachers had tried, and failed, to eradicate.

"What old days, Hamish?" she replied.

"His days on the frontier. And of the times before then, when our family was still in England."

"Perhaps he did. I don't know. I don't remember."

"I *think* I remember," Hamish said. "They were terrible stories. Very bloody. I never listened to him much, but I wish now that I had."

"For goodness' sake, Hamish, why bring that up now? Those days are long over. It's the twentieth century!"

"Yes, but those scalps," he said. "Don't you remember the Injun scalps on the porch? How they hung from the rafters?"

"Scalps? Don't be ridiculous. There was no such thing. How barbaric!"

But Hamish insisted; he was certain he wasn't making it up. "I remember them quite well," he said. "He used to tell the story of how he took them whenever we had company. How it felt like skinning a 'possum. Remember?"

Ellen laughed. "Our father, telling such stories!" she said. "Honestly, Hamish, I think you've been reading too many novels! What makes you bring this up in the first place?"

Ordinarily, Hamish would have fallen silent here, for he'd never quite been able to bring himself to tell his sister what he was thinking: modern Musgroves were cursed. But that was before reading Freud's little book. What he said instead was:

"I think that I would like to go to Europe, and visit a psychiatrist."

It was a Friday evening, and they'd been sitting quietly in the parlor, which was how they spent every evening. Nothing could have prepared Ellen for such a statement. She looked as if she'd been shot through the heart. She put one hand to her chest and used the other to steady herself, even though she was already seated.

"A . . . what?" she quavered.

"A psychiatrist," Hamish repeated. "A mental doctor."

"A *mental doctor*? What—what—what—"

"There's no need for excitement, Ellie. Everything is fine. It's—it's just an idea I had."

"But, Hamish! What on earth for?"

"Well, because it's *new*," Hamish told her. "It's the modern way of looking at things. There's this fellow, Freud"—he pronounced it "Frood"—"who lives in Europe. In Vienna, to be exact. He has the most amazing ability to talk to people and figure out what's wrong with them. And I simply thought that perhaps I should go and meet him, and have him tell me what's wrong with *me*."

"But, Hamish! There's nothing wrong with you!"

Hamish had rather expected her to say this, but now that she had, he was at a loss for words. He looked around at their apartment, which they'd moved into five years earlier. For thirty-five years previous to that, they'd lived in a house, but as they'd gotten older they found it too much to maintain. Hamish's back troubled him after decades spent huddled over a desk, his left arm twisted around awkwardly so that he could scrawl figures with his wrong hand, while his vision had dimmed and blurred; and the ever-plumper Ellen had found it increasingly difficult to climb the stairs. It was she who'd insisted they move to a smaller place, one that would require less work. Come to think of it, it was she who'd always insisted on everything. Hamish had not envisioned spending his entire life in the company of his sister. He'd hoped to have children and grandchildren, and be the patriarch of a vast and happy clan.

But none of that had happened. Nothing, in fact, had worked

out quite the way he'd thought it would. His entire life had been one of boredom, sadness, and frustration. Musgroves were still cursed, he thought; only now the curse took a form more appropriate to the world they lived in.

The world, in Hamish's lifetime, had become a very different place—almost *too* different. Automobiles chugged up and down the streets, and from every manufacturing facility came the crash and whir of automatic machinery. None of these things had been known in Hamish's youth. It was as if they'd been installed overnight. Young people now, too, were an entirely different kind of person—they went to moving-picture shows and soda fountains, and "spooned" without shame, and used jargon that no one else could understand. One could hardly tell whether they were being disrespectful or not, though Hamish suspected the latter. And there was a railroad now that stretched clear across the continent. Instead of sailing all the way around the tip of South America and back up again to get to California, a journey that used to take months, one could go overland, and be there in a matter of weeks. And in Europe, soldiers were slaughtering each other with devices of war that had never even been heard of before, or imagined.

Things in general seemed to be moving about ten times as fast as they had when Hamish was a boy. There was no room in a time like this for ghosts and family curses, Hamish realized—not, at least, in the traditional sense. No one believed in such things anymore. Yet that didn't mean they had ceased to exist. They'd merely changed, like everything else, to infect the one thing that *hadn't* changed: the human heart.

"Yes, there is something wrong with me," Hamish said now. "Look at what has happened to us, Ellie. Five of our brothers and sisters gone almost as soon as they came into the world, and now Margaret and Olivia taken by influenza just this year. Seven of us dead. And you and I living here like rabbits in this city, old and alone and—"

"We are not alone!" Ellen interrupted, sounding panicked. "We have each other!"

Hamish looked at his sister.

"Ellie," he asked quietly, "why did you never want to marry?"

Ellen always had her hands occupied with some small task: knitting, or cross-stitching, or, in later years, a newspaper word-puzzle. At present she was engaged in making a pair of booties, intended for the granddaughter of a woman who lived down the hall. She flung her needles down now and stood, gasping for breath.

"How dare you ask me that!" she screamed at her brother. "How dare you ask me that! After all the sacrifices I've made for you!"

Hamish didn't blink; he merely sat, watching her.

"Yes, but why?" he repeated. "After all, I never forced you to stay with me. I tried to introduce you to—"

"Be quiet, Hamish!" Ellen said, imploring him now. "For God's sake, please, be quiet!"

"But Ellie," Hamish said, keeping his voice low and reasonable. "I'm merely asking—"

"Oh, go and see your mentalist, damn you!" cried his sister. "Let him find out whatever it is that's bothering you! Maybe then you can leave me in peace!"

She stormed out and went to her bedroom, where she locked the door. Even an hour later, when Hamish thought she might have calmed down, he could still hear her sobbing; he tapped gently, but she ignored him, crying her eyes out, sounding for all the world like a ten-year-old girl.

"I don't understand," he muttered to himself, heading back to his easy chair. "I simply don't understand." It wasn't like Ellen to lose her temper; he hadn't seen her so upset, in fact, since the day almost thirty years earlier, when their mother had called all the children home for the Blessing of the Stones. It didn't occur to him that these two incidents were related, that they stemmed from the same root, even though they were separated by so much time. Hamish had no idea, in fact, that for his sister, time had been standing still for well over half a century, ever since McNally came to Adencourt. What was more, he also had no idea that because he'd chosen to live with her all this time, he had been under the same, simple spell, and that all he had to do to escape it was to leave.

There is still something desperately wrong, he thought as his head drooped slowly toward his chest, Ellen still sobbing in her bedroom. *That's the only possible explanation. We are innocents. We have done nothing. Our only crime was to try to live. We must never go back to Adencourt, Ellen and I, or we might yet be taken, too*—for he felt that same old apprehension creeping over him now that had pervaded all the years of his childhood. He had no wish, like some old men, to visit the place of his birth once more. He wished he had never seen it to begin with.

I wonder if I will ever make it to Vienna, was his last thought, before dropping off to sleep.

PART THREE

18

∎

WHERE OLD MACHINES
COME TO DIE

In the afternoon, her stomach in knots, Francie headed up the plowed road on foot to the house at the top of the hill. It was not a visit she looked forward to, but she felt she had to make it. These people were going to be their neighbors, after all, and she desperately wanted to be on good terms with them. She understood, as Colt did not seem to, that such touches were vital to their happiness. Perhaps she could smooth things over—make them understand that she didn't feel the way Colt felt, and that he would not be allowed to desecrate their cemetery. She thought she understood how Flebberman felt, maybe, just a little bit. He'd grown up in that place. Those people in the graves were his people. He must certainly think they were interlopers, with no right to make permanent alterations.

Flebberman had been angry, and she was not good with angry people. They scared her, in fact. But she forced herself step by step up the hill, dreading what he would say to her, not sure what she should say to him, except that she came in peace.

The snow had begun to melt, and the trickling sounds all around her, made by unseen rivulets in the roadside ditches, reminded Francie of spring. She wondered if all this snow was here to stay, or if there was going to be a late thaw before winter settled over them for good. She hoped it would melt. She wasn't ready for winter yet. It hadn't even occurred to her until today that she would have no car of her own. It had been nearly ten years since she'd needed one, after all. And apparently it hadn't occurred to Colt, either. He'd taken off and left her without any form of transportation—or food, besides the little she'd bought at the supermarket. She was accustomed to stepping out the door, walking three blocks, and heading down into a subway station or hailing a cab. But those days would not be missed, for the station always smelled like urine, even in winter, and on hot, steamy afternoons it was unbearable.

She smoothed her hair self-consciously in preparation for being scrutinized. And she had brought a gift to smooth the way: a sort-of-new, or at least unopened, paper bag of herbal tea from a specialty shop in Manhattan. She'd found it in among the kitchen supplies and peeled off the price tag, recreasing the edges of the bag to make it look newer.

■ ■ ■

The Flebberman house sat on the crest of the hill, overlooking the valley. As she ascended, Francie saw that the Flebbermans enjoyed a view of several miles in all directions. Tarmac roads danced across the countryside as if scattered by wild magnetic forces. Farms were sprawled in the same haphazard manner over hills and valleys, one here, another there, vast spaces of pastureland and small patches of forest between them. Nothing moved against the blank canvas of the snow. She could see the river flowing by their house, as fresh and silver as the belly of a fish. They might have a hill, but we have the river, she thought. Adencourt itself sat squarely aside the road, a fortress, a monument. Francie had never seen it from this perspective before. She stopped and gazed at it for a long time, both dismayed and pleased at how ugly it was from this height. It looked, she realized, like it was built by someone who didn't have the slightest idea what they were doing. At that moment, she felt an upwelling of tenderness for the old place, as though it was not a house but a misshapen child.

She turned again and plodded up the long driveway. White paint peeled from the dilapidated Flebberman home, and snow was still heaped and humped over mysterious objects in the front yard, lending them an artistic credibility that had surely never been theirs in warmer times. At the end of the driveway was a shed with no doors; in it she could see an old pickup truck, its body stricken with rust. A hand-lettered sign in the windshield advertised that it was "4 Sail." As she climbed the plank steps of the porch, she could hear shrieks of childish excitement. She'd been watched, no doubt, from the moment she left her own front door.

"Someone's here!" she heard someone—a young girl—yell out. Then, as she knocked, an unconvincing silence fell. Behind the door tiny feet shuffled, and she heard children giggling. A moment later there were heavier footsteps, and the door opened.

A heavy woman in a loose housedress stood there with a toddler in her arms, both mother and child blinking away the brightness of the reflected snowlight, as if they were cave dwellers. She had bags under her eyes, and wrinkles that looked to be premature. Even her hair was limp and tired-looking. Terrified, Francie gave her best smile.

"Help you?" the woman said, in a monotone.

"Hello," Francie said. "I'm Francine Hart. Your new neighbor."

The woman continued to stare at her, her mouth hanging

slightly open. Francie looked away; then forced herself to look back and smile again.

"Yeah?" said the woman.

"Yes. I, uh—I just thought I would come up and say hello. And—I'm sure your husband must have told you—there was a little disagreement earlier. I just—I just wanted to come up and apologize. On behalf of myself and my husband."

"Ah-huh," said the woman. She rolled her eyes back, not in disgust or dismay but as if searching for something to say. "Where's your husband at?" she managed finally.

"Oh. Well—he didn't come. He had to go back to the city."

"Ah-huh."

Francie cleared her throat and smiled at her again, less certainly this time. She held out the bag of tea.

"I brought you this," she said. "From the Manhattan Tea Brewery."

The woman stepped backward, and two more children, about three years old, appeared on either side of her prodigious hips: twins, a boy and a girl, each chewing a finger. They stared at her, too, drool shining on their pudgy chins. The woman made no move to take the gift.

"C'mon in," she said, apparently having decided that Francie wasn't going to go away.

Francie stepped up on the jamb and teetered there for a moment. The moist smells of fresh laundry and diaper ointment wafted to her, as well as the heavy fug of bacon grease, and she struggled to repress a sneeze.

"Fleb!" bellowed the woman over her shoulder. "C'mon in," she said again to Francie, closing the door.

"Thank you," said Francie. She decided to try again with the tea. "Here, I brought—"

One of the twins grabbed the bag out of her hand, and the other, sensing goodies, went for it. They whined at each other and immediately commenced a game of tug-of-war. The woman's hand came down out of the sky, yanking it away from both of them, and with the back of her fingers she swatted each of them on the ear, expertly, a swift, whiplike flick that made them howl. Francie winced.

"That ain't for you," she said crossly.

"It's just tea," Francie told her. "Lemon roiboos."

"Fleb!" the woman called again. "Comp'ny's here! Lemon *what?*" she said to Francie.

"Roiboos," Francie repeated, in a smaller voice.

Heavy footsteps, a man's, crossed the floor above her head and came down a stairway somewhere. Then Flebberman appeared, minus his baseball cap. From the eyebrows down, his face was permanently sunburned, but his forehead was as white as paste. Upon seeing Francie he stopped, startled, and looked around quickly, as if searching for an avenue of escape. Then he appeared to remember that he was in his own home, and he grew suddenly more confident.

"Ah," he said. "Yeah." *You*, he might as well have said, Francie thought.

"Hello, Mr. Flebberman," said Francie. "I hope this isn't a bad time."

"Naw," he said.

"Well, I—look. Let me just be frank. I know we didn't get off on the right foot, and I felt badly about it. If we're going to be neighbors, I wanted us to be on good terms. So I came up—"

"She came up t' 'pologize," the woman interrupted.

"Oh," said Flebberman.

"Yes," Francie said. "That's it."

Flebberman seemed even more surprised now, as if he'd been expecting an attack of some sort. Like his wife, he rolled his eyes, casting about for something to say. His jaw worked several times until he came up with something.

"Meet the wife? Jennifer."

"Yes. Hi."

Jennifer the wife smiled again, mirthless.

"You wanna cup a coffee," she announced. "C'mon into the kitchen."

She turned, and Francie followed her, Flebberman falling in behind, all of them stepping over the twins, who were now wrestling amiably over some toy. The kitchen was a long room with ancient linoleum on the floor and water-stained walls. A pretty young girl sat working at a battered wooden table. Before her was a brown paper shopping bag cut open along its folds, and on it she was creating a sunset scene in crayon, her tongue between her lips. She looked up shyly as Francie came in.

"'Melia," said Flebberman. "Say hello."

"Hello," said the girl, who was about nine years old, and looked as if she was on loan from a different family. Her hair was neatly pigtailed, and she wore a dress and knee socks. In her face Francie saw a sharpness that was utterly absent in the rest of her brood.

"Hi, there," said Francie, smiling, sensing a kindred spirit. "That's a pretty picture." The girl smiled back—the first Flebberman to do so.

"Getcher ass up outa there and let us sit," said Jennifer.

"Aw, do I hafta?" the girl said.

"We could sit in the livin' room," Flebberman said to his wife.

Jennifer sighed loudly. "Well, I ain't gettin' a whole tray set up just to haul it all the way out there," she said. "We can sit in here just as good, can't we?"

Francie, dying inside, spoke up quickly.

"I really didn't mean to stay long," she said. "I just wanted to come and say hello. Meet everyone. And—" She was going to say "apologize" again, but she stopped herself.

"No, it's awright," said Flebberman to her. To his wife he said, "Get out the plates and the silverware, for Chrissakes. And put that kid down. He don't have to hang on you like a monkey every damn minute."

"You know how he gets," said Jennifer warningly.

"Well, try 'im once," said Flebberman. "You ain't gonna carry

him like that for his high school graduation, I hope." He turned to
Francie and raised his eyebrows. She saw that this was supposed
to be a joke, and was simultaneously relieved that the ice had been
broken and panicked to realize that she didn't get it. She managed
a smile. Jennifer put the toddler down. Instantly he erupted in terrified screams, looking at Francie with wide, wet eyes. He dove for
his mother's leg and buried his face in her doughy calf.

"Fer cryin' out loud," said Flebberman. "This kid is scared a
everything."

"Hey there," Francie cooed. She bent down and wiggled her fingers at him. He turned around and stopped screaming, cramming
three fingers in his mouth.

"Well, lookit that," said Flebberman, pleased.

Jennifer Flebberman stared narrowly at Francie for a minute, as if
trying to figure out what kind of trick she was pulling. Then, without a word, she took some paper plates from a bag on the counter
and dealt them out onto the table as though they were cards.

"It's just because I'm new," Francie said. "It doesn't mean anything."

■ ■ ■

They sat at the table and ate cake with plastic spoons, while the
twins swooped in and out of the room and the toddler crawled
around their feet, cooing to himself. Jennifer did not offer to brew
any of the lemon roiboos tea. Francie suspected it was going to
end up in the garbage after she left.

It was not a squalid house, but it wasn't exactly clean, either.
She hadn't been offered a tour. From her chair in the kitchen she
could glimpse brown pile carpet in the living room, a disembow-
eled sofa, a picture window that looked down the hill to the
south. The girl Amelia stayed in the living room, peering sometimes around the corner. Francie could tell she was interested but
shy, and she was not invited to sit with the grown-ups.

"This place was built about forty years after yers was," Flebberman told her over the cake. To Francie's immense gratification, he had warmed up to her considerably, and he was now in a talkative mood. "Branch o' the same fambly as them. Used to be some other name, somethin' German. Flavia somethin'. Flavia-Hermann, that's it."

"Flavia-Hermann," Francie repeated.

"Somehow it got turned into Flebberman somewhere along the way," said Flebberman. "Prob'ly durin' one of the wars, when they didn't wanna sound so German."

"And they were related to the Musgroves?"

"The guy that built the house yer livin' in—that would have been the Corporal—"

"The Captain," interrupted Jennifer.

"—the Captain, I mean—he woulda been three or four generations back from my mom's Aunt Helen," Flebberman said. "I don't know what that makes him to me, some kinda great-great-great-uncle or somethin'. They had ten kids, and five of 'em died. Imagine that? And no boys to carry on the name. No more Musgroves left a 'tall, and we here are the last of the Flebbermans ourselfs. 'Course I got two boys a my own. Haw haw. Go forth and spread the seed, my son!" he said, in the direction of his feet. The wet-mouthed toddler, laughing, pounded on Francie's toes.

"That house was a hairloom," said Jennifer Flebberman bitterly.

"Now, it sat empty twenny-fi' years," Flebberman reminded her. "And we couldn't a 'forded to buy it anyway." To Francie he said, "Aunt Helen left it to my mom, but she had to sell it. Couldn't even 'ford the taxes. And the bank was the only one who would take it." He shook his head. "Old place oughta be on the Hysterical Register, you wanna know what I think. You folks got any plans for remodelin'?"

"We like the place just the way it is," Francie said. "Some of the bathrooms need to be brought up-to-date. But we'd like to keep it hys—historical."

Flebberman, finished with his cake, leaned back and crossed his arms. "Uh-huh," he said. He glanced quickly at his wife, who was eating her cake in tiny, vicious bites, without looking up. Francie decided it was time to change the subject.

"It just occurred to me as I was walking up here that I'll be needing a vehicle of some sort," she said. "My husband went back to the city and left me without a car. How much are you asking for that pickup truck in your driveway?"

Amazement crossed Flebberman's face. "You wanna buy *that* thing?" he said, incredulous.

"Does it run?"

"Sure, it runs, but . . . ."

"Show it to 'er," said Jennifer quickly.

"Yeah, yeah, sure, I'll show it to 'er. Might be better off with a two-legged horse, but I'll show it to her," said Flebberman. He stood up and frisbeed his paper plate in the direction of the garbage can. It bounced off the wall and dithered crazily on the floor, like a dropped coin.

"Plate fell," he said to his wife.

"I'll get it," she said sullenly.

"Lemme get my boots on," he said to Francie.

■ ■ ■

They stepped outside again and Francie breathed deeply, grateful for the fresh air. Flebberman led her around the house to the shed and got in the old pickup truck. He started it up after several tries and eased it out onto the driveway, where it sat shivering, belching blue smoke. Thanks to Bondo and rust, the truck itself was no discernible color, though it might have been red once. He got out and slammed the door, but it bounced open again, accompanied by a shower of rust from underneath. Embarrassed, he pushed it gently, leaning into it until it clicked.

"Forgot about that latch," he said. "You got to hit 'er just right or she don't shut. Push 'er, see. Yeh don't ever slam 'er."

"I see," said Francie.

"You know how to drive a stick?"

"As a matter of fact, yes."

"Well, that's good, 'cept when I put the new transmission into this thing I kinda got things a little backwards. I oughta show ya what I mean." He paused, considering. "She don't have long left. You sure you want 'er? She's gonna need work. A lotta work."

"Will it be the kind of work I can hire you to do?"

Flebberman sniffed proudly. "Hell, yeah," he said. "I can fix anything that don't breathe. And some things that do. And she runs better when she's warmed up, anyway. She needs any new parts, I can pull 'em outa the yard. You know I gotta junkyard?"

"A . . . a junkyard? No, I didn't know."

"C'mere," Flebberman said. "Lemme show ya while she's clearin' her throat."

Francie followed him back onto the porch, which wrapped around the house on three sides. Stepping onto the side that was hidden from the road, Flebberman waved an arm expansively, and Francie saw a vast area behind the house that was covered in piles of snow, with the dismembered limbs and torsos of rusted machines peeking through. An access road led to it from the far side. There was a sign, facing the road, which she couldn't read.

"Flebberman and Sons Used Auto Parts and Wrecking Yard," said Flebberman helpfully. "I got five acres of dead cars down there. Plus all kinds of other stuff. You name it, I probly got it. This is where old machines come to die." He grinned.

"My goodness," said Francie, genuinely impressed. "You would never know this was here."

"Naw. I keep it out of sight of the road. Everybody needs a junkyard, but nobody likes to look at one. I been buyin' people's junk since I was just outa high school. An' we got this place pretty cheap, 'cause it was already in the fambly. I did wanna turn it into a used car lot at one point in time, but . . ." Flebberman's words trailed off. "Never got around to it, I guess."

"There's always time," said Francie.

Flebberman looked at her.

"Yeah," he said. "I guess."

"Well. How much do you want for that truck?"

He pursed his lips. "How's five hundred sound?"

Francie nearly laughed out loud. She had been prepared to offer two thousand.

"Five hundred is fine," she said. "If a personal check is all right."

"Hell, yes," said Flebberman. "A personal check is fine."

"It still has our New York address on it. Is that okay?"

"It ain't like I don't know where you live," Flebberman said.

They went around to the front of the house again. Francie took a check from her wallet and filled it out on the quivering hood of the still-running pickup. Flebberman looked at it in disbelief and tucked it in his pocket.

"Anything ever goes wrong with it, just bring it on up here," he said effusively. "I can give you parts at cost, no prollem."

"You're very kind," Francie said. "And, Mr. Flebberman . . ."

"You can call me Randy."

"Randy. I am very sorry about that episode with my husband this morning. I'm serious about not letting him remove the cemetery. I just wanted you to know that."

Flebberman nodded, shuffling one foot in the snow. "Yuh," he said. "Good. Okay."

"We didn't want to get off on the wrong foot. Sometimes Coltrane makes up his mind about things without really talking them over with me first."

"Yuh. Well, I know how that is." He cast a glance over his shoulder at the house.

"I don't want you to worry. Really. I'm not going to let him do anything that would anger you, or . . . dishonor your family."

At that phrase Flebberman drew himself upright and met her gaze frankly.

"That's it," he said. "That's just what it is. You hit the nail on the head there. Dishonor."

"Yes. Well, just so you know I understand. And I'm on your side."

Flebberman nodded, convinced. "Sit in there, I'll show ya how to get this thing goin'," he said.

Francie got in the driver's side and Flebberman slid in next to her. The interior of the cab was misty with a strange gasoline-flavored haze. Flebberman turned on the radio and fiddled with the volume. Country music blared through one tiny speaker somewhere in the dashboard.

"Other speaker don't work," he said. "I can fix that up for ya. But this is a good radio. Gets both kinds of music."

"Both kinds?"

"Country and western."

Flebberman grinned at her. Francie laughed; she had to stop herself from crying with relief. He likes me, she thought. I will belong.

"There's yer clutch," he said. "Go ahead and push 'er in."

Francie did so, and the truck began to coast down the driveway toward the road. When she tried to put it into first, however, she found that nothing happened. Alarmed, with the truck picking up speed, she asked, "What do I do?"

"Wiggle it hard, then slam it over to the side. It ain't so much backwards as it is sideways. Sorta."

She did as she was told and the truck bounced to a halt, engine roaring, Flebberman bracing himself on the dashboard.

"It's a li'l embarrassin'," he said. "This was the first transmission I ever did myself. It ain't quite up to snuff."

"I'm sure it will be fine," Francie said. "It does give it a unique character."

"You hit it right on the head again," Flebberman said, with a satisfied air. "Got a nice way with words."

"Yes, well—"

"Now, reverse is a li'l tricky, too. Just push in on yer clutch, and then push down—"

"Down?"

"Yup, down—and then move it over to the right—no, don't look at that diagram, it'll just confuse ya."

Francie managed to find reverse and hit the gas. The wheels spun madly for several moments. Flebberman kept his hands folded in his lap as parts of his driveway were flung into the air.

"All righty," he said calmly, "less clutch."

Francie let out the pedal too suddenly, and the truck shot backward up the hill again. She stopped.

"This is hard," Francie said.

"Ah, you'll get 'er," he said. "Takes a li'l practice, is all."

"Thanks."

"Welcome."

They sat for a moment, the truck vibrating underneath them.

"I meant to tell you I found some things in the attic that belong to you," Francie said. "Some old comic books. Your name was in them."

Flebberman snorted. "Comic books?" he said.

"Some are quite old. And there are several older books. They might be worth something."

"Naw. Not them old things. B'sides, I forgot all about 'em. They been up there for years an' years."

"Well, maybe when I get my computer hooked up I can go online and get some quotes for you." Noting his expression of silent confusion, she added, "On the Internet."

Flebberman nodded. "Yeah," he said. "Well, that's somethin' I don't know nothin' about. The Internet. Never done it." He fiddled with the door handle, not opening it, just playing idly. Francie could tell he liked being this close to her. He smelled of gasoline himself, or possibly engine oil. He was too shy to meet her gaze. Sneaking a glance at his hands, she saw that there were black half-moons on each fingernail, and the backs of them were tattooed deeply with embedded filth, worn into the creases of his skin.

"You really think they might be worth somethin'?" he asked.

She shrugged. "Who knows? It can't hurt to look. They're in good condition."

"Well," Flebberman said. "Wouldn't that be a hoot an' a half. Sure could use the money, if they are."

"Well, in that case I'll be sure to check," Francie said. She knew without looking that Jennifer Flebberman would be standing at the window, watching them. She ventured, "I used to like science fiction, too, when I was little."

"Huh. Most girls don't."

"I know."

"Spacemen an' all that? Really?"

"Really."

"Hah," said Flebberman in wonder.

"Well, I'll let you know if I find anything out," said Francie. "And thank you very much. Pleasure doing business with you."

Flebberman took this as his cue to disembark. Sliding out the door, he said, "I'll see if I can't dig up the title to this old thing somewheres. Yer gonna need that to get 'er registered. I'll stop by with it, maybe tomorra."

"All right. Thanks again."

Flebberman nodded and shut the door.

■ ■ ■

Francie headed back down the hill to Adencourt, feeling the ragged hum of the truck's engine through the springs of the seat. She pulled into the driveway, remembering just in the nick of time to depress the clutch before she hit the brake. The truck slid smoothly to a halt and she turned it off, feeling accomplished.

"I'll figure you out, truck," she said. "Yee ha."

She went upstairs to the bedroom and got out of her clothes, intending to change into something that didn't smell of gas. Then, changing her mind, she went to the window and pressed her nipples against the chill glass, savoring the shiver it sent down through her middle. She looked out over the frozen landscape once more, remembering suddenly that glass was transparent— she could be seen, for heaven's sake! And here came a car! She dove quickly for the bed and slipped in under the sheets. Excited, she waited for the car to pass. Then she ran her hands over her breasts, down over her abdomen and the mound of her pubic bone. She wasn't sure why, but she was suddenly and undeniably aroused. It couldn't be Flebberman. What was it, then?

Well, maybe it was Flebberman a little. He wasn't in the least attractive, but he was certainly capable. And he had those hands. Filthy, but strong. She imagined them—just for fun, not meaning it—being on her instead of her own as she slipped a fingertip in her mouth and then ran it over her clitoris, back and forth. His dirty mechanic's hands on her pink flesh. The wrongness of it was exciting; Flebberman touching her, Flebberman tonguing her, Flebberman bringing her to climax. How odd. How very unlikely. Yet she arched her back, shuddering, and listened to her own low moan, surprised at the intensity of her orgasm.

She hadn't come that strongly in a long time, she thought, catching her breath. Years. Since going on the medication, in fact.

Well, then, she thought as she caught her breath, exhilarated. I guess it's a good thing I stopped taking it.

■ ■ ■

Later that afternoon, as the dead late-autumn sun was going down, Francie went downstairs and read a few more entries in

Marly Musgrove's awkward hand. Milking cows, planting vegetables, visits from neighbors, the names of more children. The dry record of years slipped under her fingers, the pages feeling like the skin of some kind of delicate, extinct animal. No mention of Flavia-Hermanns, of whom Flebberman was one. A strange name, both Roman and Teutonic. Perhaps even a royal name, once upon a time. A name that could be a "hairloom" unto itself.

When it got dark, she turned off the lights and wandered from room to room with a candle, unafraid, accompanied only by the dim light and the cracking of the house's inner timbers. She was the only passenger on a masterless ship. She called aloud to angels and demons alike, just to see who would flutter forth from the darkness, but was disappointed to find that all remained silent. Nothing came out to greet her, not even so much as a mouse or a moth.

Francie stood in front of one of the second-floor windows, holding the candle, staring at her own reflection. She was wearing her favorite diaphanous, old-fashioned nightgown, and she had unpinned her hair to let it fall to its natural length, past her shoulders. With extreme pleasure, she noted that she looked like some kind of nineteenth-century version of herself. Anyone passing on the road now and happening to look up would receive the fright of their lives. But the road remained silent, as it had for most of the last two centuries.

So Marly Musgrove had been widowed, or otherwise abandoned. Something had happened to the man she called the Captain. He had left, and died. She'd gleaned that from the diary. Marly, too, had lain awake in her bedroom, looking up at the ceiling, alone. Perhaps she, too, had wandered the house in the darkness, peering into the bedrooms of her children to make sure that their sleep was sound and untroubled.

The idea of partaking in this ritual herself tickled her. She picked up the candle again, its wick diminished now but its flame still determined, and walked along the hall of bedrooms on the second floor. Which child had slept in which room? She tapped on the first door, as Marly herself must have done—pretending, her bowels clenching with excitement and fear.

"Hamish?" she called gently. "Everything all right?"

Yes, Mother, she heard the reply, faint but surely real—wasn't it?

She moved down to the next room, tapping again. "Lucia? Honey? Are you having nightmares again?" she called.

No, Mother. I'm asleep.

"That's a good girl." She went to the next room, tapping again. "Ellen? My darling? Do you want anything?"

No, Mother. I love you.

"I love you, too," she called through the door.

And good night, my sleeping ones, she thought; directing this—as Marly also must have done—to the children in the cemetery.

She headed back up the stairs to her own bedroom, blew out the candle, and got into bed, the only light now coming from the half-moon that reflected off the snow outside. She lay under the comforter, so new that it still smelled of chemicals, looking out through the glass at the small bit of sky she could see from that angle. She remembered having read somewhere that old windows looked distorted because the glass in them was still fluid. It seemed solid, but in reality it was still flowing slowly, at glacial speed. This idea pleased her poet self greatly. She imagined that she could slow herself down too, so that she was aging at the same rate at which the windows flowed, entering some new dimension of time wherein the world outside seemed to pass by so rapidly that from her point of view it was as ephemeral as a shooting star. It occurred to her that this was what things must look like to the dead Musgroves in the cemetery, too. They would be sitting there, relaxed, like in Thornton Wilder's *Our Town*, watching the years pass by as though they were moments. Would they still be there in an aeon? In two? Or would they fade, as all the things they knew gradually returned to oblivion?

Time can be manipulated, Francie thought as she drowsed off. I can live at whatever pace I want, in whatever time I want. I can go back and forth from Marly's world to mine. I *can* have children, if I want. They are mine now. We can share them, Marly and I.

∎ ∎ ∎

When she slept, she dreamed of a rampaging horse with flying hooves, and hot breath spouting from its flaring nostrils. It passed directly over her, so close that she could see its veined and rippling underbelly, and the hooves came down on her head over and over, like sledgehammers, but she felt no pain. And then she dreamed she was with the children again, all five of them, the ones who had been waiting for her since the last time they had said goodbye.

19

RUMORS

Colt spent that night in the apartment, spreading himself out in glorious, solitary diagonality on the bed. And for the first time in six years, he overslept.

Some years ago, Forszak had initiated a standing rule in the office that if you made more than $100,000 in any given month, you could take the rest of the month off. Few traders hit that mark, and those that did were so flush with success that a holiday was the furthest thing from their minds. They just wanted to keep going, like an old lady at a slot machine that was spewing quarters. But there were no standing rules about anyone being late—*that* was nothing more than amateurish. Forszak had not said people could be late whenever they wanted, no matter how successful they were.

Cursing himself for this slipup, Colt showered, dressed quickly, and dashed out to grab a cab to the office. Remembering to check the mail, he grabbed the few envelopes that were in the box and stuffed them into his coat pocket as he was going out the door. He managed to make it to work just as the opening bell rang on the televisions, and for the next three hours, he sat and stared pensively at his screens, occasionally speaking into the phone in terse monosyllables, sometimes diving for his keyboard when a plump prospect presented itself. He didn't remember the mail again until lunchtime, when he put his coat on once more to head out with Joe, Buddha, and Raoul for some shish kebab. Glancing surreptitiously at the envelopes, he saw that two were credit card statements, one was junk mail, and one was from the New York State Department of Corrections. He blanched and hurriedly stuffed them back in his coat before the others could see. That was all he needed, for the other guys to know that he was getting letters from the prison people. He would never live it down. He decided to wait until he got back to the office to read it.

Just before their orders were served, Raoul and Buddha got up at the same time and went to the bathroom. Joe took advantage of their absence to lean over and whisper, his lips nearly touching Colt's ear:

"Heard you went out for a drink with Forszak yesterday."

Colt started, nearly spilling water on himself. "You mind not breathing in my ear, please?" he said.

"Sorry," said Joe, pulling back. "Is it true?"

"Yes, it's true."

"Whadja talk about?"

"Nothing. The usual shit. Why?"

Joe folded his arms, doubt written on his face.

"Just wondered," he said. "There's rumors in the air."

"So fucking what? There's always rumors in the air. This place is worse than a high school with the rumors," Colt said.

"Yeah, but *these* rumors are different. Big shake-up coming."

"He didn't say anything about that, Joe. And I haven't heard a thing. I swear."

"I'm nervous, is why I ask," Joe said.

Colt rubbed his forehead tiredly. Even though he'd overslept, he felt like he could have used another few hours in bed. He hadn't slept that well in years. Could it be because it was also the first time he'd slept *alone* in years? Francie's dreams were always action adventures—she swore, laughed, lashed out, occasionally sat up and delivered lengthy monologues. If he never again had to put up with *that* part of being married to her, he wouldn't miss it.

"Joe," he said, "you're like an old woman, for Chrissakes. If the cleaning lady forgets to empty your trash can you think it means they're letting you go. What do you have to worry about, anyway? Your earnings been down?"

Joe nodded—looking, despite his jowls and gray hair, like a shamefaced small boy. "A little," he admitted.

"Well, fuck it. You've been raking in coin hand over fist all your life. You oughta retire before you drop dead, anyway. Enjoy your life a little bit, before they have to zip you up in a body bag at your desk. Like what happened to that guy on the twenty-eighth floor last year, remember? Imagine that. Work all your life so you can drop dead? No, thanks. He was only forty years old!"

"How you talk. You're not ever gonna retire any more than I am. Besides, I'm sixty-three years old, I'm paying two alimonies, two college tuitions, and a mortgage," said Joe. "I am not the green machine everyone thinks I am. Keep that to yourself, Coltie. That's between you and me."

"Believe me, I don't have enough free disk space in my brain to remember half the sob stories people tell me," said Colt. "It's already forgotten."

After lunch, walking back to the office, Buddha pulled on Colt's coat sleeve to slow him up, while Raoul and Joe walked on. Colt yanked his arm away, irritated.

"Unhand me," he said. "What's the matter with you?"

"Word is, you were out with Forszak yesterday after work," Buddha muttered, inclining his smooth, bald forehead confidentially toward Colt. "True?"

"Jesus Christ, was my entire life story printed in the *National Enquirer* this morning? Yes, I was out with Forszak. No, I haven't

heard any rumors. No, I don't know what's happening. Satisfied?"

"Not in the least," said Buddha. "In fact, you might say that I
am in a heightened state of dissatisfaction."

"You think I'm lying."

"No, I don't think you're lying. I think you just don't know."

"So?" Colt said.

"So, you know how it works. The only guy who doesn't hear
the rumors . . ."

" . . . is the guy everyone's talking about," Colt finished. "Holy
shit, Bood, if I didn't know better I'd think you guys were trying
to make me crazy. First Joe with the questions—"

"You talked to Joe? What did Joe wanna know?" Buddha interrupted.

"Nothing. Forget about it. Go molest someone else."

The two men walked on together silently. They entered the
building and went to the elevators. Colt, as usual, headed for the
stairs—part of his health regimen. He was already on the second
floor when he was surprised to hear the door open and close behind him, and then a pair of shoes scurrying upward. He didn't
even need to turn around to know who it was.

"Coltie—" came Raoul's voice.

Colt turned.

"Yes," he said. "It's true. The SEC is coming tomorrow and
you're all going to jail. Except for me. I turned state's witness.
Now fuck off."

Raoul paled and stared at him in panic.

"Jesus, I was *kidding*," said Colt.

"Oh, man, don't *do* that," said Raoul, crumpling on the stairs.
"You scared the shit outa me, Colt!"

"Raoul, what the fuck is going on around here?"

"I don't know," said Raoul miserably. "I was hoping you would.
Everyone's talking, but nobody's saying anything. It's weird."

"Is there some *reason* you should be afraid of the SEC showing up?"

"No. I swear there isn't, Coltie. But that doesn't matter. When those guys bust down the doors, it's always the little brown guys like me they haul away first. Tell me, please, Coltie. They say there's a big shake-up coming, that they're cutting loose all the dead wood. Please, pal, I'm beggin' ya. If you know anything . . . do I need to start looking for another job?"

"You wanna know what I think?" said Colt. "I think you guys are all on crack. Nothing's happening, Raoul. At least nothing I know about. That's what I told the other guys and that's what I'm telling you."

"The other guys? You mean Bood and Joe? What did *they* wanna know?"

But Colt was already heading upward, taking the stairs two at a time.

"I got two kids, man!" Raoul called upward. "I got a right to know!"

"Read the *Enquirer*, baby!" Colt yelled down. "It's all in there, every word!"

■ ■ ■

Back at his desk, Colt remembered his mail for the second time. He took the letter from the state and shoved it in his pocket; then he went into the washroom, where he ensconced himself in a stall, ripped it open, and read:

NOTICE OF PAROLE HEARING

I should have known, he grumbled. Had it already been three years? Jesus, how times flies. He read on:

BE IT KNOWN TO ALL CONCERNED THAT IN THE MATTER
OF THE INCARCERATION OF NOVA HART THERE SHALL BE A
PUBLIC MEETING OF THE PAROLE BOARD ON DECEMER 10 AT

THE HOUR OF 3:00 PM. SHOULD YOU WISH TO ATTEND, PLEASE INFORM THE BOARD IN WRITING OR BY TELEPHONE AT LEAST TWENTY-FOUR HOURS PRIOR TO THE ABOVE DATE AND TIME.

Well, that was just charming. And more than a little coincidental. The hearing was just ten days away.

How about it, Coltie? came the voice. *You gonna get me sprung this time?*

"Fat fucking chance," he mumbled, his voice echoing off the bare walls of the washroom. "You made your bed, now you lie in it."

Aw, Coltie. That's not very filial of you.

A cough in the next stall told him that someone was in there. Hurriedly Colt stuffed the envelope in his pocket again and exited the washroom before they could see who he was. The last thing he needed now was for people to know he was talking to himself in the bathroom.

▌▌▌

In the afternoon, after a dead morning, Colt sold ten thousand shares of telephone stock at a twenty-seven-cent-per-share profit, a good note on which to end an otherwise troubling day. He put on his coat without bidding good-bye to any of his deskmates, all of whom had been behaving in a subdued manner ever since lunch, anyway; and he made a point of sailing past Forszak's office without so much as looking at it, lest he give rise to a new spate of gossip. Once on the street, he got into a cab and pulled out his cell phone. He told the driver to head uptown and then called Bucks County information. An operator gave him the number of an excavating company, then connected him.

"Steinbach Brothers," said a voice in his ear.

"Yeah," said Colt. "You guys have backhoes and stuff like that?"

"Who's this?"

"Name's Hart. I got some digging I need done."

"Well, sure we got backhoes. What kinda digging?"

"A cemetery. In my backyard. I need it dug up and gotten the fuck outa there."

There was a long pause. "This a joke?"

"Hell, no. I'm dead serious. I just bought a house, and then I find out there's a cemetery on the property. Which the goddam real estate agent neglected to mention."

The man on the other end blew out a long breath. "Well," he said. "Where d'you live?"

"You know Highway 112? That old house that used to belong to the Musgroves?"

"Hold on a minnit," said Steinbach. Colt could tell from the way he talked that the man was overweight, a smoker. "You wanna dig up *that* cemetery?"

"Damn straight. Can you do it or not?"

"Can I ask why?"

Colt knotted his free hand into a fist and pounded his leg. "Because," he said calmly. "I dislike it. Its very presence in my life offends me. I don't like the idea of having dead strangers in my backyard. That's why. Clear enough?"

"I guess. It's just—I know the guy who used to take care a that place."

"Oh, you're a chum of Mr. Flebberman's, are you?"

"Yeah," said Steinbach in his chubby voice. "You know Randy?"

"We are acquainted," said Colt. "Delightful fellow. Listen, I'm really enjoying the hell out of this little chat, but I'm terribly afraid I have to get off the phone now. What are your rates?"

"My what?"

"How much do you *charge*."

"Well, for somethin' like that, it's gonna run you a little extra. There's exhumation permits we gotta get. At least I think there is.

We ain't done anythin' like this before. Well, once. But that was just one grave. That was back in 'eighty-five, when my dad was still—"

"*How much?*" Colt said, through gritted teeth.

"One fifty an hour, plus permit costs."

"Fine," said Colt. "Be out there tomorrow morning at nine A.M. sharp."

"Now, hold on there," said Steinbach. "We're booked solid for a month and a half. I won't be able to get a crew out there until January at least, and then the ground'll be like rock, an' we're gonna hafta—"

"Three hundred dollars an hour," said Colt. "Plus a small bonus for yourself, Mr. Steinbach, if the work is completed in a timely fashion. Beginning tomorrow. Will that effectively resolve any scheduling conflicts?"

"Three—"

"—hundred dollars an hour. Plus."

"Uh," said Steinbach. "Hm. Well, I think we can figure out a way to make it work. Sure. Tomorrow? Nine A.M.?"

"Correct," said Colt. "Call me on this number if you have any problems." He gave Steinbach his cell number and hung up.

"Where ju wanna go, main?" asked the cabdriver.

Colt thought. He wanted Scotch badly. Scotch, and a nice, fat, expensive illegal cigar. He gave the name of a bar on Eighty-third where he could find these things, and more.

20

CRUELTY

The next morning, after two Scotches, a Macanudo, and another blissful night alone in the apartment, Colt was back in the office—at the proper time. The market was to open at 9:30. At 9:28, his cell phone rang. Colt had just typed in several buy orders that he intended to execute as soon as the bell rang, and he already had his hands poised over the necessary keys. These buys were hot picks—Internet stocks he'd been watching for weeks, stalking them as a panther stalks a fat, wounded gazelle. Part of him wanted to ignore the ringing, but he'd never been able to bring himself to leave a phone unanswered. After all, one never knew who it might be. The president, maybe, calling to commend him for being an upstanding American citizen. Stranger things had happened.

"Hello?" he said.

"You asshole," said Francie.

"Oh, hi, honey," Colt said, in a voice loud enough for Raoul, Buddha, and Joe to hear, since they were all listening anyway. "Everything okay?"

"There's some kind of machine in the backyard, and they're digging up the cemetery," Francie said. "So, no, everything is not okay. Coltrane, why is this happening?"

"I'm sure I haven't the foggiest idea," Colt said. "Was there anything else? We're about to open for the day, and I'm just the teensiest bit busy right now."

"Colt, how could you do this?" she said. "I thought we were going to *talk* about it, at least!"

"It's my house, isn't it?" Colt said.

Joe, Buddha, and Raoul all looked up. On television, the bell clanged and the shouting started. Colt stabbed frantically at his keyboard.

"I have to go!" he said. "Market's open!"

Francie sighed. "Coltrane, I was hoping to tell you this in person, but . . . I want a divorce."

Colt swallowed the acid that rose in his throat. "Yeah?" he said as he punched at his keyboard. Errors sprang up on the screen.

"Yes. I do. I've been thinking about it, and . . . well, bearing in mind everything that's happened between us recently, and . . . the fact that we do seem to be drifting . . ."

"Well—Francie—this isn't really the time to talk about it."

"See? You think even the market opening is more important than discussing your marriage! That's called mental cruelty, Coltrane!"

"Francie," Colt said, lowering his voice, fighting the urge to jump through the phone and throttle her, "I hate to break it to you, but the market opening *is* more important than talking to you. Okay? This is how I make my living. You know that country house you love so much, that you happen to be sitting in right now? Well, I bought it. With money I earned from this job. If you prevent me from doing my job, you are preventing me from earning money. Which means I can't buy things. And neither can you. You know the fucking market opens at nine-thirty. So you call me with one minute to go, and you make me miss it? *That* is mental cruelty. It's also *really fucking stupid*!" He barely managed to keep his voice down.

"How could you get a vasectomy without telling me⸮" Francie shrieked, so loud that Colt was afraid the three stooges could hear. He looked at them quickly, but they were all pretending to ignore him. "How could you do it⸮ *That's* what I call cruelty!"

"Right, well, I have to get off the phone now," Colt said.

"No! No! I will not be put off by you again! I demand your full and complete attention right now, Coltrane! This is not just a job I'm talking about here. It's more important than that! It's our lives!"

"I have to *go*, goddammit," Colt said.

"Coltrane, I have never in my life felt so betrayed. By anyone." He could hear the tears coming in her voice.

"Well then," he hissed into the receiver, "why don't you write a poem about it⸮"

He wished he hadn't said that, because then she started to cry, and it was like a punch in his gut. Once he had loved her for the way she saw the world in broad strokes of emotion, and admired the way she'd tried so hard to capture it in words—and always failed. Had he ever told her that⸮ Probably not. Maybe he should tell her now.

"Our marriage is over, Coltrane," she said, weeping.

Too late.

At that moment, he had a flash of how the whole business must look to her. And he thought: she must think all I care about is money, that money is the most important thing. Well, it's not. Not forever, anyway. But right now it is. Because you have to make sure you have enough. It's fine and dandy to sit around writing poems or taking vacations or whatever. But before you did anything else, you had to make sure you had enough. And we do not have enough, not yet. Not even close. And I, it seems, am the only one who understands that.

"I agree," said Colt.

When she didn't say anything for a long moment, he hung up.

"Everything okay, Coltie?" asked Buddha. "Everything hunky-dory?"

Colt looked at the television screen; the market had shot up already by twenty points. He should have been in on the action from the first second. Now he would be playing catch-up all day.

"It's all good," said Colt.

He pulled his chair in closer to his desk and focused hard on the television, trying not to blink.

"It's all good," he said again, though now they really were ignoring him.

■ ■

The phone rang again about four minutes later. It was Wayne Steinbach.

"Uh, we got a situation here," he said.

"I can't wait to hear it," Colt said. It was 9:46 A.M., and he was already weary. More than anything, he wanted to go home and get back on the couch.

"Randy Flebberman is down here and he's madder 'n a bull at a ball fry."

"A bull at a *what*?"

"You know, when they castrate the bulls and fry up their balls?"

"I was not aware of that charming custom," said Colt. "Is that before or after you marry your sisters?"

"What?"

"Nothing. Tell me what Flebberman is doing."

"Well, he says he's gettin' a lawyer and an injunction and all that stuff."

"He doesn't have an injunction yet, does he?"

"Well . . . I dunno. He's sayin' he's gettin' one, is what I'm tellin' ya."

Colt sighed. Now the stocks he'd targeted had completely lost their attractiveness, *and* his wife was leaving him. And now this. It was not going to be a bad day; it was going to be a terrible day. He pounded his fist on his desk. Everyone's computers shook. Joe, Raoul, and Buddha looked at him again, this time in alarm.

"Tell me this one thing. Is he waving a piece of paper around in the air?" he asked Steinbach.

"No."

"Then he doesn't have an injunction."

"How d'you know?"

"Because the first thing people do with injunctions is wave them around in the air. Look, Steinbach, this is a waste of time. I own that land and I don't have to have dead people on it if I don't want to. Understand? I hired you to do a job, you said you would do it. That's a verbal contract. Verbal contracts are binding, just like paper ones. Ask any lawyer. I can take your ass to court."

"Now look. Randy Flebberman is a friend of mine," said Steinbach, his voice growing higher. "I went to high school with him. Hell, I dated his wife once. Before she was his wife, I mean. I knew he wasn't gonna like it, but if I'd a known he was gonna take it like *this*, I wouldn't a done it at all!"

"Are you ready to go to court with me, Mr. Steinbach?"

There was a long moment of silence; Colt hoped Steinbach wouldn't know that he wasn't in the least legally bound to complete the job, as long as he hadn't accepted any money yet. He waited.

"No," Steinbach said finally.

"Right. Then I've said all I have to say. Good day to you, sir."

Colt hung up and met the stares of his coworkers.

"Dead bodies?" said Raoul.

"On your property?" said Joe.

"What's goin' on, Colt?" asked Buddha. "Your wife finally find out where you been buryin' your enemies?"

"Would you guys mind your fucking business?" Colt said,

louder than he'd meant to. Then, having attracted the attention of *everyone* in the office, he decided a break was in order. He got up and put his coat on.

"Where you goin'?" asked Joe. "It's not even ten o'clock!"

"My morning is shot," said Colt. "Fucking wife, fucking Steinbach, fucking you guys. I need a break. I'll see ya later." And he left, with the eyes of the entire office on him—for a split second, before they were drawn back to their screens.

■ ■ ■

Twenty minutes later, Colt was wandering slowly through Central Park, his hands deep in his pockets and his collar up around his ears, although it was actually getting warmer out—it looked like the snow they'd already had might have jumped the gun on winter. They could be in for another week or so of fall weather before things got really shitty again. That would be good, he thought. He hadn't been ready to winter in, not yet.

By force of ancient habit, he headed up to the Swan Pond. When he was a boy, he had loved to come up here and watch the big white birds glide along the top of the water, admiring their aristocratic elegance. It was one of the few memories of his childhood that was pleasant. If he had any money, which he usually didn't, he used to buy a handful of food from the vending machine and toss it in the water, little by little, drawing it out so he could stay a long time. The ducks would come in, too, vying for a chunk of the action, but the swans always chased them off. Colt remembered now how that made him feel: proud. Because they were eating his food. He admired swans for not being afraid to take what they wanted—shame never entered the picture for them. Just like him. There was no shame in doing whatever you had to do to survive, even if it meant crawling on your belly through shit and mud all the early years of your life. That was nothing to be ashamed of—as long as you were crawling uphill.

It had been a long time since he'd come here. Both the ducks and the swans were gone now, driven south by the early storm. All that was left were pigeons. Colt had always hated pigeons. Disappointed, he started wandering back down toward the south gates of the park, where he'd come in.

So Francie wanted a divorce. As he'd told her, that was not unexpected. It wasn't the first time he'd thought of it himself, either. Several times, in fact. Why hadn't he gone ahead with it? Because there seemed to be hardly any point—he was too busy to justify it. For all the hours he'd spent working every week, they might as well have been separated, anyway. Funnily enough, they only saw each other about as often as a recently divorced couple might—a divorced couple on slightly better than amicable terms, that is, who had perhaps agreed to continue sleeping together every once in a while just to take the edge off the loneliness.

The real truth was—and this was something he would have been ashamed to admit, even to Forszak—he was simply more interested in making money than anything else. Well, that in itself was not so unusual, in this business. But he cared about it more than sex, even, and that *was* unusual, and that was the part he was ashamed to admit. A lot of the guys in the office ran around on their wives. By no means all, but some. It almost seemed to go hand in hand with the kind of work they did. Yet Colt had never done it—not for lack of opportunity, and not out of virtue, either. He had simply always been puzzled by what the point of all that fooling around was. Soon enough, everything new became old; all acquisitions eventually became another liability. Then you ended up like this Joe, who had left his first wife to move on to the second, and then on to a third; it was probably only a matter of time before Number Three found out he was shtupping a woman in Commodities. And all he had to show for it was two alimony suits and an ulcer. Jesus, what a clusterfuck!

For Colt, things were different—precisely because it was all the same. Money and women, that is. They meant the same thing to him, but money was more easily handled, more easily controlled. And really more exciting, too. Something he never admitted to anyone, not even Francie, was that sometimes, sitting at his desk, surrounded by all the chaos and excitement and fear, he got a hard-on. The whole mess was so turbulent that he would grow wood right there in front of everyone, hidden only by the three-quarters of an inch of whatever the hell fake stuff his desk was made of. When he scored hard on a stock, it got harder. And then he would go into the bathroom and whack off. Sometimes it happened twice a day, so that by the time he got home he had nothing left to give, anyway.

And Francie—it seemed like the longer she was on the meds, the less she came on to him. She was content to sit in her chair in the corner of the apartment and read her goddam Emily Dickinson. He would stagger in around six or seven or eight o'clock, eyes bleary, groin drained, eat dinner and go to bed. And that was their marriage: a whacker and a poet; a wealthy man, his lonely woman.

In some Arab cultures, Colt knew, all the man had to do was walk around his wife in a circle three times and say, "I divorce thee, I divorce thee, I divorce thee." Something like that around here would be an innovation, he thought. Now I have to deal with lawyers.

And I hate the fucking lawyers.

■ ■ ■

Colt bought a bag of peanuts from an intrepid vendor who hadn't yet packed it in for the season. He ate a few and amused himself for another twenty minutes by throwing the rest of them at the pigeons. Then he went back to the office. When lunchtime came, he didn't go with the other guys. Even after four o'clock, he stayed on, trying once again to penetrate the murkiness of the

Eastern market. No after-work drink invite from Forszak this time. He was the only one left.

What gods control you¿ he asked the silent screen, as it scrolled its endless litany of numbers before him. What's the key to unlocking your secrets¿ What mountain do I have to climb to find it¿

But the screen, as always, told him little beyond the facts.

And I need the facts behind the facts, Colt thought. I have the answers, all of them. Problem is, I don't know what the questions are.

But some questions were beyond the range of mortals, even the great Coltrane Hart. At nine o'clock he went back to his favorite bar, where he had some more Scotches and another cigar. A few women talked to him, but he was merely polite, and did not encourage them to come home with him, though he knew he could have without much effort. And it occurred to him for the first time in years, looking around at these strange and hungry females who were attracted by his clothes, his scent of money, his expression of power and control, that none of them was nearly as beautiful as Francie, and certainly not half as smart.

And he thought: I think it's a pretty safe to say that I have royally screwed up.

21

---■---

DISINTERMENT

The snow wasn't going to stay after all. They had been re-prieved by the sun and warming wind, though Francie knew these had only delayed their sentence rather than commuted it. It was good enough for the living, though it meant nothing for those who had been yanked from their beds and been spirited away. Like the poor Musgroves.

To Francie, it felt like the secret police had come—as if, some-how, it was against the law in Colt's world to be dead. She stood in the yard and looked at the mess that the backhoe had made of the earth. And my husband is their secret chief, she thought—he's the invisible man in the invisible office, handing out the orders that make people disappear.

Even the giant old stump that had protected Marly's stone was a casualty, lying slanted half in and half out of the hole, its roots exposed—like a molar torn from an old man's mouth. The excava-tors had opened the graves into one large, common pit, and the bottom of the hole, which for so many years had been the resting place of the sleeping six, was now a mess of chewed-up yellow-

and-brown mud. Meltwater trickled down the sides of the pit, pooling there into an unhealthy quagmire.

■ ■ ■

The disinterment of the Musgrove family remains had been one of the worst things Francie had ever had to watch. She almost *couldn't* watch it; she would have preferred to stay in the house, hiding her head under a pillow, like an ostrich. But when Flebberman arrived, beside himself with rage and grief, she knew she couldn't just pretend it wasn't happening.

Steinbach's trio of men first plucked the stones out of the earth, putting them in the back of a dump truck. They tossed them casually, as if they were nothing more than rocks, and they clattered and broke in the truck bed.

"Goddamn it!" Flebberman had howled at them. "Wayne, you tell them yahoos to watch what they're doin'!"

Steinbach, who could barely meet Flebberman's eyes, had a word with his men. For a moment, Francie thought everything was going to be all right—suddenly all was understood, and so they could just go home, couldn't they? But then the backhoe ripped into the soil, chewing a large swathe above where Francie imagined the Musgroves' middles would be.

Flebberman lost what little self-control he still possessed.

"Steinbach!" he screamed, over the backhoe's roar. "I thought you and me was friends!"

Steinbach pretended he couldn't hear him.

"How can you do this?" Flebberman screeched. "Stop it! Please, Steinbach! Stop it right now!"

Francie felt her heart was breaking. Steinbach looked up at him finally, hangdog, and shook his head.

"Can't!" he said.

"Why not?!"

"Contract. He offered me twice the usual rate, Randy. I had to take it."

"Yeah, right," said Flebberman. "And all them little Steinbachs gotta have new shoes. Izzenat right?"

Steinbach didn't answer.

"Well, I just hope no one ever digs up yer family's bones!" he spat, screaming over the engine's noise. "Or yer gonna know just how I feel right now!"

Flebberman turned to Francie, who had been dreading this moment. She was the wife of the man who had ordered this desecrtion, after all. She was Elena Ceauşescu, Imelda Marcos. She cringed, and waited for what he was going to say to her.

But he didn't scream. Instead he came and put his face close to her ear, so that she could feel his breath. Involuntarily she closed her eyes, waiting to see what he would do. She would not have been at all surprised had he sunk his snuff-yellowed teeth into the firm flesh of her neck.

But he didn't. Instead he spoke.

"Where is he?" he asked, so quietly she barely heard him.

She hadn't expected that. It all seemed so obvious then—the reasons people sought revenge. They didn't just do it for no reason, for petty slights. They were driven by something greater than themselves; they were made mad with outrage. She understood now. And, though she knew that whatever was going to happen was probably not a good idea, she also knew it was one thing she could turn her back on—for reasons of her own. As long as it didn't go too far.

It never occurred to her not to tell him. Whatever he did to him, Colt had it coming.

"New York," Francie said.

"Where?"

Francie shook her head. He was even closer to her now—she could smell tobacco on his breath, and sweat and engine oil on his body. His arm brushed ever so lightly against her right breast, and she felt it all the way to her toes.

"I shouldn't tell you," she said, knowing she was only seconds away from doing so.

Flebberman nodded, understanding.

"I still have yer check," he said. "Is that address still good?"

Of course—the check she'd written for the truck. Francie said nothing. She nodded, the movements of her head barely perceptible. Then she closed her eyes again.

When she opened them several moments later, Flebberman was handing one of Steinbach's men something. Then he got into his truck. Francie saw that the something was a roll of money. The workman turned to his fellows and grinned; they gathered around him, and he divvied it up, a small handful to each. Steinbach himself hadn't noticed this, because Flebberman had chosen a moment when he was occupied with the roots of the tree, which had become tangled around the bucket of the digger. The workman saw that Francie had noticed, however, and he looked at her, then significantly at Steinbach, then held a finger to his lips. Francie stared dumbly. She had no idea what he meant. She nodded, because she knew that was what she was expected to do. The man smiled again and put his money away.

She stayed for another few minutes. When the bones began to come up, she went into the house. She could no longer force herself to bear witness. She went into the house and put her hand on the phone in the kitchen, where she could still see the wicked arm of the backhoe as it swung up and down, ripping into the sacred earth.

22

THE NECROPHOBE

Colt awoke with the worst hangover in recent memory. Before even opening his eyes, he knew that this was going to be another very bad day. A thick coating of sour slime lay over his tongue, and his eyes were crusted shut. Groaning, he tried to pry them open, but light pouring into his retinas made him cringe, and he hid his head under the blankets. He had fallen asleep on the couch, he realized. In the apartment. Where had he been? What had he been doing?

Oh yes—he remembered now. How many Scotches had he had? Endless. Wait now. Here came a memory, as fuzzy as an old movie. There had been a lengthy, if somewhat incoherent, conversation with someone in the bar. That's right. An old, heavily tattooed man. A war hero, though from which war he couldn't remember. Possibly the Revolution. He was that old. They'd bought each other beers and slapped each other on the back, commiserating on the faithlessness of women. The veteran had been divorced three times, he'd said. Colt vaguely recalled pouring out the whole story of Francie in a great, big soppy mess, a recollection that caused him to wince now with embarrassment. He'd grown emotional and weepy. Good Lord. How many Scotches? He began to remember—they'd killed most of a bottle between them. Enough to poison a horse.

"Jesus Christ," Colt said, into the stale air of the apartment.

"Jesus Christ is right," said a voice, from the other side of the room.

Colt sat up as quickly as he could—which was not quickly at all—and tried to look around. Squinting and blinking, he could make out someone seated in the far corner of the room. At the same time, he became aware of a tremendous need to urinate. It was so bad he knew that he was only a step away from wetting himself.

"Who the fuck are you?" Colt said.

Before the answer could come, he struggled to his feet and went into the bathroom, where he released a thunderous cataract of urine into the bowl. From that position, he was just able to turn his head far enough to see the person's foot as they sat in the chair, waiting for him to come out.

"Hello?" he called. "Who is that?"

There was no answer.

Colt pissed for nearly a full minute. Finally, he came out of the bathroom, clad only in his underwear, greatly relieved now; and there, as cool as a cucumber, was the neighbor from Pennsylvania, that short, hairy little guy with the tow truck. What was his name again? Colt blinked at him uncomprehendingly.

"Flebberman?" said Colt. "What the fuck are you doing in my apartment? How did you get in here?"

"You left the door unlocked," Flebberman said. "Here I was ready to wait all morning for you ta come out, and you made it so easy for me." He wrinkled his nose. "You musta really been tanked last night. You smell like a bum."

"I—I left the door *open*?"

"Yup."

"And so you just walked in?"

"Yup."

Colt rubbed his face. He collapsed on the couch again, his stomach rebelling. He wanted to lie down again, and if it hadn't been for the incongruity of Flebberman in his place, he would have.

"I'm confused," said Colt.

"Lemme see if I can explain it for ya," said Flebberman. He got up and crossed the room, and then Colt felt something cold and hard smash into his left cheekbone. The pain blinded him, and he fell on his side onto the cushions of the couch, struggling to remain conscious. For a long moment afterward, embarrassingly, all he could do was whine. He had never been hit that hard before. It stunned him so badly that he felt almost as if he was about to float out of his body. It even seemed, for an instant, that he did, and that he could see himself lying there, and Flebberman standing over him.

"Hey," said Flebberman, shaking him by the shoulder. "Don't pass out on me. You got a big day ahead of you."

"Unh," said Colt. "Why—why'd you hit me?"

"You'll find out, shitbird," said Flebberman. "Sit up. C'mon. Get dressed."

The little man's voice was quaking with anger. Colt pushed himself up into a sitting position, his face now numb, an alarm bell going off inside his skull.

"Oh, my God," he groaned. Tears of pain dripped down his cheeks.

"Yeah," said Flebberman. "Start prayin'."

"What—what did you hit me with?"

Flebberman pulled a pistol out of his snowsuit and showed it to him quickly before tucking it back in. "That," he said.

"You have a *gun*?"

"You better believe it. That li'l tap was t' letcha know I'm serious."

"What—what's going on?"

"Yer gonna find out," said Flebberman. "Now I'm tellin' ya one more time. Putcher fuckin' clothes on."

A flash came to him then—he had it. "This is about that cemetery, isn't it," he asked.

"Oh, yeah," said Flebberman. "You better believe it."

"How did you even know where I live?"

"Yer wife."

"Francie told you where to find me? Did you—did you hurt her?"

"Hell, no. I like yer wife. She deserves better'n you. She wrote me a check. It had this address on it. Now get up offa there and get dressed. Move slow."

Colt got up.

"Can you hand me my pants?" he said. He could feel his face already swelling. "They're on the chair behind you. You were sitting on them."

Flebberman reached behind him without looking and felt for his pants. He tossed them over and Colt worked his legs into them.

"Get the rest a yer clothes on," said Flebberman. "Get dressed for outside."

"Where are we going?"

"You'll see," Flebberman said. "I ain't in an explainin' mood right now."

"My other clothes—I have to go into the bedroom."

"Hurry up. I'm right behind ya."

Colt went into the bedroom and found some socks and a sweater, which he pulled on. As he turned around, Flebberman's fist—small, but almost sharp, like a spear, and driven by an arm that was wiry and deceptively strong—drove itself into his stomach. He fell onto the floor and curled into a ball, gasping for breath. He could sense the little man standing over him. When he could speak again, he said:

"I'm gonna kill you for this."

"We'll see about that," Flebberman said. "We'll see who's gonna kill who today."

Colt coughed. "Why do you keep hitting me?"

"To let you know who's boss."

"Okay," Colt croaked. "I believe you."

"Do everything I tell ya to. Don't do nothin' else. Nothin' funny. Unnerstand?"

"Yeah. I understand."

"This ain't my usual style," Flebberman said. He seemed to have grown even angrier, his voice growing higher. "I don't b'leeve in this kinda thing. I'm a peaceful man who never wanted to bother nobody, and never wanted nobody to bother him. But you brought this on yerself. An' now yer gonna pay. Now get up."

Colt did as he was told. He felt on the verge of throwing up, but he managed to control it. That blow to the stomach had almost done it. He couldn't take another one like that.

"Don't hit me again," he said.

"Do what I tell ya and I won't hafta. Go back in there."

Colt half crawled and half walked into the living room.

"Hold on a minnit. Toss that coat over here before you put it on."

Colt did as he was told. Flebberman searched through all the pockets. He took out Colt's keys, went to the window, opened it, and threw them out.

"Hey," Colt said weakly.

"Shuddup," said Flebberman. "I don't want you getting' yer hands on anything sharp. Believe me, I'm on to you. Yer tryin' ta plan somethin'. Don't. I'm mad enough to kill ya right now."

Colt decided that to say nothing from now on would be the wisest course of action. He put his coat on and waited, miserable. More than anything he wanted a glass of orange juice, and then to get back into bed. He wondered how long he would be able to stay on his feet.

"Now," said Flebberman. "This is how it's gonna work. We're

gonna go downstairs to my truck. You walk in front. I keep the gun in my pocket. You try to talk to anyone, you try to run— blammo. That's it fer you."

"You'll get caught," Colt said.

Flebberman came toward him again and Colt cringed, doubling over and putting up his arms to protect himself.

"Yeah, that's what I thought," said Flebberman. "Big tough New York City businessman. Not so tough now, are ya. Now— yer gonna drive."

"I'm sorry," said Colt, hating himself for saying it. "I'm really, really sorry. If I'd have known it would upset you this much, I really wouldn't have done it. I just—"

"I'm tellin' ya, shuddup!" said Flebberman dangerously.

"I—I just want to say that I was within my rights. It was my property."

"You want another whack?"

"No. Please don't. I'm just telling you. From my point of view."

"You don't know shit," said Flebberman. "There's higher laws than the ones on the books, which it seems you never heard of 'em anyway, so I dunno why I'm even tryin' ta explain it to ya. Go to the door."

Colt went to the door, Flebberman close behind.

"I can't lock it without my keys," he said.

"Yer door wasn't locked to begin with, remember?" said Flebberman. "Let it go. If you live through this day you can just buy more fancy shit to replace all the shit that's gonna get stolen. Yer rich enough, anyways."

■ ■ ■

Flebberman's tow truck was parked outside. The plow blade was still attached, and for some reason this detail struck Colt as amusing, or at least it would have if he hadn't been so terrified. Flebberman in the City. Flebberman's New York Adventure.

He got in the driver's side and Flebberman sat next to him, placing his gun on his lap. Sneaking a glance, Colt saw that it was a revolver from prehistoric days, a veritable relic. Rust had discolored the barrel, and he wondered if there was any chance it actually worked. Better not find out, he thought. It certainly worked well enough for pistol-whipping purposes. Besides, he was not up to any fancy Hollywood maneuvers. All he wanted was to do what he was told and get out of this situation. Then—vengeance. If he was still around to deliver it.

He started up the truck, put it into gear, and headed toward the Holland Tunnel. It was so early that the commuter rush hadn't started yet, and they had the tunnel mostly to themselves. They passed a police car headed into the city. Colt looked after it wistfully in the rear-view mirror.

"Don't even think about it," said Flebberman.

"I wasn't."

"Yes, you were. Y'see this gun?"

"Yes. I see it."

"It belonged to my dad," Flebberman said. "It's a fambly hairloom." Colt could feel his eyes burning into the side of his face. "I hung on to it all these years. See, I happen ta take great pride in my fambly history. All of it. An' I get kinda pissy when fancy-pants out-a-towners think they can come in and do whatever the hell they want. That includes the diggin' up of cemeteries that's been sittin' there for a hundred and fifty years in peace and quiet, which it shoulda been left there forever. You follow me?"

"Yes. I follow you."

"Problem with you is, yer an asshole," said Flebberman. "Yer name is Hart but you don't have one. Know what that is?"

Colt shook his head.

"Ironic," Flebberman said triumphantly. "That is what you might call an ironic situation. There, I bet you thought an ignorant redneck like me wouldn't know such a ten-dollar word. Isn't that right, Fancy Pants?"

"I never thought that."

"Yeah, you did. You think your shit don't stink and everyone who ain't from New York is just a stoopit fool. Doncha? You think you're better'n everyone. Maybe you been askin' for somethin' like this for a long time. Maybe you had this comin'. Ever think a that?"

"No."

"Eggzackly," said Flebberman. "Eggzackly my point. You follow me?"

Colt didn't follow him at all, but he deemed it smarter not to say so.

"I follow you," he said.

"Now is the time when yer life should start flashin' before yer eyes," Flebberman said. "Start thinkin' about all the things you shouldn't a done in yer life. And all the things you shoulda done. This is it fer you, shitbird. Take a good hard look at yerself. It was only a matter a time before somethin' like this happened to you. An' if I hadn't a done it, somebody else woulda."

Colt's blood went cold.

"Are you thinkin'?" Flebberman asked.

"Yes," said Colt. "I'm thinking."

■ ■ ■

They emerged from the dank, riverine darkness of the tunnel and into New Jersey, the city behind them now, and they passed through a landscape of concrete lots, gas stations, and tenement buildings, a dead world where nothing grew, save for weeds in the cracked cement. Flebberman shook his head, disgusted.

"Don't know why anyone'd ever wanna live here," he said. "Place is a godforsaken hellhole."

Colt decided against responding. If he was going to rant, let him rant.

"People live like rabbits. Hardly have room to stretch yer arms.

Cities ain't natural. Animals don't live in cities. Not even monkeys. Gorillas and such. They spread out. That's what we're supposed to do, too. Problem is, some people are too stoopit to know what nature wants from 'em. Certain things oughta be done a certain way."

They came to a toll booth. Flebberman tucked the gun out of sight underneath his snowsuited thigh.

"I don't have any money," said Colt. "I forgot my wallet." He waited.

Cursing quietly, Flebberman took a couple of wrinkled bills out of his pocket and handed them over. Colt paid the attendant and they edged away from the booth.

"That's two bucks you owe me," Flebberman said. "Goddam stoopit rich bastard don't even have two dollars on 'im. Good God!"

This statement, bizarre as it was, actually gave him hope— maybe he didn't intend to kill him. For the last few minutes, he had been wondering if Flebberman intended to drive him out to some remote area and put a bullet in the back of his head. But now he didn't think so. It seemed that the little man had something in mind. Now he was more hopeful that he would make it through this, somehow. And he was already plotting the various delightful ways in which he would help himself to the dish that is best served cold—revenge.

■ ■ ■

Soon they were on the Pulaski Skyway, an elevated road arching over a continuous vista of dead industrial land that was criss-crossed by railroad tracks, populated by factories and vast yards of rusted shipping containers. Marshland, flat and gray, appeared beneath them, the water rainbowed with chemicals. Flebberman shook his head again.

"Lookit that," he said. "You think anything can even live in that water?"

"Are you asking me?" Colt said quietly.

"Yeah, I'm askin' ya. Look around you. This is what cities do to the land. Nothin'll ever grow here again, I can tell ya that. All ruint and polluted to shit. Jesus, it makes me sick what people do."

Colt could feel the man glaring at him as though he was personally responsible. Again, he deemed it wiser to remain silent.

When the time came, according to Flebberman's directions, he took the turnoff for the turnpike, and they continued through New Jersey, the factories now giving way to small towns, one after the other, marked only by highway exit signs. He didn't have to ask to know that they were headed toward Plainsburg, but beyond that he had no idea where he was taking himself.

They rode along in silence for well over an hour, until they came once again to the Delaware Water Gap and crossed into Pennsylvania. Then they rounded the bend and headed up into the hills, but as they drew closer to Plainsburg, Flebberman told him to keep going along the interstate. So they were going somewhere else.

"You gonna kill me?" Colt asked finally; for this was the question that had been lurking in the back of his mind for the last couple of hours.

Flebberman snorted.

"B'leeve me, I thought about it," he said.

Colt didn't ask anything further. When the time came, he could fight—that much he was sure of. He was much larger than this man, and no doubt stronger; but that didn't matter as much as taking advantage of the right moment. He would get him in a headlock and snap his neck, he decided. That would be the way to do it. Just grab him under the chin and pull his head around sharply, until he felt the wet crack of bones breaking like green sticks, and then he would let him fall to the ground. If it came down to it, that was what he would do.

He almost looked forward to it. And as he had these thoughts, adrenaline began to seep into his system. His hangover was forgotten now, and he forced himself to ignore the throbbing in his face and the dull ache in his gut where he had been punched. He felt himself growing stronger.

"Pull off here," Flebberman said.

They got off the highway and headed around the exit ramp to a stop sign. Just as Colt had feared, they were in the middle of nowhere. He turned right as directed and continued along for another few minutes, until they came to a sign that said DUMP.

"Take that road," said Flebberman.

Colt did as he was told. The road turned to rutted dirt now, soft and muddy, with mountain ranges of filthy snow on either side. Although it had seemed just a short time ago that winter had settled in to stay, now everything was thawing, and the world was a wet mess. The tow truck pushed slowly through the muck for another mile, until the road ended without warning. That was it. Nothing more. He stopped the truck and leaned back in his seat, waiting.

"Get out," said Flebberman.

Colt got out. Flebberman slid out after him, pointing the gun at his back.

"Move a few steps forward," he said.

Colt moved until Flebberman had positioned himself right behind him, the barrel pressed into his spine.

"Now," Flebberman said, "walk dead ahead."

They walked until the ground dropped out from underneath them. They were above a huge hole in the ground, Colt saw now. Not a hole—a canyon. Looking down, he realized that they were at a landfill. Before them was spread an endless vista of acres of trash. In the distance, he could see a bulldozer moving lazily over the top of the garbage. There was no snow left here; the heat of decomposition had melted it. The bulldozer was too far away to call to the driver for help. Maybe too far away to hear a gunshot, even. The smell hit him as the wind changed, and Colt gagged as decay filled his nostrils. He covered his mouth with his hand and tried to breathe through his fingers.

"Don't smell too good, does it," Flebberman said.

"No."

"I imagine this is the first time a shitbird like you has ever smelled so much garbage. You probably think it just disappears every morning, all by itself. Like magic. This is what cities do to the world, shitbird. They fill it up with crap. An' the same with the people who live there. Everything they touch turns ta shit. Now keep movin'."

"Is this where you're going to kill me?"

"That depends on a lotta things, Fancy Pants," said Flebberman. "Right now we got work to do. Or you do, that is. Now go."

"Down there?" Colt pointed down the side of the landfill.

"That's what I said."

Clearly, arguing was useless. Colt scrambled down the embankment, crabwise. He could hear Flebberman sliding along behind him. They descended for perhaps fifty feet, until they were on top of the far reaches of the garbagescape. Colt could scarcely breathe now; the smell was almost strong enough to knock him out. He retched again, and this time he vomited. The contents of his stomach splashed on the ground and onto Flebberman's boots. Flebberman stepped out of the way, cursing. Sour bile from last night's excesses burned Colt's throat and mouth. He wished desperately for some water.

"I should make you lick that off," Flebberman said disgustedly.

"What are we doing here?" Colt croaked.

"I dunno! You tell me. Look around. Take a good look and tell me what you see."

Colt looked; all he saw was garbage. Miles of it.

"What am I supposed to be looking for?" he asked.

"Oh, fer Chrissakes. Look down, shitbird."

Colt looked down. There, at his feet, he saw several flat white stones, some of them broken into pieces. Nearby were scattered what could only have been human remains—a thighbone, part of a skull, other miscellaneous pieces that he couldn't identify. For several moments he made no connection, but then he realized that there could have been only one reason why Flebberman had brought him here, and there could be only one cemetery that he could possibly have been concerned with. It was the Musgroves.

"Oh, my God," he said.

"That's right," said Flebberman. "This is where they ended up! After all that time a restin' in peace where they belonged, this is where they ended up, 'cause a you!"

"I don't understand," said Colt, beginning to panic. "I didn't— they told me they would be reburied in a cemetery! I didn't know this was what Steinbach was going to do! I swear!"

"It wasn't Steinbach," said Flebberman. "Wayne Steinbach knows better than this. He's a decent man. It was one a those idiots he has workin' for him. Took the hundred bucks extra I gave 'em to make sure they got to the county grave, which is where they was supposed to go in the first place, and dumped 'em here instead. His helper told me. Called me last night late and told me what happened 'cause he felt guilty about it. A hundred bucks I gave 'em! An' he took it, an' this is what he did! 'cause it was closer!"

Colt turned. "Flebberman. Mr. Flebberman. Randy. I swear. I didn't mean for this to happen. I—I'll do whatever I have to to make it right. Right now. I promise. Just don't—"

"Yer goddam right you will!" Flebberman roared. There were tears streaming down his face, and he held the gun to Colt's chest. Colt stepped backward apprehensively. "Yer goddam right you will!"

"I know. I know I will. Just—why don't you go after the guy who dumped them here? Isn't this his fault? I'm asking you. Please. Be reasonable."

"Believe me, he's gonna get what's comin' ta him, too. But none a this woulda happened if it wasn't for you. You started it.

Now you finish it. Pick 'em up!" said Flebberman. "Bring 'em up
the hill! Every bit! Every blessed piece!"

"I—"

"Do it!" said Flebberman. "Or else!"

He raised the gun threateningly to Colt's face.

"All right," Colt said. He looked down at the bones. "All right.
I'll do it. Just—give me a minute to—there's something you
don't—"

"No," said Flebberman. He cocked the gun and pressed it to
Colt's temple. "No nothin'. You have five minutes to get all of 'em
back up in the truck, or yer gonna be joinin' 'em."

"Okay," said Colt. He heaved again, bending over, but there was
nothing left in him to throw up. "It's just—I have this thing
about dead bodies. I can't make myself—"

Flebberman's knee came up into his face, knocking him backward into the garbage. He felt the dry stones underneath him, and
he touched something slimy—he didn't dare look to see what it
was. He scrambled upright and tried to throw up yet again, and
once again failed. Blood streamed down his nose—he could feel it
trickling off his upper lip, a small Niagara.

"This is gonna make me really sick," he said quietly.

"I don't care," said Flebberman. "Get to work."

Colt got to work.

23

∎

THE MORGUE

He would remember the wall in the morgue for the rest of his life. He ought to—he'd been staring at it long enough. It was blue tile, with white grout. Well, of course the grout was white. Grout didn't come in any other colors, did it?

Grout. He remembered that in one of the public bathrooms at Cornell, some wag had taken a pen and written "Grout Expectations." On the grout. It was sort of funny. The joke had caught on, and a few days later, someone else had written "A grout time was had by all" in tiny letters, between the tiles. After that, it was like an explosion of grout jokes. "Grout Fishing in America." "Some men are born grout—others have groutness thrust upon them." "No grout about it." Grout jokes. Who knew that college could be so edifying?

Colt was aware of the two people standing behind him, waiting for him to turn around. They'd been waiting for a long time, and they probably thought he was either rude or crazy, but he didn't care. He was prepared to wait them out. One of them was the medical examiner, an elderly man with salt-and-pepper hair.

The other was a woman, black, much younger. An examiner-in-training, perhaps. They both wore white coats and glasses, his small, gold and round, hers large and ovoid. They had met him at the information desk and led him down here, and he'd followed them calmly enough at first, until they ended up before the viewing window. Then he'd turned away, because he knew he just couldn't do it. There was no way. He just couldn't.

"Mr. Hart?" said the older man. "Are you all right?"

Colt felt the man's hand on his shoulder. He shrugged it off, embarrassed at the suggestion that he wasn't man enough to handle this, that he needed consolation. He pulled his jacket on tighter and straightened up.

"I'm fine," he said, in his best stockbroker's voice.

He was only twenty-one that year, but he'd been working on that voice for a while already, and he had it down pretty well. It was a voice that was supposed to inspire confidence in his customers. He'd already used it to talk himself into a job, just a week after graduation. That had been less than a month ago. Three whole weeks into his new, adult life, his past successfully stowed behind him for all time, and then this had to happen. He felt like everything was ruined. Everything. He was going to have to start forgetting all over again, and it was going to be a lot harder now. It was a setback. It was a disgrace. People were bound to find out about it. The wrong people, too—his boss, his customers, his colleagues. And they would never let him forget it, because that was the way those people were. They never let you forget about anything. It was their way of keeping you down, of preventing you from realizing your own dreams—because that would only remind them all the more that they had failed to achieve theirs.

"Think of it this way, son," said the medical examiner. "You're doing her a service. It's the one last thing you can do to help her."

Colt reached into his pocket for a tissue and wiped his nose.

"How come you didn't get my father to do it?" he asked. "This is really his responsibility, isn't it?"

He could feel, rather than hear, the two looking at each other. The woman spoke up.

"We were unable to locate him," she said. "She had you listed as next of kin. We understood that they had separated some time ago."

"Yeah? Well, she was wrong," Colt told the wall. "I'm not her next of kin. I haven't even seen her in almost five years. She's nothing to me. Neither of them are anything to me. I didn't even know they were separated. That's how close I am to them. So, I don't know what the hell *I'm* doing here."

There was a long silence.

"I put myself through school, did you know that?" Colt said to the wall. "I just graduated from Cornell last month. Fifth in my class. I paid for the entire four years by myself. She never offered me anything. *Anything.*" He paused, not sure if any of this was sinking in, not even sure why he was telling them. Surely they didn't care, he knew. They must have had better things to do. They were probably waiting for him to get on with it so they could put her away in her refrigerator, or wherever they were going to stick her.

"Congratulations," said the medical examiner.

"Thank you," said Colt.

There was another long pause.

"She *is* behind glass, sir," said the examiner-in-training. "And she'll be several feet away."

They waited. He still didn't turn around.

"Tell me again where they found her?" Colt asked the wall. "An alley, they said?"

"Ah," said the medical examiner. "I thought the police had . . . gone over that with you."

"I wasn't listening," Colt said. "Tell me again."

He heard the medical examiner clear his throat. "Yes," he said. "It was an alley. Under some boxes."

"Where?"

"Ah—I don't know."

"In the Bowery," murmured the woman.

Colt almost laughed. "The Bowery?" he said. "You mean right around the corner from where I grew up? That's something. That's really something. I wonder if she could see our old apartment when she was shooting up. I wonder if she could see my old bedroom window," he said.

Then he began to cry. He couldn't help himself. It burst out of him like cats from a sack. He leaned his forehead against the cool blue tiles and tried to stop, but he couldn't.

"We understand how difficult this is," said the woman. "Believe me."

"No, you don't," said Colt. "Believe *me*." But his words were unintelligible, because he was crying too hard. He punched himself on the leg to make himself stop. It almost worked. He did it again and again, over and over, several times, until he felt the man's hand on his arm, holding him still. He stopped hitting himself, but it had done the trick. He wasn't crying anymore.

"All right," he said, wiping his nose again. "I just have to know. How bad is it?"

Neither said anything. He could tell they were looking at each other again, trying to decide how best to explain it.

"Come on. Tell me. I want to know. How long was she there?" Colt demanded. "How long was she under those boxes?"

"Two weeks, at least," said the medical examiner. "Maybe a little more."

"Two weeks, maybe a little more," Colt repeated. "Did the—did the rats get at her?"

They didn't answer that one.

"All right," he said. "I'm going to do it now. I'm going to look. Right now."

But still he couldn't bring himself to turn around. He stared at the wall for a while longer. Never, he reflected, had he wished more strongly to be somewhere else. And that was saying something.

"Look," said the woman. "Just think of it as something you're doing for her. A last service. It'll be over in a minute. If you don't ID her, she can't be given a proper burial. She'll be listed as Jane Doe and cremated. She won't have anything but a number. You don't want that, do you?"

"I told you, I don't care. I don't owe her anything."

"Not even for giving birth to you?"

He laughed, surprised at how unpleasant his own voice sounded—more like a bark.

"Please," he said. "I'm sure I was a mistake. An inconvenience. I practically raised myself. Ever since I was little. I had to feed myself, take myself to school. They didn't want me." He blew his nose again. "It's not like they abused me. That almost would have been better. At least that would have showed they knew I was alive." He paused, thinking. "How did you find out who she was, anyway?"

"Fingerprints," said the medical examiner. "She—had a criminal record."

Colt laughed again, this time in astonishment. "Great," he said. "My mother, the convict. What'd she do?"

"You'd have to ask the police," the medical examiner said. "That kind of information has no bearing on our investigation. We simply treated her as a human being, and no less."

Colt sighed.

"Will she have a sheet over her?" he asked. "I don't want to—I don't want to see—"

"You'll only see her face," said the examiner-in-training. "That's all."

"I—I've never seen a dead body before. I don't know—"

"It's all right," said the medical examiner. "It'll be over in a second. You only need to look at her long enough to know that it's her. We're sorry about the—her condition. We've cleaned her up as much as we could."

"You did?"

"Yes, sir."

"Well," said Colt. "Okay. Here I go."

He turned on his heel like an officer on parade. Then he opened his eyes.

The rats had been at her, all right. No amount of cleaning up in the world was going to fix that.

He closed his eyes again.

"Yes," he said. "That's my mother."

Then he fell to the floor.

■ ■ ■

The medical examiner caught him in time, but Colt was too big for him to support on his own, and the examiner-in-training, who had not yet dealt with a fainter, was too slow. Colt slumped to the floor, bumping his forehead on the tile.

"You have to be ready for that," the medical examiner told his protégé. "You never know when they're going to go, so you always stay just behind them. You don't want them to get hurt when they land."

"I'm sorry," said the examiner-in-training. "I haven't seen that before." She knelt and took Colt's head in her lap, patting his face lightly. The medical examiner watched her disapprovingly.

"The poor baby," the examiner-in-training said, feeling Colt's smooth cheeks. "He's barely even old enough to shave."

"Thing is, they can sue us for not catching them," the medical examiner said. "If they get hurt."

He tapped on the window to tell the orderly it was okay to take the body away.

24

—■—

THE COLLISION

Colt was behind the wheel again.

They had nearly gotten stuck in the mud heading out of the dump, and for one terrifying moment he thought Flebberman was going to make him take the bones out of the truck again and carry them. If that had happened, he would have had to kill him right then and there. Or be killed himself. It wouldn't have mattered, at that point. Bringing them up the hill, armload by armload, nearly had been more than he could take.

The tombstones hadn't been so bad, but the few mortal remains of the Musgrove family, stained a deep death-brown by their years in the earth, had clacked sickeningly as he pulled them from the trash and placed them—with a tenderness he did not feel—in the back of the tow truck. He would have preferred to fling them as far from himself as possible. He knew what the consequences of that would have been—"blammo," as Flebberman put it. But he almost did it, anyway.

They left the dirt road behind and got back on the county highway. The truck gave a final lurch as it heaved itself up onto the pavement, like a sea creature making the evolutionary transition to land. Colt groaned aloud as his stomach protested this latest outrage to his equilibrium.

"Not that I give a shit, but you don't look so good," said Flebberman.

Colt didn't answer. He was still sweating, not from exertion but nausea. He'd tried to throw up four more times, again with no results. Now his ribs ached as if he'd been in a wrestling match, and his throat burned with stomach acid.

"Please," he said. "Do you have any water?"

His voice was as ratchety as a bullfrog's. Flebberman, after a dubious moment, reached behind the seat and retrieved a half-empty plastic bottle of soda. Colt guzzled the entire thing in seconds. The soda tasted as if it had been in the truck for two or three months, but it was the best thing Colt had ever drunk in his life.

"Whatsa matter with you?" Flebberman asked. "You sick?"

"I told you," Colt said, tossing the empty bottle to the floor and wiping his mouth. "I have this—thing about bodies. I can't deal with them. They freak me out."

"You mean yer scared of 'em."

He shook his head. "Not just that. Different. I can't explain it. I just—you know how people have irrational fears of things? Like spiders? Or water?"

"Yeah," Flebberman said, settling back in his seat with a self-satisfied air. "Yer scared."

Colt fumed. No, he was not scared of bodies. He just hated them. Ever since that day with his mother's body, when he'd had to look at her, he couldn't even so much as walk into a funeral home without breaking out into a cold sweat. When loved ones of friends passed away, he sent a bunch of flowers and stayed well clear. The only funeral Coltrane Hart would ever attend again was his own.

The roads were deserted, and wet with melting snow. Colt drove slowly.

"Yep," said Flebberman. "Not near so big and tough as you think, Fancy Pants. Izzn't 'at right?"

Colt gritted his teeth and said nothing. He squinted; up ahead, cresting a rise, he could see a car coming in the opposite direction. They had passed plenty of other cars so far, and he had hoped against hope that one of them would be a cop—all to no avail. But this one looked like it had emergency lights on top of it.

Be a cop, he thought. Please be a cop.

Flebberman had seen it, too. He sat up straight and pointed the gun at him again, keeping it low.

"Don't even think about it," he said.

Colt turned to look at Flebberman, letting scorn show on his face. Suddenly, he felt as if he really didn't care what happened to him; he had had it. That was it. He was not going to take anymore. Everyone has a breaking point, and Colt had reached his. Now, even though there was still a gun pointed at him, he felt as if he had the upper hand, because he suddenly no longer cared whether he lived or died. He only wanted to make this little man suffer before he missed his chance.

"Is that thing even loaded?" Colt asked.

"What?" Flebberman shouted disbelievingly. "Of course it's fuckin' loaded! You wanna find out the hard way?"

Colt grinned. He gunned the engine.

"Yeah," he said. "I sure do."

Flebberman's eyes grew wide.

"Go ahead, shoot," said Colt. "I don't give a shit."

He stepped harder on the gas and looked again at the car that was coming at them. It was indeed a police car—a state trooper, from the looks of it. Hallelujah. Colt hoped the trooper was wearing his seat belt, because he was going to need it.

"Hang on, cop," he muttered. "Sorry about this."

In the moments just before the collision, he looked at Flebberman again. The little man's mouth was open wide with panic. He looked like he was trying to yell, but nothing was coming out. Colt grinned again.

"Who's afraid now?" he asked.

Then he swung the wheel hard to the left. There was the bone-jarring force of the vehicles colliding, not head-on but front to end, in the shape of a mason's compass. The noise was so loud that Colt's ears rang with infernal bells, in the split second before he was knocked out against the side window. This was the last thing he was aware of, for a length of time that he could not measure.

25

∎

THE CONFESSION

Later, after the excavators had left, Francie sat in her new wing-back chair, reading the diary in an effort to soothe her nerves. She had covered most of the early years already, trying to read be-tween the understated lines to get a sense of what Marly had ac-tually felt, or at least what she had thought about—but there were precious few clues to go by. None, in fact. Marly reported the events of her life as matter-of-factly as if they were happening to someone else, and as far as her inner life went, the world of her emotions was as mysterious as the surface of Pluto. As the years went by, large gaps of time began to appear between entries—they were still made only on Sundays, but intervals began to oc-cur: first weeks, then months. Francie, frustrated, skipped ahead in the hopes that some great epiphany would have come over Marly Musgrove, or that some kind of authorial instinct would have finally taken over after her own personal pump had been primed; but there was nothing beyond the usual style of entry. "Chopped wood—planted garden—made butter—mended socks."

Francie was beginning to discover, to her disappointment, that there was no literary genius lurking behind the apron, no out-pouring of the soul, no feminine wisdom to be passed down through the ages—which was, more than anything, what she'd been hoping for—some kind of connection between hearts that would span the decades and show her how to be a better woman.

But there was nothing except socks and butter. Marly Mus-grove was just a person, nothing more and nothing less.

■ ■ ■

Francie closed the diary and rubbed her eyes, yawning. It had somehow become afternoon, and the orange sunlight angled thinly through the windows and warmed her slippered feet. The house creaked and moaned as usual, as it did every time the wind shifted or the temperature changed. Just like a ship. Weigh anchor, Francie thought. Set a course for the open sea.

On a whim, she opened the diary near the end. Marly had kept the journal for almost twenty years, finally allowing it to peter out in the early 1870s. The date on her tombstone was 1888. So, that was that. Francie was disappointed to realize that she would never know what Marly's thoughts had been in the days before she died. Nor would she ever know *how* she had died. Would there have been anything revealing in those final moments, perhaps? A deathbed awakening of higher consciousness? Some kind of state-ment that it had all been worth it, that one had only to surrender to life's pain to find its sweet reward?

There was absolutely nothing like that. On the last day Marly had seen fit to record, she had helped a cow give birth to a calf and begun to empty the house in preparation for spring cleaning.

But then Francie saw, to her surprise, that there was one final entry made in a different handwriting. It slanted the other way—which Francie recognized immediately as being made by someone left-handed. She sat up straighter, her interest renewed.

It was a single entry, but a long one. Someone had finally written her true thoughts in this book—but it wasn't Marly.

The entry was dated May 16, 1888. She read:

I must unburden myself here, in this book, in which my departed Mother had undertaken to tell the simple story of her days, and allow it to bear silent witness to what I have done. I cannot go to my grave with this secret, for its weight is too much to bear, though it was not myself as a grown woman who committed the crime I am about to relate, but myself as a little girl. I hope that this fact, more than any other, will give the Reader reason to seek some room in his heart to forgive me, although I know that even the allowance which we accord the carelessness of youth knows its limits, and that I have far, far surpassed those, generous as they may be.

Nearly thirty years ago, we had a brother, Henry, whose remains are buried in the family plot next to his brothers and sisters. When he was just a year old, Henry wandered away from the house and drowned in the stream. I had been watching him, though my parents had not instructed me to do so and did not know that I did this. I was watching him not to protect him, but to wait for opportunity. Evil child that I was! Whence came this black-heartedness in me? I shall never know, nor shall I ever forgive myself. It was a childish notion that took root in me and grew in twisted fashion, a demon plant whose seed flourished because of something I saw, and one that poisoned all the rest of my days. If I had the courage, I would have taken my own life years ago. Oh, but that I had! But I shall live out my appointed days and meet my judgment when the time is right. Having taken one little life already, I cannot take another— though it be a life that has no value to it.

I drowned little Henry. Now it is written, I cannot un-write it. Why I did this is hard to tell, even to myself. But I must try. I had thought something happened, a year earlier, to get my mother with child. A man had come to Adencourt, a man of dark temperament and unhealthy character—and I had seen evidence of this in both his body and his soul. He was the medicine salesman, McNally, and he brought great harm on my family, and might have brought more, had my mother not seen fit to bring her own punishment on him. I will not write that deed here, for that is a matter for her own judgment, and it is not for such a one as me to condemn her, for what she did was no doubt right

I thought, simple, foolish idiot that I was, that Henry was the child of McNally, not of my father. He was the only child of us to have yellow hair, like McNally's. The rest of us were dark. And so I decided that something must be done to get rid of him. All was not right in our house. We had been plagued with misfortune after misfortune. Something was eating away at us, I knew not what—until McNally came, and Mother did what she did, and then Henry came some months after. And I, nine years old, reasoned that Henry must be done away with. When he was a year old I took him to the creek and held him under, until he stopped his strug-gles, and saw that another Musgrove child had left this earth and gone on too early to his reward; a year in which I had hesitated, and planned, and waited for confirmation that this plan was either right or wrong. I waited also for my courage to gather itself, and on one dark day, after Henry had already learned to walk, it did. When his little body surfaced and collected in the eddy of the great boulder across the road, I had already come back to the house, and taken pains to conceal the evidence of what I had done—for already I knew that I had made a terrible mistake, one that could never be unmade. Hamish was the one who found him, and Father

brought his little body up from the river, and we laid him to
his rest. The shame that burned in my heart from that day
to this has left a mark on my soul that I feel must be visible
to all.

Oh, Henry, Henry! I hope, when we shall meet in the
hereafter, that your little soul has the wisdom to look into
my heart and see what purpose hid there, not out of a desire
for evil, but for good, and that you shall not judge me too
harshly. But I know also that should your desire be for
vengeance, it shall be yours. I shall not attempt to escape my
fate. Nor could I leave this house for the last time, on the occasion of the funeral of our mother, without dropping, if
only for a moment, this weight that I have carried for so
long. Evil is the heart of woman! Evil is the heart of a girl-
child who had seen too much, and become affected by it,
through no design of her own! How I have suffered, will
continue to suffer, all the rest of my miserable days, and
throughout eternity!

Ellen Musgrove

Well, thought Francie.

She closed the book and set it quickly on the floor beside her.
Her heart was racing, as if she'd been running; she realized that
she'd been holding her breath as she read, and she let it out.

Henry's tombstone would have been one of the illegible ones,
she thought. And Ellen's name wasn't to be found in the cemetery
either, unless it too, was, illegible—but then, she was one of the
few children who had survived into adulthood. She must have
been buried somewhere else, then. Not here.

And she was a murderer.

Francie picked up the diary again and reread the entry. She
thought she had it after that: Ellen had believed, at one time,
that her mother had been raped by this McNally. And there was

something about McNally the girl feared—maybe something more than the childish fear of strangers. So Ellen had drowned her little brother because she thought he was McNally's child, and because she had hoped this final sacrifice would bring an end to the suffering of the Musgroves. Francie thought she understood what that meant—it was all for the children, the others that were lost. So many had died that it must have seemed to the little girl as if they really were being punished for something—as if, lurking behind the clouds, there was a host of irritable deities who had to be appeased, or they would make their wrath felt in terrifyingly random ways. It was not the first time in human history that the ignorant had made this desperate bid to assure their own futures, she thought. Think of the Aztecs, cutting out the hearts of the best and brightest of their youth; think of the Puritans at Salem.

Ellen had written that Henry's body had collected in the water near the "great boulder." Francie hadn't yet been to explore the river, but she remembered a large rock peeking up over the road. She put her boots and jacket on now and traipsed down the driveway, to visit the scene of this crime.

In Indiana, Francie remembered, Michael and she had played on the banks of a creek much like this one—for this was truly a creek, not really a river, at least not anymore. Somewhere near the source of this water, a dam must have been installed, for it seemed inconceivable that such a feeble trickle of water could have carved out this whole valley. In Indiana, they'd caught crawdads and minnows, and made little boats out of leaves, and waded back and forth in exploration of the creek's bed. It was easy to imagine the Musgrove children doing the same thing, one hundred fifty years ago. Less easy to imagine was herself doing to Michael what Ellen said she had done to Henry. To see that little face looking up at her from under the surface, terrified and uncomprehending, and feel the thrashing of his chubby limbs growing weaker and weaker, until finally they stopped—no. Not even in her darkest moments could she ever have imagined herself doing such a thing.

Ellen Musgrove was a monster.

The river was about fifty feet wide, though once, she could see, it had been wider, and probably deeper. Rocks like dinosaur eggs lined the bottom, having tumbled over each other these last ten thousand years to end up here. It wouldn't have been comfortable wading—there would have been a lot of twisted ankles. The trees flittered like the hands of a mute, their dry finger-bones clacking in the wind. She found the boulder Ellen must have meant—no one could ever have moved it, not without setting men and equipment to the task. This rock would have been sitting here long before the first people appeared, in the path of the receding glaciers. It would have seen everything. Francie dug her toes into a crevice and pulled herself onto its back.

It was a great, large, warm rounded rock, its top clear of snow, and if the water had been deeper it would have made a perfect diving platform. From her perch, feeling like a princess on an elephant, Francie looked down into the stream. Indeed, the current swirled into a pool that had carved out a place at the base of the rock, and only in this place did the water lie still, becalmed, filled at the moment with small sticks that had followed the same path as Henry's body.

How horrible it must have been for them all. She could imagine the boy, limp and dripping, being plucked from the water, carried across the road and into the house, the wailing of the family members filling the air—yet again. Each young death would have been a fresh blow to them, each one more than they could bear. And Ellen, the nine-year-old murderess. Would she have cried, too? Did she know what she was doing, or was she just responding to some ancient and unconscious urge to save her tribe from yet more suffering, fulfilling a need to eliminate the strange and the unwanted? She had done what she believed was right. Francie understood that much to be true. Beyond that she understood nothing.

This poor family, she thought. How these people must have cried. They had all suffered—but no one but the diary knew of the burden that Ellen had carried all her life. The diary—and now Francie.

Suddenly, Francie remembered the butterfly pin she'd found in the secret room under the stairs. It had been woven from blond hair. She had assumed it was a girl's, because it was so long and pretty—but she realized now that it must be Henry's. His had been the only blond hair in the family, Ellen wrote. It would have been cut from his head before he was committed to the earth, and woven into a remembrance of him. Ellen must have been the one who placed it down below the stairs—along with the diary, and her old rag dolls, and that strange bottle of snake oil. She must have done so in the hope that someone would find it someday. And when that happened, what did she hope for then? Did she hope that finally her spirit would be released, because her guilt had finally been revealed? Had she lacked the courage to confess to anyone before her own death, choosing instead to let the diary do the confessing for her?

"Ellen," said Francie aloud, to the water. "How could you do it to him? How could you?"

She received no answer, except the gentle trickle of the frigid water over the egglike stones, which seemed once again to be an echo of her voice, in some strange, liquid language.

"I can't forgive you," Francie whispered. "It's not my place to forgive you. There's no one left who can do that, Ellen. And even if I could, I wouldn't. How could you do it? How could you kill that baby?"

The water was whispering explanations back to her—explanations she could almost understand, with her poet mind. But whatever it was saying was too faint, and too old, to hear.

26

FORGIVENESS

In the dream, or perhaps nightmare—or perhaps it was real—
Colt was sitting in a courtroom. He knew that he was dead because it looked just like a courtroom on earth, except there were
no walls, ceiling, or floor. All around him was an impenetrable
black nothingness, as if he had ended up in some part of the universe where stars had not reached yet. They were floating in a
void, and a void was precisely what Colt had always imagined
death to be—just a big black bowl of nothing, with a helping of
nothing on the side. Nothing with nothing in it.

Yet here he was, sitting at the defendant's table. So he was
wrong—there was *not* nothing. And there was a judge in front of
him. Or, rather, there was *someone*, sitting up on the bench—but
he couldn't make out any features. In fact, the judge didn't appear
to have a body at all. He—or she, or it—was just an amorphous
black shadow, invisible against the nothingness. Yet still he could
sense its presence.

"How do you plead?" asked the shadow.

"Plead to what?" Colt said. "I didn't do anything! This is all Flebberman's fault!"

The shadow grunted knowingly.

"If you didn't do anything," it asked him, in a suspiciously familiar voice, "then why are you *here*?"

Colt felt suddenly short of breath.

"I'm ready to wake up now," he said.

There were whispers, as if the shadow was conferring with someone else.

"All righty," it said brightly. "You can wake up. But we'll see you back here soon, and we'll expect an answer then."

"Oh, no, you won't," said Colt. "I'm not coming back."

"Yes, you are," said the judge's voice. "You're not as slick as you think you are, you know."

■ ■ ■

When Colt awoke, he didn't know if it was morning or night. Shades were drawn over the windows. He knew only that he had been asleep for a long time. Scant illumination came from an open doorway. He knew there was someone with him, but he couldn't see who.

"Hello?" Colt called. He was shocked at how pathetic and weak his voice seemed. Was this the same "stockbroker's voice" that he'd been honing for the last twenty years? He sounded more like a Cub Scout with emphysema.

He heard soft footsteps, and a face appeared in his field of vision. It was a woman. A nurse, with shoulder-length gray hair, and a pink sweater on over her white uniform.

"You're awake, finally," she said. "Hi there, Coltrane. My name is Wanda."

Colt struggled to speak. "Dead?" he managed to cough.

Wanda smiled. "No, you're not dead. You're in the hospital in Allentown, Pennsylvania. You had a car accident on the highway, and they had to bring you all the way here because you were in pretty bad shape. Do you understand¿"

Colt nodded, relieved. So the courtroom *was* a dream.

"Throat hurts," he said.

"You had a tube in, that's why. You were in surgery to repair your arm. You might find it hard to talk for a few hours yet."

"Arm¿"

"It's broken in three places. They had to put some pins in, to hold everything together. Your left arm. Don't try to move it. How do you feel¿"

"Bad," he said. "Judge¿"

"I'm sorry¿"

He shook his head, as if to say "Never mind."

"Spine¿" he said.

"Your spine¿ What about it¿"

"Paralyzed¿"

"No," said the nurse. "You're not paralyzed. Can you feel your toes¿" She reached down and tickled his bare feet. To his immense relief, Colt could. Of all the things he feared going wrong with him, paralysis was at the top of the list of fears, followed by severe burns, followed by flesh-eating disease. He wasn't burned, and he didn't feel as though he were being eaten. If all he had was a broken arm, he'd gotten off relatively light.

But what was he doing here at all¿

Oh, yes. He remembered now. Flebberman. The dump. The accident. The police car.

"Cop¿" he said, coughing again. His throat felt as if it had been scrubbed with steel wool. "Cop hurt¿"

"The trooper you hit, you mean¿"

Colt nodded.

"He was a little banged up," Wanda told him. "But he's all right. And the man who was in the truck with you is all right, too."

"Not dead¿"

"No, my goodness," said the nurse. "He's not *dead*."

"Shit," said Colt.

Wanda appeared startled. "Maybe you shouldn't talk about it," she said. "Not to me, I mean. The police are waiting outside to ask you some questions. They've been hanging around. When you feel ready."

"Ready," said Colt. "Ready now."

Wanda raised the head of the bed, which made his head swim. She held a cup of water for him, and he sipped from a straw, coughing again with the effort of swallowing—much more difficult than he remembered it.

"How long out?"

"You were out for about a day," Wanda said. "You were unconscious when they brought you in, and you started to come to, but they put you out again for surgery. It's the day after you came in. You've been here just over twenty-four hours."

"Ready," said Colt. "Cops."

"If you're sure. I'll bring them in now."

■ ■ ■

Wanda left, and a moment later two policemen entered, large, muscular men in the dark gray uniforms of the Pennsylvania State Police, with bulky pistols strapped to their sides and wide-brimmed hats resting precariously atop their heads. One had a mustache, the other was clean-shaven and baby-faced. They introduced themselves as Witherspoon and Riller.

"You're Coltrane Hart?" Witherspoon said. He was the one with the mustache.

Colt winced. "Too loud," he said.

"Please keep your voices down, officers," said the nurse. "He has a concussion. That's why the shades are drawn. He'll be very sensitive to both light and noise."

"Sorry," said Witherspoon.

After glancing from Colt to the troopers doubtfully, the nurse left. Witherspoon leaned over until his face was inches from Colt's ear.

"You hit my car," he said, in a stage whisper.

"Sorry," said Colt. "Flebberman, gun. Kill me."

"Yeah, we know," said Witherspoon, straightening up. "I just wanted to let you know that was a new car. Brand-new. I just had it waxed."

"Come on, Ed," said Riller.

"Really sorry. Kidnapped me," Colt told them. He coughed. "Water?" he said hopefully.

The baby-faced Riller picked up the cup from the nightstand and held it under his chin. Colt sucked at the straw again, the water soothing his ruined throat, until it was gone.

"Thanks," said Colt. To Witherspoon he said, "Didn't mean to hurt you."

"But you can confirm that you hit me on purpose?"

Colt nodded. "Life in danger," he said.

"I figured. Mr. Hart, can you explain to us exactly what was going on there between you and Mr. Flebberman? We haven't been able to figure it all out, and he's not talking."

"Kidnapped," Colt said. "From my apartment. At gunpoint."

"Do you know Mr. Flebberman?"

Colt nodded.

"Was this a personal thing, then?"

"Oh, yeah," he said. "Very."

"I see." Witherspoon and Riller exchanged glances.

"The gun wasn't loaded, you know," said Riller. "Of course, there's no way you could have known that. But there were no rounds in the cylinder."

Colt felt a hot tide of shame rising up from his chest and into his face. Not loaded? He had been duped by an unloaded gun? "You sure?"

"Yeah, we're sure. It's still a crime, though. We're just trying to determine exactly which charges to file against Mr. Flebberman," Witherspoon said.

"All of them," said Colt.

"All of them?"

"Prison time. Death sentence. Gas chamber."

"The law doesn't make that provision for kidnapping, sir," said Riller. "But he is in deep trouble. Transporting you across a state line was his biggest mistake. That's when it went federal. The FBI will be wanting to talk to you."

Colt's eyes widened in delight. "Federal?" he repeated. "Good! *Big* trouble."

"Yes," said Witherspoon. "Big trouble. What we'd also like to know about, though, is the human remains in the back of the truck. What, uh . . . what's the story there?"

Colt felt himself growing ill again at the thought of those slimy bones. He closed his eyes until the feeling faded.

"He made me," he said. "Pick them up. Touch them. From the dump."

"Were you fellows out grave-robbing or something?" asked Witherspoon.

"No! Told you. Forced me. The dump!"

"You got the remains from the dump?"

Colt nodded.

"What were they doing *there*?" asked Riller.

"Mistake," Colt said. "Not my mistake. But he blamed me."

"Someone else dumped them there?"

"Yes. Exactly." He wanted to explain further, but his throat had begun to feel as though it was closing up on him. He shook his head. At that moment the nurse came in again and shot a worried look at the troopers.

"You boys should leave," she said. "He needs to rest."

"All right. We'll have to come back to this," said Riller, sighing.

"Sorry," said Colt.

"Thanks for your cooperation, sir."

The troopers left. Wanda the nurse gave him something for the pain, and he slept again.

■ ■ ■

"Well?" inquired the shadowy judge, in that same familiar voice. "Has the defendant made up his mind?"

Colt looked around. He was dismayed to find himself back in the courtroom. Glancing down at himself, he saw that he was no longer in his hospital gown, but wearing one of his good work suits.

"Wait a goddamn minute here!" he said. "I don't even know what I'm charged with!"

The judge sighed.

"If you really want to go through this charade, we will," he said—it was definitely a man's voice, at least, though nothing about him had become any more distinct; he was still just a dark shadow behind the bench. "The list of charges is quite long, though. It would take several months to read out loud."

Colt laughed in disbelief. "Several *months*?" he repeated. "Come on. You've got the wrong guy here. I think you think I'm someone else."

"No, you're the right man, Mr. Hart. We know all about you."

"In that case," said Colt, "I want a lawyer."

"You have a lawyer," said the judge. "He's standing right next to you."

Colt looked to his right. There, also wearing a suit, his hair neatly slicked back, was Joe.

"Hiya, Coltie," said Joe. "How's tricks?"

"Joe?" he said, incredulous.

"That's my name," said Joe. "Don't wear it out."

"Joe, you're not a lawyer!" Colt said. "Come on! This is ridiculous!"

"I wasn't a lawyer on Earth, but I am here," Joe said. "We all have different jobs." He leaned in to whisper confidentially. "We really don't have time to get into everything," he said. "Not now. Just go with it. I'll explain later."

Colt began to panic.

"What about a jury?" he asked. He was just stalling for time, and he could tell the judge knew it—but Joe pointed off to his right.

"There," he said.

In the jury box that had suddenly materialized, Colt saw twelve people—seven adults in varying stages of middle age, all wearing nineteenth-century costumes, and five children, some of them infants.

"Now, wait just a frigging minute!" Colt said. "What kind of selection process do you people go through here? This is insane! You can't have babies on a jury!"

"The laws here are a little different," the judge said. "You'll figure them out eventually."

"He is *so* guilty," said one of the babies.

"Damn straight he is!" said one of the men, who had an iron-gray handlebar mustache. "String him up!"

"Patience, Captain Musgrove," said the judge.

"Patience my ass," snorted the Captain. "I changed my mind. I want to testify. I don't want to be on the jury anymore."

"Everyone will have their turn," the judge said. "I promise."

"Now hold on!" said Colt. "He can't be a jury member *and* a witness! That's not fair, even if I did dig him up!"

"So you admit it?" the judge said, pouncing. "Ha! Let the record show that—"

"Ah, hold on just a second there, Your Honor," said Joe. "Strictly speaking, he didn't dig up the Captain. The Captain is buried in Gettysburg."

"Next to a damned Rebel, yet!" the Captain roared. "The indignity of it!" He turned and glared at the woman next to him, but she ignored him, looking calmly ahead, saying nothing. The other jury members tittered to themselves at this outburst. Disapproval radiated from the direction of the bench.

"What—wait a—I don't admit anything!" said Colt. "I want to wake up again, right now!"

The judge sighed. There was the sound of voices conferring again, and then a hammer banging, though no hammer was in sight.

"So ordered," he said. "But you're running out of chances here, Coltrane. You're going to have to go through with this sooner or later, you know."

■ ■ ■

When Colt awoke again in the hospital room, still with no idea what time of day it was, he could sense that again there was someone else in there with him. He squinted into the gloom and recognized a familiar shape.

"Francie?" he asked.

"Hello, Colt," said Francie, getting up from the chair by his bed-side, where she'd been curled up, waiting. At first, Colt could barely make out her features. Then details swam into focus, and he saw in the dim light that she was wearing a flannel shirt and jeans, her hair pulled back into a ponytail. Her expression chilled him; she seemed as detached as if she was at a stranger's funeral. "Thought I'd stop by to see how you were doing. The police called me to let me know. I—I'm sorry this happened to you. I knew Randy was mad at you, but I didn't know he was *this* mad."

"God, I've been having the most terrible dreams. What time is it?"

She looked at the clock on the nightstand. "It's one A.M.," she said.

"I'm losing track of time," he said. "I have a concussion."

"That's what they said."

"How—how did you get here? Michael drive you?"

"I drove myself," she said. "In my new pickup truck. Michael's in Denver. Or somewhere. I don't know where he is, actually. I threw him out."

"You bought a pickup truck?" he asked.

"Maybe now isn't the best time to bring this up, but you did go away and leave me without a car. In the middle of the country. That wasn't very considerate of you."

A light went on in Colt's head. "Did you buy it from Flebberman?"

"Yes."

"So *that's* how he found out where our apartment is. He said you'd written him a check." Colt glared at her. "He kidnapped me," he said. "Did you know that? That son of a bitch snuck into the apartment and pointed a gun at me. And he hit me with it! In the face!"

"He *was* pretty upset, last I saw him," Francie said. "But the police said the gun wasn't loaded."

"As if that mattered! Did you know what he was planning to do to me?"

"Of course not!" said Francie. "I knew he was going to do something, but I didn't think it would go that far."

"I bet you hoped it would," Colt said bitterly. "I bet you wish he'd killed me."

"Colt, please," said Francie. "That's not true."

"Huh."

"Look. It's late, and I want to go home and go to bed. I just wanted to see how your arm was. They said it was pretty bad. I guess they were understating it a little."

Colt hadn't even looked at his arm yet—he hadn't been able to bring himself to. He glanced down fleetingly now and saw that it was encased in plaster, and there were two tubes coming out of the cast, each running with a yellowish fluid. Revolted, he looked away.

"Jesus," he said. "Are those things coming out of *me?*"

"They're drainage tubes, the nurse said. They keep you from building up fluid under your incisions."

"They look pretty gruesome. Listen, Francie. When this goes to court, what you have to say is going to be important. You have to tell them Flebberman was acting crazy. He *was* acting crazy beforehand, wasn't he? I know he came over to the house while they were digging up the—while they were doing the digging. Ranting and raving and so forth. Steinbach told me. *And* he threatened to kill me."

"Well, Colt—you have to see things from his point of view to really understand what was going through his mind."

Colt stared at her in disbelief. *"His point of view?"* he said.

"I mean—I'm not saying what he did was right, but—"

"But you understand why he did it."

"You acted with total disregard, Colt," said Francie. "Total disregard."

Colt laughed up at the ceiling. "I don't believe this. My own wife thinks that the guy who kidnapped me at gunpoint was justified. Holy shit!"

"Colt," said Francie. "I'm sorry you're hurt. I'm not saying you deserved it. But you did have something like this coming. And you have for a long time."

Colt was stunned into speechlessness. He looked at Francie to see if she was joking, but her face was clear and calm. Flebberman had said the same thing, he remembered. So they were all in league against him.

"Oh, go to hell," he said. "Get out."

"And I still want a divorce," said Francie. "So I would appreciate it if you would stop referring to me as 'your wife.' "

"You'll get your goddam divorce. Don't you worry about that."

"Thank you."

"You're nuts, Francie, you know that?" Colt said. "Totally nuts."

"No, Colt, I am not nuts," Francie said, as she headed for the door, "at least not according to the way I see things. Maybe in your world I am, but then I never belonged in your world. And you never belonged in mine."

"You got that right!"

"And let me tell you one other thing," Francie said.

"What."

"This could all stop right now, with you. You can make this all go away."

"How?"

"Forgive him."

"Forgive him? Francie, you don't know what the fuck you're talking about! I don't want to forgive him! I want to kill him!"

"Then it's not going to stop," said Francie from the doorway. "It's going to go on forever. I can tell you that right now."

"Nurse!" Colt shouted, coughing, his throat sore again. "Nurse!"

The nurse came bustling in—a different one, a black woman with rustling starched skirts. "I hear you, honey," she said. "I hear you. What is it?"

"Get that crazy bitch out of here," Colt said.

"Who? Your wife? Why you wanna get her out?"

"She's *not* my wife," Colt said. "She's my ex-wife."

"I was just leaving anyway," Francie said.

"Maybe you better, miss, wife or no wife," said the nurse. "We can't have him gettin' too upset."

"No, we can't have that, can we?" Francie said. She left the room without a backward glance.

"My, my," said the nurse. "Can't have this. Can't have this at all." She deftly injected something into the IV tube in his arm, and immediately Colt felt his head begin to swim.

"What's your name?" he asked woozily.

"Betty."

"Betty? What is that stuff you guys keep giving me?"

"You sleep now, honey," said Betty. "It's just a little special somethin'."

"Did you whip it up yourself?" Colt asked, drowsing off. "Or is it a pharma . . ."

He slept again.

■ ■ ■

"No," Colt said. "I refuse to be back here." He turned to see Joe by his side again, wearing his suit. "Joe," he said, "tell them I refuse to be back here."

"He heard you," Joe said wearily.

"That's really too bad," said the judge—he, too, sounded tired now, though how a shadow could grow tired Colt had no idea. "It's time to get started. First witness?"

"Wait a minute," said Colt. "There are no witnesses! There is no trial! I question the authority of this court! I question you!"

There was dead silence. He could feel the shadow scrutinizing him.

"Hm," it said. "That's interesting. What about me do you question, exactly?"

"I question your ethics," said Colt. "And I question your motives. You won't even show your face! You're nothing but a shadow!"

"Colt," said Joe warningly, "be careful."

"Shut up, Joe. You're fired."

Joe stood up abruptly, snapping his briefcase shut. "Best news I've heard all day," he snarled. "Now I can go fishing. See ya when I see ya, Coltie." And, in the blink of an eye, he was gone.

Colt gulped.

"So," said the shadow, "you want to see what I look like, is that it? You want to know who I am?"

"You got it," said Colt. He stood and crossed his arms, the left one of which was miraculously back to normal, with a brave defiance he did not feel. "Or I'm outa here. And nothing can stop me."

He could hear murmurs coming from the jury box, but he didn't even look in their direction.

"Very well," said the shadow.

The darkness lifted slowly. As it did so, astonishment came over Colt's face.

"Oh, my God," he said. "*You?*"

"Yes, me," said the judge. "Who the hell else did you think it would be?"

Colt blinked several times, but his eyes were not playing tricks on him. He was looking directly into his own face—and into his own eyes. The judge was him, and he was the judge. And the longer he looked at himself, the more he forgot who was who.

"Is this hell?" he asked miserably.

The judge, smiling, nodded.

■ ■ ■

"Yup," he said. "Sure is."

When he awoke a third time, it was to the sound of voices in the hallway. Now he could see daylight trickling in under the shades, and he raised the head of the bed with the remote control. There were two women arguing outside his room.

"Hey," he called. "What's going on out there?"

Yet another nurse stuck her head in the open door.

"Mr. Hart," she said. "There's a woman here to see you. She says she needs to talk to you right away."

"Well, who is it?"

The other woman in the hallway also stuck her head in. Colt didn't recognize her, but he thought he had a pretty good idea of who she might be. In the half-light he could see a flowery print housedress under a fake fur coat. Tears were streaming down the woman's face.

"He din't mean it!" she said.

"Ma'am, you cannot disturb the patients," said the nurse. "Now if you'll just—"

"It's all right," said Colt resignedly. "Let her in."

"All right. But the children have to stay outside."

"Children?" Colt said. "What children?"

"You three siddown and shuddup," said the woman over her shoulder. "Momma'll be right out." Colt could hear small voices raised in protest, and the exasperated sigh of the nurse.

"Not even supposed to be on this floor," she said. "I don't know how you got them this far."

"Please," said the woman to Colt, standing in the doorway. "He din't mean to do nothin' but scare ya!"

"Mrs. Flebberman, I presume," said Colt.

"I—yeah—yes, sir. I'm Randall's wife."

"Charmed."

"I'm here t'ask ya—quit it!" She said this in the direction of her feet. Colt could see a small pair of hands reaching through the doorway and clinging to her ankles. Mrs. Flebberman shook herself loose and came further into the room, wiping her cheeks with the back of her hand. "Please," she began again. "Randy don't have a mean bone in his body. He just—"

"He could have fooled me," Colt said. "I'm not sure we're even supposed to be talking about this."

The woman nodded, crying harder. "I know it," she said. "But I had to come down. It's just—Mr. Hart. I'm here ta make a—a *emotional plea*!"

"An emotional plea?"

"I got four kids," she said, gasping. "If he goes ta jail, I don't know what we're gonna do! We're gonna be broke!"

Colt rolled his eyes. "Don't you think he should have thought of that sooner?" he asked. "Before he decided to break into my apartment and kidnap me with a gun? Jesus, lady! Your husband isn't too bright, is he?"

The woman sniffled.

"Maybe he din't go ta college like you," she said. "But—he was upset. Real upset. He never meant ta hurt ya. He told me he was just gonna make you put them bodies back in the earth, where they belonged. And then—"

"And then what? What did he think was going to happen next? I would just forget about the whole thing?"

"I know, I know!" said Jennifer Flebberman. "I ast him not to do it! I told him it was crazy, but he was so damn mad, he wouldn't listen! I never seen him like that before!"

At that moment a child crept into the room then, a toddler, followed by another. The nurse who had been standing in the hall said, "Now that's it. Really. You must leave at once, or I'm going to call security."

"I'm goin'," said Jennifer Flebberman. "Just—please understand. Mr. Hart. Sir. Please. If he goes ta jail, we're gonna lose everything. Everything."

"And you want me to drop the charges," said Colt. "Just like that. I've been traumatized within an inch of my life, and I'm laying here in a hospital bed with half a ton of metal in my arm—my *broken* arm—and I'm just supposed to forget about it?"

"We'll do anything," said Jennifer Flebberman. "Anything you say. We'll give you whatever you want. Just—"

"Ma'am," said a deep male voice in the hallway, which Colt took to be that of a security guard. "If you don't leave the premises immediately, I'm going to escort you off."

"All right, I'm goin'," said Jennifer Flebberman.

"What I want is justice!" said Colt.

"All he wanted was fer them ta be left in peace!" Jennifer said, before she stepped out into the hallway again. Colt could hear her rounding up her children, all of whom were crying now. He flung his good arm over his eyes and shuddered. Good Lord. What a mess.

"Please!" Jennifer Flebberman shouted one more time, as she was heading down the hall.

The nurse came in again—this time he didn't even bother to see what she looked like. As soon as you got to know one, she was replaced by another. It was hurting his head to keep up.

"Sorry about that, Mr. Hart," she said. "She sort of snuck by us."

"Nurse," said Colt. "No more visitors. None. Please."

"All right, Mr. Hart," said the nurse. "We'll put a sign on your door that you should be left alone."

"That," he said, "would be greatly appreciated."

"Do you want some more pain medication?"

"Jesus, no," he said. "It's giving me nightmares."

"I'll speak to the doctor about changing it to something else."

"Never mind," said Colt. "I'd rather suffer than take the chance of going back to that courtroom."

"What courtroom?" she asked.

But Colt, exhausted, had fallen asleep again, this time on his own.

27

JUDGMENT

Colt was in the hospital in Allentown for a week. He continued to refuse more pain medication; his arm felt like molten lead was seeping through it, searing him from the inside out, but he had decided to put up with it rather than take more drugs. The result of this was that he was given to letting out screams at unpredictable moments. He had begun to feel as though he had some form of Tourette's syndrome. But he remained firm, and refused all further needles.

The police came to see him one more time, and this time he gave them a full account of everything that had happened, beginning with the moment he'd woken up on the couch. He talked for an hour, screaming intermittently, making sure they got down every detail. Flebberman was still not talking, they said. He was sitting in a holding cell at the county jail, and all he did was cry. They hadn't gotten a word out of him.

"Well, I'm telling you the truth," Colt told them. "I'm not—gaah!—making any of this up."

"We don't think you're making this up," Riller assured him.

"Everything we've found fits with what you told us."

"So you can put him away."

"Well, he'll be arraigned," said Witherspoon. "And unless he pleads guilty there will be a trial. But so far, like we said, he hasn't been talking. He's not cooperating at all."

"He's scared, that's why. He knows he's going down for a long time. Oh, Jesus!" he shouted.

"He certainly feels guilty about something," Riller said, edging away from the bed.

Colt stifled another scream, succeeding in turning it into a groan, and waited to catch his breath.

"How long could he get put away for?" he asked.

The troopers shrugged. "That's not really our area," said Witherspoon. "That would be up to the judge."

"Yeah, I know. I just wondered, you know, in your experience . . ."

"It would be a long time," said Riller. "You can bet on that."

"But he might not, too. Right? With plea bargains and all that kind of stuff?"

"You really would have to wait and see what comes up during sentencing," said Witherspoon. "Remember, it's federal now. Those guys don't slap you on the wrist."

"Yeah," said Colt. "The thing is, his wife came to see me."

"She did?" The cops were surprised.

"Yeah. Asking me for—for leniency."

Witherspoon and Riller looked at each other and then at Colt.

"He's got four kids," Colt said.

"Yeah, well, he shoulda thought about them before he committed the crime," said Riller.

"That's what I said."

"You dug up his family cemetery, right? That's what happened?"

"I ordered it done, yeah. Ouch!"

"People can get funny about that kind of thing," said Witherspoon. "Some people are really touchy about their families."

"Yeah," said Riller.

"So he could plead that he was temporarily deranged," said Colt. "Right? Or something like that?"

"Usually that only works in lovers' quarrels," Riller said. "I never heard of a case like this before, actually. It's pretty unusual. There's been some stuff about it in the papers."

"There has?" Colt was surprised. "What kind of stuff?"

"Just articles. It's a weird one. No one's ever heard of anything like it before."

"Yeah, well, that goes for me, too," Colt said.

"It would depend on if it goes to a jury," said Witherspoon. "If he pleads not guilty by reason of temporary insanity or something like that. It would be up to the jury to decide if they believe him or not."

"*We* really can't advise you on anything," said Riller. "*Our* job is to collect information and enforce the law."

"But if this guy's a dangerous criminal," said Witherspoon, "and you can get him put away, then you have an obligation to do that. For the good of society."

"Yeah. I know," said Colt.

"You take care, Mr. Hart," said Riller. "We'll see you again."

■ ■ ■

Each day, the doctor who had performed the surgery appeared to check on Colt. He shone a penlight in his eyes, frowned at his arm, and examined the fluid that ran from the drainage tubes into the quart-sized plastic bags hanging from the lower arms of the IV stand. The doctor seemed impossibly young, even though he had already lost most of his hair, and there was a liberal sprinkling of freckles across his face that made him look a little like Howdy Doody.

After his last examination, Dr. Doody said, "You're looking good, Mr. Hart. Your bones are knitting, and there's no infection. I think you can probably go home this weekend."

"What day is it?" Colt asked. "I keep losing track of time in here."

"Friday. You could be discharged on Sunday, maybe."

"When can I go back to work? Monday?"

"Monday?" The man laughed. "Are you kidding?"

"No. I'm not kidding."

The doctor stopped laughing. "What is it you do that's so wonderful you can't wait to get back to it?" he asked. "Most people would be asking how long they could get away with staying home."

"Stocks," said Colt. "I'm a trader."

"Oh, yeah? Trader, huh? You got any hot tips?" asked Dr. Doody. "I hear the only way to make money on the market is to play with big money. Millions. Otherwise, they say it's hardly worth it."

"Depends on what you mean by 'worth it,' " Colt said.

The doctor grinned. "Well, lessee. I have about two hundred and fifty thousand dollars in student loans to pay back. And they're projecting that in the next five years my malpractice premiums will outstrip my earnings by . . . well, I forget how much, but it's not like it even matters. Once you have more money going out than coming in, it's time to get a new job. Basically, I need to make a million dollars as soon as possible." Dr. Doody laughed again. "Any ideas?"

"Yeah," Colt said. "Buy low and sell high."

Dr. Doody's smile disappeared.

"Come on," he said. "Everyone knows that."

Colt sighed. How was he to explain the hours of research that went into determining a stock's worth? It was complicated, and there was no substitute for it; you had to have an idea of what a company was worth to know whether their stock was a bargain or not. But even more complicated was the other part of it, the part he didn't understand himself, which was that every time a kid fell off his bike in Iowa, the shudders traveled two thousand miles through the earth and rippled through the exchange floor in

New York, manifesting themselves as the tiniest tick in the digital numbers. The market was simply a reflection of the universe, but there was no way a man of science would believe that. Colt almost didn't believe it himself—although he knew that it was true nonetheless.

"I can't tell you how to get rich," he said.

"Yeah, but what do you buy?" Dr. Doody prodded him. "I mean, how do you decide what to invest in?"

"It's a feeling," Colt said. "It's like a sailor looking at the horizon in the morning. You ever do any sailing?"

"Some."

"Well, you know how they say red sky at night, sailor's delight, et cetera?"

"Yeah?"

"It's kind of the same thing. Sailing is both an art and a science. You just trust your gut, no matter what the signs say. If it looks like a nice day but they've got a bad feeling, some guys won't go out."

"You're talking about superstition," said Dr. Doody.

"Yeah. If you want to call it that. Sailors can read charts and wind direction and all that. But they're also the most superstitious people there are. The second most, I mean," he corrected himself. "Traders are the first. Everyone I know carries some little thing with them, like a rabbit's foot or something."

"Yeah? So what do you carry?"

Colt permitted himself a wan smile. "A ring," he said. "But I lost it. And you can see what the consequences of *that* were."

"Yeah, well, thanks, anyway," said the doctor, making a note on a chart. "I'll be in tomorrow." Dr. Doody went away as suddenly as he had come, leaving Colt with the distinct impression that he had just been diagnosed as being full of shit.

Colt didn't care. Most of the time, he lay in agony, not wanting to talk to anybody. The staff were puzzled by his refusal of more pain medication, for clearly it was so bad that at times he could hardly speak; he could only clench his teeth and moan like a wounded animal, tossing his head from side to side. Yet he refused everything they offered him, for Colt knew he was damned if he was going back to that courtroom—literally—and he preferred to do his suffering here on earth.

When the nurse named Betty was on duty again, she came in and laid a hand on his forehead, clicking her pink tongue.

"We're not givin' out medals, y'know," she said.

"It gives me nightmares," he told her, wincing as the broken ends of his bones moved yet again, ever so minutely. "I had three. I can't handle another one."

Betty laughed out of her abdomen. "Honey, why on earth not?" she said. "What are you so afraid of?"

"They said I was going to be sentenced."

"Who said that?"

"The judge."

"Oh," Betty said knowingly. "You had *that* kind of a nightmare."

Colt was surprised. "You know the kind I mean?" he asked.

"Happens all the time in here," Betty said. "People dreamin' of their judgment."

"Other people have the same dream?"

"Sure they do," Betty said. "People who saw their own death close enough to touch it, anyway. Has the same effect on 'em. Well, not all of 'em. But enough. The smart ones. They tell me all about 'em, too. You think you're any more different than anybody else? Don't you know we're all the same?"

"Sure," said Colt. "Everything is connected. I knew that." He caught her eye and went on earnestly, "Did you know this? A car crash in Paris shows up on the Dow later that very same day. The question is—how? That's what I've never been able to piece together. I know it works—I just don't know why, or how, or even when. Nobody does. At least nobody that I know of. But someday, someday someone's gonna come along who can see everything all at once. He'll be able to read the stock board and tell you what's happened at every moment all over the world. He'll be like . . . plugged in. The One. The Reader. Everything is already connected, but until he comes along, no one's gonna know how it all works."

"That's right, honey," said Betty, who hadn't really been listening—Colt had been rambling on and off since he came in, and she heard only a select few words. "Jesus *is* connected, like you say. And them dreams is just your mind lookin' back over your life and figurin' out what you didn't do that you should a done, and what you done that you shouldn't a." Betty fluffed his pillow up for him and felt his pulse. "You got any regrets?" she asked casually, as she glanced at her watch.

"Regrets? Yeah. About a million of 'em," said Colt.

It must be the pain making me talk this way, he thought. Because I know damn well I don't regret any decision I ever made. Except for not throwing Flebberman out the window before we ever left my apartment.

"Well, who don't? You lucky," Betty said. "You still young. You got plenty of time to set things right again."

"I'm almost forty years old," said Colt. "I don't feel as young as I used to."

"Gracious, honey, who does?" laughed Betty. "I'm forty-three, but some mornin's I know what it's like to be seventy. 'Specially in my feet."

"You married?" Colt asked.

"Oh, yes," said Betty. "And so is you, so don't get fresh."

Colt managed a smile. "Not for long, I'm not. How's my pulse?"

"Crazy. Like you runnin' a marathon. Now, izzat because of my girlish figger or is it your arm hurtin' again?"

"Both."

"You sure you don't want somethin' to help you sleep?"

By now the pain had made Colt half-delirious, and things had begun to swim in and out of focus; the bounds of reality were blurred, like the smudged outlines of a chalk drawing, and he stared at Betty in her shimmering white uniform as though she'd just descended from a cloud.

"Are you an angel?" he asked.

Betty smiled. She put her hand on his forehead again.

"You be surprised how often I hear that, too," she said. "You go to sleep now. I think you're tired enough."

And, encouraged by her warm, dry hand on his skin, he slept.

■ ■ ■

Francie didn't come to see him again—no surprise there—nor did Jennifer Flebberman—no surprise there, either. No one came to see him, in fact, nor did anyone send cards or flowers—none of which, when he thought about it, came as a surprise, either. Sympathy, in his business, was the one commodity no one wanted to trade in, because you might as well cut someone's throat as pity them. Yet later that day he began to wonder why Forszak hadn't at least sent him a note or something, to acknowledge the fact that he still existed—and only then did it occur to Colt that no one at Anchor Capital even knew where he was.

"Betty!" he called, pressing the buzzer on the side of his bed.

Betty came to the door, wiping her hands on a tissue.

"Now, Coltrane, what is it?" she said. "I do love to say that name. He was always one o' my favorites. You finally change your mind about that medicine?"

"No," he said. "I just realized no one at my job knows where I am. They might think I've just disappeared or something. Can you help me use the phone?"

"If you want," she said. She came in and dialed the number he dictated, and held the phone up to Colt's ear as it rang.

"Anchor Capital, this is Jeanette speaking, how can I help you?" purred the receptionist.

Colt paused. Something in Jeanette's voice struck a familiar and none-too-pleasant chord in him. Even though the Snake Pit was sealed off by glass doors, he could still hear the occasional muffled shout, and it went through his head like a bolt of lightning. Just imagining himself in there made him tired and achy all over.

"Jeanette. It's Colt Hart."

He heard her gasp. "Mr. Hart!" she said. "Everyone's been worried sick about you!"

Yeah, right, he thought.

"I can't talk long," he said. "Just tell Forszak I had to take a little time off. Had an accident."

"An accident? My God, are you all—"

"Jeanette, I really can't talk. My head is killing me. Tell Forszak I'm all right and I'll be back in—well, a few days."

Colt caught Betty's eye then and noted her wry smile of amusement. She shook her head, as if to say, *Oh, no you won't.*

"Is there anything you—"

"Good-bye, Jeanette," said Colt, pressing the hang-up button.

"That's right. You just think about getting better. That's all you need to worry about right now," said Betty, taking the phone away from him.

∎ ∎ ∎

On Monday morning, the doctor told Colt he could go home. His plaster cast had been replaced with one of fiberglass; this was supported by a strut that rested on his hip and held it out at a ninety-degree angle to his body. He looked, he thought as he regarded himself in the mirror, like a half-trussed chicken.

It was just after noon when he was released. Betty had not been in that morning, and Colt realized, with a sinking heart, that he wasn't going to see her again. He had grown attached to her. On the spur of the moment he went to the nurse's station and asked one of the nurses to hold a piece of paper for him, while he wrote on it:

Dear Betty,

Thanks for everything. You saved me.

Coltrane Hart

"She'll like that," said the nurse. "She always likes to hear things from her patients."

"She's a hell of a nurse," said Colt. "You're all good nurses."

"Why, thank you," said the nurse, one he hadn't met yet.

"I feel like I've been here for a year," Colt told her.

"That's normal," she said. "Lots of people feel that way. A day in the hospital is like a month outside, we always say."

"I hope that doesn't apply to the people who work here, too," Colt said.

The nurse tittered. "Sometimes it seems that way," she said.

"I don't know how to explain this," Colt said, "but I'm going to miss being here. I almost don't want to leave. I've gotten used to it."

"That's normal, too," the nurse said. "One look at your bill will probably cure you of that, though."

"I don't even want to see it," said Colt.

"You can just take it down to the business office," said the nurse, handing him a folded sheet of paper. "They'll handle you down there."

"All right," said Colt. "So long. And thanks."

■ ■ ■

He hired a car to take him back to New York, and rode in the back, in silence, letting the chauffeur babble on about his grandchildren—the pain was still bad enough that it took up most of his concentration. It was with extreme relief that he climbed the stairs to their apartment. He felt automatically in his pocket for his keys, only to remember that Flebberman had thrown them out the window. He cursed. There was certainly no point in going out to look for them now. Then he remembered that he hadn't even locked the door to the apartment—how could he? Which meant that it had been sitting unlocked for an entire week.

A lifetime in New York had taught Colt that you never went into your apartment if you had the slightest reason to suspect there was someone else in there—because the odds were that someone *was*, or had been. But he had nowhere else to go, and besides, the ride from Allentown had exhausted him. He wanted nothing more than to sit on his own couch, tune the television to MSNBC, and take a nap. Hesitantly he tried the knob. The door swung open, creaking too loudly. Colt winced. If anyone was inside, they would know he was here now.

At first glance, everything in the front room appeared to be where it was supposed to be. Scarcely believing his good fortune, Colt took a few hesitant steps inside, remembering just in time to swing his arm out of the way so it didn't collide with the door frame. It was going to take him a while to get used to that. No lurking burglars clobbered him on the head, no junkies were nodding off in the corner. Perhaps he'd beaten the odds—he'd gotten away with it. Score another one for Mayor Giuliani, he thought. With a sigh of contentment, Colt slammed the door and locked it—safe.

Then he turned around again and let out a yodel of surprise. There before him, having just appeared in the kitchen doorway, was a nude man with long hair and a heavily bruised face.

"Holy shit!" said the nude man. "What are *you* doing here?"

"Gaah!" said Colt.

He turned and tried to make his escape, but having already forgotten that he'd just closed the door, he ran into it, the fingers of his upraised arm slamming directly into the fireproof steel and sending shock waves from his fingernails all the way up to his shoulder. For several moments he couldn't even speak, and the world around swam in and out of focus. When he could draw breath again, he let out a howl that bespoke all the suffering that had been brought upon him over the last week, and he thought, not for the first time: Just cut the fucking thing off, and let me be done with it.

"Colt, man! It's me!" the nude man said.

Colt, still in agony, turned to look at him. The man's face was as black and blue as if he'd been used for batting practice, but he recognized the long hair, and the whiny voice.

"Jesus, Michael," he said. "What are *you* doing here?"

28

■

THE OFFER

Michael helped Colt into the living room and sat him down on the couch.

"The door was open," he said. "So I let myself in. I didn't know where you were, but I didn't think you'd mind—not after you heard what I went through."

"What *you* went through?" Colt said. "Look at me! Do I look like I give a flaming crap what you went through?"

"You are looking pretty banged up. Where'd you get the busted wing?"

"I got kidnapped. And then there was a car wreck."

"Kidnapped! What? That shit is fucked up! Is Francie all right?"

"She's fine. She wasn't involved. It was our lovely neighbor out in Pennsylvania. He was upset over that cemetery that you two found. I had it moved, only—there was a problem."

"No fucking way," said Michael. "That is so fucked up!"

"Yeah. Well put. What *did* happen to you?" Colt asked. "You look like you got attacked by a hockey team."

"It was a street gang," Michael said. "See, I was sort of wandering around, trying to figure out what to do with all that—"

"Listen, Michael," Colt said. "Before you say another word, do me a favor and put some clothes on."

Michael looked down at himself.

"Oops," he said.

■ ■ ■

It was a drug deal gone bad, Michael explained to Colt, when he had thrown on his jeans and poncho.

"Drug deal? What drug deal?"

"I had a few pounds of pot in my bus. I'm surprised Francie didn't tell you about it," he said. "I thought for sure she would."

"Francie and I are getting a divorce," Colt said. "There's probably a lot of things she hasn't told me."

Michael's eyes widened. "No way!" he said. "Now *that's* the best news I've heard in years."

"Thank you," said Colt. "Please go on."

"Serious, bro. Nothing personal, but you guys really don't—"

"I knew what you meant," said Colt. "Now would you please continue?"

"Well, at first I thought I would go back to Denver and try to find the guys it belonged to."

"The guys what belonged to?"

"All this pot I ended up with by mistake," Michael said.

"Michael. Nobody ends up with pot by mistake," said Colt.

"Yeah, well, whatever. What I'm tryin' to tell you is that I had all this pot I had to get rid of that didn't belong to me. But then I thought, no way, Denver is crazy. The cops out there are probably looking for me, and they *definitely* wouldn't understand. Plus, it's a really long ways. So I decided to just get rid of it, like Francie told me I should. So, like, I was riding along the interstate, throwing little bits of it out through the hole in my floor—"

"The floor of your bus?" Colt interrupted. "You were scattering marijuana along the thruway through a hole in the floor of your bus?"

"Well, I *tried* to. Remember how I told you it was all rusted out? But it took forever. A handful at a time, you know, so no one would get suspicious, and I'm still trying to steer, y'know. It was a little on the tricky side. And by the time I got into the city I still had five bricks left. It wasn't such a great idea. So I'm like, well, shit—I should just try and sell it. So I went up to Queens, and I found these guys on a street corner, and I asked them real casual-like if they were interested, and next thing I knew they were beating the shit out of me and helping themselves." A mournful expression came over Michael's face. "They took everything," he said. "My dope *and* my bus. I'm lucky they didn't kill me."

"I'll say," said Colt.

"So then I needed somewhere to hole up for a while. I couldn't even tell the cops about my bus, man, or they would have found out about the pot. It's gone forever. And then I came here to see if you were around, because I knew you were back in the city, and I thought, I know the Coltster can't stand me, but I was hoping you would understand and have mercy, man. You weren't here, but when I tried the door—well, it was open. Why was that, by the way?"

"Another long story," said Colt.

"Yeah, right. So—is Francie still mad at me?"

"I didn't know she was."

"She threw me out," Michael said mournfully. "She told me it was time for me to grow up."

"Score one for Francie."

Michael looked doubtful for a moment. Then he gave Colt a broad grin.

"Looks like we're in the same boat!" he said. "She fired us both!"

"We are *not* in the same boat," Colt said. "We're not even in the same ocean."

"Yeah, okay, whatever. All I know is, here we are in New York, both of us all fucked up, and no Francie. You know, if she was here she'd be all like making us chicken soup and stuff." Michael sighed nostalgically. "The universe is trying to tell us something," he said. "That's why we both got our asses kicked. It's trying to say that we were on the wrong track. Francie was right about me, dude. She was right about you, too. We're both a couple of losers."

Colt decided to let that comment slide—he didn't have the energy for an argument. "Look. How long were you planning on staying?" he asked.

"Well—I don't know. I don't have any money, see. Or vehicle. Matter of fact—I'm pretty much the way I was when I was born. I got nothing. Not a thing. So I was sort of hoping that maybe I could, you know, hang out here for a little bit until I get back on my feet again?"

Colt rubbed his forehead.

"That's cool," said Michael, getting up before he had a chance to speak. "I just thought you might need some help. But whatever. Just let me get my shoes and I'll—"

"No, wait," said Colt.

Michael sat down again expectantly.

"I do need help," said Colt. "I can't—I'm working on one arm, here. I need someone to—"

"I won't wipe your ass," said Michael quickly. "But I can do everything else."

"I can wipe my own ass," Colt said testily. "Jesus, I didn't say I was totally helpless. But I can't get dressed by myself. And I need someone to go shopping and get food, and do the cooking and the cleaning and all the rest of it. I was going to hire someone, a private nurse or something, but as long you're here, you might as well do it. If you want."

"Okay," said Michael brightly. "How does five hundred a week sound? I can—"

"How does room and board sound?" Colt said. "If you think

I'm paying you, you're crazy. I'll put you up and I'll feed you, but that's it. At least for the first little while. After all the freeloading you've done, I think that's a fair deal."

"Right you are," said Michael. "A fair deal it is." He giggled. "You know, it's kind of funny, isn't it? I mean, here we are, you and me, stuck together, kind of like we were—"

"Don't," Colt said. "The irony of it is almost too great for words."

"So, what should I do first?"

"Laundry."

"Okay. Just show me where your dirty clothes are and I'll—"

"Not mine," Colt said. "Yours. I can smell those jeans from here."

"Gotcha," said Michael.

In the morning, he decided he was going into the office. Not to work—he wasn't ready for that yet. Just to walk in and show his face. He had to make an appearance if he was going to keep his job. Unless they'd already replaced him, that is. It was impossible to put on a suit, so he told Michael to cut a long slit in the left sleeve of one of his sweatshirts in order to fit it over his cast, and he pulled on his most respectable pair of chinos.

"So, I'll just hang out here until you get back?" Michael said.

"No. You're coming with me," Colt told him. "You will open and close doors, you will pick things up for me and put them down, you will do everything that I cannot do with one hand."

"You seriously want me to go to your office with you? With all the fat cats and capitalist pigs?"

"I'm sure you'll find they're not all that bad," Colt said. "You might even learn something while you're there."

Michael laughed. "Yeah, right," he said. "Capitalism 101. How to Exploit the Masses."

"Exploitation is on the twentieth floor," said Colt. "We're in Trading. And trust me when I tell you that the masses are perfectly adept at exploiting themselves."

They took a cab to Sixth Avenue. When they got out, Michael stood and gaped at the structure of which Anchor Capital was a tenant, leaning back as the magnificent glass-and-steel wall of it faded away into nothing more than a point overhead.

"Holy shit," he said. "You watch those clouds go by, it makes you want to fall over."

"So keep your eyes on the ground," said Colt, heading for the entranceway.

Michael helped Colt through the revolving doors and pressed the elevator button. They attracted not a few curious looks from the other office people waiting there—Colt knew they made a dubious-looking pair. There was a time when he would have been mortified to be seen with Michael, with his shaggy, almost-dreadlocked mane and his unshaven face, but now he was beyond caring. It was as if the pain he'd suffered through the last eight days had somehow cleared his head of all extraneous material—there were a lot of things he simply didn't have the energy to care about anymore. They got out on the thirty-third floor and headed for the receptionist, who at first stared at them in bewilderment, then leapt to her feet.

"Mr. Hart!" she said. "It's good to see you!"

"Yes, well, here I am," said Colt.

"Are you all right?"

"I'm fine."

"I got a little banged up myself," Michael said. "It happened up in—"

"Michael," said Colt. "Open the door, and don't speak to anyone unless you're spoken to. That rule is in place until we leave the office again. Understand?"

"Right," Michael said.

"Can you buzz us in, please?" Colt asked the receptionist.

"Right away, Mr. Hart," she said.

■ ■ ■

He could feel all eyes upon him as they entered. There was a moment of silence as everyone took him in; then he was greeted with a barrage of shouts. Colt gave a general wave and headed for his desk, ignoring the questions that were thrown at him. When Buddha and Raoul saw him coming they jumped up.

"Holy shit, Coltie!" said Raoul. "Where the hell have you been?"

"Raoul. Bood. What's up?"

"'What's up,' he asks us," said Buddha. "As if he didn't look like he'd just gone through a meat grinder. What happened, Colt?"

"Car accident," said Colt. "In Pennsylvania. I just came in to make sure I still had a job."

"Of course you still have a job," said Raoul. "Are you kidding? I mean, you'd have to ask Forszak for sure. But you're probably the one guy in the office who could take off for a whole month if he wanted to and still have a job waiting for him when he got back."

Colt tried not to show the relief that washed over him. He said, "This is my brother-in-law, Michael."

"What's up, dudes," said Michael.

"See, Michael? They're not so bad. Look, guys, I left some orders hanging. I just wanted to find out what—"

"We handled them for you," said Raoul. "Colt, there's—"

"How did GE do?" Colt said. "Did the Erie company get that locomotive order?"

"Yes, and you made fifty cents a share," said Buddha. "Congratulations. Coltie, listen, we've got some—"

"And I had a stop order in for some tech stocks," Colt said. "Are those still going, or are they—"

"None of them hit the limit yet," Raoul said. "Colt. Seriously. Listen a minute. We got some bad news."

"Hey, wait a minute," said Colt. "Where's Joe?" He'd just noticed that Joe's seat was empty, and his things had been cleared off his desk—all except the dippy-bird, which for the first time in Colt's tenure at Anchor Capital was standing still.

"That's the thing, Colt," Buddha said. "If we'd a known where you were, we would have called. Listen, Colt. I'm sorry to tell you this, but Joe's dead."

Colt felt for his chair. Michael slid it behind him and he sank into it, suddenly as heavy as a rock.

"Jesus Christ," said Colt. "Are you serious? You're not pulling my leg?"

"We wouldn't pull your leg on something like that," said Buddha.

"Yeah," Raoul said. "It happened last week."

"It was his heart," said Buddha. "On the subway. He was on his way home, and he just keeled over."

"I can't believe it. I just can't believe it. We were just talking about something like this," said Colt. "About how you can spend your whole life . . .ah, crap. Poor Joe."

"I guess there was a med student on the train who tried to give him CPR," said Buddha. "But he died instantly. Just like that. It was over in a second. Dead before he hit the ground, the coroner said."

"Funeral was on Monday," Raoul said. "Everybody was wondering where you were."

"Where *were* you, Coltie?" asked Buddha.

"I was in Allentown, in the hospital," Colt said. "I got racked up on the highway."

"You gonna be okay?"

"Yeah," said Colt. "Soon as this thing comes off, I'll be as good as new."

"Poor old Joe," said Raoul. "I guess he's making trades in heaven now."

"No, he isn't," said Colt. "He's a public defender."

Raoul and Buddha looked at each other.

"What was that, Coltie?" Raoul asked.

Colt shook his head. "Nothing," he said. "It's just kinda weird,

is all. Dream I had. How was the funeral? Did all his wives come?
His ex-wives, I mean?"

"Ah," said Raoul. "Well—I dunno."

"Probably," said Buddha.

"Waddaya mean, probably?" Colt said. He looked at the other
two. "You mean—you guys didn't even go?"

"Well, Colt, I mean, c'mon," said Raoul. "It was at one o'clock
on a Wednesday. If it had been on Sunday or something, then sure.
But—"

"I can't believe it," Colt said. "So his poor widow, or whatever
she is, is supposed to keep him on ice just so you guys can fit it
into your schedule? Bood, you went, at least. Tell me you went."

"Well, Colt, don't get that way about it," said Buddha. "Joe
woulda understood. He knows the score."

"You gotta be fucking kidding me," Colt said. "Neither of you
guys went? Did anybody from the office go?"

"Forszak went," said Raoul.

"Forszak can afford to take off," said Buddha. "Colt, don't be
that way. It was nothing personal."

"Nothing personal? How many years you been friends with
this guy? Five, six? And you can't even take the time to say good-
bye to him?"

"I said good-bye to him when he left work that day!" said
Raoul. "You never know when it's gonna be the last good-bye!
Okay, Colt? You just never know! And nobody ever got anything
outa goin' to these things anyway. It's depressing, is all. It's like—
flowers and music and praying. When did Joe ever go in for those
things, anyway? It don't make sense. If he'd a had it his way, we
all woulda gotten shitfaced and played cards or somethin'. Or
gone to a strip joint."

"You go for his wife, not for you!" said Colt. He stood up again
and put his face just inches away from Raoul's. "You dumb mother-
fucker, you don't go for yourself! You don't go just because it's con-

venient! You go for the other people! You go for his family, so you can shake their hands and tell them how much you liked him! That's why they have funerals, you assholes! For the living people! Not for the dead! For the living!"

"Jesus, Colt," said Buddha. "Get outa his face, will ya?"

"Yeah, Colt, what the hell?" Raoul said, backing up. "I know you're upset. Believe me, we're upset too. The whole office is—"

"You guys are a disgrace," said Colt. "You can't take five seconds outa your money-hungry lives to say good-bye to your friend and offer your condolences to his family? You make me sick. You really do."

There was silence. Several other traders had stopped what they were doing to listen.

"We did keep an eye on your trades for you," Buddha said. "We're not completely selfish."

Colt threw his good arm in the air. "How long did that take you?" he asked. "Five seconds? If that?"

"What, you're pissed at us because you think we're too greedy?" Raoul said. "There's the pot calling the kettle black."

"It's not that, for crying out loud," said Colt. "It's about drawing the line! It's about yourselves! Jesus, you guys! Didn't you learn anything from Joe dropping dead? I mean . . . I don't know. Maybe it's because I've been sitting in a hospital for the last week, half outa my mind and with nothing to do but stare at the ceiling. I been doing a lot of thinking. A lot of thinking. And you know what I think now?"

"What" said Buddha, sullen.

"I think you shoulda gone. You really shoulda gone. Not just for Joe, you guys. But for yourselves."

The phone on Buddha's desk began to ring.

"Good for you, Colt," said Raoul. "You've succeeded in making us feel like shit."

"Good," said Colt.

Buddha picked up the phone, listened, and said "Yessir." He put it down again and turned to Colt.

"Well, Mr. Sensitivity," he said. "Forszak would like to see you in his office."

Colt turned to look at Michael, who was standing against the wall, listening.

"You wait here," he told him. "I'll be out in a little bit."

■ ■ ■

Forszak always kept the shades in his office pulled low, to make it easier to see his computer screens. Instead of fluorescent lights, he had floor lamps, which cast a warmish yellow glow around his vast work space. The effect was comforting; it was like visiting a kindly grandfather in his living room.

"Have a seat, Coltie," said Forszak. "I wish you'd of told us sooner about your accident. Believe me, if I'd have known, I woulda called. I just figured you were taking some time off, as is your prerogative. As one of my top earners."

"Poor Joe," said Colt. "I can't believe it." He sat down on one of the couches that was against the walls.

"Yeah, poor Joe," said Forszak. "It was a shocker. He was a good friend of yours, wasn't he?"

"Sat next to him ever since I came in," Colt said. "It just—it kinda makes you think."

"It sure does," said Forszak. "It's shit like this that can make you take stock of your entire life and wonder what it all adds up to."

"That's it. That's exactly what I mean." Colt felt chagrined suddenly as he remembered Forszak's story, and all the losses he had suffered. "Of course, it's nothing compared to what you've been through," he added. "But for me—"

Forszak waved a hand dismissively.

"It's all relative, that's true," he said. "For me, a guy Joe's age passing away is not such a great tragedy, not on the face of it. You can't say he was too young, you can't say he never had a chance. You can't even say he suffered. He hit the ground like a sack of wet cement. It's sad for the ones he leaves behind, of course. But it only becomes tragic if he didn't do what he set out to do. Maybe Joe left a few things undone, but at least he lived in freedom. He was able to make his own decisions about how his life would be spent."

Colt nodded. "You're right there," he said.

"Now listen. There's been a few changes in the time you were gone," Forszak said. "I thought I should probably tell you about them as soon as possible, because there are some decisions that have to be made."

Colt stiffened, wincing as his arm sent him another reminder of the accident. "Yessir?" he said.

"First of all, I'm happy to say that my launch date has been moved up," Forszak told him. He got up from his chair and went to one of the windows, pulling the shade up so he could look out over Sixth Avenue. Colt squinted in the brighter light. Across the street he could see the windows of the building opposite, and beyond it there were clouds drifting over the city. "I'll be leaving next week."

"Next week?" Colt echoed.

"Yeah. So I'm afraid my visit to your new country place is gonna hafta wait until I come back."

Colt had forgotten all about that, even though it was planning for this visit that had been the beginning of the end of things, when one thought about it; for he had wanted to have the cemetery gone before Forszak and his wife showed up. His apology seemed so ridiculous that it was all he could do to keep from laughing.

"Well, we'll just have to reschedule, sir," he said. "My, uh—Francie will be disappointed, but she'll understand. Under the circumstances. Congratulations."

"I can hardly wait," said Forszak. "I may not look like it, but I feel like I'm ten years old again. I'm leaving for Russia in two days. I'll be gone for at least a month."

"A month. I see."

"I got confidence things will run smooth while I'm gone. The other partners will be in and out to keep an eye on things."

"Yessir."

"There is something else, which I been meaning to bring up with you for some time," Forszak said. "I was waiting until just before my launch date to talk to you about it. It's something I meant to see through before I left, because let's face it—there's a chance I won't come back, y'know."

"You mean—you might stay in Russia?"

Forszak smiled. "No, Coltie," he said. "I mean there's a chance I could die on my way to the moon. Or on the moon. Or on my way back from the moon. Space travel is still in its infancy, Colt. We're like the pioneers setting out across the plains. Things go wrong all the time."

"Oh," said Colt. "I hadn't even thought of that."

"And in case I *don't* come back, I wanted to make sure that you get the chance to become a partner yourself. I want to get the paperwork done before I go. So that no one else can interfere."

Colt leaned back on the couch and stared at Forszak in amazement. "You want to make me a partner?" he asked.

"A junior partner. To start. You got all the right qualities, Colt. And, most important, you got the capital. You've been doing very well since you came here, and I know your habits. You have a few million put away by now, don't you?"

Colt stuttered, taken aback by the directness of the question. "Ah—in various forms, yes."

"How much are you liquid for?"

"A—a couple million, sir."

"Would you be willing to reinvest that in the firm? And keep on doing what you're doing, at a substantially greater percentage than you're getting now? The rewards would be very great, Colt. No matter what the market does. There's a correction coming along some time soon. Everybody and his grandmother knows that. Maybe you want to wait until that has taken effect. But on the other hand, this offer might not be open then." Forszak shrugged. "Depending on what happens to me."

"I understand," said Colt. He was being offered something that every trader dreamed of—the most lucrative situation that existed, in fact. It was the chance to become disgustingly wealthy. If he played his cards right, he could double his money in the next five years. And double it again five years after that. And by then he would only be fifty years old. Coltrane had to smile. He had dreamed of this moment since he was eight.

"I'm sure you'll agree it's a wunnerful opportunity," said Forszak.

"I agree, sir, it is," said Colt.

"So then I assume you'll—"

"Do you mind if I take some time to think about it?" Colt said.

Forszak removed his glasses and blinked at the younger man several times.

"Think about it?" he repeated.

"Just—to consider all the factors," Colt said.

"To consider all the factors."

"I've been through a lot in the past week," said Colt. "And to be perfectly frank, I'm not sure what I want right now."

"I see," said Forszak. "Well, I gotta tell ya, I'm surprised."

"My wife wants a divorce," said Colt.

"I'm sorry to hear that." Forszak appeared surprised by the new tack this conversation was taking.

"Yeah. Well. She's pretty pissed off at me for a lot of things."

"I see," said Forszak.

"I know you understand," said Colt, getting up. "You told me about your kids, how you hardly talk to them. Let me ask you something. Was it worth it to carry things this far? To this level?"

"My kids," said Forszak. "Well, to tell the truth, Coltrane, I don't really think—"

"You chose to work your ass off," Colt interrupted. "That's fine.

I respect that. But now you have two kids who barely speak to you. And I was just wondering if you still feel like it was all worth it."

"Of course it was worth it," Forszak said irritably. "What you don't understand, young man, is that I came from nothing. Nothing. I made all this with my bare hands. I started out on the street, damn it!"

"I know," said Colt. "Look, Mr. Forszak. I'm not accusing you of anything."

"Well, it certainly sounds like you are!"

"I'm sorry. I didn't mean to sound like that. It's just that I— well, like I said, I've been doing some thinking. About all of this. This whole life. And—"

"Aw, God," said Forszak resignedly, sitting down at his desk and putting his feet up. "You're having one of those moments."

"Sir?"

"One of those you-can't-take-it-with-you moments," said Forszak. "And so you wonder what the point is, and whether there's something more valuable than money. Is that it?"

"Well," said Colt, "I guess so. Yeah."

"I shoulda known this was coming," said Forszak. "Look, Colt. I'm not your typical unfeeling businessman. I've thought about all these things many times. I did make an effort for my kids. I tried to be around them as much as I could, given the circumstances. And you know what? They're a couple of spoiled little shits. They grew up the opposite of the way I did. They had everything instead of nothing, and now they feel like nothing is enough. Me—I think to myself, well, that's too bad, but I'm still here. I'm still Igor Forszak, and sometimes I'm still the little kid who came stumbling out of the camp more than fifty years ago, more than half starved to death and crawling with lice. And I still feel like I felt that day. You know what that feeling was?"

Colt shook his head.

"Wide open," said Forszak, spreading his arms out in front of him. "Anything could have happened to me. That was the happiest day of my life, and not because I was free. It was because I had absolutely nothing to lose, and I knew I was finally on my way back up. Because anything was going to be better than what I had just come from. Somebody coulda handed me a shit sandwich on rye and I would have been happy about it, because it was more than I had. You see my point?"

"I think so," said Colt.

"That's what all this has been about for me," Forszak told him. "Not having lots of money. Just having that feeling. I never quite got it back again, but I'm still chasing it. That feeling like I could do absolutely anything I wanted, and that everything was something to be grateful for. I'm almost at the peak here, Coltrane. Almost at the top. Can you think of anything higher than actually going to the moon? It's the pinnacle of our civilization. It is the most advanced thing a man can do—to actually leave Earth, to escape our gravity."

Colt was silent, looking at the floor. He could feel Forszak staring at him, breathing heavily. Then he took some papers out of a drawer and laid them carefully on his desk.

"You know what?" he said. "You're at a crossroads here. I see that very strongly. So, you have some thinking to do. I'm gonna leave you these papers. I've already signed my part. You just have to sign yours. You don't have to make up your mind right away. You can take them home with you and think about it for as long as you want. If you don't sign them, you throw them in the fire. Understand? If you do sign them, you take them to my lawyer. His name is on the letterhead. He'll fix everything." Forszak gathered the papers into a sheaf and handed them over. Colt rose and, after a moment of hesitation, took them.

"This was what everyone was talking about," he said. "There was a lot of rumbling before I got hurt. People knew something was coming."

"Oh, that," said Forszak. "I dropped a few hints that we were gonna downsize. I like to do that every once in a while, through the secretaries. You know, feed them false info and tell them to spread it around. Keeps people on their toes. Plus, it distracts them from the real rumors. Only way I can keep a secret around here."

"That's a good one, sir," said Colt.

"True story," said Forszak. "Now go away, if you please, I have a lot to do." Forszak smiled again. "You'd be amazed at how complicated it is to get ready for a trip to the moon. There's a million things you have to bring, and you're not allowed to carry any of them with you on the ship. So why bring them?" He shrugged. "Who am I to ask this? I just do what I'm told."

Colt held out his good hand, and he and Forszak shook.

"Good luck, sir," said Colt.

"Thank you, Coltrane," said Forszak. "Look up in the sky a coupla weeks from now. Maybe you'll see me waving."

29

HEADING NORTH

"Y ou okay, man?" Michael asked Colt, as they stood on the curb outside, waiting for a cab. "Kind of a bummer about your friend, huh?"

Colt remained silent. He struggled into his seat and allowed Michael to strap him in. Then Michael closed the door and got in on the other side. The driver half turned in his seat, waiting for directions.

"West Village," Colt told him.

"You okay?" Michael asked again.

"I'm fine," Colt said. "Would you stop asking me that?"

"Was he a good friend of yours?"

"We ate lunch together every day for more than five years."

"So I guess that means you liked the dude."

"Michael," said Colt, "you have this amazing ability to make even the most profound events seem no more significant than a skateboarding competition. Do me a favor and either talk like a big boy or shut the fuck up. I'm serious."

"Whoa," said Michael, hurt. "Sorry." He fell silent for a time, but then, his monkeylike mind having jumped into yet another tree, he spoke up again.

"What did your boss want in there, anyway?"

"Nothing," said Colt.

"Is that nothing as in nothing important, or nothing as in I should mind my own business?"

"You're starting to catch on," Colt said.

He was still holding the sheaf of papers that would make him a partner, if he signed them. How many times had he dreamed of this moment? Times without number—times beyond counting. He wanted to sign them, he really did. He even already knew that he was going to sign them. There was no soul-searching involved; this was the most important moment of his life. It was that simple. And yet there was something that was making him wait, and he didn't know what it was. Something important. If it came just like this, he thought, would it be real? Was this the way it was supposed to be, or were other things supposed to happen first?

Because, the thing was, even though this was right and good and the way it was supposed to be, there was something missing. And it was driving him crazy trying to figure out what it was.

Maybe it was what happened to Joe. Poor Joe. He wondered what his last thoughts had been as he fell to the filthy floor of that subway car. Did he even know what had hit him? Probably not. He'd probably just been wondering what he was going to have for dinner, or trying to calculate how much he would have to earn this month to pay off his alimony and still have enough left over for himself. Wondering if he would have enough to buy Christmas presents for everyone. Joe had needs, both small and great, just like everyone else. And then his last glimpse of earthly life turns out to be the candy wrappers and discarded newspapers and half-empty plastic soda bottles under the seats of the subway cars. How depressing could things get?

And then there was Christmas. Jesus, Christmas wasn't too far away now, was it? It always seemed to come out of nowhere, and

Colt always just gritted his teeth and endured it until it was over. He hated Christmas with a passion. Just like everyone else he knew—except Joe, who'd loved it. Colt would have preferred that it be just another workday. New Year's was a holiday he could get behind, but Christmas? He hadn't enjoyed it as a kid. Mostly because he always knew that it was never going to be anything special. If his parents remembered to get him anything, it was always something he had no use for. A bike once, even though there was no place to ride it, and which promptly got stolen out of the hallway. A board game, even though he had no one to play it with. A G.I. Joe doll, even though he didn't play with dolls. Francie had always liked to glitz up the apartment in those stupid lights, and she had a fake tree she put up in the corner, reminiscing all the while about the real trees they used to have when she was a kid in Indiana. And she loved to make a big deal out of hanging stockings and stuffing them with things. That was another thing he should have appreciated about her and didn't, how hard she tried at Christmas. But he wasn't used to it. The whole thing seemed strange. They never had trees at all, fake or otherwise, when Colt was a kid.

What Christmas meant for Colt now was that he kept a list of Francie's measurements on file at his office, and when the holidays rolled around he hired a gift-buyer to go out and make his purchases for him, which this person did for a fee that was slightly more than nominal but still well worth it, considering how much time he saved. Four or five items of clothing, a few books, a piece of jewelry. These were dropped off in a box at the office, already wrapped, with cheery sentimental cards taped to the outside. All he had to do was sign them and lick the envelopes.

And that was it for another year.

"There's something falling out of your pocket," said Michael.

Colt was jolted out of his reverie. "What?"

"Here. Look. Is it important?"

Michael pulled the envelope from the corrections department, which had apparently been hanging half out of his pocket, and handed it to him. The notice of his father's parole hearing.

Colt stared at it as if he'd never seen it before. He opened it again, holding the envelope in his teeth while he pulled out the paper. Once again he read the details. He'd forgotten all about it; in point of fact, he'd never actually intended to do anything about it. He certainly hadn't meant to attend.

But that was before the accident. And before Joe. And the list of charges against him that the judge had said would take months to read.

"Holy shit," he said. "That's today."

"What's today?" said Michael.

"What time is it?" Colt asked him.

Michael shrugged. "I dunno," he said. "I never wear a watch."

"Buy one," said Colt. "You're going to need one, if you're going to be my assistant."

"Your assistant? But, dude—"

"Stop calling me dude. I hate that fucking word," said Colt. "Driver, go to the parking garage on the corner of Eleventh and West Thirtieth."

"What's there?" asked Michael.

"My car," said Colt.

"Your car? Are we going somewhere?"

"Yeah," said Colt. "We're going to prison."

30

■

THE HEARING

The prison was set back from the highway about a mile. It sat at the top of a hill that gave a sniper's view of the surrounding valley, at the end of a gravel road that passed over a sort of canal. One of New York State's oldest penitentiaries, it loomed like a medieval fortress that had been taken over by a race of malignant and warlike beings. Barbed wire sprouted from the ground and from the ramparts, resembling some deadly new species of flesh-shredding ivy; the ground here was inexplicably gray, splotched with stubborn patches of snow that had resisted the thaw. It was an old prison, as far as prisons went, built a century earlier out of man-sized blocks of dun-colored stone—but, weathered by the despair that seemed to emanate from the very ground, it had become ageless in the way that only institutions can.

Michael was driving—Colt was in the back, so that his broken arm could extend unimpeded—and he pulled the Camaro into the visitors' parking lot. Colt noticed that even in the parking lot, remote cameras were keeping an eye on them from the tops of the sodium-arc light poles. A sign on one of the poles said DO NOT

LEAVE VALUABLES IN CAR. PRISON NOT RESPONSIBLE FOR BREAK-INS. Now that was the funniest thing he'd heard in months, he thought. Prison not responsible for break-ins? Of course not. It was only the breakouts they cared about.

"Jeez, what a depressing place," said Michael. He turned off the car and sat for a moment, doing deep-breathing exercises.

"You mind letting me out?" Colt asked.

"Yeah, yeah. I'm just doing some cleansing breaths, man," said Michael. "Can't you feel it?"

"Feel what?"

"The negativity. The sadness. This place is heavy."

"It's a prison," Colt snarled. "It's supposed to be heavy. Now let me out."

■ ■

They walked up the sidewalk together, Michael sticking close to Colt's side, until they came to the visitors' entrance, which was a large steel door with a small window in it. They were admitted by a robotic eye that whirred and buzzed at them, and then searched and processed by a series of emotionless guards, who gave them visitor's passes to wear on their coats. Then they were sent down a long hallway. All at once, it appeared that they had entered some kind of high school. There were small, thick plastic windows in the doors, and through one of them Colt caught a glimpse of orange-clad men sitting in desks too small for them.

"What room did he say?" Michael whispered.

"This one," Colt said.

They went in one of the doors, finding themselves at the back of the room, and squeezed into the closest empty seats. The hearing room was exactly like a high school classroom, except that it had folding chairs instead of desks; at the front was a long table, where presently were seated three men and one woman. This, Colt assumed, was the parole board. A number of people were sitting around listening and watching; these must either be the families of the potential parolees, hoping for an early release—or possibly their victims hoping to delay the same. Facing the table was a lone plastic chair, and in it sat an old man. Colt couldn't see his face, but by his wizened and shrunken posture it seemed he had been in prison for a long time. His orange jumpsuit fell loosely about his shoulders, and he sat huddled into himself, looking down, as if in deep contemplation.

"Is that him?" Michael whispered.

"I don't know," Colt said. "I don't think so."

"You don't *know*?"

"I haven't seen him in twenty years."

"He doesn't know you're doing this?"

"Doing what?" Colt hissed. "I didn't say I was doing anything. We're just *here*."

The board was apparently in the middle of a hearing. The woman at the table removed her glasses now and rubbed her forehead.

"So, Mr. Alonso," she said to the wizened man in the chair, "what you're telling me is that you do feel you've been rehabilitated. Is that it?"

The old man nodded. "Yes, ma'am," he said.

"And you were admitted to a court-ordered psychiatric program as well? Did you finish that up, and how did it go?"

"Went good," said Mr. Alonso. "All done with that now."

"And what are you going to do, if you get paroled today? What are your plans?" one of the men asked.

Mr. Alonso turned around and pointed to someone seated in the crowd, or the audience, or whatever one called it; Colt could see now that the old man was toothless, his face nothing but a map of wrinkles. Following where he was pointing, Colt saw another man that looked much like him, except that he had no hair.

"That's my brother," he said. "He's been out ten years. He has a 'partment."

The free Mr. Alonso stood up and waved at the board members, who nodded at him.

"Your brother was in prison, too?" asked the woman, who, Colt surmised, was in charge of things—the chairman. Or chairwoman. Chairperson. Whatever. "For what crime?"

"Robbery," the imprisoned Mr. Alonso said.

"I see. Armed robbery?"

"I believe it was," said the imprisoned Mr. Alonso.

"I see. And you're in for robbery, too."

"I tried ta heist a Stop N' Go. Didn't get too far."

"Which means we'd have two convicted robbers living together under the same roof."

"I'm almost seventy years old," said the imprisoned Mr. Alonso. "My brother, he's sixty-three."

"Right," said the chairwoman. "But you're still both convicted felons."

"And, uh, how do you intend to support yourself?" asked one of the men on the board, who wore a brown three-piece suit, and looked as if he might be bucking for office; serving on a parole board, Colt knew, was one way to break into politics, since it looked good on a resume—and the brown-suited man looked as if he had his sights set on nothing less than the Office of the President of the United States of America, so eager and serious was his expression.

"Well," said Mr. Alonso, "there's a little savin's-and-loan we've had our eye on for quite some time now. No guards, no teller shields. We could be in and out in three minutes, as long as my trick knee isn't botherin' me."

The board remained silent for one long, stunned moment. The free Mr. Alonso rested his head in his hands. The imprisoned Mr. Alonso turned around and looked in his direction, then back at the board.

"Uh-oh," he said.

"Right, well, under the circumstances I don't think the board needs to deliberate," said the woman, glancing for confirmation at her colleagues—one of whom was apparently trying not to laugh. "At this time, Mr. Alonso, the board finds that it would not be prudent to commute your sentence to parole, and we hereby recommend that you continue to serve the remainder of your term, which is—" here she checked a paper in front of her—"three years from this date."

"Thank you!" said Mr. Alonso. He stood up enthusiastically, apparently with no understanding of what had just taken place. A guard came in to escort Mr. Alonso from the room, and the spectators began talking among themselves in a low buzz.

"He acts like they're taking him to Disneyland," said Michael.

"If that had been him" said Colt, but he didn't finish that thought.

The free Mr. Alonso got up and left the room, still shaking his head. The board member who had been trying not to laugh regained control of himself.

"You can bring in the next candidate," said the woman at the table. "Is there anyone here with respect to the case of—" she checked the papers again—"Mr. Nova Hart? Anyone here for Mr. Hart?"

Michael elbowed Colt.

"That's you, dude," he said.

"Shut up. I know it's me," Colt said. "I haven't decided if I'm going to say anything yet."

Michael raised his eyebrows. "You came all the way up here and you're not even going to say anything?"

"I told you, I haven't even seen the guy in more than twenty years," said Colt. "I wouldn't know him if I passed him on the street."

"Yeah, but he's your dad!"

"He's not my dad. He's my father. There's a difference."

"Whatever."

Michael leaned back in his chair and folded his arms. Colt took a deep breath and stood up.

"Here, ma'am," he said.

The parole board looked up as one, and their eyes went to his upraised arm, appraising him.

"And you are, sir?" said the chairwoman. "Did you notify the board that you were coming? Did you wish to address us in this matter?"

Colt cleared his throat. "My name is Coltrane Hart," he said. "I'm Mr.—ah, I'm his son. Sorry, I didn't tell you ahead of time. I wasn't sure if I was going to come or not. I only made up my mind this morning."

"Right," said the woman. "You can sit closer if you like, Mr. Hart. We're not going to bite you."

A titter went through the spectators. Colt, fighting the flush that threatened to rise to his face, went up to the front row of seats, Michael trailing close behind.

"And you are, sir?" the woman asked, addressing herself to Michael.

"Mr. Hart's personal assistant," said Michael brightly.

"I see. Please be seated."

The door at the front of the room opened again, and the same guard entered, leading another prisoner by the arm. He, too, was clad in the regulation orange jumpsuit, and if it had not been for the fact that his name had just been announced, Colt thought, he would never have known that this man was his father.

Nova Hart had once been handsome, in a severe way, with a strong, thin nose and high cheekbones, over which arched a broad and intelligent forehead; he had never been particularly strong, but in Colt's memory he was tall, with a commanding appearance, and he'd boasted a luxurious mane of black hair that had reached well past his shoulders. This man looked nothing like what Colt remembered. His shoulders and spine were curved, and his skin had faded to a pasty gray color. What little hair he had left was cropped close to his head, and had gone completely white. He seemed to have settled into himself, like a dock into a river. He was at least a foot shorter than Colt remembered, though whether that was his memory playing tricks on him or not, he didn't know. He gave no sign of recognizing his son. He shuffled to the chair that Mr. Alonso had just vacated and sat in it gingerly, as if afraid of breaking himself. Colt could only stare at him. This man is not Nova Hart, he wanted to say—there's been some mistake. But at that moment the prisoner reached up and smoothed a few strands of hair back from his forehead, and this familiar gesture triggered a memory in Colt. It was really him.

"Good afternoon, Mr. Hart," said the woman.

The prisoner nodded and mumbled something.

"You've been serving a prison term of fifteen years, and your review is now taking place as scheduled," she said. "You were last up for parole three years ago. At that time the board made the decision not to grant it to you. Do you know why that was, sir?"

The man mumbled something.

"I'm sorry," said the brown-suited hopeful. "Could you repeat that, please?"

"I was too sick," said the prisoner. "Didn't show up."

"And you chose not to reschedule?"

The prisoner nodded. He coughed, a deep, hollow sound that seemed to resonate in the frail cavity of his chest.

"Are you sick again?" asked the woman.

The prisoner nodded. "Not again," he said. "Still."

"Okay. And so—well, let me ask you this. What kind of programs have you been involved in since your sentencing that might make the board consider offering you terms of parole?"

The prisoner shrugged. "Went through some counseling," he said. "That was a while back now."

"And you were sentenced originally for trafficking drugs."

The prisoner nodded.

"Heroin, in particular. Isn't that right?"

"Yeah," he said. "That's right."

"Have you been involved in any work programs?"

"Too sick," said the prisoner. "I'm in the infirmary most of the time."

"Mr. Hart, are you still addicted to drugs?"

The prisoner shook his head. "I've been clean for a long time. Since I came to prison."

"Well, you are drawing close to the end of your term. It would be complete in another year. And your behavior has been exemplary, according to your records. The board is inclined to be lenient at this time in your request for parole, but there's some questions we need to ask you first, in order to make sure that you're going to be able to support yourself."

There was a long silence, during which the board first pondered the man before them, and then looked as one at Colt. He still had not spoken, and still his father hadn't noticed him.

"I can't support myself," said Nova Hart. "You better just leave me in here."

"Are you saying you don't want to be paroled?" said one of the men.

"Sayin' there's no point," said Nova Hart. "I'm too sick to work. I don't know anybody anymore. Don't have any money. No point. I didn't file this request anyway. It went through automatic. You better just lock me up again."

"Was there anything you wanted to add, Mr. Hart?" the woman asked Colt.

The prisoner shook his head and stood up. "That's it," he said.

"Wait a moment, sir," said the woman. "I was speaking to the gentleman behind you."

The prisoner turned, an act that seemed to take a very long time, and his gaze traveled over his son and went on, uncomprehending. Colt stood up and cleared his throat.

"Ah," he said. "Yes."

The prisoner stared at him first in surprise, then in astonishment. Then he recognized him, and he swayed backward, as if hit by a gust of air.

"Jesus Christ," he said. "Look at you."

"Do you recognize this man?" asked the woman. "Mr. Hart?"

The prisoner nodded, his wrinkled neck lost among the folds of orange cloth that swathed him. His voice trembled with emotion when he spoke.

"Yeah, I know him. Hello . . . Colt."

"Hello," said Colt.

"Well," whispered the old man. "Well, well." He sat back down again and leaned forward, rubbing his eyes. Colt noticed, for the first time, that he was in handcuffs.

"To the younger Mr. Hart, I am addressing myself," said the woman. "Was there anything you wanted to say in this matter?"

Colt stared at her, mute, overwhelmed.

"Mr. Hart?" she prompted him.

"Ah," said Colt, "anything I wanted to say?"

He could feel the eyes of the room upon him.

"Yeah, I have something to say," he said. "Where should I start?"

31

---◼---

A HISTORICAL DIGRESSION
(CONLUDED)

On a balmy May afternoon in 1888, Marly Musgrove was walking across the yard of Adencourt from the kitchen to the pump, carrying an empty bucket in one hand and her grandson, Lincoln Flavia-Hermann, who was less than a year old, in her other arm. Marly's Bavarian son-in-law, Kloot, had just bought a new horse, a dun-colored, two-year-old mare that stood about fourteen hands high. The horse was nervous. To relax her, Kloot was giving her a brushing, but his efforts only seemed to make her more skittish. She'd been uneasy about moving in the first place, he recalled later. She'd seemed calm enough as he was leading her away, but as they approached Adencourt, her nostrils grew wide and she began to dance from side to side, as if she smelled a predator. Kloot thought a good brushing-and-currying would calm her down and help her get used to her new surroundings, but stupidly he hadn't thought to tie her reins to the hitching post. He would later blame himself for the consequences of this careless omission; for, as the horse grew more spooked, he was having a harder time holding her—until finally she ripped free and tore across the lawn, racing, Kloot would later explain in his mangled English, "like the Devil himself was licking her rear."

Marly had just finished drawing a bucket of water for washing dishes. Lucia had been after her for the last couple of years to install indoor plumbing in the house, but Marly wouldn't allow such a luxury, even though she had been granted a war pension for the Captain's service; plumbing seemed to her like something that belonged only in the homes of the very rich. As the horse was speeding across the yard, Marly was distracted by the small boy in her arms, her first and only grandchild. The bucket dangled loosely from her fingertips, and as she stumbled over a stray piece of firewood, water sloshed against her leg.

"Would you look at what Granny did to herself?" Marly cooed to the baby, oblivious to the seven-hundred-pound animal running blindly toward her—Lucia would later say she had suspected for some time that Marly's hearing was going bad, and had urged her to see the doctor about it, but Marly applied the same logic to her body that she did to her house: any improvements made to the basic structure of things was vanity. Even so, no one could understand why she didn't at least feel the vibrations of the hoof-beats, for even a small horse can set windows and plates to trembling when it runs. Marly set the bucket down to get a better grip, still holding the little boy. Kloot Flavia-Hermann had already begun to scream her name as the horse bore down upon her, but—again inexplicably—Marly either didn't hear him, or simply didn't have time to respond.

It was all over in a moment. The horse passed over the two of them and continued on down the road. She would later be found back in her stall at her former owner's farm, shivering and rolling her eyes. In her wake, she left two human bodies: one sitting upright, too stunned even to cry, and the other lying prone in the dirt yard, blood seeping from her ears, one eye shut, the other open and grotesquely turned back into her skull. Piecing everything together later from what was left of the outlines in the dirt, curious neighbors and the traveling doctor would determine that the horse's hooves could not have missed the little boy's head by more than half an inch. That he was alive was a gift; that he was unharmed, a miracle.

But those same hooves had crashed into Marly's head with the force of sledgehammer blows, and her skull was crushed practically into powder along the right side and top of her head—so much so that the undertaker later had to remove her brain entirely, in order to prevent it from leaking out of her ears.

Once again, the scattered Musgrove children were summoned by telegram. The gathering this time was much more subdued than it had been for the Blessing of the Stones. Marly had only been in her fifties, and no one had expected her to go so soon; although, being a Musgrove, Hamish would think later, what they *really* ought to have said was how lucky she was to have lived as long as she did. Olivia and Margaret showed up with their Philadelphia husbands once again, and once again Hamish and Ellen took the train in from Pittsburgh, arriving at the house in a hired wagon.

Marly lay in a coffin in the outer living room, having already been dressed, washed, and laid out by the undertaker and his staff. Her children and the neighbors from several miles around kept up a vigil that lasted through most of the night. Toward sunrise, the neighbors went home to rest, and the children filed into their old bedrooms with the docility of trained pets returning to their cages. The Philadelphia husbands did not give any thought to keeping their wives company, but settled for bunking together in one of the empty bedrooms, for comfort—though neither would admit it, both of them were terrified of the old house, and were sure it was haunted. It went without saying that no one would sleep in Marly's bed, though it was the most comfortable.

In the morning, Lucia was the first to rise. She brewed pots of coffee and fried ham steaks and eggs, and soon, awakened by these delicious smells, the others began to drift downstairs. Ellen was the last to get up. When she came into the kitchen, where the others had been eating in shifts at the small table, her appearance gave her sisters a shock. Her face was smeared with dust, and her dress, which she had not bothered to change out of before bed, was torn along the sides, as if she had been dragged for some ways down the road.

"Ellen!" Lucia said. "What on earth happened to you?"

Ellen looked bewildered. She smoothed her hair back self-consciously and stared at everyone staring at her.

"Why, I don't know what you mean," she said.

"You're filthy! And your dress!" Lucia cried. She went to her sister and spun her around, pointing to the tears in her clothing. "Were you sleepwalking?" she asked.

"I—yes, I must have been," Ellen said quickly. "I think I remember waking up in the barn." She gave a faint smile.

Hamish looked skeptically at her bare feet, which were clean. Had she been walking around in the barn at night, he thought, she would have certainly had to step through the manure that Kloot Flavia-Hermann rarely bothered to clean up.

"First time I've ever heard of a sleepwalker stopping to put on their shoes," he remarked.

"Now, Hamish, you know very well that sleepwalkers do strange things," said Lucia. "And Ellen has often walked in her sleep before. Remember the time Mother heard a noise, and found her on the porch roof?"

Hamish did remember that time, and so did Ellen; she also remembered that she hadn't really been sleepwalking, but had merely crept out of bed to explore the house at night, something she did often, though she had never been discovered before that time. Marly's assumption that she was sleepwalking was a charitable one, made for her own peace of mind, for girls who left their beds at night to amuse themselves could not be trusted in the slightest; it was easier for Marly not to believe such a thing. Otherwise, she would have had to tie Ellen into bed.

"*I* remember that," said Olivia. "Though I am rather mortified to think that she hasn't grown out of it by now."

"*Et moi aussi*," said Margaret, sniffing.

"Ellen hasn't sleepwalked in years," said Hamish. "It's being back home under these trying circumstances that's doing it to her."

There was a general murmur of assent and understanding—Hamish could always be trusted to come up with the right explanation in a pinch. Thus diagnosed, Ellen shot her brother a grateful look, and scurried back upstairs to clean herself up and change her dress.

■ ■ ■

The funeral was held that afternoon. The same minister who had consecrated the graves the year before arrived around one o'clock, in a black surrey drawn by two black horses. Since after breakfast, the mourners had begun to gather once again in the living room to bid farewell, and by noon their numbers had swelled to more than a hundred. Marly had not been the most outgoing of women, but she had been respected in the community. Laid out now in her black dress, a silk kerchief tied under her chin to keep her mouth closed and to hide the worst of her injuries—ruined head propped on a small pillow, hands folded at her waist—the adult Musgrove children could scarcely believe how small death had made her. In their memories, she would always loom as the largest figure any of them had ever known, eclipsing even their frightening military father, whom Olivia and Margaret barely remembered—but now they suddenly noticed that she was really only a tiny woman, barely five foot four, and that whatever spirit, had possessed her mortal self and lent it such stature had fled for good.

The minister intoned a blessing over the casket, which was then closed. As Marly's face disappeared from view for the last time, Hamish felt a terrible tightening in his chest, and he sensed that the floor was falling away beneath his feet. Ashamed of himself, he had to be supported by the Philadelphia husbands until he regained his equilibrium. His sisters, unrestrained by the dictums of manly comportment, set up a collective moan that grew into a low wail as the coffin was transported out of the front door.

Hamish recovered enough to assume his position as one of the pallbearers. The men moved a step, then paused, then took another step, then paused. In this solemn manner, accompanied by the periodic thud of a muffled military drum that had thoughtfully been provided, as a tribute to her war-widowship, by the local militia, they headed around the house and toward the family plot. The mourners fell into line behind, forming an undulating black-clad dragon of grief, the head of which had already stopped at the open grave site just as the tail was leaving the house.

When all had gathered, the minister spoke for a lengthy time. He reminisced about Marly's girlhood, of which he had known nothing, and spoke of the great sadness and hardships that she had endured in her life, but that were now coming to an end, as she was laid to rest among the little ones who had left her too soon. The minister once again read the names of the dead Musgrove children aloud, and the living Musgroves cast an anxious eye at Ellen, dreading a repeat of last year's performance. But, to their mixed relief and surprise, Ellen remained calm, even dry-eyed—almost detached. It seemed to the others as if, in her mind, the funeral was already over, and she was back home in Pittsburgh. When the service was over and the coffin lowered into the ground, each of the children threw a shovelful of dirt on top of it, and then stood back as each of the mourners did the same. By the time they were done, the hole was nearly filled in. The undertaker's men had only a small job to finish, and then there was a new grave at Adencourt.

It was, the children knew, to be the last. Though they hadn't discussed this with each other, each of them had a fervent wish *not* to be buried at Adencourt, although for very different reasons: Olivia and Margaret because it was too unfashionable; Hamish because he intended never to return to this cursed place again, either in life or in death; and Ellen because, in addition to the reasons she shared with Hamish, she couldn't bear the idea of sleeping side by side through all eternity next to the little brother she had drowned. It was enough, she felt, that her soul would be tormented in hell for all eternity—it was too much to think that her very bones would be made restless, too. Lucia was the only one who wouldn't have minded. She had rarely left Adencourt in life, and saw no particular reason to leave it in death, either. But then again, being of an unspiritual mind-set, Lucia didn't believe that *where* a person's remains lay made any particular difference. She would be happy to be buried next to her husband in the Lutheran cemetery closer to town, when her time came.

The funeral over, all the mourners went back into the house for supper. Then they bid farewell to the siblings and went home in their wagons. As the dust settled in the driveway, the women set about cleaning the place once more. They scrubbed it from top to bottom, beginning in the attic and working their way down to the basement. They had not planned to do this, it being a strange end to a day of sadness; but they found themselves at a loss, and fell to work as a substitute for conversation.

Ellen and Lucia worked together in their mother's bedroom, first sweeping out the corners and shooing an invisible amount of dust into the hallway, then getting on their hands and knees to scrub the floor with soap and water. Eventually, Lucia got around to opening the closet that had held their mother's few dresses. It had been years since she'd had occasion to go in there, and she was given a turn by the headless dressmaker's dummy that greeted her mutely, like some forgotten guest who had wandered in there long ago.

"I'm burning this old thing," she declared firmly. "It's always given me the fantods."

Ellen agreed with her. They cleared the closet of a number of items that nobody had any use for, now that Marly was gone, and carried them out behind the barn, where Hamish set fire to them with a sense of grim satisfaction. Then the two sisters went back upstairs to finish their work. Only then did Lucia spy the door to the hidey-hole, which had been concealed behind a pile of boxes.

"Goodness, I'd all but forgotten about that place!" she exclaimed. "It's been ages since I was down there."

"Nor me," Ellen said—quickly.

"I wonder if I could still fit in."

"Oh, no, Lucia," said Ellen, ushering her out of the closet and firmly closing the door. "You and I are much too plump to be crawling around down there. Why, what if we got stuck? The boys would have to tear the house down just to get us out!"

Self-consciously, Lucia placed her hands on her waist and smoothed her dress.

"You're right," she said. "I'm as fat as a house, ever since Lincoln was born."

The childless Ellen colored to her forehead; she had deserved that, she thought.

"Well," she said, "at least you have a reason to be fat."

Thus satisfied at having drawn this small amount of blood from each other, the sisters left Marly's bedroom, closing and locking the door firmly behind them.

■ ■ ■

It would be some months before Lucia and her husband would finally allow themselves to move in there, now that Adencourt was theirs, and then the closet would once again be crammed full of boxes of scraps and cast-off items. The passage to the hidey-hole was closed off to little Lincoln as he took his first steps in the living room, then graduated to climbing stairs, then to exploring the empty bedrooms on the second floor. Lincoln believed that he had a host of invisible playmates who made their residences there, and whom he was accustomed to visit on a daily basis, chattering away to them in a made-up tongue. He would often attempt to introduce his parents to these playmates, and would be frustrated by the fact that they couldn't see them; to him they were as real as anything else, and most important, they kept him from growing lonely. But by the time he grew into a tall, lanky boy, even Lincoln had ceased to be aware of the presence of the spirits of his five aunts and uncles, none of whom had lived on earth as long as he had, and who were therefore unequipped to trail him into the mysterious reaches of adolescence, and beyond.

This was why neither Lincoln nor any of his descendants was to discover the diary that Marly had kept secret from everyone, but which Ellen had stumbled upon the night that she rose from bed and rummaged, grief-stricken, through her mother's possessions, inhaling the lingering scent of her body on her bedclothes, fingering her meager collection of jewelry, pilfering the butterfly pin that Marly had woven from Henry's long blond hair, finally discovering the journal at the bottom of a steamer trunk, hidden by a pile of undergarments. Here, finally, she had found a place where she could record her confession of what she had done, hoping to feel relief at finally unburdening herself of her terrible secret; hoping also—in vain—that she would find some solace in writing it in the same book her mother had written, in her childish, uneducated hand, as if it were a chronicle of just another household tragedy.

When she had finished her confession, she crawled agonizingly down through the darkness into the hidey-hole, nearly becoming stuck several terrifying times. There, in the place she had not visited in more than twenty years, she deposited the artifacts of her guilt, among the rag dolls that she herself had left down there years earlier and forgotten about, as well as the empty bottle of the poison that had consumed her father as he consumed it—another item she had stolen so she could examine it, in an effort to understand. It was her greatest hope, as well as her fear, that the diary would one day be discovered by someone who had it in them to understand the reasons why that thing had happened, and who possessed, perhaps, the ability to see through the veil that ordinarily conceals the lives of those who live in the same place at different times from one another's view; someone who could—by some miraculous chance, through some generous way of seeing through time—see poor Ellen as she really was, and forgive her.

PART FOUR

PART FOUR

32

THE TURKEY OF BLISS

They rode along in near-total silence for the first hour, Michael humming some inane tune to himself, Coltrane sitting in the back with his legs splayed out to either side, and the old man in the passenger seat with his hands folded quietly in his lap, as though he were still in handcuffs. He'd brought what he said were all his earthly possessions. They fit into a clear plastic bag, which he kept tightly between his feet, as if afraid someone was going to steal them. The countryside of upstate New York flowed rapidly by. With all green gone from the earth now, neither Colt nor Michael saw anything in the scenery worth looking at; this was the season of dying, when the world went into lockdown. But the former prisoner preoccupied himself with staring out the window. "Beautiful," he kept whispering to himself. "Beautiful."

After an hour of this, Colt felt it incumbent on himself to make some other form of conversation.

"You feeling all right?" he asked.

The old man half turned in his seat.

"Say something?" he asked. His voice was as scratchy as sandpaper.

"I asked if you were feeling all right. I overheard you saying that you were sick."

"Oh, yes, fine, fine," said his father. He turned forward again, but after several moments a thought occurred to him, and he turned once more and asked, "How are *you* feeling?"

Colt bobbed his head from side to side. "Could be better."

The old man hesitated, as if afraid of transgressing some boundary. "How'd you break your arm?" he asked finally.

"Car accident."

"Bad one?"

"Pretty bad."

"Anyone else get hurt?"

"No. Just me."

The old man nodded, and after a moment he resumed looking out the window. After another interlude of several minutes, he said, "This is a nice car. I guess it wasn't the one you had the accident in."

"Nineteen seventy Camaro with a three-speed shift and a two-hundred-horsepower V-eight engine," said Colt automatically.

His father nodded in admiration. "You've done well for yourself."

"Well enough."

"I always knew you would," said his father.

▋ ▋ ▋

Half an hour later, they were back in the city. Michael pulled up in front of the parking garage and handed the keys to the attendant. Nova Hart waited for Michael to let him out—to Colt it seemed that he was actually awaiting permission to leave the car—and then he stood clutching his plastic bag to his chest, looking neither to the side nor straight ahead, but down at his feet. When he saw Colt struggling to get out of the backseat, though, he offered him his hand, and, after a moment's hesitation, Colt took it. The old man's skin was cool and leathery against his, and he let go as soon as he had recovered his balance, wiping his palm quickly and secretly against his pants.

"You live by here?" Nova asked.

"It's kind of a walk," said Colt. The sun was below the buildings now, and there was a chill breeze, but the slight warming of the past couple of weeks had continued, and it felt more like a fall evening than a winter one. "You feel up for a walk?"

"Oh, sure," said the old man. "I'm up for a walk."

"Probably feels good to stretch your legs, doesn't it?" Michael asked. He had kept silent up till now, occasionally shooting glances at Colt's father in the car. Colt wondered if Michael saw something in him he liked; perhaps he had the idea that Nova Hart was some kind of counter-revolutionary hero, imprisoned for his beliefs. Well, maybe a talk with the old man would fix that misconception.

At that moment, Colt realized for the first time why it was he had always disliked Michael so much, perhaps even hated him. It was because he was nothing more than a Nova Hart–in–training, a younger version of his own father. More than anything, Michael reminded him of Nova as he had been thirty years ago: irresponsible, bumbling, selfish, a little stupid, concerned only with when the next party was and how he was going to get there. Imagine Michael with a kid, and you would have my dad, he thought. And then imagine Michael progressing to heroin. And then abandoning everything.

"Sure does," said Nova. "Real good."

They fell into line on the sidewalk, Michael in front, Nova in the middle, and Colt behind. He couldn't quite bring himself to walk next to his father. It was about a mile to the apartment, and the old man walked slowly, his gait no longer the far-stepping stride that Colt remembered struggling to keep up with, on the rare occasions that they had gone anywhere together. It was all he could do now to avoid stepping on his heels. The prison had given him a new set of clothes—jeans, a blue work shirt, a thin denim jacket, and a black knit cap that sat cockeyed on his head. He walked like someone who kept expecting to bump into a wall. Every hundred paces or so, it seemed, he would pause for a brief instant, almost in disbelief, before he kept going. After the third or fourth time of this, he turned, and with a sheepish smile said:

"First time in a long while I can walk more than a hundred paces in a straight line."

"Why's that?" Colt asked.

"That was the size of the exercise yard," he said.

■ ■ ■

Colt had by now replaced the locks on his door, and he fumbled one-handedly with the keys until Michael took them from him and let them in. Then he closed the door again and locked it, and his father stood in the living room, still clutching the bag to his chest, staring at the floor. Michael disappeared into the bathroom and closed the door. A moment later they heard the sound of him urinating. The two of them were left alone for the moment.

"This is where you live, huh?" the old man asked.

Colt nodded.

"Nice place," said his father. "You married?"

"Was," said Colt. "We're getting a divorce."

"Oh. Too bad. I woulda liked to meet her."

"She doesn't know you exist," Colt said matter-of-factly, struggling out of his jacket. "I told her you were dead."

Nova nodded just as matter-of-factly, his expression changing no more than if Colt had informed him it was going to rain tomorrow. "Where's she live?" he asked. "You have any kids?"

"We bought an old country place out in Pennsylvania not too

long ago," Colt said. "That's pretty much what started it all, I guess. The divorce, I mean. Didn't know it was going to happen that way, but there you go. When I look back at it, I can see the whole thing started because of that house. Don't know why. She's out there now. Probably stay there." He swallowed. "And no, we didn't have any kids. I didn't want them."

His father nodded again. "What do you do, Coltrane? You still go by Coltrane?"

His father's use of his name surprised him. He stuttered for a moment before answering.

"Yeah, I still go by Coltrane," he said. "What'd you think, I woulda changed my name?"

"Wouldn't of surprised me."

Colt pondered this—it was something that had never occurred to him. "I'm in finance."

"Oh. Finance," said Nova, nodding, impressed. "Stock market?"

"Yeah."

"Yeah," said his father. "Well, you always were good with money."

"Someone had to be, in our family," Colt said. "Our so-called family, I should say."

"Yeah," his father agreed, again with no perceptible change in his expression, or in the sound of his voice. Colt felt he could stand there and throw bombs at him all day and he would just look around blankly and nod. The old man was like a punching bag—he would just keep coming back up for more. Why the hell did I bring him back here? he asked himself, for what he was sure wasn't going to be the last time. At my age, I'm suddenly looking for a father figure? No. That's crap. There must be something else.

Now his old man was looking around at the living room, at the plush sofa and chairs that had cost nearly six thousand dollars, the empty walls where Francie's pictures had hung, the giant television in the corner with its DVD player and cable box. "Looks like you've done well," he said.

"Yeah. I've done all right. You want anything? A drink, or something to eat?"

"Naw," his father said. "Chow's usually at six. I don't get hungry until then. You kinda get used to being on a schedule like that."

"Well, sit down then. If you want."

The old man sat down gingerly on the couch and then let himself fall back into it, pure relief on his face. "Ooh," he said. "Softest thing I've sat on in years. Can I sleep on here?"

"If you want," Colt said.

Michael came out of the bathroom. Colt felt in his pocket and came up with a wad of cash.

"Here," he said, handing it to him. "Take this and go get us some sandwiches. Maybe some beer. You want a beer?" He addressed this to his father, who shook his head.

"Can't drink," he said. "Medication."

"Get a six-pack of something good," he said to Michael.

"Right," said Michael. "What kind of sandwiches?"

"I don't care. Smoked meat. You like smoked meat?" He addressed this also to his father, still unsure what to call him.

"Sure," said his father. "I guess. Been a while. I almost don't remember if I do or not."

"Get some Montreal smoked-meat sandwiches. And some beer. And some chips."

"What kind of chips?"

"I don't care. Any kind."

"All right," said Michael. "I'll be back in a little while."

"Don't take too long. I'm hungry," Colt said. He looked at his watch and saw that it was five-thirty. "You don't get hungry until six?" he asked his father.

"Like clockwork," said Nova.

"I'll be back by then," said Michael. He pocketed the money and let himself out. Colt locked the door again after him. Then he sat down on one of the chairs.

They sat for several moments, the only sound that of the city outside. Finally his father said, "Sure was surprised to see you up there."

Colt snorted. "Yeah," he said. "That makes two of us."

The old man appeared puzzled. He cocked his head, but didn't ask for an explanation.

"I wasn't really planning on coming, is what I mean," Colt said. "It was just a spur-of-the-moment kind of thing."

"Oh," said his father. "Spur-of-the-moment."

"Yeah."

"I see." He nodded.

"You can set that bag down, if you want," Colt said. "No one's gonna take it from you."

The old man looked down at the bag he held in his arms. "Oh, yeah," he said. "This stuff. It can all go in the incinerator. It's just old clothes."

"You didn't have any books or anything?"

"Naw. They didn't let us have much."

"Right."

Nova set the bag down at his feet. "You just kinda get used to hanging on to whatever you've got in there," he said. "Even if it isn't much."

"So you'll be needing some new clothes," Colt said.

"I guess I will, at that. Sooner or later. These ones are pretty new. When you're a guest of the state you get new clothes every year. Kind of a big deal when it happens. Something to look forward to."

The two men sat, not quite looking at each other. Colt began to tap his foot on the floor and then made himself stop.

"Sure was surprised to see you," his father said again.

"Yeah, well. Like I said. Spur-of-the-moment."

"You never came to see me before. Not that I blame you."

Colt didn't reply to this. Idly he picked up the remote and turned the television on to MSNBC, muting it. Instinctively he followed the trail of stock quotes as it raced along the bottom, shaking his head in dismay.

"Tech stocks are gonna start taking it in the shorts," he said. "I gotta get outa there."

"Stock market," said Nova. "I never understood much about it."

"The bubble's too big," Colt said. "That's all. Just too big. It's gonna pop soon, and a whole lotta people are gonna be crying."

"You make a lotta money at what you do?"

Colt was amused by the directness of the question, and for a moment he wondered at the motives behind it—but the old man simply seemed to be curious. "Yeah," he said. "I do."

"Good. I always knew you would."

"Yeah, you said that before," Colt said. "Only thing is, I'm wondering how you possibly could have known that."

His father looked at him, and Colt felt for a moment that he was looking into a watery-eyed version of himself, as he might appear in another twenty-five or thirty years. The idea of it gave him a feeling like vertigo, and he fought the shudder that ran down his spine.

"I dunno," his father said softly. "You were always so self-sufficient."

"Yeah, well. I had to be. Otherwise I would have starved to death."

Nova shifted on the couch, absently testing the springs with his hands.

"Ah, Colt," he said. He shook his head. "You don't know how many times I wished I could do things differently."

"Yeah," said Colt. "You don't know how many times I wished that you had."

That was out now, at least, and he felt a grim sense of relief, as though he had just lost ten pounds. His father looked down at his feet again and shifted uncomfortably on the couch.

"I thank you," he said, "for getting me out of there."

"You were gonna be out soon, anyway. It sounded like they were going to let you go no matter what."

"Yeah. Old man like me. They got no reason to keep me in there anymore. I'm past being a danger to anyone, I guess. Just a burden on the state now. I—I just wanted to let you know. I don't blame you for not coming to see me. Or coming to the trial. Or any of that."

"Yeah, well, good," said Colt. "You wanna know what I blame you for?"

The old man wouldn't look up.

"Okay," he said querulously.

"I had to identify Mom," Colt said. "Who died in an alley after an overdose. And she was laying there for two weeks. That's what I blame you for."

"Colt, you gotta understand. We were split up. I hadn't seen her for—I don't know how long. A few years. I was in Mexico when she died, Coltie. I didn't even know she was gone. Was—was there a funeral?"

"Yeah, sort of," said Colt. "A service. Me and about five other people, one of whom was some kind of priest or something. The other ones I didn't know. They tried to talk to me but I didn't want to talk to them. They looked like—junkies, I guess. Losers. I didn't want anything to do with them."

"They couldn't have been junkies," said Nova. "Junkies always have better things to do than go to funerals. They must have been someone else."

"Well, whoever they were. Old hippie friends of yours. I wondered where you were. What the hell were you doing in Mexico?"

"Cheap black tar heroin. On the beach."

"That the stuff you were trying to smuggle when you got arrested?"

His father nodded.

"Well," said Colt, "you wanna know what I think? I think it serves you right for being such a stupid asshole."

Nova laughed quietly and nodded yet again. It was getting rather maddening, this nodding, thought Colt.

"Oh, you think it's funny?" Colt said.

"No, I—"

"You think it's funny I had to leave home while I was still in high school because my parents kept stealing my lunch money to get high? Or maybe that I hated my own parents so much that I never wanted to see them again? You think that's funny?"

"No, no. I wasn't laughing because it's funny."

"Then why?" Colt demanded.

"Because it's good," said Nova. "For you to tell me how it is. Lay it down for me, son. I need to hear it. It's almost all over for me, anyway. I don't have a long time left. I kinda thought it was all gonna end for me any day now in prison, and here I am, in a luxury apartment in the middle of New York City." He shook his head. "I'll tell you one thing," he said. "My life sure is full of some strange surprises."

"Yeah," said Colt. "Tell me about it."

"Why was it you came and got me, anyway?"

Colt ran his hand through his hair and sighed.

"It's funny," he said. "Part of me really doesn't know. And part of me does. I had this car accident, like I told you. And I think I must have almost died. I—kept having these dreams, but they weren't dreams. Like I was being . . . judged. I guess. And they were going to read this list of charges against me. Only—I knew they weren't going to be crimes."

His father was nodding as though this was the sort of conversation he had every day. "Uh-huh," he said. "What were they, then?"

"Regrets," said Colt.

"Oh. So you got some regrets."

"Yeah. And there was something else, too."

Nova looked up at him expectantly.

"I, uh—I kept hearing your voice in my head," said Colt. "Kind of like you were watching everything I did, and passing judgment on it. Letting me know whether it was a good thing or a bad thing." He almost laughed. "It used to drive me crazy. I tried everything to stop it, but nothing worked. Not even loud music, or booze, or anything. It just made it worse. So I thought—I don't know. I was tired of running from it, I guess. I wanted to see if it was really your voice, or if it was just something I made up. And now—"

His father was looking at him frankly, curious, interested.

"Well?" he said. "Which was it?"

"I don't know," said Colt.

Shyly his father looked down at his hands.

"That's funny," he said. "I used to pretend I was talking to you. In my head, I mean."

"You did?"

The old man nodded. "I had to keep you alive somehow," he said. "You were all I had left. Even though I didn't deserve you. Make no mistake, Coltie. I know I don't deserve you. I never did. You were an accident, did you know that?"

Colt closed his eyes and turned his head away, his guts aching.

"Well, I guessed that, more or less," he said.

"We never planned on having you. I know that's probably not an easy thing to hear. Maybe I shouldn't tell you this. But I have a reason for wanting you to know. Because later, after you were gone, I realized how lucky I was to have had you at all. By then it was too late. I used to talk to you all the time, and I would pretend you were listening. I didn't even know what you looked like anymore. I didn't even know if I would recognize you when I saw you again. But when I saw you today, I knew it was you right away."

Colt was staring at him bemusedly, listening.

"Sometimes," his father went on, "I wasn't even sure that you had ever happened. I wasn't sure you were real. When you're locked up long enough it seems like you've never been anywhere else, you know?" He shook his head. "No, you wouldn't know. You've never been locked up. But what I mean is—I was hoping you were real. That I didn't just dream you up. And that we were still connected. Somehow. Even just a little bit. And—I guess maybe—"

The door opened at that moment, and Michael came back in, bearing two brown paper bags. He set them down on the floor and, after locking the door again, reached into one of them and came up with a sandwich wrapped in white paper. He handed it to Nova Hart, and then handed another to Colt.

"All they had was smoked turkey," he said. "Hope that's all right."

Colt waited to see if his father was going to finish what he was saying, but his attention was fully taken up by the sandwich now. He watched his father unwrap the paper to reveal a long baguette sliced down the middle, a riot of lettuce and tomatoes and slices of turkey erupting from the sides. Nova picked up a tomato and stared at it like a lover; then he popped it in his mouth and chewed it slowly, closing his eyes in rapture. Obviously he was not going to finish what he was saying until that sandwich was gone. It was probably the best food he'd had in fifteen years, Colt thought. Colt opened his own sandwich, picked it up and took a bite.

"Yeah," he said. "Smoked turkey is all right."

33

—■—

GETTING READY

In the days since her obligatory visit to Colt in the hospital, Francie had busied herself with getting Adencourt in order. Not the *whole* house—that task was far too large. Instead, she concentrated on the parts in which she would spend most of her time: the bedroom, the kitchen and living room, and the oak-paneled den, which she had decided to turn into her office. Not office: Colt had an office. She would have a writing room. Of all the rooms in the house, it was the best to work in. The east wall had a large, deep window that looked out over the property. From there she could see the barn, its spine snapped as if under some tremendous weight, and the stunted apple trees, which—if they still blossomed—would fill one corner of her view with white petals, come spring. And she could just see the pile of earth that marked where the cemetery had once been.

She went to an antique shop in town and purchased a used draftsman's table, which the owner was kind enough to deliver for her, since it weighed more than she did. Here she could scatter her papers and books at will, when eventually she retrieved them from New York; and she could lean on her elbows and stare out at the yard in an endless daydream that would rest her mind and prime it for the work that lay ahead of her.

There were still, she felt, some impediments to her creativity. First was the terrible wound in the earth where the Musgroves had lain—she was going to have to have that filled in, for it pained her to look at it. Second, and more to the point, was the fact that she still had not had a good idea for a poem. She had many ideas, to be sure, but none of them was the kind of idea she used to have, years ago. Now, she could only hunt wistfully through the corners of her mind, lamenting the loss of the light that had once shone there and praying for its return.

Her third concern was of a more venal nature, and that was simply the fact that she had no money. Throughout their marriage, she had relied on Colt for her spending money, never giving a thought to savings of her own; she saw now what a mistake that had been. Colt had given her a household spending account in their first year together, into which he dumped a pile of cash every month. From it, she had withdrawn the money to pay their bills, as well as to buy whatever things struck her fancy: usually books or antiques, occasionally clothes. She had never been much of a clothes shopper. Perhaps if she'd had girlfriends to go out with, she would have shopped more, but when she looked back at the last decade of her life in the city, she realized she had never made any close friends—besides Walter, who owned the bookstore and was her only fan, and whom she hadn't seen in months, anyway. That, too, she thought, must have been one of the effects of Benedor. She had spent most of her time alone, reading, walking, going to movies. That was it. It had been a long, dry season for her, a season that stretched over ten years; but now it was coming to an end, and even though it was winter outside, she could feel something like a warm spring rain falling, soaking in, waking things up.

And that was very good indeed, but it didn't change the fact that she was flat broke. She had at most a few thousand left in her account. It pained her to think that even after the dissolution of their marriage, Francie was going to have to depend on Colt for her survival. Even her new desk had been paid for with one of the credit cards that was in her name but paid for by him, and it was only a matter of time before that card was taken away. Part of her dreaded that moment, and part of her welcomed it, so she could be free of him; yet another part suggested that she go out and indulge herself in a massive spending spree at his expense, one last hurrah before the cord was cut. But if she hadn't been a binge shopper during her marriage, she couldn't see herself becoming one just because she was getting divorced. She was simply going to have to figure out a way to make it on her own. And as long as the house stayed hers, she knew she could find the strength to do it. She had begun to develop that unshakeable strength that comes from standing in one's proper place in the world.

■ ■ ■

Amid the cleaning and organizing and setting up, Francie heard nothing from Colt himself—but she did get a call from his lawyer, one Mr. Gibbons, who had begun the divorce paperwork, and was calling to tell her that she ought to get a lawyer of her own as soon as possible. Yet the formalities of the divorce itself did not interest her in the slightest. As far as she was concerned, it might have been something that was happening to someone else, on the other side of the world. She had only one true concern, beyond how she was to survive: that she should be allowed to keep Adencourt for herself.

Mr. Gibbons, who seemed affable enough for a lawyer, said that he would convey back to his "client" her wish that things proceed as rapidly and smoothly as possible, and her desire to retain "the Pennsylvania property."

"Can't we just get divorced?" Francie asked Mr. Gibbons. "I

mean, nothing personal, but do lawyers really need to get in the middle of it?"

"That's actually up to you," said Mr. Gibbons. "If you want to contest the divorce, or if you want to ask for something, then it's going to be up to lawyers to sort it all out. I know that my client is eager for things to proceed smoothly."

"I was married to your client for almost ten years," said Francie. "Your client is an asshole."

There came a knock on the door, and Francie interrupted Mr. Gibbons in the middle of his reply to tell him that she had to go. When she answered the door, she saw Jennifer Flebberman, who over her housedress was wearing a hooded sweatshirt. Men's workboots came up to her stubbly ankles. Her lips were blue, and her teeth were chattering.

"For heaven's sake," she said. "Mrs. Flebberman! What are you doing out in this weather with no coat on? Come in right now!"

"I just—walked down the hill," Jennifer Flebberman said. "Din't think it was all that cold out 'til I got halfway down."

Having discovered another, drier stash of wood in the basement, Francie had a fire going all the time now, and she led Jennifer Flebberman into the living room and pulled the wingback chair closer to the hearth, forcing the woman to sit down.

"Where are your children?" she asked.

"Melia's watchin' 'em," said Jennifer. "I ain't got long."

"Was there something I could help you with?"

"Oh, I—" Jennifer started and stopped. "I jus' don't—" Interrupting herself again, the graying woman began to sob brokenly, leaning forward and putting her face in her hands. She cried so hard she couldn't speak. Francie put a hand on her bony shoulder and tried to console her, but she cried on and on, trying to get control of herself and failing several times. When most of her tears had run their course and she was able to speak again, she said, "I jus' had ta talk to yeh. I don' know who else ta talk to!"

"I understand," said Francie.

"I don' know what we're gonna do! My kids need their dad! I—
I jus' can't b'leeve Fleb would go and do something like this, and
leave us hangin'! I thought—I don' know. I thought maybe if I
come down here ta see yeh . . . we could work things out a little
bit."

"What's the situation, exactly?" Francie asked. "How much
trouble is he in?"

"Big trouble. Lots of it. Kidnapping. Deadly weapon. State
lines. All of it. They're talkin' about him like he's some kinda
killer, when he ain't! He's the kindes', sweetes' man I ever knew,
and if we don't get 'im back, we ain't gonna make it! We're gonna
have ta move, and lose the house, and I don' know what all's
gonna happen ta the kids!"

"You have my fullest sympathy," said Francie. "If you ask me,
my husband got what was coming to him. And I don't blame
Randy one bit for doing what he did."

Jennifer looked at her with wide, wet eyes. She wiped her nose
on her arm and tried to stop crying.

"I'm ashamed to be askin' yeh this," she said, "but I don' work,
and we din't have much savin's. An' there ain't too many people
we can ask for help. I thought—oh, I hate askin' yeh this when I
hardly even know yeh—but your husband has such a good job,
and—" Her voice trailed off, ashamed and hopeful. Francie nodded.

"You need money," she said. "Is that it?"

"Yes," said Jennifer Flebberman. "Please. I'm sorry. I really am.
But I don' know what else ta do."

Francie sighed. "I don't know how to tell you this, but my husband and I are getting a divorce," she said. "And I didn't have
much savings of my own. You and I are in the same boat, Mrs.
Flebberman."

"You can call me Jenny," said Jenny.

"Jenny. He and I are not exactly getting along right now. So he's
not likely to give me anything I ask for. I have a little money of my

own. I could let you have some of it. Would—would a thousand be all right?"

Jennifer Flebberman nodded. "That would see us through a couplea months," she said. "If we're careful."

"And I have another idea," said Francie. "Your husband left some boxes of comic books up in the attic. They've been there for years. I had already mentioned to him that I might take them into the city and have a friend look at them. Some of them might be collector's items."

"Really?" said Jennifer Flebberman. She had calmed down now, and she looked at Francie with new eyes. "You think so?"

"They're not worth millions, or anything. But there are a lot of them. They might bring in a few hundred dollars. And then—well, maybe by then things will have changed." Francie was already plotting what she was going to do to get Colt to drop the charges against Randy Flebberman, or at least lessen them; if it came down to testifying against Colt, to prove that he had it coming, she would, she thought, with pleasure. Oh, wait—spouses weren't allowed to testify against each other. Or was it that they weren't allowed to testify *for* each other? She couldn't remember. She hadn't watched enough television. Damn it, she thought. The more I don't know, the more I need the lawyers after all.

"I'll go into the city tomorrow," said Francie. "First thing. Once I talk to Walter and get some idea from him of what they're worth, I'll get back to you. And I'll try and have a talk with my husband. Or ex-husband."

"I don' know how I could thank yeh for that," said Jennifer Flebberman.

"We're neighbors, aren't we?" said Francie. "We have to help each other out."

34

———————■———————

ONCE MORE TO THE APARTMENT

As long as Francie was going back to the city, she thought she might as well stop at the apartment to retrieve the boxes in her closet. They contained her old papers from college, a number of bookmarked and underlined poetry anthologies, and ten aging copies of *Poems from My Sinister Hand,* and of all the things she owned these were the only ones she really would have regretted losing if Colt decided to throw them away. She didn't want to see him; she was content to talk with him through Mr. Gibbons. But she still had a key for the apartment, and, knowing him, she figured that he would have gone back to work as soon as possible. He wouldn't let something as insignificant as a broken arm ruin his chances for making money. Not the Colt she knew.

She loaded her old-new pickup truck with Flebberman's comic books and headed into the city, confident that she had timed her visit to miss seeing Colt completely. It was a covert mission—he would never even know she'd been there. She'd mastered the idiosyncrasies of the truck's transmission by now, and she had to laugh at herself as she chugged through the Holland Tunnel—the last time she'd gone under the river, she'd been a different person, leading a different life. She never would have imagined herself in the flannel shirt and jeans that had already become the uniform of her Pennsylvania self, driving a pickup truck full of comic books.

Upon arriving at the apartment, she was disconcerted to learn that Colt had changed the locks. It took her several attempts to figure this out; she thought perhaps the key was just sticking in the deadbolt, but no matter how she rattled it, it refused to open. Francie cursed. So he hadn't changed after all. He was just being subtle about how he was going to make her life miserable, that was all. Out of frustration, she banged on the door.

"Damn you!" she said. "You asshole! *Now* what do I do?"

But much to her surprise, the lock clicked and the door creaked open.

"Francie?" came a small voice—not Colt's.

"*Michael?*" Francie said.

Michael was hiding behind the door, and he peeked out now, timid as a mouse.

"Are you—hi," he said. "Are you still mad?"

Francie was unable to believe her eyes. "Oh, my God, Mikey," she said. "I thought you went to Denver!"

Michael opened the door wider now and stood there, grinning at her sheepishly. "Nope," he said. "I came here instead."

"What on earth are you *doing* here?"

"I got rid of all the—the *stuff*," he said, looking up and down the hall to make sure no one was listening. "Just like you wanted me to. And I've been helping Colt. He gave me a job."

"He gave you a *job*?"

"Yeah. I'm his assistant. You coming in?"

Francie stepped in and Michael closed the door behind her. She stared at him a moment longer, as if still unable to believe her eyes. "Oh, Michael, you little weirdo," she said, holding out her arms. He fell into them gratefully and squeezed her around the middle. "I'm so glad to see you."

"You're not mad anymore?" he asked hopefully.

"I'm sorry about that, honey," she said, kissing his ear. "I just—"

"I know," said Michael. "I was being really stupid. And I'm sorry. I learned my lesson, believe me. I'm not running errands for any more friends."

"Or picking up girls in parking lots?"

"Or that, either."

"Where is Colt? That bastard changed the locks on me."

"He had to," said Michael. "Flebberman threw away his keys."

"He did?"

"Yeah. He didn't do it because of you. He had no way to lock it otherwise."

"Oh." Deflated now, Francie felt slightly foolish. "Well, where is he, anyway? Not here, I hope."

"He's out clothes shopping with his father," said Michael.

Francie cocked her head and stared at him, not sure she'd heard him right.

"What did you say?" she said. "Clothes shopping? With his—"

"Father," Michael said. "We went and got him out of jail."

Francie shook her head, as if to clear her ears. "You got Colt's father out of—"

"Yeah. He was paroled. Colt stuck up for him and they let him out early."

"Mikey, you must be confused," Francie said. "Colt's father is dead."

"Oh, right," Michael said. "Shit, maybe he wanted to tell you about this himself. Well, too late. His father wasn't dead. He was in prison."

Francie sat down on the sofa. "Good Lord," she said, stunned. "What next?"

Michael shrugged. "I dunno," he said. "That's all I know. Listen, Francie, when you meet him, try and act surprised, okay?"

"Michael," said Francie, "I won't be acting. I can promise you that."

"I'm really glad to see you again," he said. "I was sort of afraid you would never want to see me again. After all the—"

"Of course I would want to see you again," Francie said. "I can't explain what I was going through, Mikey, it was just—"

"I know. It was that freaked-out supermarket, right?" Michael said.

Francie laughed. "I told you, the supermarket had nothing to do with it. I was going through something really strong, Mikey. Something really powerful. And I'm out the other side of it now, and I feel—better."

"I heard you guys are getting divorced," Michael said.

"Yes. That's true."

"Well, you know what I say—better late than never."

"That's true of me in a lot of ways these days, Michael," said Francie. "I know exactly what you mean."

"That Colt, though—he's full of surprises. I'm starting to think he's not so bad. He did give me a job, after all."

"How much is he paying you?"

"Well—nothing. At first. But he's letting me stay here. Which is cool of him. He said maybe later he would put me on the payroll."

"I'm proud of you, Michael," Francie said.

"And then he goes and springs his dad from prison."

"This I have to see," Francie said.

35

EVERYTHING IS CONNECTED

Colt had taken his father to a department store with the intention of making only a quick foray into the men's department, but as soon as they came in the front door, Nova seemed to become paralyzed and disoriented. It had been fifteen years since he'd worn anything but an orange jumpsuit, he told his son, and he was afraid he'd forgotten how to wear other kinds of clothes. Colt told him that was impossible; you didn't forget how to wear clothes. It wasn't like riding a bike, after all.

"No, but you forget how to act when you're wearing them," Nova said.

"Come on," said Colt, growing impatient—for the last five minutes they'd been standing by the front door, and the security guards were beginning to look at them with suspicion. "It's not like you're going for a job interview. You just want something to wear that doesn't scream 'convict.'"

Nova looked around with wide eyes at the huge store, and the crowds of people moving through it. Tinny Christmas carols drifted down from the ceiling—the happy, unconscious sort of crap they played to keep you shopping, Colt thought. He tried to remember what had happened to Thanksgiving. It must have only just passed, but he had no memory of it. He and Francie always had a turkey dinner, at least. But this year, of course, there was nothing. He hadn't even noticed it was missing. And now it was somehow December.

"Everything about me screams 'convict,'" said Nova. "Everything. Do you know I can't even take a crap any more unless I've been given permission?"

"There are some things I don't need to know," said Colt.

"Can I help you with something, sir?" said one of the security guards, a large man with a crew cut and a blue blazer, finally coming over to them.

"We're just looking," said Colt.

"I haven't been out in public in fifteen years," Nova told the security guard, who raised his eyebrows.

"All right, you don't need to tell your life story to everyone you meet," Colt said. He took his father by the elbow and steered him toward the men's department. They went up the escalator to the second floor, with Nova latched firmly on to the moving handrail and peering over the side at the shoppers below. They entered a landscape of ties and shirts, and once again Nova froze.

"Are you kidding? I don't need any of this stuff," he whispered.

"Come on. We'll just get you a couple of pairs of khakis or something. Some more denim shirts. You have to have more than one outfit . . . Nova." Colt still wasn't sure what to call his father. "Dad" was out of the question. "Father" sounded ridiculous.

"I'm not going to need it."

"Yes, you are."

"No, Colt, really."

They were approached now by a matronly woman in a skirt suit, who exuded the scents of brand-new fabric and flowery perfume; Colt could hear the plump sausages of her thighs, encased in dark panty hose, whisking together as she walked.

"May I help you gentlemen?" she inquired sweetly.

"Here you go," said Colt to his father. "This man—my father, I mean—needs a few new things. But he's not sure what he wants."

"What style of clothing?"

"Casual," said Colt. "Some chinos, some shirts, a pair of shoes." He'd forgotten that he himself was dressed in the only thing he could wear over his upraised cast, which was a sweatshirt with one arm scissored neatly up the seam, and a pair of jeans; yet he was pleased to see that the saleswoman bowed her head deferentially just as if he was dressed in his best suit. Maybe she recognizes me, he thought. "I'll just hand him over to you," he said, "if you don't mind."

"Won't you come with me, sir?" said the saleslady. With his eyes wide and his expression suddenly beatific, it seemed that Nova had already become entranced by the woman. Colt realized, with some amusement, that it had likely been fifteen years since his father had been this close to a female, at least one that wasn't in uniform.

"I'll be right over here," Colt told his father, pointing to a row of armchairs. "And then we'll get you a suit."

Nova Hart shot an anxious look over his shoulder as he was being led away. Colt made himself as comfortable as he could on one of the chairs and perused a magazine, waiting. About fifteen minutes later the saleslady reappeared.

"Excuse me, sir," she said. "The gentleman . . ."

Colt looked up. "Yes?"

"He's locked himself into one of the changing rooms, and he won't come out."

Colt struggled to his feet. "Well, maybe he's just trying stuff on," he said.

"I think I heard him—well, crying," said the woman. "Is he ill?"

"Crying?" Oh God, he thought.

"Come this way, sir. I'll show you where he is."

The woman brought Colt to the dressing rooms and pointed to one of the Venetian-style doors. Colt tapped on it.

"Nova?" he called. "Are you in there?"

There was no reply, but he heard the snuffling and honking of a nose being blown.

"Nova," he said. "Come on out."

"No," his father replied through the door. "It's too—"

"Too what?"

"—big," he said. "Too big."

"You're scared? Is that it?"

"I'm not scared," said the old man irately. "I just feel better in here, that's all."

"You can't stay in there all day, you know."

"It's just . . . the walls."

"The walls? What about them?"

There was a long pause.

"I miss them," came the reply.

"Is your father agoraphobic?" asked the saleslady.

Colt turned to her—he'd forgotten she was there. "No, he's a—yes," he said. "An agoraphobic."

"I'm not . . . whatever you're calling me!" said Nova Hart. "I'm a con!"

The woman's eyebrows rose the same way the security guard's had, and she took a tiny step backward.

"All right, all right," said Colt, embarrassed. "Come on out, Nova. We'll go home, if it makes you feel better."

"It would," said Nova, but still he didn't open the door.

"I'm sorry, was it something I did?" said the saleslady. "I can't imagine—"

"No, it's not your fault," said Colt. He tapped on the door again. "Nova, come out and we'll go home."

"Make her go away," Nova whispered. "I can't come out while she's there."

Colt looked at the saleslady again. "I think he means you," he said. "It's nothing personal."

"Oh," said the saleslady. "Well, I certainly am sorry."

"Nothing to be sorry about."

The saleslady whisked away again, looking back once over her shoulder.

"All right," said Colt. "She's gone."

The door opened, and Nova stood there in the doorway, face red and flushed. "I—I don't know what came over me," he said. "Can we go now, please?"

"Yes, okay. We're going."

"I don't really need any clothes," he said. "I only need one suit."

Colt sighed. "All right," he said. "Why do you only need one suit?"

"Just something halfway decent, to be buried in. If I'd stayed in the joint, they would have taken care of all that. Funeral expenses and so on. They never shoulda let me out."

"What on earth are you talking about?" Colt said.

"Didn't they tell you, at the prison?" said Nova.

Colt stared at him. "Tell me what?" he said.

"I'm dying," his father said as they stepped onto the escalator. "I have AIDS."

Colt felt a chill creep up from the bottom of his spine. The old man had related this as casually as if he was telling Colt he had a cold.

"No," he said. "They didn't tell me that."

"I was sure they would have," said Nova, without much emotion. "Kind of like when you adopt a puppy from a shelter. They tell you everything that's wrong with it. So you know what you're dealing with."

"Nobody said anything."

"Well," said his father. "Shame on them. That would have been a lot easier than me telling you myself. Now let's get out of here," his father said. "Please? I can't take it anymore."

"All right," Colt said. "We're going."

■ ■ ■

They waited for a taxi for several minutes in silence. Colt couldn't think of what to say, or rather, he couldn't think of what to *feel*. Was he supposed to be sad about this? A part of him said yes, but another part of him remembered a time when he would have been almost happy to hear that his father was dying, or dead. And that had not been so long ago.

They got into the taxi and Colt gave the driver directions.

"You're mighty quiet all of a sudden," said Nova.

"I'm just—taking it in."

"I got it from dirty needles, you know. Not from—the other way."

"Right," said Colt.

"I could tell you were wondering."

"No, I was just—well, yes. I was wondering."

"Yeah. You never know with us prison types." Nova grinned.

"Jesus," Colt said. "Come on."

"Relax. Just a little joke."

"Why didn't you tell me sooner?"

"Because, I really thought you already knew. Besides, it's not like I just found out. I've had it for years. For a long time I just had that HIV business. It didn't turn into anything. But now—I'm starting to develop symptoms. Coughing a lot. Lesions on my lungs. I have to take a lot of medication."

"When did you get it?" Colt said. "You told the parole board you hadn't been using any drugs since you came to prison."

"That was a lie," said Nova. "You tell them that because they don't like to hear how corrupt the prison system is. You don't want to remind them of what a joke the whole thing is. They have this happy little fantasy that prison is a place where people get rehabilitated, and where bad things never happen." He laughed disdainfully. "Those motherfuckers are so full of shit, I'd like to cut every one of their throats," he said. "You know where I got the stuff from? The guards," he said. "They smuggled it in up their asses. They packed it in balloons, and up the poop chute it went. Those guards are looser than the biggest queens in the pen. We bought it from them. And we shared needles, us prisoners. We only had one or two. We had to sharpen them against the wall, they got so dull."

Colt felt vaguely nauseous. "How long did that go on?"

His father shrugged. "Years," he said. "I don't know exactly. I really am clean now, though. Have been for a long time. But at first, it wasn't any different on the inside than it was on the out-side. It's a fucking joke. Just so you know your taxpayer dollars aren't accomplishing much."

Colt chose to ignore that comment. "So you got it from one of your prison buddies."

"Yeah."

"Jesus."

"I'm telling you, boy. It was a mess in there. The whole system is a big joke. Don't ever go to jail. It makes you crazy just trying to figure out how things work."

"I don't plan on it," Colt said.

"Good."

"So," said Colt. "Well, I'm—sorry. That you're sick."

Nova looked at him.

"Thanks," he said.

They were silent for a long time, the cab stopping and starting in the traffic. After a while Nova turned to Colt again and asked, "Do you believe in God?"

Colt was surprised. "In God?"

"Yes."

"Well—no. As a matter of fact, I don't."

"Oh. Why not?"

"I don't know. Because it seems like a kind of primitive idea, that's why. Like the kind of thing people believe only because it makes them feel better. Why?"

"I just wondered if it's because of me that you don't believe, or if you had another reason."

"Well," said Colt, "we weren't exactly a churchgoing family."

"No," said Nova. "I never could stomach it when I was a kid, either. But I guess I been thinking about it a lot more lately."

"Do you? Believe in God?"

"Me?" Nova frowned. "I don't know. All I know is, I used to pray that I wouldn't die in prison. I didn't think anyone was listening. But then—you came along."

Colt snorted. "I'm not God."

"No. I know that. What I'm saying is, maybe something sent you to my parole hearing to get me out."

"I don't know why I went to that parole hearing," said Colt. "Maybe God is as good a reason as anything else. But I didn't hear anyone talking to me."

"No. Of course not. That's not really what I meant."

"Well, what did you mean, then?"

"I guess I just wonder that if there really was a God, and he really did send you to the prison, maybe you wouldn't even know about it at all. In case that's the way it works. I don't know. I'm really just guessing."

"Huh."

"Yeah? Waddaya think?"

"I don't know," Colt said. "It's not something I ever think about."

When they were just a few blocks from the apartment, still stuck in traffic, Colt said, "You wanna know what I do think about?"

"Sure."

"It's not going to make any sense. And it doesn't have anything to do with what we were talking about. But I was just thinking about this idea I have. Kinda hard to explain."

"Try me."

"It's about the stock market," Colt said. "Did you ever notice—well, no, you probably never did. It's . . . it's got to do with the way the market is connected to the rest of the world."

"I see," said Nova.

"It's something that just calms me down to think about," Colt said. "It makes me feel like there really is a reason for everything. It has to do with—I don't know, with the way the universe works, or something. See, all those numbers, when you put them together in a matrix, they form a pattern. You look at them one way, they're just values, and that's it. They don't have to do with anything else. But you look at them another way, and things start to emerge. You see how world events have an impact. This is not just conjecture—it's real. A natural disaster happens, or a war, and the market reacts. That's not hocus-pocus."

"Right," said Nova.

"So then one day I started thinking, if big things have a big impact on the market, then little things must have a little impact. See what I mean? I'm not talking about things that make the newspapers. I mean the little everyday things that happen to everybody, all the time. Those things must show up, too. Because you know why?"

"Why?" asked Nova.

"Because everything is connected," said Colt. "The more you're in the business the more you realize that. Everything is connected to everything else. Joe Shmoe in California wakes up on the wrong side of the bed, has a bad day—that shows up in the numbers. Somehow. Don't ask me how. I'm still trying to figure it out. But I know it's true. It has to be." He glanced at his father to see how he was digesting this information. "It's not something I ever talk about with anybody," said Colt. "But you asked me if I believe in God. I don't, but I do believe in this. Not just in the stock market. In that everything is connected. I know we all believe it, all us traders. Or something like it, anyway. A lot of us carry good-luck charms, did you know that?"

"No. What's yours?"

"Well, I lost mine," said Colt. "A couple of months ago. I guess I knew that was when things were going to start falling apart for me. But I pretended not to notice. Or to care."

"Yeah, but—what was it?"

"It was a ring," said Colt. "A simple little gold band."

"Why that? What did that mean?"

"It was Mom's," Colt said. "The day I moved out, I took it with me. I wanted something of hers, but I knew she wouldn't give me anything. Or she would give me the wrong thing. And I didn't want to tell her I was leaving, anyway. I just wanted to go. So I went into your room and I took this old ring out of her jewelry box. I wore it on a chain around my neck for years. But it fell off when we moved, I guess."

"I remember that ring," said Nova. "It was her father's. Solid gold. His wedding ring."

"Yeah. It had engraving in it. Initials and a date."

"Yeah, that was it. Good thing you took it, you know. When you did."

"Why?"

"Because she probably would have ended up hocking it for dope. That's what happened to all our stuff. She looked for that ring. I remember. She was hoping to get twenty bucks for it, but we never could figure out what happened to it."

"Oh," said Colt.

There was another long silence.

"You know, that idea you have—how things are connected. To the numbers."

"Yeah?"

"It's pretty good," said Nova. "It's not so different from what other great thinkers in other times have believed. Did you know that? The ancient Chinese sages believed something very similar. I mention them because I've always found them kinda interesting. I would read about 'em in the library. The Taoist masters. They thought that if you were good enough at meditation, you could see the nature of everything reflected in everything else. Didn't matter what you looked at. A flower. A bug. You could see the entire structure of all creation, mirrored in that one little thing."

"Yeah," Colt said. "That's it."

"That's what you mean?"

"Yeah. Exactly what I mean."

"Far fucking out," said Nova Hart, as they finally emerged from the shiny snarl of cars that clogged the intersections and pulled up in front of the apartment.

36

TO LIVE AT ADENCOURT

Colt opened the door to the apartment and entered. Then he stopped, surprised, for there, sitting next to Michael on the couch, was Francie.

"Oh," he said. "Hi."

"Hi," said Francie.

"The Coltster!" said Michael.

Nova Hart trailed him in, and he, too, stopped upon seeing Francie. "Hello there!" he said.

"The Novarama!" said Michael.

"Oh, my God," said Francie, staring at Nova. "So you *are* real."

Nova smiled, pleased. "Yes!" he said. "Depending on what you mean by 'real,' of course."

Francie stood up. "I'm Francine. Francine Hart," she said. "For the moment."

"Yes, I heard the bad news," said Nova, shaking her hand. "I'm Nova Hart."

"It's a—a great surprise to meet you," Francie said. "It's funny, but Colt never said anything about you to me." She looked at Colt archly, but he pretended not to notice.

"Yes, well, I don't blame him," said Nova. "You certainly are a very beautiful girl." He looked at his son, who studiously avoided his gaze, too.

"Thank you," said Francie. "Colt, can I speak with you in private, please?"

"Ah, okay," said Colt. "Sure. I guess."

■ ■ ■

They went into the bedroom and Francie closed the door. Then she turned and put her hands on her hips.

"You're just full of surprises," she said.

Colt shrugged, with his good arm. "What can I say?" he said.

"Why didn't you ever tell me your father was alive?"

"Why do you think?"

"You were ashamed."

He nodded. "That's pretty much it," he said.

"And yet Michael tells me you're responsible for getting him out of prison."

"Yeah. That's true. But they were gonna let him out, anyway."

"But you took him home with you."

"Yeah. Obviously."

Francie shook her head. "I don't understand," she said.

"Yeah, well, neither do I, to tell the truth," said Colt. "It just seemed like the right thing to do. At the time. I wasn't really thinking when I did it."

"Well, Coltrane Hart," said Francie, "in all the time I've known you, I have to say that is a first. You could have told me about him, you know. I wouldn't have judged you for whatever it was he did."

"That wasn't the point," Colt said. "I guess I felt like maybe it was time to . . . well, not start over, exactly. It's a little late for that."

"What *did* he do, by the way? He didn't kill anyone, did he?"

"He was trying to smuggle heroin from Mexico," said Colt. "So he could sell it and get rich. He got caught at the border. And I didn't tell you, not because of what you would think. I didn't tell you because I didn't want to know him anymore. There's— there's a lot of history there, Francie. A lot of stuff happened to me that I just wanted to put behind me. When I was a kid, I mean. He may seem like kind of a neat old guy now, but he was a miserable father. Really bad. And for a long time I just wanted to pretend that it had never happened. But—"

"But you figured out you can't do that," said Francie.

"Yeah," said Colt. "That's right."

"Yes," said Francie. "Well. I don't really know what to say. It's weird, Colt. We've been together all this time, and all of a sudden I feel like we've only just been introduced."

"Yeah, well," said Colt uncertainly. "So you just stopped by to—"

"Yeah, right. I just wanted some of my old stuff," said Francie. "My papers and books and so on."

"Yeah. Okay. Well, you know where they are."

"Yeah. And there was something else I wanted to talk to you about."

"What?"

"Jennifer Flebberman came to see me yesterday."

"She did? What did she want?"

"What do you think she wanted?"

Colt rubbed his eyes tiredly. "Yeah," he said. "Don't tell me. She wants me to drop the charges against her husband. And you agree with her."

Francie folded her arms. "Yeah," she said. "I do."

"Because you think I had it coming. That's what you said to me in the hospital, when I was lying there in agony. That I deserved it."

"Well, Colt—"

"Don't say it again. Just don't. I already know what you think."

"Fine," Francie said. "That woman has four children, Coltrane. They're already in trouble financially. If Randy Flebberman goes to jail—"

"I know, I know," said Colt. "I already dropped them."

Francie stared at him for a long moment, not sure whether she believed what she was hearing. "What did you say?" she asked finally.

"The charges. I dropped them. I called the police yesterday and told them I wasn't going to press charges. I guess she just hadn't heard yet. He's going to be trapped in bureaucratic limbo for a while, and there's nothing I can do about that. But he's going to be home soon."

"Oh, my God," said Francie.

"Yeah. You misjudged me." Colt smiled, a self-effacing grin, a look that said, for once, that he had been wrong and was now trying to make things right. "I've been thinking about a lot of stuff, you know. I had a lot of time to think in the hospital. And—there was this dream I had. Three dreams, actually. More like nightmares. And I realized I never should have tried to move that cemetery. All this—" he gestured to his broken arm—"and everything else besides, happened because of that. It's like—I don't know. Signs."

"Signs?"

"From—wherever. I don't know. The universe or whatever."

"Holy shit," said Francie. "I do believe Coltrane Hart has had a spiritual awakening."

Colt bristled. "Now, hold on there," he said. "It's not like I've found Jesus or something. I mean, I'm not suddenly going to start going to church or anything like that."

"Oh, no," said Francie. "God forbid." She smiled.

"Good one," said Colt. "Very funny."

"Well," said Francie, "what can I say? I'm glad."

"I thought you would be."

"Oh, and I found something of yours." Francie plucked an object from her pocket and handed it to him. "Up in the bedroom," she said. "In the floor. It was kind of stuck between a couple of floorboards. I don't know what happened to the chain."

It was his good-luck charm—his mother's ring. Colt took it and held it in his palm.

"Wow," he said. "I thought this was gone."

"Well, there you have it," said Francie.

"Thanks." He stuck it in his pocket and patted it. He was about to open the door, but something in her expression told him she had more to say. "Was there something else?"

"Yes. I heard from your lawyer."

"Oh, yeah. Gibbons."

"He wants me to get a lawyer of my own."

"Yeah, well, you know, you should. I mean, it's just the way it's done. I guess. So they can do all the arguing and stuff for us. That way we don't have to hash it out ourselves. It's a lot easier that way."

"Well, I thought I would talk to you first," said Francie. "Just to let you know what it is I want."

"Uh—okay. I guess that's all right."

"I want the house," said Francie. "That's it. Nothing else. No money, no stocks. Nothing from your portfolio. Just the house."

"Oh," said Colt. "That's it? You're sure?"

She nodded. "It's the only thing we've got that means anything to me," she said.

"What are you going to do for money?"

"I don't know. But I can take care of myself. I can get a job somewhere. Maybe in Plainsburg."

"In Plainsburg? Is there even a job market in Plainsburg?"

"It's not your problem, Colt," she said. "I can handle it. I just wanted to tell you."

"Yeah. Okay. Well. I don't have a problem with that. It's already paid for, anyway, and to tell the truth, I sort of regretted buying it. Not sure it's ever going to appreciate."

"*I* appreciate it," said Francie. "And that's all that matters."

Colt drew a deep breath. "There's, ah—there's something I wanted you to know, Francie. I mean, something I felt like I should say to you."

She waited, hands in her pockets.

"And that is that I'm—well, I'm sorry."

Once again Francie wasn't sure she had heard him right. "You're sorry?" she repeated. "Is that what you said?"

"Yeah."

"For?"

"Well," he said, "I guess everything."

"I might need to hear some specifics," Francie said.

"Well, hold on now," said Colt. "This is not me coming crawling to you on my knees. I'm just saying, is all. I have feelings of—of sorryness. In a general way. About everything."

"Coltrane, clarify," said Francie. "If you're apologizing to me for something, I'd like to know what for. That's all."

"Right. Well—the, uh—the whole thing about kids. And all that."

"You mean the fact that you had a vasectomy without telling me."

"Yes. That."

"You're sorry for that?"

"I am," said Colt. "I mean, I had my reasons, and you know what they were, so I guess there's no need to go into it all over again. But some stuff has happened to me in the last couple of weeks that's kind of—changed me, I guess. And I can see now that maybe I didn't handle that whole issue very well. And I just wanted to let you know that it wasn't anything personal."

Something in Francie's face softened then, it seemed to him. She shifted on her feet, staring up at him. Colt found it not as hard as he'd thought it would be to look at her as he was saying these things.

"It wasn't personal?"

"No. It really wasn't. It wasn't that I didn't want to have kids with you. It was just that I didn't want to have them, period."

"Right."

"So, just so you know." He paused. "Did you, uh—did you think it was personal?"

"Well, to tell the truth, Colt, yes, I did," said Francie. "And I think it would have been damn near impossible not to take it that way, just so *you* know. It would have required a level of self-control that no human possesses, not to take something like that personally."

"Yeah. I know. Well, I really am sorry about it. And it really wasn't personal. And another thing," said Colt.

Francie waited.

"I know you told me you wanted a divorce," he said, "and if that's what you want, then you can have it. And you can have the house, too. I won't fight you on that. But I just had to say this one thing, which is this. And that is—"

Francie still waited, not saying anything.

"I don't know if *I* want a divorce," he said. "I mean, I'm not mad enough at you to justify that. It just doesn't make sense. I'm not mad at you at all, in fact. You didn't do anything. I know you were the one who asked for it. And I'm not saying that you have to come back to me or anything. I'm not begging you to forget all about everything. That's not what I'm doing."

"I see," said Francie. "What are you doing, then?"

"What I'm doing is—I mean—I don't know. I just wanted to ask you if you really felt like a divorce was . . . well, was necessary."

"I guess I don't know what necessary means, in this context," she said.

"You don't?"

"No. But I do know what I need. And that is I need to be on my own. To do my own thing. I guess that's what's necessary."

"Oh."

"One thing I have to tell you, Colt," said Francie, "is that a lot has changed with me, too. You remember when we met, there at the museum, ten years ago? How we were then?"

"Yeah."

"That was not me," she said. "Or rather, that wasn't the full me."

"It wasn't?"

"I've changed, too," she said. "A lot. Maybe even more than you have. For one thing, I was barely twenty-one years old then, and now I'm thirty. That's a big difference. But I don't know. We both changed, I guess. And that's what makes me wonder if we even belong together anymore. What I realized is—" She stopped herself, putting a hand to her throat. "Oh, shit," she said.

"You okay?" Colt asked.

"Yeah," she said, wiping her eyes on her hand. "Did you ever . . ."

Colt waited.

"Did you ever think that we were together for the wrong reasons? Because we only needed each other? Not because we loved each other?"

Colt frowned. "I don't know," he said. "I never thought about it that way."

"Oh," said Francie. "Because the thing is, I have."

"I see," said Colt.

"I never knew you as I was, when I wasn't on those pills," said Francie. "And you never knew me. You never knew what I really was like, the real me. You only saw the medicated me. And that wasn't me. It was only half me. You never saw me do all the things I could do. I stopped wanting to do *anything*. And that wasn't who I was. I used to have dreams, Colt. I used to be really ambitious. Like you. I had goals, and I was all set to go after them."

"I thought they helped you, those pills," said Colt.

"Helped me, maybe. At first. They helped me not be so scared. But then, after I stopped being scared, I just kept on taking them. And I see now—" here she put a hand over her mouth again, pausing before she could go on—"I see now that I was taking them just so I could pretend I was happy."

"Happy. With me."

She nodded.

"Right," said Colt. "So you were . . . what? Lying?"

"Um," said Francie, her voice quivering, "okay, if you want to look at it that way. I don't think that's fair, but I could see how you might feel a little—well, cheated maybe. Out of being with the real me. If that's how you feel. I don't know."

"Okay," said Colt. "Well, I guess it doesn't matter. Not any more. Not if it's over."

"No," said Francie. "Not if it's over."

"So."

There was a long, dead pause. Francie struggled to breathe; she sat down on the bed. Colt put his hand on her shoulder and sat down next to her, but she got up and moved away from him.

"No," she said. "Don't."

"Sorry."

"I should go," Francie said.

"You don't have to. Not because of me. You can stay if you want. Michael's here. You can hang out with him."

"No. I really have to go."

"All right."

She stood up and went to the door.

"Francie," Colt said.

She turned. "Yeah?" she said.

"For what it's worth," he said, "I always saw you doing something big. And I used to wonder sometimes what was holding you back. Whatever that thing is, whether it was the pills, or something else—even being with me—I just want you to know something."

She waited.

"I'm glad it's gone," he said.

Francie managed a smile.

"Thanks," she said, and she walked out of the bedroom, leaving him looking after her.

37

SOLD

She was the last of Walter's customers to get the news.

In the past, Walter had kept long hours, opening early and often not closing until ten at night; since the only other thing he did besides sell books was sleep, he often used to say, he might as well be sitting behind his register. He had never, in Francie's experience, been closed. But pulling up in front of the bookstore, she saw with sinking heart that the lights were off, and there was a sign taped to the door. She didn't need to read it to know what it said, but she forced herself to get out of the truck and look anyway.

CLOSED FOREVER

it said, in Walter's bold, regal handwriting.

"Oh, shit," said Francie. "Oh, Walter!"

She pressed her face to the window, shading her eyes from the glare. Walter hadn't even removed his stock yet—all his books were still on their shelves, waiting for creditors to come haul them away, no doubt. And yet—

Francie had to look twice to make sure her eyes weren't playing tricks on her. She knew exactly where *Poems from My Sinister Hand* had been sitting, just a foot to the right of the cash register, leaning on its own small Plexiglas display rack. But now it was gone. She squinted harder to see if maybe it had just fallen over or something, and that was when she spied a handwritten note taped to the rack, written in the same hand, in red marker:

THIS BOOK HAS FOUND A HOME

Francie could hardly breathe.

Someone had bought her book.

She continued to lean against the window for a long minute, resting her forehead on it, covering her face with her hands as if she was still looking inside, although her eyes were shut.

When she had gotten control of herself again, she turned and got back into her pickup truck. She started it up and wrestled with the gear shift, listening for the satisfying *chunk* it always made when she put it into first.

Then, in a cloud of blue smoke, she pulled away from the curb, heading back toward the tunnel and out of the city, back to the place where she belonged.

EPILOGUE

Less than two weeks later, there came a knock at her door, and when she went to see who it was, there stood a free Flebberman in his familiar snowsuit and boots, smiling a chagrined half-smile.

"Hello, John Dillinger," she said. "I half expected to see you in stripes."

Flebberman laughed self-consciously. "Yeah," he said. "I guess that's about right."

"So they sprung you in time for Christmas?"

He nodded. "I prob'ly got you to thank for that," he said. "You puttin' the bug in yer husband's ear."

"Believe it or not," Francie said, "he did it on his own. As far as I can tell."

Flebberman was taken aback. "You gotta be kiddin'," he said.

"No, I'm serious. Unless the ghosts of Christmas past, present, and future ganged up on him."

This seemed to be too much for Flebberman to take in. He simply stood there and stared at her, his mouth hanging slightly open, as always.

"He let me go?" he said finally. "Why?"

"He's been reborn," said Francie. "Don't tell him I said that, of course, because he'll deny it. But that's what happened. You want to come in? Not packing heat, are you?"

Flebberman blushed. "Naw," he said.

"I never had you figured for a stick-up artist, anyway," said Francie. "It didn't seem like your style."

Flebberman stepped in and scraped his boots on the mat. Another snowfall had come the night before, not much more than a heavy dusting, but this time it had stayed; particles of ice scattered around the foyer as he shed his boots and entered the living room. The thawing season was over, and things had begun to freeze again. It would be a cold Christmas Eve tonight, and a solitary one for Francie, but it was the way she wanted it. She had refused Colt's offer to spend the holiday with him and his father in the city, and Michael had gone back to Indianapolis to see their parents. Once upon a time, not very long ago, the idea of spending Christmas alone would have terrified her. Now, however, she looked forward to it.

"What can I do for you?" Francie asked.

"I, uh—got somethin' I wanted to ask ya," he said.

"Yes, and now that you're here I've remembered I have something to show you," said Francie.

"Yeah? What?"

"No, you go first."

"Well, the, uh, mortal remains—y'know, the fambly—the police got 'em now, and they said we could come get 'em back, if we got a reburial permit. Which I got already. I wanted to ask ya—could we—can I, I mean—put them back? Where they belong?"

"Of course we can," said Francie. "We can do it today, if you like."

"Not today. I gotta go pick 'em up yet," Flebberman said. "At the police station. Not lookin' for'ard to seein' cops again, but waddaya gonna do. How about day after tomorra?"

"That would be fine. I don't have much else going on. Now, wait here a minute," said Francie.

She went upstairs to the master bedroom and retrieved Marly's diary. Bringing it back downstairs, she said, "I thought you might want to see this. I found it under the stairs."

Flebberman took the book in his reddened and callused hands, opening it carefully to the first page. "What is it?" he asked.

"It's a diary," Francie said. "What's really important is who it belonged to."

"Who?"

"Marly Musgrove."

Flebberman took the book to the wingback chair and sat down, his snowsuit whiffing and zipping. "Holy Jeez," he said, staring at it in amazement. "You gotta be kiddin' me."

"No. It's the real thing."

"You found it *where*?"

"Under the stairs," said Francie. "There's a secret kind of space, just there." She pointed to the wall under the main staircase. "You get to it from the closet in the master bedroom. You never knew about it?"

Flebberman shook his head. "No," he said. "I had no idea nothin' like that was there."

"I'll show it to you. It's quite something. I found all kinds of things down there."

"Kinda hard to read," Flebberman said, turning the pages of the diary one by one. "Funny handwriting. You read it?"

"Yes. All of it."

"Anything good?"

"Well—"

Flebberman looked up at her expectantly.

"I'll let you read it for yourself," she said. "Take it with you. It's yours, anyway. It belongs to your family." And that is how you should find out about what happened to Henry, she thought. You shouldn't hear it from a stranger—not from me. If Ellen's spirit—or Henry's—was still restless, forgiveness had to come from one of their own family, and from no one else.

"Awright," Flebberman said. "I really—" He fumbled his words, turning red all the way up to his ears. "I don't know what ta say," he finished lamely.

Francie smiled.

"That was very eloquently put, Mr. Flebberman," she said. "And the feeling is mutual."

■ ■ ■

Francie awoke late the next morning and spent most of the day curled up in the wingback chair, fire crackling, notebook open on her lap. She forgot it was Christmas. Most of the time she stared out the window, but occasionally she scribbled a line or two, and then reread what she had written with a small smile of pride. The next day, having made a trip to the state police barracks in Allentown and retrieved, with official permission, the remains of the Musgrove family, she and Flebberman replaced the bones in the gaping hole in the rear of the property. They had been placed in a canvas bag labeled HUMAN REMAINS, and Francie watched as Flebberman carefully maneuvered a bulldozer borrowed from Wayne Steinbach, pushing the pile of half-frozen dirt back over the pathetic gray bundle that was his ancestors. There was no way to sort out the bones, it being impossible to determine who was who; Flebberman had made the decision to leave them in the bag, and let the few remaining fragments of the Musgroves rest together.

"Ain't like it matters now," he said. "After all they been through. Most important thing is, they're back where they belong."

Francie agreed. Together they patted the earth into shape with shovels, and then they laid the shattered fragments of the tombstones on top, piecing them together as best as they could.

"I should at least offer to buy new stones," said Francie. "It seems like the least I could do, considering my role in all this."

But Flebberman said, "Naw. Way I see it is, everything's bound to go back to the earth sooner or later. People shouldn't interfere, that's all. It ain't right to hurry it up, but it ain't right to slow it down, either. Know what I mean?"

"I certainly do," said Francie.

"Everything should just be left alone," Flebberman said firmly. "Besides, it would just run to more money. And I got legal expenses comin' outa my ears now. Which I deserve," he added, shamefaced.

"How much are your expenses?" Francie asked.

Flebberman shrugged and leaned on his shovel. "Lawyer, impound fees, bond money, more legal fees, a fine for stealin' from the dump—even though it was things that belonged to me—you wouldn't b'leeve it. I didn't even know it was against the law to take things outa the dump in the first place. And I gotta pay for the damage to the cop car. Maybe thirty thousand dollars in all. Prob'ly more."

"And you don't have the money?"

Flebberman came as close to laughing as Francie had ever seen him. "Nope. I never had that much money in my life. But I got an idea."

"What's that?"

"Well," he said, "I got good credit. That's one thing. And I can get a loan. You remember that idea I had I was tellin' you about, the one about havin' a used car lot?"

"You—you want to open a used car lot? Here?"

"Not here. In town. It just seems like the right time to do it. I ain't never gonna make enough money to pay back what I owe, not doin' what I'm doin'. We just been scrapin' by fer as long as I can remember. But I been thinkin' about the future, you know, 'specially when it looked like I was gonna be spendin' the next twenty years in the slammer. I started thinkin' about all the things I wanted to do and never did. Funny the way bein' locked up works on yer mind. An' I thought, Gawd, if I ever get outa here, I'm not gonna waste one more second of my life. I'm gonna do all the things I wanted to do, plus all the things I shoulda done. An' that car lot was number one on the list. Besides spendin' more time with my kids, I mean," he added. "I could make it work. I know I could. I even know where I wanna put it. I ain't gonna get rich, but I could be doin' a damn sight better than I have been, and in a few years I could have all my debts paid off and start puttin' money away fer my kids besides. Waddaya think?"

"Brilliant," said Francie. "Perfect. Do it. Let nothing stop you."

"Yeah," said Flebberman. "That's what I think, too."

■ ■ ■

He had brought something to show her; it was a photo album, filled with images of Flebberman's family. Most had been taken in the last fifty years, and there were palm-sized snapshots in both black and white and color. The one she liked best was a large print of an old man in a rocking chair, looking out a window, leaning his chin on a cane.

"Who's that?" asked Francie.

"That," Flebberman said, "was old Uncle Lincoln. Really my great-uncle, I think. Story is he survived gettin' run over by a horse when he was just a baby. He died when I was little. I don't 'member him." He paused to think. "That was the same horse that killed Marly," he said, remembering. "Marly was Lincoln's grandmother."

Francie leafed through a few more pages until she came to what looked like a postcard, a very old one. It was a picture of an old-looking city, and underneath it said "Vienna."

"What about this?" she asked.

"I dunno about that," Flebberman said. "I've always wondered about it. Take it out and see if anything's written on it."

"Really? It might tear."

"Not if you're careful," Flebberman said. "Go ahead. I always wondered who sent it, anyway."

The postcard was pasted into the album. Francie got a sharp knife from the kitchen and gingerly fitted it between the postcard and the paper backing. With a surgeon's skill, she worked it back and forth until the postcard came free. On the back, in scrawled handwriting, she read:

May 12, 1919
Dear Ellen,

All is well with me. Hope you are same. I love Vienna & may stay longer. Do not worry.

Fondly,
Hamish

"Oh, yeah," said Flebberman wonderingly. "I heard about this guy. He's the one moved ta Yurrip when he was an old man."

"I read about him learning to walk," said Francie. "In Marly's diary."

"I never did hear what ever happened to 'im after that," Flebberman said. "I wonder if he died over there, or if he came back."

"Maybe you could find out."

"How?"

"The Internet," Francie said.

"The Internet has my fambly in it?" Flebberman said, dubious. "I dunno."

"You can get access to records," Francie said. "You can send e-mails to request information, too. I bet you might be able to find something. You could even find out about the name Flavia-Hermann, if you wanted."

Flebberman pursed his lips. "Wow," he said.

"We'll do it when I get my computer hooked up," Francie said. "I'll show you how it works."

"'Preciate it," said Flebberman. "That, and everythin' else you done." He smiled at her shyly, showing his snuff-stained teeth.

She walked him to the door and watched as he headed down the driveway toward the road. He turned when he had left her property, and smiled at her.

"You're a good neighbor," he said.

Francie smiled back.

"Happy New Year, Randy," she called.

Flebberman pointed his boots toward his house and started walking, moving neither quickly nor slowly, but going at the only pace he had ever known in his life. Francie remained at the door even after he had crested the hill, just looking out across the road at where the great boulder rose up over the embankment. She stared out also at the valley spreading away in all directions, thinking how big it was, and how quiet. The air was as still as the inside of a church, and the cold was slow to touch her, but when it finally crept inside her clothes and she began to shiver, she closed the door again and went back to her chair by the fire, and there she stayed.